PRAISE FOR THE NOVELS OF
Mimi Matthews

Gentleman

"Tartly elegant...A vigorous, sparkling, and entertaining love story with plenty of Austen-ite wit."
-*Kirkus Reviews*, starred review

"Matthews ups the ante with a wildly suspenseful romance..."
-*Library Journal*, starred review

"Exhilarating, complete with mystery, adventure, and plenty of shocking reveals. This page-turner shouldn't be missed."
-*Publishers Weekly*, starred review

"Readers who love lots of intrigue and historicals that sound properly historical will savor this one."
-*NPR*

Fair as a Star

"A kindhearted love story that will delight anyone who longs to be loved without limits. Highly recommended."
-*Library Journal*, starred review

"A moving friends-to-lovers Victorian romance... Historical romance fans won't want to miss this."
-*Publishers Weekly*, starred review

The Winter Companion

"Fans of the 'Parish Orphans of Devon' series will adore this final installment, reuniting the orphans and their loves."

-Library Journal, starred review

The Work of Art

"Matthews weaves suspense and mystery within an absorbing love story. Readers will be hard put to set this one down before the end."

-Library Journal, starred review

"If all Regency Romances were written as well as 'The Work of Art,' I would read them all…[Matthews] has a true gift for storytelling."

-The Herald-Dispatch

The Matrimonial Advertisement

"For this impressive Victorian romance, Matthews crafts a tale that sparkles with chemistry and impresses with strong character development…an excellent series launch…"

-Publishers Weekly

"Matthews has a knack for creating slow-building chemistry and an intriguing plot with a social history twist."

-Library Journal

"Mimi Matthews writing style could almost trick one into believing her a contemporary of Austen, Brontë or Gaskell."
-*The Silver Petticoat Review*

A Holiday By Gaslight

"Matthews pays homage to Elizabeth Gaskell's *North and South* with her admirable portrayal of the Victorian era's historic advancements…Readers will easily fall for Sophie and Ned in their gaslit surroundings."
-*Library Journal*, starred review

"A graceful love story…and an authentic presentation of the 1860s that reads with the simplicity and visual gusto of a period movie."
-*Readers' Favorite*, 2019 Gold Medal for Holiday Fiction

The Lost Letter

"Lost love letters, lies, and betrayals separate a soldier from the woman he loves in this gripping, emotional Victorian romance…Historical romance fans should snap this one up."
-*Publishers Weekly*, starred review

"A fast and emotionally satisfying read, with two characters finding the happily-ever-after they had understandably given up on. A promising debut."
-*Library Journal*

JOHN EYRE
A Tale of Darkness and Shadow
Copyright © 2021 by Mimi Matthews

Edited by Deborah Nemeth
Cover Design by James T. Egan of Bookfly Design
Interior Design & Typsetting by Ampersand Book Interiors

Paperback: 978-1-7360802-2-1

This book is a work of fiction. Names, characters, places, and incidents are products of the author's imagination or are used fictitiously. Any resemblance to actual events, locales, or persons, living or dead, is entirely coincidental. All rights reserved, including the right to reproduce this book or portions thereof in any form whatsoever.

Except for use in review, the reproduction or utilization of this work in whole or in part, by any means, is forbidden without written permission from the author/publisher.

"The Star" by Ann and Jane Taylor originally appeared in *Rhymes for the Nursery*, published by Harvey and Darton, London, 1806. It is used in this work by right of public domain.

Jane Eyre by Charlotte Brontë was originally published by Smith, Elder & Co., London, 1847. Excerpts, quotations, and references are used in this work by right of public domain.

Dracula by Bram Stoker was originally published by Archibald Constable & Co., London, 1897. Excerpts, quotations, and references are used in this work by right of public domain.

JOHN EYRE

A Tale of Darkness and Shadow

MIMI MATTHEWS

USA Today Bestselling Author

For my mother, Vickie.

This story was written entirely for you.

ONE

Lowton, England
October 1843

John Eyre stood over the freshly turned heap of earth, his head bent and his gloved hands clasped behind his back. The sun was breaking over the bleak Surrey Hills, a slowly rising rim of molten gold. It burned at the edges of the morning fog that blanketed the valley, pushing back the darkness, but doing nothing at all to alleviate the bone-numbing chill that had settled into his limbs.

Lady Helen Burns's newly dug grave was located behind the church in a section reserved for those poor souls who had died outside of the grace of God. Unconsecrated ground. The final resting place of the village's suicides and unbaptized infants. None had been blessed with so much as a simple marker. No cross, headstone, or marble angel to commemorate their passing.

Until now.

Helen's humble plot was adorned with a tablet of gray marble. John had commissioned it himself. It didn't state her name, or the date of her untimely death. Had it done so, Sir

William would have no doubt demanded it be removed. Helen was still his wife, and therefore his property, even in death.

In lieu of Helen's name, the stonemason had recommended a quote from the Bible. Something dire, from the book of Lamentations. "The crown is fallen from our head: woe unto us, that we have sinned!"

John would have none of it.

Instead, he'd ordered the stone to be chiseled with a solitary word of Latin: *Resurgam*. It was the promise of resurrection. Eternal life in the hereafter, free of earthly woe—whether the church believed she merited it or not.

It had been an act of defiance. Yet how pathetic it looked in the early morning light, that small stone with its single word, propped over a hastily dug grave.

She had deserved better.

"I thought you would come." The Reverend Mr. Brocklehurst approached, the tread of his footsteps nearly silent on the frost-covered grass.

John's muscles stiffened. The beginnings of another headache throbbed at his temples. Megrims, the village doctor called them. Symptoms of a highly strung individual with far too much on his mind—and on his conscience.

Whatever they were, they were coming with more frequency of late. Even during those hours when the pain was at an ebb, the shadow of it still lurked behind John's eyes.

"A sad end for an unhappy soul." Mr. Brocklehurst came to stand beside him. He looked down at Helen's grave with an expression of pious regret. "Though I cannot but think it mightn't have come to this had you never offered her your... sympathies."

John failed to conceal a flinch at the thinly veiled accusation. "I was kind to her, and she to me. There was nothing more to it than that."

There hadn't been. Not on John's part.

But Helen had come to view their friendship in a different light. She'd seen him as a savior. A man who might help her to escape the prison of her life.

He hadn't helped her in the end. He'd been too concerned about his own future. Too respectful of the bonds of matrimony.

"In these cases," Mr. Brocklehurst said, "kindness can often be a cruelty."

John gritted his teeth. He had no patience for the man's homilies. Even less for his insinuations that John's friendship with Helen had hastened her demise. He had enough to reproach himself with on that score without being lectured to by a clergyman.

"You're young yet," Mr. Brocklehurst went on. "You'll soon learn."

Young? At seven and twenty? John felt as old as creation. Weary in body and soul. After Helen's death, he'd been quite ready to lie down and die himself. But that was all over now. It had to be. Guilt was a bog—a mire. He wouldn't permit it to suck him under.

"Where will you go?" Mr. Brocklehurst asked.

"Far away from here." John inwardly winced to hear the lingering bitterness in his words. In the preceding weeks, he'd thought the last ounces of emotion had been leached from his soul. Nothing remained, save a firm resolve to start again somewhere else. To move forward, safe in the knowledge that he would never make the same mistakes again.

And yet that trace of bitterness remained.

It was a result of being here. Of seeing her small, ignominious grave.

"To another school?" Mr. Brocklehurst coughed. "I think that unwise."

JOHN EYRE

John's fingers curled into an unconscious fist. He had the sudden urge to strike Mr. Brocklehurst right in his smugly sanctimonious face.

An uncivilized impulse.

It was restrained by the same shackles of propriety that had prevented John from saving Helen. They bound him up tight, suffocating his baser instincts into inaction.

As if he would ever strike a man of God. Or anyone, come to that.

He wasn't a man of violence. He was a man of letters and learning.

"I've taken a position as tutor in a private household," he said.

He'd placed the advertisement over a month ago. And then he'd waited.

And waited.

He'd begun to despair of ever receiving a response when the letter of enquiry had arrived from Mr. Fairfax of Thornfield Hall in Yorkshire. It was a brief missive, penned in spidery handwriting, offering a situation with two pupils, at a salary of forty pounds per annum.

It was precisely what John required. A remote locale, far away from Lowton. A place where he could focus anew on his teaching. It was more than work to him. It was his vocation. Given time and space, he hoped he could rekindle his passion for it.

"And Sir William has seen fit to give you a reference?"

"Not he," John said. "It was her ladyship."

"She knew you were leaving, then."

John made no reply.

Of course Helen had known he wished to go. She'd known he found the situation untenable. He'd told himself it was for the best. That in his absence, she might resume the normal course of her life. Not in happiness—for John was aware that such an emotion was impossible when married to the likes of Sir William—but with a spirit resigned to doing her duty as a wife. The same spirit with which she'd endured her situation before John had come to the village and taken up his post as schoolmaster.

He hadn't reckoned she would find it too much to bear.

"She has gone to God now," Mr. Brocklehurst said.

John's head jerked up. Anger flared in his breast. "You can say that? Yet you have consigned her here, to this piece of land, where God does not exist."

"God exists everywhere."

"I no longer believe that."

Mr. Brocklehurst murmured a rebuke. "You are grieving, sir. But you mustn't question God's plan. You mustn't lose your faith."

John bent to retrieve the portmanteau that sat at his feet, his hand gripping tight around the leather handle. His trunk had already been corded and sent on ahead. All that remained was to get himself on the stage.

His gaze raked over Helen's grave one last time before he turned away. "I already have."

Three days later, John arrived in the village of Millcote at half past seven in the evening, his headache in full force. The George Inn was but a ramshackle building near the Yorkshire coast. Nothing much to speak of. A mere stop on the stage. John removed his hat and gloves as he entered. The door slammed behind him, shutting out the rain that had followed him all the way from Lowton.

"Evening, sir." A grizzled gentleman in his shirtsleeves approached, hastily donning his coat. The innkeeper, John presumed.

"Good evening." John glanced around the common area. A pendant oil lamp hung from the ceiling. It cast a shifting pattern of shadows on the empty tables and chairs. "Is there no one else here?"

"No, sir. None save the wife and me, and yon coachman. Will you be wanting a room?"

"I shouldn't think so. That is, I was expecting to be met by someone from Thornfield Hall."

The innkeeper gave him a blank look.

"Do you know of the place?" John asked.

"Aye. I know of it."

John waited for the innkeeper to elaborate, but the man said nothing more. John suppressed a flicker of impatience. "Has no one been here today from Thornfield?"

"No, sir. We've not had anyone here today excepting the stage. Not with the storm coming."

John's new employer, Mr. Fairfax, might be reluctant to send a carriage out in such miserable weather. If that was the case, John had little choice but to remain here awhile.

He requested to be taken to a private room. Once there, he removed his frock coat and cravat, and bathed his face with cool water from the pitcher at the washstand.

There was no mirror available. He didn't require one. He knew the limits of what could be achieved with his appearance.

He'd never been considered handsome. Not in the traditional sense. Though tall enough, he was too slight of frame and too plain of feature. His black hair, high forehead, and dark eyes spoke of book learning and quiet contemplation. A man who was all interior thought and emotion. Not a man of action. Not a hero who could have ridden to Helen's rescue and saved her, damn the consequences.

A breath shuddered out of him.

It was this blasted headache. How was a man to think straight?

The innkeeper had placed John's portmanteau on a bench at the end of the bed. John opened it, withdrawing a small, rigid leather case. Inside, arrayed in three neat rows, were more than two dozen glass phials of laudanum.

The village doctor had prescribed it for the worst of John's headaches, but in the aftermath of Helen's suicide, John found himself relying on the drug more and more.

On a good day, a single phial could be made to stretch to several doses.

Today was not a good day.

Relief wouldn't be enough. He wanted—*needed*—oblivion, if only for a few brief moments.

Uncorking a phial, he swallowed the entirety of the contents in one grimacing gulp. It was sickly sweet. Increasingly familiar—as was the muzzy-headedness that followed.

He lay down upon the bed and closed his eyes.

And he must have fallen asleep, for when next he opened them, the candle at his bedside had guttered, and his room was swathed in darkness.

A knock sounded at the door.

John sat up, running a hand through his disheveled hair. His mouth was dry as cotton wool. "Yes? What is it?"

"Coachman's come from Thornfield, sir. Looking for a Mr. Eyre."

"I won't be a moment." John swiftly put himself in order, gathered his things, and hastened downstairs.

John Eyre

The coachman stood at the open door, droplets of rain clinging to his oilskin coat. He eyed John's trunk, which the innkeeper had left in the passage. "Is this all of your luggage?"

"Only that and my portmanteau." John followed the coachman outside. A one-horse conveyance awaited. The coachman hoisted John's trunk onto the roof and secured it with a length of rope.

The rain had slowed to a drizzle, the air redolent with the fragrance of wet earth. John saw no evidence of stars in the night sky nor any sign of a moon to light their way. A lamp hung at the front of the carriage, on the right of the coachman's box, but all else lay in darkness.

"How far is it to Thornfield?" he asked.

"Ten miles." The coachman opened the door of the carriage and waited while John climbed inside. When he was settled, the coachman fastened the door. Seconds later, the carriage shook as he took his place on the box and gave the horse the office to start.

John leaned back into his seat as the carriage lurched into motion. Their progress, over the course of the next hour, was leisurely. Necessarily so given the darkness, and the evident age of the carriage. The vehicle was neither dashing nor well-sprung. Which suited John very well. He had no desire to be employed by a person of fashion. A simple country life, that was what he required. Someplace quiet and orderly where he could teach his new pupils in peace.

In his letter, Mr. Fairfax had described the two boys as being shy but eager to learn. They were ages six and seven. A bit younger than the children John had taught at the village school in Lowton.

He prayed he was up to the task.

Older boys were more trouble, but one could talk with them. Reason with them. They weren't babies just out of the nursery.

But beggars couldn't be choosers.

Mr. Fairfax's letter had been the only reply to John's advertisement. He hadn't held out much hope of receiving another offer of employment. Certainly not one that would take him so far away from Lowton.

He rested his head against the rain-streaked window as the carriage rolled through the mud. The laudanum had left him with a dull headache, and a familiar sense of queasy malaise that wasn't likely to leave him until he'd properly eaten and rested. It was going on midnight. Would the housekeeper at Thornfield have something prepared for his arrival? A cold collation, perhaps? Or a slice of leftover kidney pie?

The thought of food did nothing to settle his stomach. Rather the opposite. A surge of nausea rose in his throat. He let down the window and thrust out his head. Damp night air filled his lungs.

"You all right, sir?" the coachman called down.

"Quite well. Just needed a bit of air." John's answer appeared to satisfy the fellow. He made no attempt to stop the carriage. Indeed, he gave the plodding horse a brisk smack with the reins as if to speed the creature's pace.

John kept the window down. The fresh air was welcome, and he could see better without the barrier of the streaked glass. A halo of light shone from the swinging carriage lamp. Enough for him to get an impression of the passing scenery. Trees and shrubs and twining brambles. It wasn't a welcoming landscape. Less so at this time of year, as autumn marched inexorably toward winter.

There didn't appear to be any houses hereabouts. The scattered fences and pitched roofs he'd spied as they left the

George Inn were long behind them. Only emptiness lay ahead. A vast stretch of countryside engulfed in a silvery mist that clung to the branches and swirled along the edge of the road.

Thornfield Hall must reside in a valley, for as the carriage rolled on, the mist appeared to grow heavier, settling over the ground and partially obscuring the way in front of them.

In time, they approached a crossroads. The stone edifice of a crumbling old church loomed to their right, its tower rising defiantly against the night sky. Its bell tolled the hour as they passed. One chime. Two chimes. And on and on, all the way to midnight.

The sound faded behind them as the carriage turned down the left branch of the road. It was still echoing softly in the night when John saw her.

And it was a *her*, however noncorporeal. She seemed to materialize from the mist ahead of them, a mere shimmer of vapor coalesced into the form and figure of a woman. *A lady.* A beautiful, beribboned wisp of one in a full-skirted gown.

John blinked hard to clear his eyes, but the figure remained. White and ethereal. She stood in front of the oncoming carriage, one hand held out in front of her. The gesture was unmistakable. Halt, it said. Don't come any farther.

The horse plodded on, no change in its gate.

John's pulse leapt in his throat. "Stop!" he called out to the coachman. "There's someone ahead!"

The coachman slowed the horse. "What's that?"

"There! A woman in the road! Can you not see her?"

"Ain't no one in the road, sir."

John blinked again. This time, when he opened his eyes, the lady was gone. Only the mist remained. His heart pounded. "She was there. I saw her."

The coachman gave a low chuckle. "That'd be the Millcote mists, sir. Always do play tricks on folks. Reckon you'll get used to them." He clucked and the horse walked on, forward and through the very mist where the lady had been standing seconds before.

John sank into his seat, his forehead beaded with perspiration. His pulse beat an erratic rhythm at his throat. Perhaps it was the Millcote mists, whatever those were. Either that or the dose of laudanum he'd taken at the inn. He didn't know which. All he knew was that he *had* seen a lady in the road. He knew because he'd recognized her.

It had been Helen.

Two

Thornfield Hall
Yorkshire, England
October 1843

John was half asleep inside the carriage when it finally came to a rattling halt. The coachman jumped down from the box to open a pair of sagging iron gates. Resuming his seat, he drove the carriage through, the gates swinging shut behind them with a resounding crash.

They ascended a long drive, and at length, came to the front of an enormous stone house. Mist rolled about it, above and below, obscuring the architecture from view. What windows John could make out were dark. All but one—a small curtained window from which a glow of candlelight weakly flickered.

The carriage stopped in front of a tall wooden front door. It creaked open on hinges desperately in need of oiling. A white-haired gentleman garbed in a worn black suit emerged, his eyes cloudy and his back slightly hunched with age. He held a branch of candles aloft in one gnarled hand.

"Mr. Eyre?" he queried as John disembarked from the carriage. "Welcome to Thornfield Hall. Do come in and make yourself warm."

Clutching his portmanteau, John followed the manservant into the house. The butler, he presumed, or some sort of steward. The fellow led him across a square marble-tiled hall and through one darkened room and then another, before ushering him into a much smaller chamber. A fire blazed in the hearth, and candles flickered from atop tables both high and low.

John's eyes were briefly dazzled by the light. It took a moment for them to adjust. When they did, he was at once put at ease by the picture before him.

It was a cozy room, with walls covered in figured silk paper, a floor carpeted in a thick floral Aubusson, and a polished brass carriage clock that quietly ticked the passing seconds.

Two velvet-upholstered armchairs, backs draped in crocheted antimacassars, resided in front of the fire. An inlaid mahogany table stood between them. A tea tray sat atop it, holding a painted porcelain teapot, two cups, and a plate of sandwiches.

The butler set the branch of candles down upon the mantel. "Do sit down."

John took the chair nearest the door. It wasn't, he suspected, the butler's favorite. It had an unrumpled look about it.

"Your journey was rather dreary, I fear." The butler sank down in the chair opposite. He poured out a cup of tea and offered it to John. "Jenkins will take his time."

John thanked the butler as he took the teacup. "The horse was obliged to walk. There was a great deal of fog about." He sipped his tea. It was scalding hot, as though it had just been prepared. "Mr. Fairfax has retired, I presume."

"I am Mr. Fairfax, sir."

"You?" John couldn't conceal his surprise. The gentleman in front of him must be in his late sixties at least. "Forgive me. I assumed the boys were your sons."

Mr. Fairfax gave a hoarse laugh. "Heavens, no."

"Your wards, then?"

"They are the wards of Mrs. Rochester, sir."

John went still. Slowly, he returned his teacup to the tea tray. "You have me at a disadvantage. I was under the impression that *you* were my employer."

Another laugh. "Bless me, is that what you thought? Goodness no, Mr. Eyre. Thornfield Hall is the home of Mrs. Rochester. Her ancestral home. I am only the butler—the manager. Mrs. Rochester commissioned me to find a tutor for the boys." He gestured to the plate of sandwiches. "Eat, please. You look slightly ill, if I may say so."

"A trifling headache. It's plagued me since I left Surrey."

"I'm sorry to hear it. Do you require anything for your comfort? A headache powder, or—"

"Thank you, no. Food and rest will be sufficient." John helped himself to a sandwich. "I shall be well enough in the morning." He paused. "Is there a Mr. Rochester?"

"No, indeed. Mrs. Rochester is a widow."

John considered the matter as he finished his sandwich and drank his tea. He'd never before been employed by a lady. Even Helen had been subservient to the wishes of her husband. It was he who had paid John's wages and seen to the needs of the students at the village school—albeit begrudgingly.

What sort of lady was this Mrs. Rochester? A wealthy one to be sure. Thornfield Hall was a formidable structure, and the interior—what John had seen of it—appeared well appointed. Yet there was a smell of neglect about the place. Of damp and disuse.

"I am glad you are come," Mr. Fairfax said. "It will be pleasant to have a companion. The winters can feel quite lonely here with no one but the servants for company. They're agreeable enough, but one can't converse with them on terms of equality."

John began to warm to the old man. He knew what it was to want for companionship. In Lowton, he'd had no real friends. No one to talk with, save Helen.

His tired mind formed a hazy image of her. But not of her. Of the creature he'd seen from the window of the carriage. An apparition, silvery white, standing in the center of the road. The memory of it sent a faint shiver down his spine.

He should never have taken that last dose of laudanum at the inn. Not when he was already exhausted and in a lingering state of grief. It was foolish. Self-indulgent. He downed another swallow of tea. "I hope you will find my company as agreeable as you've anticipated."

"Oh, I'm sure I will, Mr. Eyre. Already I begin to feel my spirits lift, just to have you here in my parlor, taking tea with me. But I won't keep you sitting up all night for my own amusement. If you've finished eating, I'll show you to your bedroom." Mr. Fairfax rose and retrieved the branch of candles. "It stands between mine and that of the boys. You will want to be near them, I think."

"Thank you, yes." John followed Mr. Fairfax from the room. The butler first stopped in the hall to bolt the front door, and then, having removed the key from the lock, he led the way upstairs.

The staircase was made of dark oak, with a wide, curving banister and steps that seemed to go on forever. A high stained-glass window rose above it. The sort of window that appeared more suited to a church than to a stately country house. Rain fell steadily against the glass.

John Eyre

"We haven't yet escaped the storm," John said.

"That is no storm, sir. It's just a wee bit of rain and wind." Mr. Fairfax guided John down a long gallery lined with closed doors. An unsettling chill pervaded the darkness. "The real storm has not yet come."

"You expect it soon?"

"Undoubtedly." Opening one of the bedroom doors, Mr. Fairfax gestured for John to precede him inside. He came after him with the branch of candles. "I shall light a fire for you."

John was grateful for it. In the room he'd rented at the boarding house in Lowton, he'd never been allowed to have a fire. The proprietress had been stingy with coals, refusing to permit anything more than a single small fire in the parlor each evening by which her boarders had huddled to warm their frozen hands and feet.

"There." Mr. Fairfax stood. The fire in the grate crackled behind him. He looked about the room. "It is small, I grant you, but the furnishings are in the modern style. All of them excepting your bed. That dates to the fifteenth century, I believe, though it still has a practical use. Come, let me show you."

The great oak monstrosity at the center of the room was shaped like a bed, certainly, but instead of being hung with heavy curtains, it was enclosed on all sides by carved panels of wood.

"A box bed." Mr. Fairfax slid one of the panels open, revealing the mattress, pillows, and neatly folded coverlet inside. "I sleep in one myself. It does a splendid job of keeping out the cold and damp." He looked over his shoulder, his bushy white brows lowered. "You're not wary of enclosed spaces, I trust? If so, rest assured that you have nothing to fear. It opens from the inside as well as the outside."

"It looks..." John faltered. What it looked like was a medieval cupboard—or worse. A tomb. But he was practically asleep on his feet, and the bedding appeared comfortable enough. "It suits me," he managed finally. "I was always cold in my previous lodgings."

"You won't be so now, I promise you." Mr. Fairfax lit a candle for John and then bid him good night, adding, "We breakfast at eight. I shall see that the boys are brought to the dining room."

"Thank you. Good night." John fastened the door behind Mr. Fairfax. The coachman had brought in his trunk. He rifled through it until he found a linen nightshirt. He changed into it, and then—after washing, and winding his pocket watch—he climbed into his new bed.

It was strange to be enclosed on all sides by wooden panels. Strange, and yet somehow rather reassuring. He felt oddly comforted. A fact which stood in stark contrast to the bleakness of his life in the months preceding his departure from Lowton. There had been no comfort in them. No warmth.

First had been his decision to leave his position at the village school. A decision only reached after weeks of heartsick anguish. And then Helen had taken her own life. It had been a blow from which John felt he'd never recover.

He'd wanted to shut himself away. To weep at the injustice of losing her. But he hadn't the luxury of mourning Helen, nor the right. The best he could do was to hold to his plans. To leave Lowton forever and start afresh somewhere else.

Thornfield Hall was to be that place.

He was here now, warm and safe, in a new home and with a new position. It was an opportunity to wipe the slate clean. A chance to move forward—away from Helen Burns and the tragedies of the past—and into a brighter, more promising tomorrow.

The prospect of it brought John a rare measure of peace. At once weary and optimistic, his eyes slid shut and he fell into a deep and dreamless sleep.

John woke at dawn, as was his custom. Sliding open the panel of his box bed, he blinked against the sunlight shining in through the curtains that framed his chamber window. His eyes were always more sensitive to the light after a dose of laudanum.

Rising, he washed and dressed in a plain black frock coat, vest, and matching trousers. He took care that the cuffs and collar of his white linen shirt were clean, and that his cravat was knotted in a fashion that was neither too dandified nor too simplistic. First impressions were important, and as he fully anticipated meeting both his pupils and his new employer at breakfast, he intended to start as he meant to go on—neat, smart, and unpretentious.

Having threaded his watch chain through his waistcoat and assured himself of a clean handkerchief in his pocket, he at last ventured forth.

Thornfield looked far more welcoming in the daytime than it had in the dead of night. More luxurious, too. As John descended the oak stairs, his gaze took in the oil paintings on the walls, the crystal chandelier that hung overhead, and the great clock below with its case of carved ebony. He had no experience with such grandeur. In Lowton, the finest house had belonged to Sir William, and though it had been large and well-appointed, it had been nothing very awe-inspiring.

Across the hall, the front door stood half open. A sign that the servants were up and about, though he saw none of them nearby. Curious, he opened the door and crossed over the threshold.

Cold air nipped at his face as he stepped outside. The rain had stopped for the moment, and a shaft of early morning sunlight shone down through the dark clouds onto a well-tended expanse of lawn. It was abutted by a great meadow and an array of knotty thorn trees as strong and broad as oaks, which at once explained how Thornfield had acquired its name.

He turned to survey the front of the house. It had been too dark last evening to get more than the barest impression of its size. Now, however, he could appreciate the full height and breadth of it. Made entirely of worn gray stone, it was three stories high, with battlements along the top.

Brown hills rose in the distance, embracing the property at the front and the back and giving it a feeling of seclusion. There was no evidence of any other dwellings. No sign of a neighboring village, nor even of a neighbor. It must be that Millcote was the closest thing to society in these parts. And that some ten miles away.

No wonder Mr. Fairfax had admitted to being lonely here.

The thought had no sooner crossed John's mind than the butler appeared at the door.

"You're an early riser, Mr. Eyre," he said.

"That I am." John went to join him. "I've been exploring."

"So I observe. And how do you find Thornfield?"

"I like it very well. What I've seen of it." John paused, adding, "It's bigger than I realized."

"Yes, it is a grand place, though not at its best at the moment. A great house requires the presence of its mistress. I can only hope that Mrs. Rochester will one day decide to come and reside here permanently."

John's brows lifted. "She doesn't live here?"

"She visits when she's able—when her affairs permit it. Which isn't as often as I'd like, I must tell you." Mr. Fairfax's rheumy eyes softened with memory. "Ah, but you should have seen Thornfield in the old days, all lit up for a ball or a party. It was a sight to behold. People came for miles to dine and to dance. Mind you, I was only a lad of eighteen when first I came here, employed as a footman by the mistress's grandfather. And proud I was of it. But that was a long while ago. More than fifty years, at least. A different time."

"It's hard to imagine," John said. "The location seems quite isolated."

"Not entirely. There's Millcote, of course. And Hay—a village beyond that hill, not but two miles away from here."

John squinted into the distance. Mist swirled over the hills and atop the meadow, making it difficult to see. "No neighbors?"

"A few of them on the other side of Millcote. The Eshtons and the Ingrams. But I don't expect you'll meet them. The Eshtons have gone to London for the winter, and the Ingrams are lately in mourning. They receive no visitors." Mr. Fairfax escorted John back into the house. "Mrs. Rochester is still in mourning herself. She prefers a quiet life now. It wouldn't be suitable to be entertaining. She won't even permit the vicar to call when she's in residence."

If the vicar was anything like the Reverend Mr. Brocklehurst, John didn't blame her. The man had no idea of how to comfort a grieving individual. His God was an unforgiving one—a God of fire and brimstone, with no love or Christian charity about him.

"You're not likely to meet him," Mr. Fairfax said. "Not here at Thornfield. But there are services at the church in Hay should you care to attend."

John didn't care to, personally. He hadn't been lying when he told Mr. Brocklehurst that he'd lost his faith. It was hard to nurture any sort of belief in the wake of Helen's loss. At the same time, he knew his duty. "If Mrs. Rochester desires it, I will accompany the boys."

"The boys?" Mr. Fairfax shut and bolted the front door. "Goodness me. The boys are in no fit state to attend church. Mrs. Rochester would never hear of it."

John felt a flicker of unease. No fit state? Were the children ill?

As he was meditating on the question, a creak sounded on the oak staircase. John stopped where he stood in the hall and looked up. The hairs rose on the back of his neck.

Two little boys descended the steps hand in hand. They were small and startlingly thin, with heads that seemed large in proportion to their bodies, and dark, sunken eyes surrounded by deep shadows. Their black hair was shorn close to their scalps, and what skin was visible outside of their clothes had the appearance of wax—pale and bloodless.

"Here they are," Mr. Fairfax said. "Boys! Come and meet the gentleman who is to be your tutor."

John studied the boys as they came into the hall, schooling his features into what he hoped was an expression of benign greeting. He prayed his face didn't betray his alarm, for the two children *were* alarming to look at. A pair of animated corpses with empty staring eyes. A young woman in a black stuff dress and white apron followed behind them, urging them forward. Their nurse, John presumed.

"This is Stephen," Mr. Fairfax said. "And his brother, Peter."

"Good morning, boys," John said. "I'm pleased to make your acquaintance."

The children stopped in front of him, still holding hands, their sunken eyes cast downward. Their nurse whispered a reassurance to them in muted French.

A sudden thought occurred to John. He turned to Mr. Fairfax. "Are they foreigners?"

"Their nurse, Sophie, is French, and Stephen and Peter were born on the Continent, I believe, though heaven knows precisely where. Mrs. Rochester adopted them during her travels. It's she who gave them their names, after Saint Stephen and Saint Peter. The poor mites. They've had a trial in getting here. Mrs. Rochester says they took ill on the voyage, but she's confident they'll regain their health once treated to good food and a little sunshine."

A little sunshine?

The children looked as though they'd never been exposed to sun in their lives.

John turned his attention back to them, wondering how the devil he was meant to communicate. He had a smattering of French and Italian, but couldn't converse in either language with any degree of fluency. "Do they speak any English?"

"Forgive me, Mr. Eyre," Mr. Fairfax said, "I thought I'd mentioned it. Stephen and Peter do not speak at all."

Three

*Letters from
Miss Bertha Mason to
Miss Blanche Ingram.*

*Hotel des Anglais
Cairo, Egypt
Monday, 13 June 1842*

Dearest Blanche, —

Forgive my long delay in replying. I have only just this morning arrived in Cairo and found a whole stack of your letters awaiting me. You will think me a bad correspondent. I assure you I'm not. Only a very tired lady who has spent far too much time of late on crowded conveyances and not enough of it seated in front of a writing desk.

What a journey I have had! There is so much to tell you that I don't know where to begin. First, the weather: do you remember those summers so long ago when we would strip down to our shifts and bathe in Mr. Eshton's pond? The heat of those days is nothing to the blazing sun of Egypt. It's so indescribably hot here, my dear, that it's all I can do to breathe. But I love it for all that, which I suspect owes more to my current state than any tolerance for the temperature.

At last I'm free to travel as I will! You alone will not take such a proclamation as being indecorous. You know what I suffered living under Mama and Papa's thumb, and then again when I was obliged to mourn them. Their loss will always be a great pain to me, but I can't help but be thankful for it now I'm in full control of my fortune and my destiny.

I say full control—what I mean is, as much control as I can exercise given the constant meddling of our family attorney, Mr. Hughes. You would think that a year and a half on the Continent in the wake of losing my parents would have been enough to satisfy his ideas of propriety. All those months spent in mourning, and the tedious ones that followed after, visiting European museums and taking tea, as bored and restless as ever I was in England.

Mr. Hughes was opposed to my coming to Egypt. He subscribes to a traditional view of womanhood. Believes our place is in the home, and all of that. He's even gone so far as to advise me to marry. And perhaps I shall do, eventually. But not right away. I've resisted the bonds of matrimony this long. I won't tumble into them the very instant I'm taking my first steps of freedom.

You will say that there's no danger of falling into matrimony at my age. At eight and twenty, I'm all but an old maid. But believe me, dear, my fortune will compensate for a great deal. With some men—I shan't call them gentlemen—it will even compensate for my strident personality.

Thus, I am resolved to be on my guard. When I do marry, it will be for love, and not because I have been compromised by a fortune hunter. My maid, Agnes, remains with me wherever I go, as does my manservant, Mr. Poole. You were right about him. A man of few words, but brawny and capable. He never asks questions, simply does what I tell him to do.

Tomorrow we visit the pyramids and the Sphynx. I've been advised to hire a native translator, known as a dragoman, to accompany us. And I mean to do so directly after I've finished this letter.

What else can I tell you? I have seen the Mediterranean Sea at moonlight, the chaos of the bazaar at Alexandria, and have ridden down the streets of Cairo on the back of a temperamental donkey. I have begun to feel that my life before leaving England was a long and terrible dream. I don't mean to imply that all of it was unhappy. There were many moments of joy, your friendship chief among them; however, the greater the distance I've traveled, the more alive I feel. Things are brighter, more fragrant, engaging all of my senses.

Which isn't to say that I don't still look the part of a dull English spinster. But I mean to remedy that. This evening, if there is time, I will purchase more suitable clothes at the bazaar. It's too hot for silk and taffeta, and all of my blacks and lavenders make me look a full decade older.

With that, I must close, my dear. The bell is ringing for tea. Please write back when you can with all the news from home.

Your loving,
Bertha

John Eyre

Hotel des Anglais
Cairo, Egypt
Thursday, 14 July 1842

Dearest Blanche, —

The most extraordinary thing has happened. A gentleman doing excavations among the ruins at Thebes has discovered the entrance to an intact tomb. It was hidden beneath the debris of several other tombs, and no one had any notion of its existence until earlier this week. Tomorrow evening they are finally going to open it, and speculation among the hotel guests is high as to what might be found there.

I am determined to be present for the opening, and wish you could be here to witness it as well. It seems only yesterday we were both marveling over reports of ancient Egyptian tombs in Papa's archaeological journals, and dreaming we could view mummies and funereal artifacts in situ. But I won't reproach you for refusing to accompany me on my travels, though I do believe you might have given it more consideration than you did. How much fun we could have had together in Paris and Rome!

All that aside, I must admit that a year and a half on the Continent has done little to prepare me for the experience of Egypt. This past month has gone by in a whirlwind. Along with Agnes and Mr. Poole, I have seen all of the sights and made friends with many of the residents of the hotel. But I yearn to expand my horizons beyond the other British guests, some of whom I've already encountered multiple times during my travels across France and during the voyage to Alexandria. Our dragoman, Farouk, has been a great help in that regard. He seems to know everyone in Cairo and has a passing acquaintance with the foreman at the dig, as well. He promises to introduce me to him when we arrive in Thebes.

We will be traveling up the Nile by steamer ship first thing in the morning. The heat has only increased since last I wrote. We've been obliged to keep indoors in the middle of the day, only emerging in the early dawn hours or later in the evening after the sun has set and it's grown a little cooler. When they open the tomb, they will do so by lantern light. It's all quite thrilling, my dear. I cannot think how I will manage to sleep tonight knowing the treat that lies before me tomorrow.

Until then, I remain, your loving friend,
Bertha

Hotel des Anglais
Cairo, Egypt
Tuesday, 19 July 1842

My Dear Blanche, —

You will find this a disappointing letter, I fear. As you can see from the direction, I have returned to Cairo. Thebes did not live up to expectations at all. I arrived there on Friday for the opening of the tomb, only to discover—along with the rest of our party—that the sarcophagus was empty. Farouk explained that it had been ransacked, probably many hundreds of years ago. There were broken jars and some pieces of statuary but no sign of the mummy who had been interred there. It was all quite deflating.

But I haven't returned to Cairo empty-handed. While in Thebes, I met the most delightful lady. Mrs. Wren is a widow who is touring Egypt as I am. She's been here since the spring, and knows ever so much about the place. She took me under her wing at the dig, and yesterday accompanied me back to Cairo. Indeed, she was already staying here, at a nearby hotel. I can't think how it is we've never encountered each other until now.

You would like her very well, my dear. She's older than we are—somewhere in her middle forties, if I was to hazard a guess. Yet still rather strikingly beautiful, with dark hair and eyes and a sun-bronzed complexion. The very picture of a lady traveler in her flowing robes and veiled hats.

Mrs. Wren is intelligent, as well. I've observed her speaking flawless Arabic to the servants, and equally flawless French to the maître d'hôtel. Her father's people were English, but she was born on the Continent and has spent many years living in Eastern Europe along with her brother. I have not met him as yet, but Mrs. Wren promises to introduce me this evening at dinner. If Mr. Rochester is half as charismatic as his sister, I'm sure I will be smitten.

I must stop now to bathe and change. I shall write again tomorrow with a full report. God bless you, my dear.

Your loving,
Bertha

Four

Thornfield Hall
Yorkshire, England
October 1843

John pulled back the faded velvet curtains, letting in the cold gray light of morning. The library at Thornfield Hall was a cavernous room lined with bookcases that stretched up to the ceiling, and scattered about with heavy chairs and tables on which books were stacked in no particular order. Mrs. Rochester had determined that it must be used as the schoolroom. And it wasn't entirely unsuited to its role. A cabinet piano resided in the corner, and near the bank of windows a globe stood in a wooden frame, alongside an inlaid drum table covered in maps of the world.

Most of the books in the library were dusty tomes of history, philosophy, and archaeology. Relics of an age gone by. Among them a single shelf had been allocated for John's use. It was stocked with a variety of elementary works, along with several volumes of light literature and poetry. He supposed that Mrs. Rochester believed these were all a tutor would require, and indeed, they might have been, had his students been capable of understanding English.

As to that capability, John had no notion. Seated at their makeshift desks, Stephen and Peter were as mute after a week of study as they'd been when John had first made their acquaintance. For the last seven days, he'd read to them and talked to them and made attempts at teaching them their letters. But how much was truly getting through?

There was only one activity the boys had exhibited any interest in.

John gestured to the cold hearth. "Shall you light the fire this morning, Peter? Or perhaps you, Stephen?"

The boys' eyes remained wary, but John knew enough of children to recognize the slight change in their posture.

"Come," he said. "Both of you, up."

Pushing back their chairs, the two boys slowly came to join him in front of the fireplace, their every movement as halting and jerky as a pair of automatons. As if they were, in each instant, willing themselves to move forward against their own better judgment.

Initially, John had found their lack of coordination disturbing. And he still did, to some degree. He couldn't discern whether their awkwardness was due to physical infirmity or if it was merely a symptom of profound mental reticence. They were uncertain of him, if not outright afraid. Knowing that, John was careful never to speak harshly or approach them with too abrupt a movement.

He knelt down and motioned for them to do the same. It was a ritual he'd unknowingly started on his first day of instruction when, on arriving in the library, he'd discovered that the servants had failed to light the fire.

Since then, John had come to look on the library as his own domain. One in which he would have to tend to drawing the curtains and lighting the fire each morning. He didn't resent the fact. Indeed, it was an opportunity for the boys to learn practical skills. They eagerly helped him to kindle a fire in the hearth, and then to light the table lamps from little twists of paper.

"Mind you don't burn yourself, Stephen," John said as the lad thrust his remnant of paper into the fire. "Well done, both of you. Very good job, indeed." He gestured to their desks. "Back in your seats, if you please."

The boys complied without a word.

Time had passed when John had wished for a quiet classroom. Now, he found himself longing for words—any words. Were the boys truly mutes? Mr. Fairfax claimed not to know.

Stephen appeared to be the eldest, though not by much. It was he who always took his brother's hand. A protective gesture, or so it seemed. As if Stephen wanted to keep his brother close for fear of losing him.

Even now, sitting side by side, the boys often looked to each other for reassurance. When taken along with their waxen skin and malnourished bodies, it made John fear that the pair of them had been through some harrowing ordeal. Were they the orphans of war? Of pestilence? Two waifs Mrs. Rochester had saved from a life in the street?

Or perhaps they were merely what Mr. Fairfax had said: two boys who had lately fallen gravely ill.

John was no stranger to illness himself. An epidemic of influenza had robbed him of both of his parents, leaving him an orphan at the age of five. An undersized boy who had been obliged to rely on a charity school for his board and keep—and for his education. Not all of the teachers there had been kind to him. Many had been short-tempered and cruel. It had made John all the more determined to show kindness to his own pupils. Especially those without benefit of a mother and father.

"This morning," he said, "we will turn our attention to drawing." Stephen and Peter sat still at their desks while John distributed paper and charcoal pencils. He pulled a chair up in front of them to demonstrate. "Pick up your pencils, thusly. Between your thumb and first two fingers. Not too tightly, Stephen." John gently loosened the boy's fingers. Stephen flinched at the contact. "It's all right," John said. "Do you see how I'm holding mine? Light but firm."

When he was confident they understood, John drew the outline of a simple flower on the edge of his paper. He was gratified when the boys copied the figure on their own papers with unsteady hands.

"What about this?" John sketched the trunk and branches of a tree. "Can you draw the same?"

For the next hour, he engaged the boys in copying the various figures he sketched onto his pad. John was a competent draftsman and had filled many a pleasant afternoon sketching a landscape or a portrait of someone he'd met. But today's work was nothing worth preserving in his portfolio. It was all basic outlines and shading.

Intermittently, he produced a letter next to a figure. An A for apple, or a C for cat. The boys dutifully copied, though whether they understood the meaning or not was another question entirely.

"Excellent, Stephen. Very well done, Peter." John rose from his chair and returned to his place in front of the bookcases. "Now, I'd like you to draw something of your own devising. Anything you choose. The globe. The door. Or perhaps a book, or this candlestick? Or something you alone can see?"

He urged them on with words and gestures, and at length, Stephen picked up his pencil, and hesitantly, began to draw. Peter followed his brother's example.

John suppressed a swell of pride. He couldn't communicate with his pupils through words, but he may yet do so through the medium of art. As a boy, drawing had been his own escape from loneliness. If he could convey the rudimentary techniques to Stephen and Peter, perhaps they, too, might find some measure of consolation.

It was a modest goal, but one that boosted John's spirits as nothing had in days. He felt, all at once, as if he might actually be capable of making a success of his new position.

He kept back as the boys' pencils scratched steadily over their papers. He didn't like to loom over their shoulders. This was their time to express themselves. To be creative. Only when Peter put aside his pencil did John finally approach.

He recognized the subject of the drawing at once. A feeble effort, but not the worst John had ever seen. He was determined to praise it to the heavens.

"Oh, well done, lad. The sea, I believe. You've rendered the waves beautifully. No doubt you saw enough of them during your voyage to England." John collected the paper. "I shall save it for you in my portfolio."

Peter betrayed no pleasure in being lauded by his tutor. He sat still and quiet, his back hunched over his desk.

John next moved to review Stephen's work, expecting to find a similar effort. Gazing down, he saw...

But he didn't know what he saw.

Stephen appeared to have blackened the whole of his paper with the edge of his charcoal pencil. Only a single square at the top was left unshaded. A solitary block of white. John crouched beside Stephen's desk to get a better look.

On closer examination, John saw that the shading was not, in fact, solid black. It was darker at the bottom of the page, seeming to grow faintly lighter as it reached the top. As if light were coming in through the white square and diffusing the darkness around it.

"Ah. I see," John said. "Is it a window?"

Stephen stared at him blankly.

"Window," John said again, carefully enunciating each syllable. He gestured to the bank of windows opposite. "Like that one?"

The boy's thin face registered no understanding.

John's spirits sank a little, but he was resolved not to be discouraged. "The shading is excellent. Altogether, a commendable first effort, I'd say." He took the drawing from Stephen. "I shall save this one in my portfolio as well."

Rising to his feet, John gave the boy's drawing another lingering glance. A frisson of uneasiness tickled at the base of his spine. Odd that. There was nothing particularly sinister about the sketch. It was only that the perspective was all wrong. A window shouldn't be placed so. Not on the ceiling of a room, surely. Unless it was a sort of skylight.

Then again, perhaps the white square wasn't a window at all.

As the next week slipped by, Thornfield began to feel more and more like a home to John. His duties as tutor were often taxing. Some days he felt as though he was making progress with his pupils. Others were an exercise in pure frustration. He was pushed to the limits of his creativity—forever thinking up new ways to engage the boys' interest. Drawing, globes, and counting games. Anything that might ignite a spark in their lifeless eyes.

But teaching didn't absorb all of his time. After morning lessons, and then again during those evening hours that he could call his own, John explored the house and the grounds, making full use of his pad and pencils to sketch anything that caught his eye.

No servants were ever around to impede his wanderings. Indeed, he scarcely encountered a soul. Mr. Fairfax was his only companion. The two of them often dined together in the evening in the same cozy little parlor where John had taken tea on the night of his arrival.

During the day, Mr. Fairfax kept busy managing the small staff and seeing to meals and the account books. Thornfield employed no housekeeper. What servants John observed were mostly males—several strong footmen, a coachman, and a groundskeeper. The only women in residence besides Sophie were the cook and her scullery maid.

"Is it not too much, managing such a large house with so little staff?" John asked one morning, encountering Mr. Fairfax on the stairs.

The butler was breathing heavily as he climbed, clutching the banister with one age-spotted hand. "Not usually. Most of the house is shut up. We attend only to the main rooms."

"A large enough responsibility on their own."

"Yes, but one must keep them in order. Mrs. Rochester arrives with so little notice, you see. One never knows."

"And she expects the house to always be in readiness?" John frowned. "Is she an exacting sort of mistress?"

"Not particularly so, but she dislikes a flurry of activity upon her arrival." At the end of the hall, the folding doors of the drawing room stood open. Mr. Fairfax entered and immediately proceeded to dust some figures of fine porcelain that stood on the mantelpiece.

John followed behind. Until now, he'd only spied the lavish room from the threshold, not daring to enter it on his own. It was far too luxurious, with its rich chairs and curtains, thick Turkish carpets, and walnut-paneled walls. "Is she generally liked?" he asked.

"Oh yes. Her family has always been respected. They've owned most of the land in this county at one time or another."

"But what of Mrs. Rochester herself? What of her character?"

"Oh…" Mr. Fairfax returned one of the figures to the mantelshelf. "She is rather peculiar, I suppose. She's traveled a great deal and lived in a great many odd places. I daresay she's intelligent. Clever, even. But since she's returned to England, I've had little conversation with her."

"In what way peculiar?"

"Eccentric, you might say. And others *have* said. She speaks in such a blunt manner, you see, and has such decided opinions. She was always thus. Even as a girl. It amused her to put people out of countenance."

"What of her husband, Mr. Rochester? Did you know him well?"

"Not at all. Mrs. Rochester was both married and widowed during her travels. Her husband passed sometime last winter. She returned with Stephen and Peter in the summer. A month in residence, and then she was gone again. Heaven knows where. She doesn't care to be idle."

With that, Mr. Fairfax concluded his dusting—and his tale. He offered to show John over the rest of the house. "If you're looking for the most scenic views to sketch, you won't find them from the gallery windows."

"Do you know of a better vantage?"

"The best, sir." Mr. Fairfax led the way up the stairs to the third floor and down a dark, narrow hall. They passed low-ceilinged rooms filled with oversized furnishings from years gone by—heavy bedsteads, rows of narrow chairs with carved animal feet, and Egyptian-style ottomans and settees.

Some of the furniture was shrouded in holland covers, other pieces stood bare, revealing ebony surfaces painted with gold, and giltwood tables with jackal-headed figures standing upright in place of legs.

Such garish furnishings had been popular decades ago. Gaudy imitations of the treasures found in Egypt. John thought them more tasteless than sinister. And yet, when coupled with the gloomy quiet and the cold, stale air, the relics gave the third story of Thornfield Hall the feeling of a tomb. He couldn't imagine spending a night in such a place.

"Do the servants sleep here?" he asked.

"No. They occupy smaller apartments to the back of our own. These rooms aren't in use, nor are any on the third floor."

John followed Mr. Fairfax up a narrow flight of stairs to the attics. From there, an even narrower ladder gave access to a trapdoor overhead, leading to the roof of the Hall.

"I can no longer manage it myself," Mr. Fairfax said, "but if you wish to venture up, you will have a fine prospect from the battlements."

At the butler's insistence, John made his way to the roof alone. Raindrops fell in a gentle patter, dampening his hair and collar. Leaning over the battlements, he surveyed the grounds below him: the winding road, the velvet lawn, and the great meadow with its thorn trees.

The Millcote mists were settled over the landscape like so much silver vapor, clinging to the trees and swirling all about the drive. Were he standing below, they would obscure his view. Confuse him as they had on the night of his arrival. But here, on the roof, he could see above them. Over and beyond, all the way to Hay. Indeed, he could just make out a little spire rising from the hills. The village church. Not but two miles away, and yet undiscernible when on the ground.

John inhaled deeply. His head began to clear, the fresh air whisking away the last remnants of the small dose of laudanum he'd taken the night before. Mr. Fairfax was right. This was a princely prospect, and one John looked forward to sketching when the weather permitted.

Returning to the ladder, he climbed back down into the attic. It took his eyes a moment to adjust to the darkness.

"Go ahead," Mr. Fairfax said. "I'll fasten the trap-door."

John retraced his steps down the narrow staircase to the third floor. Once there, he waited in the passageway for Mr. Fairfax. It was still and quiet as death, all the wood-paneled doors in the corridor shut, and nothing but a little window at the end of the long hall to give any light. It was in all this silence that he heard the sudden sound of a man's laugh, echoing from the darkness.

It was a chilling noise. Cold and mirthless, with nothing of humor about it—or of humanity.

John's breath stopped in his chest. He froze where he stood, listening. The laughter ceased for a moment only to begin again, louder and more inhuman than before.

There was no way of pinpointing the source of it. It seemed to come from both nowhere and everywhere, the icy vibration of it infused in the very vault-like air around him.

"Mr. Fairfax," John said as the butler descended the stairs.

"Yes, sir?"

"Who was that laughing?"

Mr. Fairfax answered, quite unperturbed, "Mr. Poole, probably."

Mr. Poole?

John had never met the man. Which wasn't saying much. He rarely encountered the servants. "You did hear it, didn't you?"

"Oh, yes. I often do. Mr. Poole has a keen sense of humor."

At that moment, the laugh sounded again in a low tone.

"Mr. Poole!" Mr. Fairfax called out.

John didn't expect the fellow to answer, for the laugh had sounded almost preternatural. Indeed, were he a superstitious man, he might have been afraid. But it was the middle of the day, and there was no other circumstance of ghostliness about the incident. Certainly nothing like the night John's laudanum-addled brain had conjured Helen out of the mists.

Presently, a door at the end of the hall opened, and a middle-aged servant emerged. He was a large man—tall, broad, and muscular—with a dull, expressionless face and a rapidly balding pate. A less apparition-like figure John couldn't have imagined.

"Too much noise, Mr. Poole," Mr. Fairfax said.

Mr. Poole bowed and returned to his room.

"He mends old furniture for Mrs. Rochester, and is always at his work all hours of the day. He's quite skilled actually, particularly in matters of metalwork. On rare occasion you may encounter him at his forge in the stables." Mr. Fairfax walked alongside John as they departed the third floor, returning to the warmer, brighter levels below. "How did you fare with Stephen and Peter this morning? Are you making any progress?"

"Some," John said. "They've had another drawing lesson."

"Oh?"

"I mean to expand upon it when the weather permits."

"If you're waiting for sunshine, sir, you'll wait a long while. Until the storm comes, we'll have nothing but fog and damp."

John had begun to doubt whether the storm Mr. Fairfax so often spoke of would come at all. Though the rain fell, and the mist clung determinedly to the landscape, the weather never worsened. It was as if Thornfield were perpetually on the cusp of a storm—or caught in the eye of one. "Children aren't made of spun sugar. Many enjoy a bit of mud. Unless... you don't suggest that the wet weather would imperil their health?"

"No more than any other boys of their age. Though Stephen and Peter *were* ill during the journey. Seasickness, I believe."

"Is that all?"

Mr. Fairfax regarded John with a look of concern. "You suspected worse?"

"Frankly, yes. They look as though they'd fallen victim to something grave. A wasting disease, or—"

"Heavens, no. Mrs. Rochester would have told me if that was the case. She was confident the children could be fed up. It's why Cook insists they eat double portions of liver and other red meats. To help them get their color back."

"Have they yet seen a doctor?" John asked.

"On their arrival, Mrs. Rochester had the surgeon, Mr. Carter, in. He prescribed a tonic. Sophie administers it to them morning and evening."

John's lips compressed.

"You don't approve?"

"Of patent medicines? No, I don't. Not for children." Most patent medicines contained laudanum. And while John didn't scruple to take the drug himself, he knew enough of its side effects to be wary of it being administered to little boys.

"Mrs. Rochester wouldn't have authorized the treatment if she didn't believe it would work. She's very discerning and has no tolerance for any nonsense."

John wasn't so sure. What sort of lady would abandon her two young wards when they were in such poor health? Why wasn't she there, tending to them and looking after them? The boys must hold some affection for their benefactress. Surely her presence would be a comfort to them.

But of course it would. John knew that much from experience.

As a newly orphaned inmate of the charitable school, he'd often longed for the soothing touch of a mother. A cool hand across his brow, or a soft voice to sing him to sleep. It was easy to imagine the boys yearning for the same calming feminine presence. When one was ailing in body and spirit, nothing could compensate for the loving presence of a mother figure. Not a nurse or a benevolent butler. Not even a conscientious tutor.

But John didn't press the matter. Not yet. He'd been in his position only a fortnight and wasn't yet in possession of all of the facts. There was time enough to learn the truth of the boys' condition. He'd question Sophie if he must. Inspect the patent medicine or even talk to the surgeon. And soon—if his mysterious employer was ever inclined to return to Thornfield—he would address his concerns with Mrs. Rochester herself.

Five

Thornfield Hall
Yorkshire, England
January 1844

John measured out a teaspoonful of laudanum from one of the phials in his case. As autumn at Thornfield had given way to winter, he'd had no luck ridding himself of his headaches. But that was no reason he couldn't combat them in a more sensible manner. It had been months since he'd last downed a whole phial in one swallow. Now, he restricted himself to small doses. Only enough to ease the pounding in his temples.

The pain always came at night. Lying within the pitch-like darkness of his box bed, John's weary brain inevitably drifted to thoughts of Helen.

He'd sworn to purge her from his heart and mind, but the guilt over her death refused to be exorcised. As he drifted to sleep, he could sometimes fancy that he saw her there, kneeling at the end of his bed, inside of the darkness with him, accusing him of abandoning her.

As if, in life, Helen had ever come anywhere near his bedroom.

A stolen kiss she'd initiated behind the village schoolhouse had been the full extent of their physical relationship. It had immediately provoked in him a storm of regret and self-recrimination.

And not only that.

It had embarrassed him.

The truth was, he'd never thought of Helen in that way. Not as a potential conquest or a prospective lover. She'd been his friend. It was no small thing, but it hadn't been a romance. It couldn't have been. For all that he'd admired her beauty, the sight of her had never once made his heart beat faster.

"I'm sorry. I can't," John had said, pulling away from her.

He'd expected Helen to be equally embarrassed. Instead, she'd clung to him almost desperately. "Please don't," she'd said. "I need you so much. It's no use pretending."

"We mustn't." He'd set her apart from him with grim determination. "You're a married lady."

It hadn't mattered that her marriage was an unhappy one. That she was starved for love and affection. He'd wanted to abide by the rules. To do what was right.

"Don't forsake me John," Helen had begged. "I couldn't bear it."

And she hadn't borne it.

John's fingers tightened on the phial of laudanum. At length, he measured out a second teaspoonful and swallowed it down. Tonight, he needed a reprieve from her ghost, and if a double dose of laudanum was the only way to get one, then so be it.

He put away his case of medicine and climbed into his box bed. Settling under the coverlet, he reached to slide shut the heavy wooden panel.

And he hesitated.

The remnants of a fire still crackled in the grate. He was loath to lose the warmth of it.

Leaving the panel open, he lay down on the mattress, his feather pillow shaping itself to his throbbing head. His eyes fell closed. And he waited. Waited for his medicine to do its work.

A queer drug, laudanum. It ate away at the edges of his consciousness, pulling him down into a hazily pleasant stupor, leaving him suspended between sleep and waking. It was in that state that John heard the strangest thing. A soft, sibilant sound. Like two snakes conversing.

But it wasn't hissing, though it sounded eerily similar. It was whispering. Two murmuring voices passing secrets in the dark. A mere thread of twin breaths, too faint to make out the words.

Gooseflesh rose on John's arms. Steeling his nerves, he poked his head out of the side of his box bed. Where on earth was the hissing coming from? Was it outside his door? He didn't think so. There was no tread on the floorboards. No shadow cast from someone passing in front of the keyhole.

A piece of wood splintered and cracked in the fireplace, drawing John's gaze. Was it the fire that hissed? He watched it for a long moment, as the laudanum infiltrated his bloodstream.

But no.

The remnants of wood sparked, but they didn't hiss. And they certainly didn't whisper.

Settling back into his bed, he reminded himself that old houses made all sorts of odd sounds. Creaks, and shrieks, and groans.

And then there were the muffled voices of those houses' inmates. The sound of their footsteps, and of their intermittent laughter.

Indeed, how many times in these past months had he heard the strange laugh of Mr. Poole? That same mirthless chuckle that had turned John's blood cold when first he'd encountered it on the third floor? Since then, he'd sometimes seen Mr. Poole in the early morning hours, down in the kitchens with a basin or tray in his hands, or out by the stables working away at something on his forge. On each occasion, John had been singularly unimpressed by the man. He was no specter—no ghoul.

The source of the whispering was likely just as unimpressive. The house settling, or the wind whistling down the chimney. Either that, or like so much late at night, it was only in John's head. A product of drugs, and of conscience, made worse by his own imagination.

Helen was hundreds of miles away, moldering in her grave. She was out of pain now. At rest. There was no reason for her to haunt him so. What harm had he ever done her except to be kind? To know her and to be her friend.

To leave her behind.

His eyes moistened. He squeezed them shut, willing himself to sleep. In the past, he'd have taken another dose of laudanum, but not tonight. He'd had enough of the stuff already. It was time to be quit of the drug. To save it for only the worst of his headache pain. He was done with relying on it. Done with using it to blot out his grief and anger.

In time, his breath became regular, his chest rising and falling as he sank into sleep. The whispering resumed right before he drifted off. John's final thought was one of sudden understanding.

It's coming through the wall.

"They're not mutes," John said.

Mr. Fairfax was seated at a wooden table in the butler's pantry polishing the silver with a blackened cloth. Candlesticks, salt cellars, serving dishes, and flatware were all set out before him. "I beg your pardon, sir?" He cocked his ear toward John. "What was that you said?"

"Stephen and Peter aren't mutes." John sank down onto the hard wooden chair beside Mr. Fairfax. "I heard them speaking last night. Whispering to each other."

"You *heard* them?"

"Through the wall of my room."

Mr. Fairfax continued polishing. "What did they say?"

"I couldn't tell. The words were too faint. But I think…I very much suspect…that they weren't conversing in English."

"A foreign language?"

"None that I could discern. But I don't believe it was French or Italian. I would have recognized the cadence of it." John didn't know why Mr. Fairfax wasn't reacting with more interest. The butler just kept polishing, intent upon his task, as if spotless silver were the most important thing in his universe. "Did Mrs. Rochester never mention where it was they came from?"

Mr. Fairfax's brows beetled. He worked his cloth over the intricate relief decoration on the branches of a silver candelabra. "Europe?"

John suppressed a flicker of irritation. "Is that a question?"

"Only what I assumed, Mr. Eyre. Where else would they have come from?"

Where else, indeed.

"Did you ask Stephen and Peter directly?" Mr. Fairfax enquired.

"Not yet." John didn't want to alert the boys to the fact that he'd heard their whisperings. With any luck, they'd whisper again—and next time he'd be able to make out exactly what language they were speaking in.

They'd already come so far under his care. Both of them could now write their letters, and perform simple addition and subtraction. More importantly, they'd grown used to John himself. There was no more flinching—no more cringing away when he beckoned them forward. Once or twice, Stephen and Peter had even appeared to look to him for praise.

Their health had improved as well. With no parents about to object to his edicts, John had been able to do as he thought best. He'd put an end to their doses of tonic—a patent liver medication that held a greater concentration of opiates than it did any ingredients of value.

He'd also seen that fruits and sweets were added to their diet, and that Sophie ceased shearing their hair down to their scalps. Some still believed that, during illness, the hair deprived the body of vital nutrients, but John had never subscribed to that view. He preferred his pupils to have healthy food, and healthy occupation, without any remnants of the sickroom following them about.

Overall, he was pleased with the progress he'd made. His pupils looked less like animated corpses and more like little boys. They behaved more naturally—*moved* more naturally. And yet…

John knew enough to recognize that Stephen and Peter still didn't entirely trust him. There were no smiles. No laughter or boyish hijinks. And there was no speech. No sounds.

At least, not until last night.

"I wonder if I should write to Mrs. Rochester?" he asked. "It would save me trying to discover the answers to my questions on my own."

"You could do so," Mr. Fairfax replied. "But she moves about so frequently. It might be months before you receive an answer. Too much time to be of any use." He gestured to an envelope on the table. "I've written to her myself, as you see, in care of a hotel in Paris."

"Paris?" John had imagined Mrs. Rochester to be in London for the winter, not on the Continent. "Is that where she is?"

"She does abide there on occasion, or in Cairo, Athens, or Varna."

John's mouth quirked. Surely the butler was joking. "I hope you haven't any pressing concerns."

"No more than usual, sir. She answers my letters in her time. As long as I remember to post them."

"I'm walking to Hay after the boys' afternoon lessons," John said. "I can take your letter with me, if you like."

"You don't mind?"

"Not at all." John had walked to Hay several times in the past months. It was a mere two miles away. And though he didn't bother to stop and scrape acquaintance with anyone in the village, the exercise never failed to do him good.

"Very well. But be careful of the Millcote mists. They're worse in the evening."

John had observed as much. The mists always grew heavier at night, making the roads a hazard. "I shall be back before sunset."

Hours later, with lessons at an end for the day, John finally set out across the meadow for Hay, bundled up in his overcoat, scarf, and gloves.

It was a chill January evening. The earth was damp beneath his booted feet, and the air was still. There was no one else about on the narrow country road. None he could see moving through the mists that gathered over the ground and along the trees.

As he walked, twilight approached, lending an air of magic to the bleak winter landscape. He was but a mile from Thornfield in a lonely lane, the chief pleasure of which lay in its utter solitude. It led all the way to Hay at a slow incline, flanked by leafless trees and empty fields.

In the distance, the moon rose over the frost-covered hills—a sliver of luminous white.

John realized, all at once, that he'd misjudged the time.

He'd left Thornfield too late to beat the darkness. Even now, the mists were thickening, beginning to obscure his view. Every footfall sank him deeper into the billows of swirling gray.

He briefly contemplated turning back. But there was no point abandoning his task. Not now he was more than halfway there.

Hastening his step, he continued on, only to be brought up short by an unsettling sound.

It emanated from within the mists ahead of him, at once recognizable: the low growl of an animal.

John's heartbeat quickened in spite of himself. Foolish. It couldn't be anything dangerous. Not hereabouts. A dog merely.

It snarled again—an unmistakable threat.

And then John saw it, moving through the mist like a shadow. His stomach clenched. Good God, it wasn't a dog.

It was a wolf.

He took an instinctive step backward as the creature approached. It was black and rangy, its teeth bared in a snarl as it padded toward him.

It wasn't real. It couldn't be. There were no wolves in England.

He recalled stories he'd learned in the nursery. Old folklore told to him by his equally old nurse. Stories of black dogs in the North of England. Animal-shaped spirits—shapeshifters and familiars—that roamed the moors. They were believed to haunt the lonely highways and byways of Britain, preying on solitary travelers.

Travelers like him.

"You're not real," he said to the wolf.

In reply, the wolf bared its teeth. Saliva dripped from its jaws.

John took another step backward, his breath burning in his lungs.

In the very next moment, a rush of wind came down the lane, accompanied by the pounding of hooves. The wolf cringed at the thunderous sound, and with a whining cry, the great creature sprang away, disappearing into the mist a fraction of a second before a horse emerged: a great black steed with rolling eyes and a frothing mouth.

Another apparition?

But no.

There was a rider atop the horse. A lady in a fitted black riding habit. Her presence at once broke the spell. She was all too real, and so was her horse. John leapt out of their way as soon as he realized it.

It wasn't soon enough.

The horse spooked at the sight of him, rising up on its hind legs in a panicked rear. Lowering back to the ground, it surged past him in a dead bolt, its rider sawing on the reins. In the next instant, it skidded and fell with a clatter, taking its rider down with it.

John ran to assist her. "Are you all right?"

"The dratted beast has slipped on the ice." The lady propped herself up on one elbow, watching her horse scramble to its feet. "He looks no worse for it, thank God."

"What about you? Are you injured?"

Gathering up the voluminous skirts of her habit, she attempted to regain her feet, only to inhale sharply as she put her weight on her right leg. "Blast it." She tested her foot again. Her face contorted with pain. "Your arm, if you please."

John strode to her side. "If you require a doctor, I can fetch the surgeon from Hay."

"Thank you, no. Your arm will suffice." She took hold of it, gripping him tightly as she stood.

John placed his hand at her waist to support her. It was a small waist, tightly corseted, though she wasn't a small woman. When standing, she was nearly of a height with him. "Are you certain?" he asked.

She briefly bent to feel her foot and leg. "I'll live. Assist me to that stile, would you? I should like to sit down a moment and catch my breath."

He helped her across the lane and stood at her side as she sank down on the step of the stile. The fall had knocked her riding hat off, and her hair had come partially loose. In the waxing moonlight, he could see her face quite clearly.

His heart gave a queer double thump.

She was beautiful, but not in the usual style. Certainly not in any style that he'd ever encountered before. There was an exotic quality to her countenance—skin that was faintly olive, an aquiline nose, and dark flashing eyes that sparked with flecks of bronze and green. And her hair! It was wild, and curling black, with the most extraordinary streak of white through it—a two-inch bolt of lightning, beginning to the right of her brow and flashing all the way to the ends of her glossy tresses.

Such an odd feature should have put him in mind of an older woman. But this lady wasn't old. Indeed, he'd be astonished if she was very much older than he was himself.

"You may go," she said. "I'm quite all right now."

"I can't leave you here like this. Not at this time of night."

"How chivalrous you are. One wonders why you're not at home yourself. The mists aren't safe after dark. Every fool knows that. You must be a stranger here."

"Not at all. I've resided here since the autumn."

"That long?" Her voice held a flicker of mockery. "Where do you live, then? Are you from Hay? Let me guess. You're the new curate. You have the look of an ascetic about you."

John bent his head to conceal a smile. "No, ma'am. I'm not from Hay, and I'm not a curate. I don't believe the vicar has one."

"No? More's the pity." She massaged her ankle. "Well? If not from Hay, then where is it you come from?"

"Just there." He gestured to the hills behind her. They were cloaked in a heavy mist. "Thornfield Hall. It's the home of Mrs. Rochester."

She was quiet a moment, her dark brows knit in a frown. "I see. And do you know Mrs. Rochester?"

"I haven't yet had the pleasure of meeting her. She's presently away from home."

The lady's gaze dropped from his face to study his simply clad figure. "You're not a servant."

"No, ma'am. I'm tutor to Mrs. Rochester's wards."

"Ah. Of course you are." She brought her eyes back to his. Her frown deepened. "Do you always stand right in the center of the road?"

"No, I—" He broke off. "I thought I saw a wild animal in the mist. A...dog."

"A wild dog?"

"Something like." He was reluctant to say what he'd actually seen. A wolf? It defied belief. "Did you happen to see anything?"

"Nothing but a man standing in my way. Has no one at Thornfield warned you not to be out after dark?"

"I expected to be back before nightfall. The time got away from me." He saw her wince again as she put weight on her foot. "I beg your pardon, but are you quite certain you don't need me to fetch the surgeon? It would be no trouble."

"No, no. But you can do me another service, if you please. Catch my horse by the bridle, would you? And bring him here so I can mount."

The horse was nearby, idly cropping a tuft of weeds. Approaching slowly, John caught the hanging leather reins and used them to lead the horse to its mistress. The creature didn't go quietly. It was a spirited beast, tossing its head and stamping its hooves.

"Calm down, you great idiot," the lady commanded. She looked at John. "I must impose on you again."

"I'm at your service."

"Can you manage to lift me up into the saddle? Or would such familiarity put you to the blush?"

John refrained from pointing out that though he may look the part of an ascetic, he most certainly wasn't one. "I believe I'm up to the task."

"Excellent." She reached out to him with an imperious hand.

He took it without hesitation. Gloved in fine black leather, it fit rather well in his own. He helped her to her feet. She released him almost at once in order to gather her horse's reins.

John came to stand behind her. "Forgive me," he said as his hands closed about her waist. She was right up against him, soft tendrils of her hair brushing his cheek. So close he could smell the elusive fragrance of her perfume. Some heady combination of sandalwood, vanilla, and spices.

Heat rose up his neck. It had been a very long while since he'd taken a woman in his arms. And this lady was no Helen Burns. No clinging vine of femininity. She was vibrant and alive. A veritable force of charismatic energy. "Are you ready?"

"Yes, but be quick about it before he takes it into his head to bolt again."

John lifted her easily and tossed her up into her sidesaddle.

She landed with practiced skill, at once taking charge of her mount, even as she found her stirrup and swiftly arranged the skirts of her fashionable black habit. "You're very strong," she said. "You will need to be."

With that enigmatic statement, the lady kicked her horse into a canter and was gone.

John stood at the top of the lane, watching as she disappeared into the mist.

Six

*Letters from
Miss Bertha Mason to
Miss Blanche Ingram.*

*Hôtel d'Angleterre
Athens, Greece
Thursday, 11 August 1842*

My Dear Blanche, —

Thank you for your sweet letter! I was delighted to hear about the arrival of a new vicar in Hay, and doubly glad to hear that he's so very amiable. You must tell me more about this promising gentleman at your earliest convenience. Not that I have any right to press you to write more often. I daresay you've long since given up on receiving timely reports of my own adventures. But I have an excuse, dearest, for you see, I have spent the past weeks on a ship traveling to Athens.

Yes, I've at last given up Egypt. The sweltering temperatures were simply too much to bear, and when Mrs. Wren and her brother invited me to accompany them to Greece,

I fairly jumped at the chance. The three of us have become fast friends, and have been spending ever so much time in each other's company.

You will be pleased to hear that Mr. Rochester is every bit as charming and agreeable as his sister. Like her, his English is, for the most part, excellent (albeit with a strange intonation), and he has a command of many other languages as well. He's never been to England as yet, but he often speaks of his desire to return to the "land of his father's ancestors," as he calls it.

How else to describe him? Words seem wholly inadequate. He's neither a dandy, nor a scholar. Not a young man, nor one of middle age. He is, in fact, rather a riddle to me, though I have been traveling with him these many weeks.

I daresay my confusion owes more to my own reaction to him than to any objective fact. And yes—in answer to your question—he's tall and handsome and all that sort of thing. But the same might be said for dozens of men, and none of their kind has ever captivated me to such a degree before. I suppose it's that Mr. Rochester has taken such an interest in me. He solicits my opinions on a range of topics and has even heeded my advice on occasion.

And you're not to think it's because of my fortune, for Mr. Rochester has a fortune in his own right. He owns property in the West Indies, as well as in Europe, from which he derives a sizable income. It is enough to fund his various pursuits—one of which, I've lately discovered, was the dig I visited in Thebes. Mr. Rochester has a particular passion for antiquities, and not only of the Egyptian variety. He's collected ancient artifacts from all over the world and keeps them in a special vault at his estate.

As to Greece, there isn't much I can say. I imagined ancient wonders, honey-covered sweets, and warm waters of sapphire blue, but the heat has played havoc with Mr. Rochester's health. To accommodate him, Mrs. Wren and I restrict our outings to the evening, just as we did in Cairo. We're up all hours of the night, talking and dining and wandering about the city. As a result, I sleep through much of the day. Agnes and Mr. Poole do *not* approve. But you know how very unromantic British servants can be. They love nothing more than tradition and routine. Anything that diverges from such is looked on with the gravest suspicion.

I shall have more time to write in the coming days. We plan to remain in Greece for the month. Mrs. Wren is looking into taking a villa. It will be more comfortable than staying at a hotel.

Goodbye for now, my dear. I promise to write again before the month is out.

I remain, your always loving,
Bertha

Villa Striges
Athens, Greece
Friday, 9 September 1842

Dearest Blanche, —

Apologies for the delay. What a domestic dustup we've had! You will never believe it, but I've been writing to you often these past weeks, and only noticed yesterday that you've yet to send a reply. On further investigation, I discovered that one of the servants at the villa has failed to deliver your letters, or to post any of mine. Heaven knows why. Mrs. Wren says it's pure laziness and has fired the girl. She tells me that she'll be taking personal responsibility for the post from now on, but I'm loath to inconvenience her with my private correspondence and have set Mr. Poole to the task.

Along with domestic troubles, we've also had a tragedy in the village to contend with. The body of a local woman was found on Friday. She was mauled by some manner of wild animal. No one knows for certain what kind of animal it was, but we have all been advised to remain on our guard after dark. It's put me rather on edge, especially as most of my activities of late take place in the evening. I'm eagerly anticipating cooler weather in hopes that Mr. Rochester can better tolerate the temperatures, and I can once again resume a daylight existence.

He and I have been spending more time together in the evenings. Mrs. Wren has lately been ill, and often retires to her room while Mr. Rochester and I dine or go out together to stroll about the village. You will, perhaps, think it not very appropriate that I should spend so much time in his company unchaperoned, but Mr. Rochester is the soul of propriety. Indeed, his manners are faultless. I frequently joke that he has the sensibilities of a much older gentleman—a courtier from centuries gone by.

But though I feel a definite fondness for him—and flatter myself that he cherishes the same sentiment toward me—that fondness has never been put into words. He's not said a thing to me that could ever be construed as a passionate declaration, nor made any attempt to do more than shake my hand. I own to being a trifle frustrated. There have been many moments when some greater expression of affection would have been welcome, and most happily so.

Have I done wrong to remain so long in company with Mr. Rochester and his sister? The villa in which we've taken up residence is in every way agreeable, but the servants answer to Mrs. Wren, not to me. I keenly feel my lack of power here, and my lack of independence. Perhaps it's time for me to strike out on my own again? Then again, it can surely do no harm to remain a while longer. The warm friendship I've developed with my host and hostess does much to compensate for my misgivings.

Enough about me. Let me hear from you, dearest! Tell me what the weather is like in Millcote, and who has come to call since last you wrote. Anything more about the vicar in Hay? Is he still as promising a prospect as you first surmised? Enclose a sketch of him when next you write, and I shall tell you precisely what I think.

I must dash now. Mr. Poole is walking into the village, and awaits my letter to post. I pray you will receive it directly.

All my love to you,
Bertha

Villa Striges
Athens, Greece
Monday, 17 October 1842

Darling Blanche, —

How pleased I was to receive your letter this morning—and how angry I am at our former servant for having disposed of your previous ones, for I realize now just how much I've missed of the goings-on in Millcote and Hay. Thank you, my dear, for so patiently catching me up with the state of things. I am, of course, overjoyed to hear that your vicar has asked leave of your father to pay court to you. Judging from the portrait you enclosed, I must conclude he's as sensible as he is handsome.

I have some good news of my own to share, though I fear you will find it comes rather too quickly. It is this: Mr. Rochester has proposed to me.

As you'll no doubt guess from my last letter, his proposal was entirely unexpected. How was I to know he was even contemplating such a course? After more than two months in each other's company, we had settled into a companionable enough relationship, but he never once made any direct overtures until last evening. (As to that, I will tell you all, my dear, but you must promise to burn this letter after reading it. If it fell into the wrong hands, it would compromise me utterly.)

You see, Mrs. Wren has been away this week. She was obliged to travel inland on a matter of business. I was given the choice of accompanying her—an unpleasant prospect, especially with that wild creature still roaming about. It's mauled another villager, can you believe it? The fellow was found near the beach in a most dreadful state. Regrettably, he succumbed to his wounds before he could describe what manner of animal had attacked him.

The villagers have been frightened. They're a superstitious people and have come up with all kinds of theories, none of which have the slightest connection to reality. Common sense says that there must be a wolf or bear hereabouts. One with hydrophobia, perhaps. It gives me shivers to think of encountering such a creature. Hence my decision to remain at the villa with Mr. Rochester. You see, I hold my life slightly more valuable than I hold my reputation. An unpopular opinion for a lady in my position, I know.

Naturally, I'm still attended by Agnes and Mr. Poole, though neither was accompanying me on this particular night. Mr. Rochester suggested we go for a walk along the beach.

The sea was in turmoil, the waves crashing mightily on the shore. It was there he first took me in his arms and kissed me. Not a friendly kiss like you and I have shared, nor a kiss one might receive from a gentleman beneath the mistletoe. This was altogether different. To begin with, it lasted much longer than any kiss I've ever had before. I won't go into intimate detail, except to say that, when coupled with the passion of his embrace, it was all rather thrilling.

Sometime later, he confessed that he had come to care for me deeply. To love me, in fact, and that it was his fondest wish that I would consent to be his wife. He even produced a ring—a blood ruby on a band of gold, not too dissimilar to one worn by his sister. A family heirloom, he said. Part of a valuable set, hundreds of years old.

Dearest, you know what my feelings have been about marriage. How determinedly I resisted the pressure of my parents and of Yorkshire society. But this is quite a different matter. I'm no longer an inexperienced girl, languishing in the country. I'm a woman, grown. A woman who has seen the world, and who knows her own mind better than she ever has before.

It's true my attorney, Mr. Hughes, has been urging me to marry. I expect he thinks a husband will manage my fortune and property better than I will myself. But Mr. Hughes's advice has had no influence on my decision. The simple truth is, I believe that marrying Mr. Rochester will be the greatest adventure of my life. He's unlike any gentleman I have ever met, or am ever likely to meet again. I'd be a fool to refuse him. And I am no fool.

Be happy for me, my dear.

Your own,
Bertha

Seven

Thornfield Hall
Yorkshire, England
January 1844

After depositing Mr. Fairfax's letter at the post office in Hay, John returned to Thornfield along the same narrow lane from whence he'd come. Walking briskly through the gathering mist, he was alert for any sign of the wolf. But the creature made no reappearance.

John began to doubt whether it had ever existed to begin with.

It had likely been nothing more than his imagination playing tricks on him again. One day the ghostly figure of Helen Burns, another the form of a ravening wolf. If there was some deeper meaning to the sightings, John couldn't discern it. All he knew—all that he was quite certain of—was that the two teaspoonfuls of laudanum he'd taken last night had been one teaspoonful too many. Better to suffer the pains of a headache than to be haunted thus.

Passing through the creaking gates that led up the drive to Thornfield, he crossed the frozen lawn and entered the house through one of the side doors. At this time of evening, Thornfield was usually quiet, its inmates settling down for dinner and bed. Tonight, however, it was bustling with activity. Footmen dashed past John in the hall. Mr. Fairfax followed after them, barking orders at everyone in his path.

"Whatever is the matter?" John asked.

Mr. Fairfax came to meet him. "Oh, Mr. Eyre. Thank goodness you've returned." He took John's hat and coat. "The mistress has arrived this very moment. And injured, too! Some thoughtless fool startled her horse on the road. She fell and turned her ankle. I've been unable to persuade her to send for the surgeon. She claims all is well, but what a foul mood she's in. And rightfully so."

John stilled for an instant, understanding sinking in.

The darkly beautiful lady he'd encountered in the lane had been Mrs. Rochester.

A leaden weight formed in his stomach as he recollected the noble turn of her countenance, the feel of her corseted waist under his hands, and the soft brush of her hair against his face. She'd been almost queenly. Vaguely seductive with her exotic perfume and imperious manner.

Good lord. He'd known his employer was a woman, but he hadn't imagined her being quite so womanly. How could he work for such a person? Not a middle-aged matron, but a lady who was almost of an age with him?

It was perhaps foolish to concern himself with such things. A lady was a lady, no matter her age, and he was only a tutor. A gentleman of no family or fortune. He could scarcely be expected to have much interaction with her. But his experience with Helen had made him wary.

"I'm sorry now that I sent you off with my letter," Mr. Fairfax said. "Had I known the mistress was returning today, I'd never have troubled to write to her. If only she could have given us some notice. But I won't complain. We're fortunate to have her home in any event."

"Does she wish to see me?" John asked.

"You, sir? Ah, you mean does she wish you to bring down Stephen and Peter. No, indeed, Mr. Eyre. She's in no mood to see the boys this evening. You're quite at liberty to retire after you dine. Alas, I will be too busy to join you. The coach will be arriving soon with her baggage from Millcote. I shall have to eat in the kitchen as I'm able. Make free with my parlor, if you like."

"Thank you," John said, "but I believe I'll dine with the boys this evening."

He'd done so on several occasion in the past months. It gave him an opportunity to be with them outside of the schoolroom and to further develop the tenuous bond they were forging.

That he *hoped* they were forging.

After washing and changing, he joined them in the nursery. A small walnut table stood in the corner. The two boys sat around it in high-backed wooden chairs.

John wondered how Mrs. Rochester would react to the changes in their appearance. Not only had their hair grown, their features had filled out a bit, too. Gone were the hollow cheeks and sunken eyes that had characterized their faces on John's arrival last year. Under his care, even their skin had improved. It was no longer deathly white, only a little pale and shadowed.

A footman assisted Sophie in bringing up their dinner, a wholesome meal of roast beef, boiled potatoes and carrots, and a tureen of pea soup.

Dismissing the servants, John ladled out the soup to the boys himself. "Mrs. Rochester has come home."

Stephen and Peter exchanged a glance before dropping their eyes to their bowls. Their faces were curiously blank.

John gestured for them to pick up their spoons. He hadn't expected them to respond, but was nevertheless disappointed at their lack of reaction. The least they could do was show some sign that Mrs. Rochester's return was of interest to them. She'd brought them into her home. Had ensured that they were looked after. Provided for.

"Perhaps you'll see her tomorrow," he said as the boys began to eat. "She'll be pleased to hear of all the progress you've made."

But on the following day, Mrs. Rochester didn't send for the boys, nor did she send for John. In fact he didn't see her at all, not even during his midday and early evening walks about the grounds. He'd quite given up on being summoned when, at half past four, as afternoon lessons were ending, Mr. Fairfax came into the library.

"Mr. Eyre," he said. "Mrs. Rochester has requested that you and the boys join her in the drawing room for tea this evening."

John was standing at the bookcase, directing the boys to put away their books for the day. He straightened to attention at Mr. Fairfax's words. "Of course. What time does she take her tea?"

"At six o'clock. You'll have ample time to shave and change."

"Should I?"

"Oh, yes. I always do before joining her in the evenings. One mustn't give her any reason to criticize. She'll have cause enough already, what with you having taken away the children's tonic."

John didn't say anything. What *could* he say? He'd known when he made the decision to put a stop to the boys' patent medicine that, eventually, he'd have to answer for it. "I see," he replied at length. "Well, I trust the improvement in their appearance will speak for itself."

Mr. Fairfax inclined his head. "Sophie should be down to fetch them directly. I'll see that she prepares them for tea. They've little jackets about somewhere, haven't they? And clean neckcloths?" With that, the butler withdrew, still muttering to himself as he went.

A gathering mass of anxiety grew in John's chest. A physical weight he could feel lodging itself beneath the bones of his sternum. He didn't know enough about Mrs. Rochester to anticipate what she might ask of him, or what she might expect. And he didn't like having to defend his methods.

"That will be all for today, boys," he said after the last book was shelved. Sophie had materialized at the door of the library, awaiting her charges as she always did. Stephen and Peter were never permitted to roam the house unaccompanied. "Go with Nurse. I'll see you again this evening at tea."

As they passed him on their way to the door, John patted each of them on the shoulder. He'd never endorsed teachers being overly demonstrative with their students. A pupil wasn't meant to be doted upon. Certainly not by a figure so briefly in their lives as a governess or tutor. Forming an attachment would only inflict unnecessary suffering on the child when the inevitable day of parting came.

But Stephen and Peter were a different case entirely. They were small and frail, and sometimes…

Sometimes, John even fancied that they were afraid.

Of what, he didn't know.

Perhaps, like him, it was only bad memories that haunted them. Some tragedy from their past. The loss of their parents or their homeland. The least he could do was offer them reassurance. To that end, he'd lately made it his habit to ruffle Peter's hair on occasion, or to rest a steadying hand on Stephen's narrow back. Initially, they'd flinched, but now they seemed to accept his attention. Sometimes, even to bask in it.

After they'd gone, John tidied the library, pushing in the chairs at the boys' makeshift desks and organizing his papers for tomorrow's lessons. Having done so, he repaired to his room where he shaved and changed into a fresh frock coat and cravat.

At ten minutes to six o'clock, he collected Stephen and Peter from the nursery. Together, they made their way to the drawing room. Mr. Fairfax was already there, seated on a damask-covered settee in front of the fire. Across from him, half reclined on an overstuffed silk sofa, was Mrs. Rochester.

She was clad in unrelieved black crepe. A mourning dress. It was fitted tight through the bodice and arms with a high neck and full skirts that spilled all about her. A jet brooch was affixed to her throat, along with a silver locket on a long chain. It twinkled in the flickering light cast from the fire and the two wax candles that stood on the mantelpiece. Another ornament of jet adorned her hair, pinned into the thick coil of plaits she wore at her nape.

Staring into the fire, she took a sip from the delicate porcelain teacup poised in her hand, not seeming to notice that anyone else had entered the room.

"Here is Mr. Eyre," Mr. Fairfax said. "And he's brought Stephen and Peter."

"Excellent," Mrs. Rochester replied, still gazing fixedly into the flames. "Boys? Come here to me."

John urged Stephen and Peter forward. The boys crossed the distance to Mrs. Rochester, coming to a halt in front of her. Stephen's hand crept out to take that of his brother.

Mrs. Rochester set down her teacup and saucer and turned to examine her two young wards. Her bronze-and-green-flecked gaze drifted over them, her brows drawn into a frown. Searching, searching. As if the two boys were a puzzle she couldn't solve.

After a long moment, she reached out and touched Stephen gently on the cheek with the back of her fingers. She touched Peter as well, a soft brush of her hand down the length of his slim arm, culminating with a squeeze of his hand. All the while, she looked into their eyes, and they gazed steadily back at her. Something seemed to pass between the three of them. An unspoken emotion, as strong as speech.

John felt it resonate. A taut silence, but not an empty one. The moment was infused with meaning, as impossible to comprehend as the boys' whispered words had been two nights before.

If Mr. Fairfax sensed it, he gave no indication. Instead, he seemed to think it necessary to fill the vast silence with an endless stream of chatter. He expressed sympathy for Mrs. Rochester's injured ankle, marveled at her patience in being confined to the couch, and gave voice to his wish that she remain in residence through the winter. He even made a point of commending John's work with the boys.

"They're much improved, aren't they?" he asked. "And it's all owing to the efforts of Mr. Eyre. His presence here has been a blessing. You can't imagine how grateful we all are for your having had the wisdom to hire him. Stephen and Peter are flourishing, I tell you. But that's plain enough to see. One hardly recognizes them from the sad figures they presented when they arrived here. I didn't like to say so then, but I was quite afraid for their health."

"Mr. Fairfax," she said when the elderly butler at last paused to draw breath, "you may return Stephen and Peter to the nursery. I require a private word with Mr. Eyre."

Mr. Fairfax cast a worried glance at John as he stood. "Yes, ma'am. As you say." He ushered Stephen and Peter from the room. "Come along, boys. I will take you back to Nurse."

The drawing room doors shut behind them.

John remained where he was, standing in respectful silence across from his employer.

Mrs. Rochester regarded him from her place on the sofa. "Are you certain you're not a curate?"

He blinked. "I beg your pardon?"

"You look the very picture of one now. Something about your face. I thought you an ascetic when I encountered you in the lane. Now it seems to me that you're more in line with a medieval reformer." She picked up her teacup from the table at her side. "Do sit down, Mr. Eyre."

He took the seat on the settee lately vacated by Mr. Fairfax.

"You've made quite a lot of changes to the rules I set out for my wards," she said. "I'd be well within my rights to dismiss you."

The very prospect of losing his employment was enough to make John's palms grow damp. He was grateful his voice didn't betray his apprehension. "Yes, I daresay you would."

"Perhaps I will do." She took a sip of her tea. "You've been resident in my house three months?"

"Yes, ma'am." John noticed, for the first time, that she was absent a wedding band. A minor thing, to be sure. And yet it seemed an odd lapse for a widow who was, otherwise, sporting such a heavy display of mourning. She was all but veiled.

Her questions continued at a brusque clip, a hint of impatience in her voice. "And you came from—?"

"I was lately employed in Surrey."

"That much I know. But where is it that you *come from*, sir? Where were you *born*? Surely you didn't spring to life fully formed. Or perhaps you did. Perhaps you're some otherworldly creature brought here to lurk in the middle of fog-bound lanes."

"No indeed, ma'am," he said gravely. "I was born in Hertfordshire." He anticipated her next question. "In a village called Letchmore Green."

"And your parents? Do they still reside thereabouts?"

"My parents are no longer living. They died when I was a child."

"I see." She lowered her cup. "How, may I ask?"

"An influenza epidemic. It took them swiftly, along with many others in our village." John had little memory of the events, except that his nurse had bundled him up in a blanket and taken him away. She'd passed him on to another family, who were fleeing to the neighboring town, before taking ill herself.

"What became of you?" Mrs. Rochester asked. "Had you any relations to take you in? Any uncles or aunts, or kindly grandparents?"

"Not a one, kindly or otherwise. I was sent to a charitable school on the outskirts of the county."

"Ah." She studied his face. "What age were you?"

"Five."

"And how long were you there?"

"Until I was twenty."

"Fifteen years! You must be tenacious of life." She paused. "Why did you not leave when you came of age?"

"I was offered a position as teacher there. It seemed wise to take it. I had little experience of the world yet, and nothing much to recommend me."

She tapped one fingertip on her teacup. "Where did you go after you left the charitable school?"

"To a boy's school in London. I taught there for many years. Nearly four altogether. When the school closed down, I was obliged to move on."

Her brows lifted slightly.

"The school's benefactor was killed in a carriage accident," he explained. "Without funding, it could no longer afford to operate."

"Is that when you removed to Surrey?"

"No, ma'am. I was employed at another school for a brief while. It was after that—some two years later—that I went to Surrey."

"And there you taught at a village school? In Lowton?"

"I was the village schoolmaster. Until last year." John's mouth went dry. He glanced at the tea tray. "May I?"

"By all means."

He poured out a cup for himself and took a drink. It was Indian tea—strong, and fragrant.

"Why did you leave Lowton?" she asked.

He lowered his cup back to its saucer. "I decided it was time for a change."

"So, you placed an advertisement in the newspaper. And Mr. Fairfax answered." A wry smile edged her mouth. "You came well-recommended. Indeed, the squire's wife in Lowton gave you a glowing character. One might even say a worshipful one."

John's stomach knotted. His gaze briefly fell to the contents of his cup. "I was grateful to her for providing it."

"Hmm." Mrs. Rochester leaned back on the sofa. The fabric of her skirts rustled over her petticoats. An alluring sound—and one John hadn't heard since leaving Lowton. He hadn't had much occasion, of late, to be in the presence of ladies. "What are your particular skills, sir? Mr. Fairfax would have me believe you an expert in all things, but you and I know better. An education from a charitable school is oft as many times one of God-fearing piousness than of reading, writing, and arithmetic."

"There *was* a great deal of religious emphasis at the school," John conceded.

Rather too much. The children had often been deprived of food and warmth. The proprietor claimed that such deprivations brought them closer to God. In reality, it had only made them weaker and more susceptible to illness. During John's time there, many children had died.

"I suppose, then, that you can quote me scripture and verse of your Bible," Mrs. Rochester said.

"If you require it. I was also taught more practical skills. In addition to reading, writing, and arithmetic, I know something of globes, a little French and Italian, music, and—"

"Drawing? Mr. Fairfax says you carry a sketchpad about the grounds, and that you've been teaching the boys to draw, as well."

"I've been giving them some instruction, yes, ma'am."

"I suppose you fancy yourself an artist."

"Not at all. I have only a modest talent, but I believe the boys *are* learning—and deriving pleasure from their efforts."

"A modest talent? I shall be the judge of that." She made an impatient gesture toward the door. "Well, Mr. Eyre? Fetch your portfolio."

He retrieved it from the library and brought it to her. She took it without a word. John returned to his seat, watching her flip through the contents with a vague feeling of uneasiness. He'd shared his portfolio before—with other employers, as well as with his students. And yet it was an infinitely personal thing. A unique expression of his vision. A glimpse at how he viewed the world, and the people around him.

She scrutinized each sketch and painting, turning them over when she'd finished with them. Some she held longer than others, her eyes drifting over the work with greater interest. "This landscape," she said as she perused a watercolor. "Is it somewhere in Hertfordshire?"

"No, ma'am. It's a place I imagined."

She turned to the next painting in his portfolio. "What of this subject? Was she also a product of your imagination?"

John's chest tightened. "No. That one was taken from life."

Mrs. Rochester looked over the portrait. It was a watercolor, like the painting before it, but there the similarity ended. There was no darkness to the delicate rendering, only light. The golden sun of a glittering summer afternoon, shining on the subject's blond hair and illuminating the perfect oval of her face. John had mixed the blue tint for her eyes with special care. A subtle shade, with a mild sheen to it. It was the only thing to hint at the sadness within.

"Who is she?" Mrs. Rochester asked.

He cleared his throat. "She was the squire's wife in Lowton."

"Ah, I see," she said. "The lady who gave you such an impeccable character." And then: "*Was?*"

"She died recently."

Mrs. Rochester's eyes briefly met his over the painting. "You begin to worry me, Mr. Eyre. It seems you've left a trail of bodies in your wake. Is there anyone for whom you've worked that still lives? Or am I, myself, now in peril?"

A flare of indignation ignited in John's breast. He reminded himself of Mr. Fairfax's words—that Mrs. Rochester was eccentric. That she enjoyed putting people out of countenance. But to make light of Helen's death? To mock the very losses that had brought him low? "Mrs. Rochester," he began. "The tragedies of my past—"

"What is this?"

John broke off. She'd turned to the next painting in his portfolio. But it wasn't a painting. It was a charcoal drawing.

And it wasn't one of his.

He leaned forward in his seat to get a better view. "I was wondering that myself. Stephen sketched it the first day I provided him with paper and pencils."

Mrs. Rochester stared down at the drawing, an expression in her eyes that was hard to read. "Did he."

"It's a subject of his own devising. Something he imagined. Or perhaps that he's seen before. A window, I thought. Do you recognize it, ma'am?"

"No. Of course not." Her face had gone pale in the firelight. "It's nothing. A child's nightmare. You shouldn't indulge them in sketching such grim scenes." And then, before John could discern her intention, she crumpled the drawing in her fist and tossed it into the fireplace. It immediately caught flame.

"Wait!" He lunged to retrieve it. "You shouldn't have—"

She turned on him in a fury. "How dare you?" Her voice was low and fierce, sending him back into his seat as Stephen's drawing burned to cinders. "You know nothing of those boys, and nothing of my reasons for keeping them the way I do. You think to dictate to me? To override my decisions as if I were some silly woman with no notion of what I'm about?"

He drew back at the heat of her words. Confused. Speechless. He'd been scolded by employers before—shouted at and reprimanded. And he'd borne it, always. There was little choice when one was in a subordinate position. But this time—*this time*—his temper rose within him at the injustice of her anger. Hadn't he helped the boys? Hadn't he made progress?

It was all he could do to respond in a civilized manner.

"When I arrived here," he said, "the children were in a terrible state."

"The children were being looked after! According to *my* orders. And here I find out that you've countermanded those orders. That you've—"

"Their tonic—"

"Yes, yes. So I understand. You think it useless. A patent medicine bought by witless fools to treat imaginary ailments. Tell me, sir, do I look like a fool?"

He answered grudgingly. "No, ma'am."

"No, indeed. There are rules in this house, laid down for the protection of those children, and for everyone else hereabouts. I owe you no explanation for anything. Even less, for after meeting you this evening, I'm hard-pressed to decide whether I wish you to remain here." At that, she closed his portfolio and thrust it back at him.

He took it from her, his heart racing. Good lord. Had he just been given the sack? He looked at Mrs. Rochester. She was, once again, half reclined on her sofa, her expression drawn inward. She appeared to have already mentally dismissed him.

"I'm sorry if I've given offense," he said. "It wasn't my—"

"That will be all, Mr. Eyre. I grow weary."

"Yes, ma'am. But if you would—"

"Enough." She waved him away.

There was nothing John could do but withdraw. Relinquishing his seat, he walked stiffly to the door and opened it. He'd no sooner done so than Mrs. Rochester spoke again, her words echoing at his back as he exited the room.

"We shall revisit the subject of your employment tomorrow," she said. "You may depend upon it."

Eight

After a restless night, John rose at dawn resolved to face the consequences of his actions. If he lost his position, so be it. He'd done what was right—what he *still* believed was right. The boys were visible proof of that.

He felt a twinge of regret at the prospect of leaving them. Or perhaps more than a twinge. His emotions had been half dead when he came to Thornfield, but working with Stephen and Peter had gone a long way toward resurrecting them. His life was beginning to have meaning again. A purpose. And now, to have it all jerked away from him... It hardly seemed fair.

It *wasn't* fair.

But such was the fate of a man in his position, existing at the whims of his betters. Which was precisely why he shouldn't have permitted himself to become attached.

Descending the stairs to the hall, he let himself out through a side door and crossed the frost-covered lawn to the adjacent meadow where the thorn trees clustered. He often walked there in the early hours before breakfast. It gave him a chance to clear his head. To rid himself of the lingering effects of the laudanum he'd inevitably taken the night before.

Only a teaspoonful last evening. A brimming one. Enough to dull the pain, and to ease him into sleep.

Head bent, he shoved his hands into the pockets of his trousers as he strode through the meadow and into the trees. A crumbling stone bench stood within the canopy of branches. He liked to sit there of a morning. To mentally prepare himself for the day ahead.

Today would require more preparation than usual. With Mrs. Rochester in residence, he had no notion how best to proceed. He didn't even know if he'd have a job by this time tomorrow.

"Good morning, Mr. Eyre."

John looked up with a start.

Mrs. Rochester was seated on the stone bench, her figure half shadowed by the bare branches of the thorn trees. She was in mourning dress again—another plain black gown with long, tight sleeves and an equally form-fitting bodice. There was nothing particularly alluring about it. It nevertheless served to accentuate the swell of her bosom and the comparative narrowness of her waist, drawing his eyes, quite against his will.

"Mrs. Rochester," he said when he found his voice. "Good morning."

"Mr. Fairfax informed me that you were accustomed to walking here."

"I am. That is...I do. Most mornings. But how..." He inwardly cursed his lack of eloquence. It wasn't his habit to become tongue-tied in the presence of a lady. "Your ankle—"

"It's much improved today. Not entirely healed, but well enough to put my weight on." A cashmere shawl was twined loosely through her arms. The soft fabric had been dyed black to match her gown. "You're surprised to see me."

"A little."

"You shouldn't be. I don't believe in prolonging unpleasantness. Better to get it over with."

"Is there going to be unpleasantness?"

"Possibly." She frowned at him. "Come here."

John approached slowly. He felt rather like a fly being invited into the web of a spider. An exceedingly handsome spider, but a spider nonetheless. He came to a halt in front of her, fervently wishing that he'd taken more time with his appearance this morning before setting out for his walk. His black hair was disheveled, absent even a single drop of macassar oil to tame it, and he wore no hat to hide its condition. Along with his rumpled waistcoat and trousers, it put him at a distinct disadvantage, especially when faced with the composed figure that Mrs. Rochester presented.

Her posture was impeccable, her spine straight as a ramrod. She wore no bonnet. Her head was bare, her dark tresses caught up in a large roll at her nape. The cold morning sunlight shone on the white streak at her temple.

His stomach clenched on an inexplicable pang of…something. Desire, he feared. It was as bewildering as it was unwelcome. Good lord, he wasn't attracted to the woman, was he? She may be beautiful—strangely so—but she was, in every other way, unconventional to an unsettling degree.

She was also about to dismiss him without a reference.

He had no reason to feel anything for her other than animosity.

"Sit down," she said in the same imperious tone in which she'd addressed him yesterday.

John was reluctant to obey. Then again, it was better than standing in front of her like some errant schoolboy waiting for his dressing down. After a moment's hesitation, he sank onto the stone bench at her side. Her heavy skirts bunched against his leg, as he angled himself to face her.

She turned to him, so close that he could see the extraordinary length of her eyelashes, black as soot, framing her bronze-flecked eyes. "Mr. Eyre—"

"Mrs. Rochester—" He broke off. "I'm sorry. Please go on."

She needed no encouragement. "I know I was harsh with you last evening. Too harsh, I suspect. And for that I must beg your pardon."

His heart beat hard. An apology was the last thing he'd anticipated.

"You must understand," she said. "I've been traveling for a long while. And when I come home, it's never for any length of time. I'm unaccustomed to staying overlong in one place. I can't abide it. Which is why I require people here at Thornfield whom I can trust to do my bidding, even when I'm halfway around the world. It's vital that my orders are obeyed."

"But the children—"

"Do let me finish."

His jaw tightened. "Of course. Forgive me."

"What I'm trying to say is that the servants here know better than to question me. They haven't any need to, nor any right. Thornfield is my house, and the children are my responsibility—solely my responsibility. Mr. Fairfax should have made that clearer, but I expect he was dazzled by all of your earnest reforms. Indeed, they're not *all* objectionable."

"Not all?" he repeated. "I don't feel that *any* of them are objectionable. Every step I've taken since I arrived has been for the benefit of Stephen and Peter. You can see that for yourself. They've flourished under my care."

Her frown deepened.

"And it hasn't been easy," he added. "Mr. Fairfax could provide me with no information about where it is they came from or what their mother tongue might be. Nothing save the fact that they'd taken ill on the journey here."

"It's the truth."

"That's all well and good, but what about the rest of it? I arrived expecting to tutor two lads who could speak and understand English. Not two sickly boys, effectively mute, who cringed away from me every time I moved in their direction."

Her lips compressed. "You find yourself not up to the task? Well, then, perhaps it's best if you—"

"I didn't say that. I only meant that I've been working at a disadvantage since I got here. Fumbling around in the dark. Trying to learn things on my own that could have more easily been conveyed to me in a letter or a—"

"Were there so many replies to your advertisement?" she asked. "Another post you could have taken that would have been more agreeable to you?"

John's temper sputtered out, her question extinguishing it as effectively as water on a coal fire. He couldn't bring himself to lie to her. "No. There wasn't."

"Then I can't see what difference it makes."

"It makes all the difference in the world if you're going to dismiss me."

"You want full credit for what you've accomplished, is that it? All that you've achieved at the expense of my rules? You have it, sir. But in future—if you're to have a future here—you must abide by those rules. Do you feel yourself capable of doing so? Or must you and I part ways?"

"That depends. Do your rules include forcing that patent medicine down the boys' throats?"

Her face hardened. She didn't reply.

It was answer enough.

John stood abruptly. There was no more reason to remain. If he must go, then go he would—and without subjecting himself to any more of her barbed remarks. "In that case," he said gravely, "I will bid you good day, ma'am."

With a stiff nod, he turned to leave. In that same instant, the winter sun blinked through the clouds, its rays shining into his eyes.

Mrs. Rochester was on her feet in a flash. "Stop," she commanded. "Don't move."

He was startled enough by her tone to obey her.

She came to stand in front of him, her skirts pressed against his legs. Reaching up, she brought her hand to cup his cheek.

And John may as well have been turned to stone.

His breath stopped in his chest, even as his pulse throbbed at her touch. Her hand was warm and soft, the feminine curve of her palm an intimate brand on his skin. But this was no caress. This was physical restraint. She held him still, forcing him to look at her as her eyes bored into his.

"Are you an opium taker?" she demanded.

His heart slammed against his ribs. "What?"

"I believe you heard the question." Her fingers tightened on his cheek. "Are you an opium taker?"

His mouth went dry. "Mrs. Rochester—"

"Don't lie to me. I can see it in your eyes. The way your pupils react to the sunlight. Damn me that I didn't notice it before."

"It's not what you think."

All at once, she let him go. He staggered back a step, his heart racing. She scarcely seemed to notice him. Turning away, she paced to the stone bench and back again, hands clenched at her sides. He thought he heard her say something to herself—muffled words whispered under her breath.

"I have a legitimate use for it," he said lamely. "The drug—the laudanum—it was given to me by a doctor. A remedy for headaches. It's had no effect on the performance of my duties."

She didn't reply, merely continued pacing, a deep line of worry etching itself across her brow. "How long?" she asked at last.

How long had he been using it? John cast his mind back to his first appointment with the village doctor in Lowton. His headaches had commenced not long after arriving to teach at the school. Not long after meeting Helen. "Just over a year."

She folded her arms. "Then you were taking it before you came here. Before you ever knew of this place."

"Only when needed to combat my headaches. I've never abused the drug." It wasn't entirely true. His laudanum usage had increased fivefold after Helen's death. It was only lately that he'd been able to successfully reduce his dosage. And even now, there were nights when he struggled to restrict himself to one teaspoon.

"But you're still taking it?" She searched his face. "How often?"

John's pulse pounded in his ears.

How often?

"Daily," he admitted.

She exhaled a harsh breath. And then she turned her back on him again and walked to the bench.

His muscles trembled with the effort it took to remain calm. For God's sake, he had no substantial savings. Nowhere he could possibly go. And if word got out that he was an opium taker, as Mrs. Rochester had so damningly put it, he'd be ruined. No one would ever hire him again. And then what? The workhouse? Death from exposure? Starvation?

He swallowed hard. "You'll wish me gone today, of course. Understandably so. But I would beg an hour or two to pack my things, and permission to say goodbye to the boys. I shouldn't like them to think that I abandoned them."

"What's that?" Her gaze jerked briefly to his. "No. No, indeed, Mr. Eyre. You're not going anywhere today. And as for tomorrow… Well." She bent her head. "An opium taker. This changes the complexion of things."

He couldn't tell if she was talking to him or to herself. Her words made no sense at all. "Do you mean that you wish me to stay?"

She shot him another distracted glance. "For the time being, yes."

"But what about our disagreements? The boys' tonic, and the—"

"I can give you no definitive answers. Not now. I need time to think." She waved him away. "Trust that we'll revisit the subject later. Until then, you may resume your duties."

He stood there a moment longer, watching her restless perambulations. And then, like a prisoner with a last-minute reprieve from the hangman's noose, he swiftly quit her presence.

NINE

For the next several days, John saw nothing of Mrs. Rochester. Mr. Fairfax claimed she was busy tending to estate business, but John never once encountered her as he walked over the grounds. Even those clear afternoons when he ventured up to the battlements with his sketchpad provided no view of Thornfield's elusive mistress. It was as if she'd simply disappeared.

At the end of the fourth day, John withdrew to his bedroom in a miserable state. Mrs. Rochester's absence was anything but reassuring. He'd begun to anticipate her reappearance—and his inevitable dismissal—with a greater and greater sense of foreboding.

It was affecting his nights as well as his days.

In such cases, he would have typically found peace in a phial of laudanum, but his ill-fated encounter with Mrs. Rochester had alarmed him. He hadn't understood her at all. Didn't know why it was she'd consented to keep him on, even if only for a little while. All he knew was that her words had shaken the very foundations of his self-respect.

Are you an opium taker?

The harsh question had replayed itself over and over again in his mind as he tutored Stephen and Peter, and in the evenings as he dined with Mr. Fairfax. It had followed him on all of his walks and rambles, haunting his footsteps like an accusing specter.

Are you an opium taker?

John had begun to wonder if anyone else in the household had ever suspected him of using laudanum. If they'd ever, like Mrs. Rochester, espied the signs of drug use in his eyes or on his face.

The very idea was enough to make him sick to his stomach—and to spur him into action.

Retiring to bed on that first evening, he'd foregone his usual dose of laudanum. And then again, each evening thereafter.

But tonight…

Tonight, his head was throbbing. Worse than that, he'd been in a cold sweat for most of the day, droplets of perspiration clinging to his brow as he'd helped the boys with their watercolors, and as he'd shared an after-dinner cup of tea with Mr. Fairfax.

Stripping off his coat and cravat, John went to the wash basin in the corner of his bedroom and filled it from the pitcher. He shrugged out of his waistcoat and tugged his linen shirt off over his head. Bare to the waist, he plunged his head into the ice-cold water.

Before the village doctor had prescribed laudanum for John's headaches, cold water baths and compresses had been his only line of defense against the pain.

Lifting his head from the basin, he dried his face and hair with a scrap of rough toweling. The cold water wasn't as effective as it once had been, but it provided a little relief. It would have to be enough.

By the time he finished readying for bed, the fire had died in the grate. Two half-melted tallow candles standing on a low chest near the door were the only source of light. John extinguished one of them and retrieved the other to guide his way across the room.

Shadows danced on the walls of the box bed as he approached. Time had passed when the claustrophobic contraption had caused him apprehension. But as the winter progressed, he'd begun to feel a measure of gratitude for the bed. It kept him snug and warm when the wind was whistling down the chimney.

Crawling under the covers, he blew out his candle, leaving it to sit on the bedside table. When a fire was blazing, he liked to sleep with the door of the bed cracked open, but there was no reason to do so tonight. He reached up and slid the door closed. It clicked shut, engulfing him in darkness.

Pain throbbed behind his eyes, making slumber elusive. For the next several hours, he drifted in and out of a fitful sleep. At length, he could do nothing but stare straight up at the ceiling of his box bed. There was no way to discern the pattern of the wood in the darkness. Indeed, the construction of the bed was so faultless that not a single sliver of light managed to infiltrate the closely fitted seams.

What time was it? Twelve o'clock? One?

He closed his eyes again.

No sooner had he done so, than a whisper of sound struck his ears. His eyes snapped open. Was it the boys again? The two of them murmuring together on the other side of the wall?

But no. This was different. Softer.

And closer.

An icy shiver traced its way down John's spine. He held his breath, listening. Perhaps he'd imagined it. Perhaps he'd—

It came again. A low slithering hiss. This time unmistakable.

Good God. Someone was trailing their fingertips over the oak panel of his box bed.

He sat bolt upright, his pulse leaping. "Who's there?"

They provided no answer. Not in words. Instead, their fingernails scraped along the wood. The sound sent a jolt of fear through John's vitals. Fear, and sudden anger.

"Enough of these pranks." He reached to slide open the door to his bed.

But the door wouldn't budge.

What the devil? He tried to force it open. "Who's out there?" he demanded again, shaking the panel with all of his strength. "What's the meaning of this?"

Bloody blasted hell. It was immoveable. As if someone had locked it from the outside.

"Impossible," he muttered. The box bed didn't have a lock on the outside of its sliding door. There was no reason for one. And yet, try as he might, he couldn't move the damned thing.

He shook it again in a burst of panic. But it was no good. He hadn't the strength to move it.

At last he lay back against his pillows, his breath coming in harsh pants.

"I'm not afraid," he said. "And I'm not amused either. This is a puerile joke by any standard. Haven't you anything better with which to torment me?"

His bold words were met with silence.

Total silence, for John could no longer discern the hiss of fingertips tracing along the bed. There were no footsteps, either. No indication that anyone had left the room.

He lay there, fists clenched, listening for a hint of his tormenter's movement, or even of his breath.

But John heard neither.

As the minutes ticked by, his muscles began to relax.

And he began to wonder.

What if it hadn't been a person at all? What if it had been a mouse or a rat? Rodents scrabbling in the dark? It was a distinct possibility. And in his present state of mind, one that would have instantly caused him to jump to conclusions. When coupled with the locked panel, was it any wonder he'd reacted as he had? That he'd believed it was a person responsible?

Sitting up, he tried sliding open the panel one final time. It held fast. "Blast it," he said under his breath. He was well and truly stuck.

Not that it mattered. He'd have been closed up inside the bed until morning in any case. He may as well try to sleep. No one would be awake to help him for several hours at least. Until then, he'd just have to make the best of it.

He lay back again into the softness of his feather pillows.

And suddenly, he felt quite tempted to laugh—or possibly, to weep. Was it madness, what was happening to him? His sanity slowly slipping away in the wake of Helen's death? The laudanum had brought her ghost. A grim occurrence. But the lack of laudanum had brought something darker—a cold, seeping fear that made him imagine all manner of sinister things

As he slipped into a fitful sleep, he couldn't decide which was worse.

John woke in the morning, sitting up in his bed and stretching as he always did. His eyes bleary from sleep, he reached reflexively to open the wood panel of his box bed. It slid back easily on its track.

All at once, the events of the previous night came back to him.

His pulse quickened. Climbing out of bed, he tested the panel again, sliding it back and forth several times. It never once became stuck. And certainly not in the way he remembered it being stuck last night—fixed so fast into the frame that no degree of force could move it.

It was a puzzle, and one he didn't care to keep to himself. At breakfast, he shared the whole of his disturbing experience with Mr. Fairfax.

"The wood swelled, no doubt," the butler said as he buttered a slice of toast. "Not surprising in this weather."

The two of them were seated in the dining room at one end of the long mahogany table. Cook had provided them with a breakfast of hardboiled eggs, sausages, kippers, porridge, and toast. A swirl of steam rose from the spout of the teapot, drifting up toward the coffered ceiling.

"I'm sure you're right." John sipped his tea. "But it *was* disconcerting."

"If you'll forgive my saying so, it sounds much like a nightmare."

John lowered his cup. "I didn't dream it." He couldn't have done. The events had been too real. His fear too vivid.

"No, indeed. But I know from experience the tricks an old house can play on one's senses. Many a night I've heard footsteps, or a phantom hand brushing the wall." Mr. Fairfax took a bite of his toast, chewing it slowly. "It's the wind, most of it. The odd sounds. That and creaking floorboards. Houses settle, you know. I won't claim one becomes used to it. There are times that even I find myself shuddering when a cold draft passes my door. One can almost envision it being a person. A sentient shadow."

"You begin to sound like my old nurse."

Mr. Fairfax's rheumy eyes met John's. "A superstitious woman?"

"What I remember of her. She enjoyed telling me bedtime stories populated with black dogs and vengeful witches. I can't say it was very soothing for a boy of five."

"We've a black dog myth ourselves in this part of Yorkshire. The Barghest, it's called. A frightening creature with outsized fangs and claws. We still get sightings on occasion." Mr. Fairfax freshened his tea from the pot. "A farmer in Hay claimed to have seen it only last summer."

"Did he? And lived to tell about it?"

"Oh, the Barghest isn't dangerous in and of itself. It's simply an omen."

"Of what?"

"The coming of death."

The hairs lifted on the back of John's neck. His mind conjured an image of the great black beast he'd seen on the road to Hay. "I hesitate to ask… Did anyone die after the sighting?"

Mr. Fairfax's expression sobered. "There are always deaths hereabouts. Fevers. Sickness. Accidents. One can't attribute them all to a sighting of the Barghest."

"What's this about the Barghest?" Mrs. Rochester entered the room. She was in riding dress, a crop held in one gloved hand.

Disposing of his napkin, John at once rose from his chair. "Mrs. Rochester."

"Mr. Eyre." She inclined her head. "Mr. Fairfax, you're not frightening our new tutor, I trust."

Mr. Fairfax's chair scraped on the floor as he stood. "I hope I'm not, ma'am."

"You aren't," John said. "Old folk tales from the nursery don't scare me. Far from it."

"No? And here I thought you a sensible fellow." She swung her crop. "Do you ride, sir?"

"I… Er, a little." He faltered. "That is, not very well."

She had a wide mouth, soft and full and disconcertingly sensual. It tugged down into a frown. "Never mind. You can accompany me to the stables. We'll see if I've anything to suit you. If not, we shall walk instead."

"Stephen and Peter will expect me in the library shortly."

"Stephen and Peter can wait. You may have ten minutes to change into something more appropriate. Meet me in the hall." With that, she turned on her heel and exited the room.

John remained, still standing awkwardly at his place at the table. What was left of his sausage and eggs grew cold on his plate. "She's very changeable."

"I expect she may appear so to a stranger," Mr. Fairfax said. "I myself never notice it."

"Don't you? I would think it plain."

Mr. Fairfax resumed his seat. "One must make allowances."

John's gaze cut to his. "Why so?"

"The mistress has many painful thoughts to harass her."

"About what?"

"She has no family, for one," Mr. Fairfax said. "They've all died within the last five years."

"Five years is a tolerable time."

"You forget, sir," Mr. Fairfax said. "She's also lost her husband. A more recent tragedy."

"Yes, of course." John paused, adding, "Her manner is such that one forgets."

Mr. Fairfax's mouth tightened almost imperceptibly. "I trust her mourning clothes serve as a reminder."

John inclined his head in silent acknowledgment. Mourning dress, indeed. She was garbed to the teeth in it, but it had no effect on her bearing. And it certainly didn't inhibit her from enjoying herself. A morning gallop? A grieving widow would refrain from such activities, surely.

Excusing himself, John retreated to his bedroom to change. He hadn't any smart riding clothes. The best he could manage was an ancient pair of Bedford-cord breeches and a coat of worn woolen broadcloth. Humble raiment for a humble schoolmaster. The last time he'd worn the ensemble was to accompany Helen into the village to call on a sick child.

Helen had supplied him with a gelding for the journey. "I'd as soon we'd taken the gig," he'd said.

Helen's face had been radiant in the summer sunlight. "No chance of that. William would have insisted I bring a maid. And I want you all to myself today."

At the time, John had been growing weary with her infatuation. But now…

The memory made his heart ache—and worse. Guilt accompanied every recollection of Helen. A heavy stone in his stomach, reminding him of all of the things he might have done differently if only he'd been bolder. Braver. Willing to sacrifice himself for her happiness.

Meeting Mrs. Rochester in the hall, his face must have shown his preoccupation. She gave him a narrow look. "We've established that you can only ride a little. It isn't because you're afraid of horses, is it?"

"No, ma'am. It's merely lack of practice."

"That's easily remedied." She pointed toward the door with her crop. "Shall we?"

He accompanied her outside, walking next to her as they made their way down the drive. The mist was thick as smoke. John had never seen it so heavy this early. "Is a storm coming, I wonder? Mr. Fairfax is forever threatening one."

"Have you seen many storms since you arrived here?"

"There's been rain and wind on occasion. And this infernal mist. It never fully dissipates. I can't fathom why."

"Thornfield is settled in a valley," Mrs. Rochester said. "It's a cradle of fog, and fog-bred pestilence. Both of my parents died in this place."

"I'm sorry for your loss."

"Don't be. Their death freed me. It also left me a great deal of money." Her tone betrayed no excess of emotion. It was matter-of-fact. Almost offhand.

John looked straight ahead as he walked, uncertain how to respond. Plain speaking was always appreciated, but to be so frank about the death of one's parents? It didn't seem right.

She cast him a wry look. "I understand you haven't yet gone to church."

"No," he admitted. "Mr. Fairfax said you preferred the children be kept away from services for the time being."

"A rare case of your abiding by my wishes." She swung her crop. "But I don't ask about the children. I ask about yourself. Why do you not attend?"

John returned her glance. There seemed no reason to dissemble. She already knew of his laudanum use. He doubted whether her opinion of him could get any worse. "I've lately lost my faith."

"In God?"

"In most everything." He bent his head, regretting the words as soon as he uttered them. "Forgive me. That's not entirely true. I still have faith in my teaching. In the good that can be done with the boys."

"You value your skill as a tutor very highly."

"I hope I have good cause."

"Oh, Stephen and Peter are much improved, I'll grant you. They look almost human now."

He inwardly flinched. It was no more than what he'd thought himself, but to hear her give voice to the sentiment made his heart hurt on the boys' behalf. "I'm pleased you recognize it."

"I'm not blind, Mr. Eyre. Indeed, I see more than a man like you could ever comprehend. Besides, it isn't their improved appearance I object to, only the means by which you went about achieving that improvement."

"My methods were nothing very extreme. Healthy food, intelligent occupation, and outdoor exercise when the weather permitted."

"And a cessation of their tonic."

"Yes. That too."

"I expect you've been on tenterhooks this week, waiting for me to dismiss you. Or has our last conversation quite slipped your mind?"

John had the suspicion that she'd delayed their conversation to achieve that precise effect. To keep him in a perpetual state of anxiety—dreading the moment he'd lose his position. Was such a fear likely to slip his mind? It bloody well wasn't. "It could hardly do that. The vice I admitted to you then isn't one I'm particularly proud of."

"A vice, you call it."

"As well as a necessity. I had legitimate cause to use the laudanum prescribed to me, but I'm the first to confess that I'd come to rely on it a bit too heavily. You were right to be upset about it."

She shot him an alert glance. "You speak of it in the past tense. Why? You haven't stopped using the drug, have you?"

"I have, actually."

Her eyes narrowed. "I didn't take you for a fool, Mr. Eyre."

"I'm sorry?"

"To stop taking it altogether? Even I know that such a course would cause a person to become ill."

"Not ill. Only, a little…" He exhaled heavily. "I don't know. Fanciful, I guess. Imagining things that aren't there."

Something passed over her face. An emotion he couldn't identify. It might have been concern. Possibly even alarm. "Such as?"

"Last night, the panel of my box bed became stuck. I was briefly trapped inside, and for a moment I…" He ran a hand through his hair, giving a short laugh. "I fancied someone was in my room. Stupid, I know. The panel opened easily enough in the morning. Mr. Fairfax thinks it was likely due to the wood swelling."

"Does he."

"As for the rest of it…" John shrugged. "One hears things in old houses."

Mrs. Rochester's pace quickened. She stared straight ahead, her jaw set. John had to lengthen his stride to keep up with her.

Up ahead, the stable emerged through the mist—a formidable structure of gray stone with strong, wood-fenced paddocks running out at either side.

"You shouldn't have stopped taking the laudanum," she said.

He looked at her sharply. "Why not?"

"For your own safety."

His brow creased. "For my safety? What does that—"

"Your health, I meant." She slowed her step as they approached the stable yard. A large man was there, bent over a forge. He was hammering a length of heavy silver chain, the clang of metal-on-metal ringing in the silence.

John recognized the fellow at once. It was Mr. Poole.

"How are you getting on?" Mrs. Rochester asked him. "Any progress?"

Mr. Poole briefly stopped hammering. His brow was beaded with sweat. "Almost done, ma'am."

"And we won't be having any more difficulties, I trust."

"None so far as I can see."

"Excellent." She looked at John. "Come along, Mr. Eyre. I've changed my mind about riding this morning. Let us walk down to the orchard instead."

Some of the tension left John's muscles. It was difficult enough to parry with Mrs. Rochester while strolling at her side. On horseback it would have been well-nigh impossible. "If you like."

She cast aside her crop in the stable yard, folding her arms as they trudged past the paddocks and down a dirt path toward the small orchard at the back of the Hall.

John had the sense that she was coming to a decision—and one he wasn't going to like very much. "May I ask you a question?"

She flicked him a distracted glance. "That depends. What is it you wish to know?"

"Only this: what was it that originally ailed Stephen and Peter? The illness they had when first they came here? Mr. Fairfax insists it was nothing but seasickness."

"You have reason to doubt him?"

"Mr. Fairfax has no firsthand knowledge of the boys. He knows nothing except what you've told him."

Her mouth quirked. "You have reason to doubt *me*?"

John flushed. Of course he had reason. Her every word—every gesture—served to put him more on his guard. She was the embodiment of a mystery to him.

Even so, he had no reason to think her a liar.

"No, ma'am. But judging from the boys' condition, I find it hard to believe their illness wasn't something of a more serious nature."

"You're right. It wasn't seasickness. Or rather, it wasn't *only* that." She readjusted the heavy skirt of her riding habit over her left arm, arranging the folds of fabric with deliberate care. "Stephen and Peter contracted a minor blood disease while living abroad. It weakened them substantially. I've been struggling with proper methods for restoring their health ever since."

"What kind of blood disease?"

"A sort of anemia. Not entirely uncommon in the region they hail from."

"What region is that?"

"A remote part of the countryside outside of Varna. You won't have heard of it."

Varna? Good lord. He'd thought Mr. Fairfax had been exaggerating when he said Mrs. Rochester traveled to such exotic places. It was all John could do not to gape at her. "Do you mean to say…the boys are Bulgarian?"

"Romani, I believe." She frowned. "It's difficult to be certain."

Her tone was discouraging, but John felt anything but discouraged. Quite the reverse. The information opened up a world of possibilities. "But that's wonderful news. There must be some Romani person living hereabouts. We could invite them to speak to the boys. To translate. It would be helpful to—"

"Quite out of the question."

He broke off. "Why?"

"The boys have no need to be reminded of the past. They have a new life here. And if I can manage their health, and see that they have a proper education, they'll soon forget what happened before."

"What happened?" he asked. "I would dearly like to know."

She didn't answer him. Not directly. She squinted into the distance. At what, John couldn't tell. It was impossible to make out the orchard. Impossible to see much of anything in these conditions. He wasn't even certain they were going in the right direction.

"I'd assumed they were orphans," he said. "Mr. Fairfax told me that you'd adopted them during your travels. That you'd named them yourself."

"I did. Stephen and Peter. The first martyrs."

A shiver went through him. It was cold as the devil outside. "What happened to their parents?"

"They're dead, I expect. Likely from the same blood disease that the boys contracted. It took the lives of a great many people in the region. You might think of it in terms of a plague."

"You don't mean to say it's fatal? Surely anemia isn't—"

"A sort of anemia, I said. Something more insidious. It leaches a person of all of their strength—of all of their will. If left untreated, they wither away to nothing." Mrs. Rochester glanced briefly in his direction. "Don't look so alarmed, Mr. Eyre. The disease hasn't consumed the children yet."

"No indeed, but it sounds dreadful."

"It *is* dreadful. But not to worry. I've had luck in combating its encroachment. And I shall continue to do so, provided no one countermands my instructions." Her expression sobered. "You realize, of course, that I shall have to replace their tonic."

His spirits slowly sank. Naturally, she would. She was one of those ladies who had a belief in patent medicines. If one didn't work, another would be tried, and then another—each of them with nothing more to recommend them than the last. "I see."

"I mean to replace yours, as well."

"You...what?" He came to an abrupt halt. "Do you mean... my laudanum? But I'm no longer taking it. I have no need—"

"Headaches, you said. Isn't that right?" She stopped to face him. The mist rose at her back, swirling around the pair of them. "You *were* speaking the truth, weren't you?"

"Yes, but I don't see how—"

"It's quite simple." She took a step closer to him. The faint fragrance of her perfume drifted to his nose. "I have a solution for your pain, Mr. Eyre. The same solution I mean to employ for the children."

His pulse skipped. He cleared his throat. "Another patent medicine? Really Mrs. Rochester, I—"

"No. It's something altogether more wholesome. A decoction of herbs, vegetables, and minerals, from an old recipe that's recently come into my possession. It contains no opiates, and will cause you no harm. But I believe it will answer."

He stared at her. "Answer to what?"

"The impasse we find ourselves at." She looked steadily back at him. "Will you promise to take it? And to not interfere when Sophie gives it to the boys?"

"An herbal tonic." He huffed. Was this the cost of securing his position? To saving himself from being cast out onto the streets in the dead of winter? If so, surely it was a small price to pay. "You're confident it will serve its purpose?"

"As to that, only time will tell. But...yes." Her eyes glittered with a strange resolve. "When administered correctly, I have great hope it will do precisely what it's meant to do."

Ten

*Letters from
Mrs. Bertha Rochester to
Miss Blanche Ingram*

*Hotel d' Orient
Varna, Bulgaria
Saturday, 19 November 1842*

My Dear Blanche, —

Forgive the delay in writing. We've been traveling, and I'm only now at liberty to respond to your (rather severe) letter. You're perfectly right to scold me for being so changeable. My only excuse is that I knew so little of the world before now. It was easy to vow that I'd never marry when the sole contenders for my hand were a trio of Yorkshire mill owners and farmers, none of whom had anything more than their bank balances to recommend them.

You ask if I love Mr. Rochester. In truth, I don't know. I feel a great physical affection for him, certainly. An attraction unlike any I've ever known. But what is love, really? Nothing but a lofty ideal, to my mind. Such ideals are easy to adhere to when no temptation exists to challenge them.

Which isn't to say that Mr. Rochester is a mere temptation. He's a worthy man, I promise you, and a fascinating one, with such a way about him. Whenever we're out together in the evenings, he draws people to him like a magnet. No one can resist his subtle charm. He could have dozens of ladies at the snap of his fingers if he wanted them, and has no reason to have "set his sights on me" as you so unflatteringly put it. No reason other than that he finds me equally worthy of attention—equally fascinating in my own way.

You and I have long been special friends, and I trust we shall always be so, no matter what direction our lives take. Do you imagine that, if you married your vicar, I would be jealous? Of course not! I would rejoice in your happiness. Can you not do the same for me?

The tone of your last letter makes me reluctant to share the following, for I know it might serve to deepen the rift between us. But here it is: Mr. Rochester and I were married last week. We are now husband and wife.

You will reproach me for marrying so far away from home. No doubt you'll say I should have waited so that I could be wed in the church at Hay, among all of my friends and neighbors. But our decision to wed in Greece owes more to logic than to sentiment. My new husband is obliged to return to his ancestral home for a short time. It is an old Bulgarian estate, some seventy miles north of Varna. He inherited it from his mother's people, and has many distant relations there who will be wanting to meet me before we return to England.

And yes, my dear, I *am* returning home. My husband is very keen on coming to England, and can speak of little else. Our visit to Bulgaria will be only a brief one. Through the winter, I expect, with plans to depart for Thornfield Hall sometime in the spring. You may write to me care of the consulate at Varna. I've enclosed their direction.

Pray don't be worried for me. I'm still quite capable of looking after myself—much to my new husband's dismay. Since the incidences of that wild beast near our villa, I've taken to carrying my Nock percussion pistol in a specially made pocket of my skirt. It seemed unimportant at the time, such that I never thought to share the fact with Mr. Rochester. But as we traveled up the coast from Athens, I had occasion to use my pistol, and fear I shocked the poor man.

The sun had set, and our coach had come to a lonely road. As I was out stretching my legs, a creature approached. I glimpsed it in the moonlight—a great beast rustling inside the bushes—and sensed it was about to spring. Drawing my pistol, I leveled it and fired. I didn't kill the creature, but whatever it was (a bear?), it fled for its life. As I returned my pistol to its pocket, I saw my husband regarding me with a very strange expression. He asked me where I had got it, and I told him that it was mine, but not to fear, for I knew full well how to use it, and all manner of weaponry, my father having taught me.

Oh, Blanche, if you could have seen the look on Mr. Rochester's face! It's a giddy feeling to surprise someone like that. And to impress them, too, for I believe he *was* impressed by my skill. He never said so, but during the remainder of the journey, I frequently observed him studying me—with a newfound respect, I daresay.

There's so much more I long to share with you. All the details of my wedding ceremony, and other, more personal details, too. But I won't do so. Not until I can be assured you will receive such confidences with a spirit of friendship. It pains me that we are at odds. What would I do without my bosom friend to confide in? Be happy for me, my dear.

Your devoted,
Bertha

Krepostta Nosht-Vŭlk
Senniskali, Bulgaria
Tuesday, 10 January 1843

Dearest Blanche, —

My sincerest apologies for my failure to write. I have been these seven weeks ensconced in Mr. Rochester's house on the Bulgarian coast, a veritable prisoner of the inclement weather. House, I say. In truth, it's a fortress, located high atop the cliffs overlooking the Black Sea, far from any semblance of civilization. It's quite medieval, really, composed almost entirely of massive old stone, with sunken doorways, broken battlements, and high iron-barred windows that admit no sunlight. Carved figures loom at every corner, worn to unrecognizability by time and weather. Wolves, I believe they once were.

The only modernization to Nosht-Vŭlk (what the natives call the estate) has been to the room in which my husband keeps his antiquities. It is a vault lined with deep shelves and glass cases of ancient texts and strange statuary, tablets, and jars. These artifacts come from all around the globe. Not only Egypt, but Asia, Europe, and even the New World. In the vault they're sheltered from light and extremes of temperature, preserved in a near perfect state.

Mr. Rochester keeps the door locked. It even has a bar on the interior so that while he's inside with his collection, no one can burst in and disturb him. I've been permitted to view his treasures on occasion, and have determined that the vault is, by far, the most comfortable room in the house.

Mind you, I'm not complaining, except to say that when combined with our isolated location, the weather has made correspondence nearly impossible. The village post is unreliable at the best of times, and the servants my new husband employs even more so. Not a one of them speaks a word of English, and though I was assured they had a rudimentary grasp of French, when I address them in it, they pretend not to understand me.

To make matters worse, my maid, Agnes, has left me, without giving the courtesy of notice. She simply disappeared one evening. I discovered her absence the following morning when she didn't come to my room to help me dress, and only later discovered that she'd hired a calèche to take her to Varna, and from there no doubt returned to Greece. She even took my pistol, if you can believe it. I daresay she was frightened. She must have been to embark on a journey in all of this snow.

It's an odd thing, for she gave no indication of fear or unhappiness. Indeed, she was a hearty creature, and a loyal one, too. The native girl Mrs. Wren has found to replace her isn't half as competent. She has a sly way about her, which makes me reluctant to trust her with anything.

Mr. Poole still abides with me, thank heaven. Though I've begun to fear that he, too, will depart any day, if not for home, then for more favorable accommodations outside of my husband's influence. I scarcely know if such a place exists hereabouts. When meeting Mr. Rochester and Mrs. Wren in Cairo, I had no idea they were such important people. The way the locals address them, one would think my husband and his sister were royalty. The villagers all but bow and scrape. Meanwhile, they look on me with expressions of suspicion, sometimes going so far as to cross themselves when they think I'm not looking.

It's strange, really, for the Bulgarian villagers we met as we traveled to Varna were exceedingly hospitable. I'd expected the same from the residents of Senniskali, the rural village at the foot of my husband's estate. However, the villagers hereabouts have not been welcoming to me at all. I begin to wonder if they're even Bulgarian. I asked Mr. Rochester about this, but he would only admit to them being a diverse group, owing to recent wars in the region. Mrs. Wren was a bit more forthcoming, telling me that most of the original inhabitants of Senniskali had died out long ago and have since been replaced with Romani settlers.

Our position high atop the cliffs means that we are constantly buffeted by sea winds. At any given time, one can hear the crash of the waves roaring more than two hundred feet below. It is an unsettling sound, made more so by the emptiness of the skies above. Unlike the Yorkshire coast, there are no sea birds squawking. No avian life of any kind hereabouts that I've seen.

I was assured we would only be staying through the winter, but now even that appears uncertain. Mr. Rochester has been consumed with business. Something about his investments in the West Indies. He hasn't confided in me as yet. I must own I am disappointed. In Greece, as in Egypt, he professed to value my opinions. Here, however, he is content to keep his own counsel.

As before, much of our time together is restricted to the evenings. He says that the sun gives him headaches and causes weakness in his limbs. I had thought his ailment a mere intolerance to the blazing heat of Egypt and Athens, but it is, apparently, something of a graver nature—a rare sensitivity, the management of which he has been navigating his entire existence. I've made it my mission to help him find a cure for his ailment, and have spent many hours in my husband's library poring over old medical texts and books of folk remedies.

I won't say that Mr. Rochester appreciates my efforts. Indeed, I suspect he hasn't wholly acclimated to being married. He still considers Nosht-Vŭlk to be entirely his. All of my attempts to learn about its management have been firmly rebuffed—as have my efforts to take household matters in hand. He has even gone so far as to forbid me from exploring certain parts of the fortress. He claims that there are floors above and below with rotting wood, and other dangerous conditions. It isn't safe, he says, to roam about unescorted. I do believe he's right about the rot, for at certain moments as I walk through the dark halls or sit quietly in my husband's vast library, I have caught the vague scent of decay.

I'm quickly learning that marriage is a union defined by compromise. Though I sometimes find my husband's directives to be senseless, I've found it easier to comply with his wishes than to engage in countless arguments. This is especially true in matters related to his health. For a man who appears to be in perfect physical condition, he has an abundance of medical issues. I sometimes wonder if they're real or imagined.

On our wedding night, for example, he asked me to remove the silver timepiece locket that I always wear. You know the one. I explained to him what it meant to me—that it held the final portraits of Mama and Papa—but he was adamant that I take it off. He claims that silver is all but toxic to him, and says that if it touches his skin, even for an instant, he breaks out in the most painful rash. I ask you, Blanche, have you ever heard of such a thing?

But you must forgive my endless prattling. Reading over all that I've written, I'm tempted to tear up this letter and start afresh. You will think me dreadfully unhappy here. Not at all, my dear. I promise you, I'm perfectly content. I'm only a little homesick, I suppose, for you and for Thornfield. Too many weeks have passed since last I received a letter from you. Are you well? Are you happy? Do write to me and set my mind at ease.

As soon as the weather clears, I shall endeavor to have a servant journey to Varna to see what's going on at the consulate. Perhaps they've forgotten to forward my mail. Or perhaps there's been a mix-up with the direction to Senniskali. Trust me to sort it out.

Until then, all my love to you, dearest,
Bertha

Krepostta Nosht-Vŭlk
Senniskali, Bulgaria
Wednesday, 15 February 1843

My Dear Blanche, —

You'll be pleased to hear that I enlisted Mr. Poole to make the journey to Varna, and he returned this morning with a whole stack of your letters. They have been sitting at the consulate, waiting for me to retrieve them. Apparently, the consulate was unable to forward them on to Senniskali. I don't fully understand why. Some bureaucratic nonsense, no doubt. At any rate, I have your letters in hand now and have read them all one after the other. They've given me such solace and have inspired more than one appreciative laugh. Your descriptions of the vicar are delightful. He sounds a rare fellow, and I'm so pleased to hear that your courtship continues apace.

Things here are much as they were in my last letter, save for one alarming incident that I must recount, if for no other reason than purely for the oddness of it, and because it has greatly affected both my peace of mind and the harmony of my marriage.

It all began with Mr. Poole. Unfortunately he was injured during the journey to the consulate. A wheel came loose on the carriage he was travelling in, and he and several passengers were thrown into a ravine. Mr. Poole escaped the accident and was able to continue on to Varna by hired calèche, however when he returned home today, I discovered that he'd hurt his arm quite badly. He's such a stoic figure, you know, and won't admit to any aches and pains. I mightn't have ever known he was hurt if he hadn't nearly fainted while climbing the stairs into the hall.

Mr. Rochester wasn't at home at the time, nor was Mrs. Wren. The two of them had left the previous night to visit Mr. Rochester's solicitor on the Wallachian border—an elderly fellow, I'm told, who is unable to come to us himself. I would have gone with them, but my husband insisted I remain. He didn't like the idea of my traveling at night, and claimed the journey would be faster if just he and his sister went, accustomed as they are to the peculiarities of the countryside.

But what to do about Mr. Poole? I haven't been in residence long enough to know of any surgeon in the area. And Mr. Poole's arm was beginning to swell up most dreadfully. Left to my own devices, I could think of nothing else but to walk down into the village and ask after a healer. Senniskali was relatively empty today. Most of the villagers had gone into town for the twice-monthly market, and others had accompanied my husband on his journey to the border. Those remaining looked on me with wary eyes.

I gestured at them, addressed them in my schoolgirl French, and—at length—did my best to utter the few words of Bulgarian that I've learned (my accent is atrocious). Initially, they drew back from me. They must have thought me a veritable madwoman. No one would so much as grant me a minute of their time. And then the queerest thing happened. An elderly peasant woman approached, clothed in loose-fitting garments—an embroidered tunic and apron worn beneath a warm scarf and coat—with a belt at her waist on which hung a variety of dried herbs and root vegetables.

She spoke a few words of English, for which I was ridiculously grateful. Through that, I learned that she wouldn't accompany me back to the house. Indeed, she outright refused. She would only see Mr. Poole if he was brought to her. Well, you can imagine my discomfiture—and his, as well. But with a great deal of patience, I somehow managed to get him down to the village so the woman could have a look at his arm.

After that, the proceedings took a surprisingly modern turn. I had expected her to treat Mr. Poole with some natural remedy, but drawing us both into her thatched hut, she produced a locked box filled with stoppered glass bottles. She mixed the contents of one of the bottles and used it to clean Mr. Poole's wound. She then withdrew another bottle, from which she urged him to drink. He proved hesitant—understandable after the scorching pain he experienced from the first treatment (which I suspect was some derivative of sulfuric acid).

I asked her what the second bottle contained and she said something in Bulgarian—or possibly Romani—which was difficult for me to discern. We went on this way, back and forth, in abject frustration, as she tried to get him to drink from the bottle, until finally she said: "Lod-num."

That, at least, I could comprehend. I took the bottle from her, unstopped it and smelled it. Sure enough, its fragrance was as sickly sweet as the laudanum Mama was accustomed to taking in the final days of her illness. Just to be certain, I tipped a few drops of the stuff onto my tongue. It was definitely laudanum, and so I assured Mr. Poole.

He swallowed the contents. The drug shortly did its work, and while he was pliable, the woman set his arm in a long splint. She then gave me three small glass phials of laudanum, which I assumed were to be administered to Mr. Poole over the course of the next several days, should his pain become too much to bear. I tried to offer the woman money, but she pushed it away. Instead, she briefly covered my hand with hers, folding my fingers tight over the phials of laudanum.

"Hurry home, my child," she said in heavily accented English. "*Morţii călătoresc repede.*"

I don't know what she said, or what language she spoke in, but I must tell you, Blanche, it fairly turned my blood to ice. I'd never seen this woman before. Didn't know who she was or where she came from. But the tenor of her voice told me that she'd just issued a warning. I was incapable of ignoring it. Gathering my wits, and the semi-alert Mr. Poole, I returned to the house and bolted the door firmly behind me.

When Mr. Rochester returned this evening, I met him at the door, anxious for the comfort of his arms. It suddenly all seemed very silly—the healer and her mysterious words. I felt so stupid to have been afraid. I opened my mouth to tell him about it, but before I could utter so much as a single syllable, Mr. Rochester's hands gripped me very hard about the shoulders. He thrust me away from him, his face contorting into a fearsome mask of anger. He demanded to know what I'd done.

I was speechless. He'd never before taken such a tone with me. I told him that I didn't know what he was talking about, and asked what he meant. He accused me of lying and said that I "reeked of the stuff." He then shook me hard, making my head snap forward and back on my neck, ordering me to tell him where I had got it.

My heart was beating like a drum. I told him that he was making no sense at all. Was it the laudanum he smelled? But surely that was impossible. I'd only swallowed a few drops, and that was just to be certain that it *was* laudanum. I explained as much, telling him the story of Mr. Poole's injury, and how the healer in the village had treated it. No sooner had I finished than he abruptly shoved me away from him, so forcefully that I nearly fell upon the flagstone floor of the hall.

He commanded me to go to my room, claiming that he couldn't be near me in my present condition. He said the smell of laudanum—or any opiate—was repulsive to him. I tried to reason with him, but he only roared at me to go, scaring me so much with his rage that I could do nothing but flee.

As I sit here in my bedchamber, I'm ashamed to reflect upon the altercation. He was being wholly unreasonable, and yet…I didn't argue. I didn't fight. I was too afraid to do either. Heaven help me, Blanche, I ran away from him and raced up the stairs like a scalded dog. Mr. Poole is here with me now, keeping vigil on a chair near the door. I didn't dare leave him outside to face my husband's wrath.

Tomorrow, I pray Mr. Rochester will be in a better frame of mind, and then I'll be able to broach the subject of his behavior. I'm certain he'll have an apology for me, as well as a reasonable explanation. But honestly, darling, it's so perplexing to me. How did he know I'd taken those drops of laudanum? How could any person have known?

I will hide this letter away until Mr. Poole is well enough to take it to Varna. Given his condition, it may be many weeks. By then, I know this incident will be nothing but an unfortunate memory. I daresay Mr. Rochester and I will laugh about it one day.

Your faithful friend,
Bertha

Eleven

Thornfield Hall
Yorkshire, England
February 1844

John was unaccustomed to visitors at Thornfield Hall. With only himself and a handful of servants in residence, there had been little point in anyone paying a social call. But with Mrs. Rochester home, the locals bestirred themselves. As a result, she was much engaged over the course of the next several days with receiving neighbors and entertaining acquaintances from town. Sometimes she even invited them to remain for dinner.

Mr. and Mrs. Eshton and their two sons called more than once. Away for the holidays, they had recently returned to the Leas, their estate on the other side of Millcote. According to Mr. Fairfax, they were—along with the Ingrams—the nearest neighbors to Thornfield.

"Mrs. Rochester practically grew up with the children of the Eshtons and the Ingrams," he explained to John one evening when the Eshtons stayed to dine. "They're quite old friends."

John was seated with Mr. Fairfax in his small parlor, drinking a cup of after dinner tea. He'd been up on the battlements sketching when the Eshtons arrived, and had seen them disembarking from their fashionable carriage. They were a well-to-do family, clothed in fine silks and smartly tailored superfine. It had been difficult to tell from so far up, but it looked as though the two sons were of an age with Mrs. Rochester.

"Only friends?" It was none of John's business. Still, he couldn't help being curious.

"The old master did cherish hopes, at one time, that there would be a match between his daughter and one of the Eshton lads. But Mrs. Rochester would have none of her father's scheming. She was resolved to have a love match."

John held his tongue. To his mind, Mrs. Rochester wasn't at all the romantic type. Quite the reverse. She seemed hard, and rather cynical. If there was any softness to her—any feminine vulnerability—he hadn't seen it yet.

Not that he'd been much in her company of late.

Indeed, after she'd secured his promise not to interfere with this new herbal remedy of hers, she'd seemed to have no more use for him. The most he'd received from her was a distant nod or a cool glance when they happened to pass each other in the hall.

It nagged at him, her dismissiveness. Especially at night, before bed, when he dutifully swallowed down a teaspoonful of her vile prescription. It tasted of roots and earth, and rather vaguely of rosewater and garlic, with a tinny aftertaste he couldn't quite identify.

But a promise was a promise.

And, to be fair, he hadn't had a recurrence of his headaches. The strange medicine wasn't laudanum by any stretch of the imagination, but who was to say that it wasn't working?

"I confess I've wondered if she'll marry again," Mr. Fairfax said. "And if one of the Eshton boys might have a chance this time around. A union between the two families wouldn't be unwelcome."

"Do you think it possible?" John asked.

"It's difficult to tell. She's changed a great deal since returning from her journeys abroad. And it isn't only that streak of white in her hair."

John gave him an interested glance. "That's something new?"

"Aye. Indeed. And the oddest thing, sir. She hadn't any white in her hair at all when she left Thornfield after her parents died. None that I ever saw. But when she returned home last summer—not three years later—there it was, bold as you please. I didn't like to enquire about it. Ladies can be sensitive about their hair. Their crowning glory, and all that. Though I did wonder, as anyone might. She never mentions it herself. Doesn't mention much of anything about her travels."

"Perhaps she's ready to settle down?"

"With one of the Eshton boys? Who can say? I never could understand her, even when she was a girl, but now…" The butler's lips pursed. He took another sip of his tea. "I expect it's more likely she'll leave us again, than that she'll remarry. Wouldn't you agree, sir?"

"I couldn't guess," John said. "We've had little interaction since she returned."

"She may yet ask you to bring the children in to her. The Eshtons will have heard of them by now and might like to see them."

John wasn't so sure. But Mr. Fairfax had the right of it. A short time after the Eshtons departed, a message was sent up, summoning John and the boys to the drawing room.

Mrs. Rochester awaited them there, disposed on the silk-upholstered sofa near the fire, wearing her usual black crepe. A long necklace of jet hung loose at her throat, and jet combs adorned the intricate coils of her hair.

On a table near the windows sat a large white box tied up in satin ribbons.

"Stephen, Peter," Mrs. Rochester said, making no move to look in their direction. "The Eshtons have brought you a present. You may open it."

John ushered the boys to the table where, with his assistance, they untied the ribbons and opened the box. Inside were layers of tissue paper that, once pulled away, revealed a beautifully rendered set of wooden blocks. On one side were pictures, and on the other, letters and numbers.

Stephen picked up the letter D and examined it, flipping it over to look at the picture of a dog on the back. Peter did the same with the letters R and C, which featured rats and cats, respectively.

"Mr. Eyre?" Mrs. Rochester at last turned her head away from the fire. Her eyes briefly met his. "Come and sit down. The children can amuse themselves."

John did as she bid him, taking a seat across from her in one of the armchairs that resided by the hearth.

"Draw your chair closer to me," she said. "You're too far away. I can't see your face in the shadows."

He'd have preferred to remain where he was. To hide himself outside the range of the low light that emanated from the fire and the flickering branch of candles that stood on the mantelpiece. But he knew better than to disobey a direct order. He drew his chair forward.

Mrs. Rochester resumed staring into the flames. She looked different this evening. Not quite so stern or forbidding. Her cheeks were faintly flushed, her bronze-and-green-flecked eyes brilliant in the firelight. John suspected she'd had wine at dinner and possibly an after-dinner drink as well. Her manner was easier, her expression softer.

She'd been among friends this evening. Had she enjoyed their company? She must have done to look so much at her ease.

A long minute passed, and then another, as she looked into the fire and John looked at her, when quite suddenly, she turned her head and caught the direction of his gaze.

"You examine me, Mr. Eyre. Do you find me beautiful?"

"No, ma'am." The reply passed his lips before he'd fully deliberated on it. A feeling of horror followed. Had he just said...?

Good lord.

If a hole in the floor had opened up at that moment, he'd have gladly jumped into it.

"Upon my word, sir, you're a man of decided opinions. And you don't cringe from uttering them, for all that you sit there as quiet and contemplative as a man of God."

"I beg your pardon. I ought to have said that questions about appearances are difficult to answer. Tastes differ so widely."

"I'm not to your taste, is that it?"

He inwardly groaned. He was making things worse, but couldn't seem to stop himself.

Why couldn't he have simply admitted to her beauty? He'd thought her beautiful before, hadn't he? Strangely beautiful.

And oddly forbidding.

He moistened his lips. "It's not that. It's only—"

"Pray, tell me, what is it about my appearance that you object to?"

"Nothing," he said. It was the truth. She may not be beautiful in the traditional sense, but she was deeply alluring. The kind of female who put every other woman in the shade.

How to say that without sounding like a demented fool? He struggled for the right words. "You are, in every way—"

"What am I? You've already admitted I'm no beauty."

Heat crept up his neck. "Please allow me to take back that answer."

"I'll allow nothing of the sort. I value a little plain speaking, even if it stings my pride." Her mouth twitched at one corner, the barest threat of a smile. "Go on. Tell me what I am, sir. A gorgon? A dragon?"

"You *are* formidable."

"At last. And does it follow that what is formidable cannot also be beautiful?"

"I've never considered it," he said. "Perhaps therein lies my difficulty."

"Beauty, you believe, is weakness? A fair damsel in distress?"

"Yes. I suppose I've been guilty of thinking that on occasion."

"How, then, do you view strength? Is it an ugly quality in a woman?"

"Not at all. It's...admirable."

Her eyes briefly sparkled with amusement. "But I'm not admirable, am I? Nor am I beautiful."

"You're exceedingly handsome."

She laughed. "A spontaneous compliment. Thank you, Mr. Eyre. I believe you've been made to squirm enough."

He smiled slightly. "I'm not squirming yet, ma'am."

"No? Then perhaps I may be so bold as to tell you what I think of *your* appearance?"

"You already have. Rather frequently."

Her brows lifted.

"You believe I look like a curate," he reminded her. "An ascetic."

"That's your manner, not your face and figure. Mind you, it doesn't help that you dress all in black."

"Would you prefer plaid waistcoats and trousers?" Brightly colored plaids were all the rage at the moment in gentlemen's suiting. They were also incredibly garish as far as John was concerned, and not at all proper for a man in his position.

"It isn't a criticism, Mr. Eyre. Merely an observation. Just as I've observed that you're really quite handsome, though I suspect you try to conceal it."

Quite handsome?

His heart beat hard. "I've never—"

"Come, sir. I know when a person is seeking invisibility. I've sought it myself on occasion. I only wonder why? Did you suffer such abuse in your last position that you decided it was better to lurk in the shadows than to draw attention to yourself?"

"A man in my profession is content to remain in the background," he said. "It's the job of others to shine."

"You're a supporting player, then? Not a hero?"

"Hardly." He was tempted to smile again. "What's heroic about a schoolmaster?"

She leaned back on the sofa. "I wonder."

Across the room, the boys were playing with their blocks. The echo of wood clacking against wood sounded along with the crackling of the fire.

"If you'd wished it," John said, "I could have brought Stephen and Peter down earlier. They might have been introduced to your guests."

Mrs. Rochester's expression of amusement faded. "I have no intention of introducing the boys to any of my guests. They're not trained monkeys to be made to perform for strangers."

"Certainly not. But they're doing better these days. They're writing their letters and numbers, and can do their sums. They haven't yet spoken to me, but—" He broke off.

Her eyes narrowed. "But what?"

"I thought perhaps Mr. Fairfax might have told you." He lowered his voice. "I heard them once, whispering through the wall."

"Whispering what?"

"Nothing I could make out. I suppose it was Romani. Which is another reason why it would be helpful to—"

"Out of the question. They'll talk on their own when they're ready. Until then, I won't have you introducing them to strangers who may or may not speak their native tongue. It would be far too disruptive."

"You'd rather they remain silent?"

"It's not a question of silence. It's a matter of timing. And right now…" She shook her head. "It's too soon."

"They've been living here since July, and under my care since October. That's more than half a year altogether. In my opinion—"

"*Your* opinion?" Her eyes kindled. "What right have you to preach to me? You, who have never set foot outside the safety of this small island? You speak of life in Hertfordshire, London, and Surrey. While I, *I* have traveled the depth and breadth of this world. I've seen its beauty, and its depravity. Have encountered evils you could never dream of. Don't think to tell me of your opinion on matters you don't understand, or I shall be obliged to crush that opinion with my experience. It will not be pleasant, I promise you."

John's mouth compressed. He said nothing.

Nor did she for several taut seconds. And then: "I suppose I've hurt your feelings."

"Not at all," he said stiffly. "I'm your paid subordinate. You may speak to me in whatever manner you choose."

"My paid subordinate," she scoffed.

He rose, deeming it useless to continue their conversation when she was lapsing into one of her foul moods.

"Where are you going?" she asked.

"To return the children to the nursery. It's past their bedtime."

"You're afraid of my temper."

"I'm bewildered by it," John said. "But I'm not afraid."

"Do you never feel passion, Mr. Eyre?" she asked. "Do you never bellow and roar?"

"What good would it do me? In my experience, talking about one's problems is far more productive than shouting about them."

"Yes, I daresay." She turned her attention back to the fire. Her voice fell quiet. He couldn't tell if she was speaking to him or to herself. "I sometimes think that I should like someone to talk to. Someone to confide in."

There was a rare vulnerability in her words. A deep thread of loneliness. It inspired a pang of sympathy within John's breast. He stilled, waiting for her to say something more.

The long moment stretched out between them, and in that silence he was struck with the rather disconcerting urge to ease this mysterious burden of hers. Despite her changeable moods, and her seemingly irrational demands, he wanted to be of service to her, even if only in some small way.

But it wasn't to be.

Mrs. Rochester had withdrawn into herself again. She waved him to the door with a distracted flick of her hand. "Away with you. You may take my wards back to the nursery."

John didn't see Mrs. Rochester again until later that week. He chanced to meet her out on the grounds when he was walking with Stephen and Peter. While the boys occupied themselves with a game of battledore and shuttlecock, she invited John to stroll with her along the edge of the meadow.

It was an icy February afternoon, the ever-present mist swirling down the drive and settling over the snow-covered lawn. John was wearing his heavy wool coat, scarf, and gloves. Mrs. Rochester was similarly bundled up in a black cloak, her hands thrust into the confines of a fur-trimmed muff that she wore suspended from a silken cord round her neck.

"I've been thinking about something you said, Mr. Eyre."

He cast her a wary glance. "Have you?"

"You told me that you had lately lost your faith."

"Ah." John had forgotten about that conversation.

"Were you in earnest?"

"I was."

"Will you tell me what precipitated your loss of faith? Mind you, you're not obliged to. Even if you *are* my paid subordinate."

He forced a grim smile. There was no reason to prevaricate. "I suppose it was the death of Lady Helen. Not but that my faith wasn't already waning."

"The wife of your former employer? She appeared young in that portrait of yours."

"She was the same age as you and I."

Her brows lifted. "You presume to know my age, sir? I don't recall having shared it with you."

"Forgive me. Another assumption of mine. But it seems to me that you can't be much older than I am. Despite your—" He broke off, his eyes closing briefly on a private grimace.

Dash it all! Was he doomed to always be saying the wrong thing when he spoke to her?

"Despite what?" she asked.

He exhaled slowly. There was nothing for it but to answer her honestly. Indeed, he was certain she already knew of what he spoke. "The white in your hair. It might lead one to think you older than you are."

Her hand emerged from her muff. She brought it to her temple, gloved fingers briefly touching the aforementioned streak. "A nuisance. I sometimes forget it's there."

John didn't reply. He could scarcely tell her that he found the streak strangely attractive. That it caught the eye—as singular and mysterious as all the rest of her.

She tucked her hand back into her muff. "We've established that Lady Helen was young. And your portrait tells me that she was beautiful. But you haven't yet mentioned how it was she died."

He hesitated before answering. "She took her own life."

Understanding registered in Mrs. Rochester's gaze. "I see." She slowed her step. "How did she do it?"

"She hanged herself."

His words were met with a long silence.

John wished he were content to let it lie. To allow the silence to subsume the gruesome reality of Helen's death—her imagined final moments as she struggled for air. But he couldn't leave it at that. The guilt was too much a part of him. Guilt and—he was ashamed to admit—anger.

"There were more seemly ways she could have done it," he said abruptly. "A pond on the grounds of her estate she might have drowned herself in. An overdose of the sleeping draught she took each evening. But either of those methods might have conjured doubt or uncertainty."

"She wanted her intention to be clear?"

"I believe so." John had long suspected it to be Helen's parting blow at her husband. An action that would result in

Sir William having to live with the unambiguous shame of her suicide. But lately John had begun to wonder if it hadn't also been meant for him. The man whom she'd begged to take her away. To save her. The man who had ultimately let her down.

"I suppose you loved her," Mrs. Rochester said.

His throat tightened. He turned his head, looking across the lawn at the boys playing. "Not in the way she wanted."

He'd loved her as a friend. Had admired her greatly. Indeed, for a time, her grace and gentle femininity had been a pattern card by which every other lady was measured and fell short. But there had been nothing of romance about his admiration. Nothing of heat or passion.

Mrs. Rochester was quiet for several minutes, the crunch of their footsteps on the frozen path the only sound as they continued down past the thorn trees. "Is that why you left your position in Lowton? Because your employer's wife fancied you?"

"What else could I have done?"

"You might have run away with her."

"On a schoolmaster's pay? But I wouldn't have been a schoolmaster any longer. I would have had no employment. And Sir William wasn't likely to grant his wife a divorce. Where could Helen and I have gone? We'd have been outcasts." John gave voice to thoughts he'd never before shared with anyone. "No. There was no future for us. The best thing that I could think to do was to leave."

"And yet…if you had loved her…"

"I didn't," he said. "Not *that* kind of love. Not the kind that moves mountains—that overcomes all odds."

At that moment the boys ran up out of the mist to join them, rackets hanging loose in their hands. Their cheeks were flushed from the cold.

Games of battledore and shuttlecock were a new addition to their time out of doors. John had had to initiate play himself, demonstrating how to toss the shuttlecock back and forth, and how to strike it with one of the light rackets. Stephen and Peter had initially been reluctant, but in the past month they'd come to enjoy batting the shuttlecock about.

Enjoy being a relative word.

John had yet to hear either of them laugh, though he was pleased to see them running and chasing each other, and even more so to observe the brightness in their formerly dull eyes.

He set his hand on Stephen's shoulder. "At this rate, you'll soon be frozen through. Another half an hour, and then we'll return to the schoolroom."

The boys trotted off again. John watched them go, satisfied that they understood his meaning.

Mrs. Rochester didn't wait long to resume their conversation. "You speak of love that can move mountains. *Can* a gentleman love in such a way? I'd have thought such strength of emotion only existed in novels and poetry."

John turned his attention back to her. "I can't speak for other gentlemen. All I know is that I've never experienced it myself. But you..." His gaze drifted over her mourning black. "I suppose you felt such a love for your husband."

"Why on earth would you suppose that?"

"Mr. Fairfax said he died a year ago. Yet you're still in full mourning. Another lady might have transitioned to shades of gray or lavender by this time. But you haven't done so. I'd assumed it was because you were still deeply grieved by his loss."

"And therefore I must have loved him greatly?"

"That's the logical conclusion."

A glint of wry humor flashed in her eyes. "My dear Mr. Eyre, what makes you think that it's my husband for whom I wear mourning clothes?"

John searched her face. It was difficult to tell if she was being serious. He rather doubted it. Their brief acquaintance had impressed upon him her perpetual habit of keeping people off balance. It was, he gathered, some manner of protective mechanism. A way to stop them from getting too close to her.

"I'm afraid you've had a great deal of loss in your life," he said.

Her expression of amusement faded. "Haven't we all? You've just admitted to having lost Lady Helen."

"She wasn't mine to lose." The truth of the statement sank into John's bones. He wasn't entirely ready for it. He was too used to feeling responsible for Helen's death. Too accustomed to his own guilt. He cleared his throat. "But your husband, and your parents—"

"Enough talk of death," Mrs. Rochester said. "It isn't why I sought out your company. I wished to speak to you of faith."

"It's not a subject I'm in any position to remark upon, not when my own faith is at its lowest ebb. Of course, if you've changed your mind about my taking Stephen and Peter to church—"

"I told you, the boys aren't to be paraded in front of strangers."

"No, of course not."

"Besides," she added, "I would have thought you reluctant to attend church on any account. Mr. Fairfax informs me that you've had several invitations to tea from the vicar in Hay, and that you've each time sent your regrets."

"True enough." The vicar, Mr. Taylor, seemed a civil sort of gentleman, eager to make John's acquaintance, and thereby lure him to Sunday services. John had politely declined his invitations, claiming to be too busy for social calls at present.

"You have no wish to meet our estimable vicar?"

"Not at the moment." John paused. "I notice that you don't attend church yourself."

"What has that to do with anything?"

"It makes me wonder if your faith is as feeble as mine."

"I daresay you think faith is measured by how often one attends Sunday services. How loud one sings from a hymnbook." Her eyes found his. Something inexplicable flickered behind her gaze. "Do you believe in good and evil, Mr. Eyre?"

The question sent a strange chill through John's veins. She asked it with such gravity. Such solemn intent. He wished he could answer with the same conviction. Instead, his answer was tepid at best. "As much as any Christian."

"Which is to say, not very much at all." Her skirts brushed against his leg. Somehow, during the course of their walk, they'd drawn closer to each other. As close as a pair of lovers sharing whispered confidences. "I know how it is. We all of us are raised on stories of God and the devil. Abstract ideas of good and bad. But what about in the real world? Do you believe in the forces of evil? And that godly people can ultimately triumph over them?"

"I would like to believe. But in our world, you must admit that evil often triumphs. Bad people prevail, while good, honest people are ground into dust. For evidence, you need look no further than the inhabitants of any workhouse."

"And yet my faith is stronger than it's ever been." She gave him a look, as challenging as her tone. "Do you doubt it?"

He opened his mouth to reply, but she forestalled him.

"I don't attend church because the essence of my belief has nothing to do with an inanimate building or with the people who populate it. My faith is solely concerned with matters of good and evil. And you must believe, sir, that I stand firmly and relentlessly on the side of good. The side of God. You would do well to determine where it is that *you* stand."

Her speech was so passionate, so unflinchingly earnest, that he felt the impulse to answer in kind—albeit with a trifle less heat. "At the moment," he said. "I stand next to you. It seems a worthy place to be."

A spasm of emotion crossed over her face, as fleeting as it was unreadable. "Would that I could be certain—" She broke off.

"Certain of what?"

Her reply, when it came, was equally quiet. "That you would remain at my side, irrespective of what comes."

"I have no plans to leave Thornfield." He cleared his throat. "So long as you're pleased with my service, and the boys—"

"Ah, yes. The boys. You wish them to continue improving. To speak, eventually."

"Don't you?"

"As to that… It's complicated." Her shoulders stiffened. "I don't expect you to understand."

"I do understand."

She gave him an uncertain glance.

"You're protective of them," he said.

Her bosom rose and fell on a deep breath. "I have tried to be."

"And yet…" He warned himself not to say it. The words tumbled out nonetheless. "You left them for months on end while you resumed your travels."

"Not because I didn't care for them. Indeed, I cared too much. If you only knew…" She stopped on the path, turning back to face the house. Its silhouette was barely discernable in the mist, only the battlements standing out strong and clear against the winter sky. "This wretched place. How often I have abhorred the very thought of it. No sooner do I arrive here than I want to leave again."

"Understandably so. It can be dreary at times, especially with the Millcote mists."

"Is that the name they've given to this effluvium?"

"It's how it's been described to me. As a phenomenon particular to this part of the country." He paused, adding, "You said it contributed to your parents' death."

"After a fashion. The dampness of it, and the chill. There's always been fog in the valley, as long as I can remember. But this…the Millcote mists, as you call them…" A frown worked its way between her brows. "This is something new."

"Whatever it is, surely it's no reason to shun the place. Not when Stephen and Peter are in residence."

"You're very decided in your opinions for a paid subordinate." There was no humor in her voice this time. No hint of amusement in her eyes.

"I want only what's best for my pupils."

"They've found in you a passionate advocate, I see."

John might have saved himself the sting of additional rebuke, but he felt himself duty bound to continue. "Were things different—were they talking and acting as carefree boys are wont to do—I wouldn't dream of pressing the subject. But despite the progress I've made with the pair of them, they still require a great deal of help. A great deal of care. As their tutor, I can only do so much. Your presence here would—"

"Do you think any of this has been easy? That I've been blessed with a surfeit of choices—for the boys, or for myself? By God, sir, you don't know what it is to navigate such a treacherous sea as I have done." She looked at Thornfield, casting such a glare over the place as John had never seen. "My instincts have served me well thus far. Had I not heeded them, I wouldn't be standing as I am now."

He tried to understand her, not entirely certain that he did. "You aren't very happy here, are you?"

"There was a time I was, though I didn't know it then."

"Was it so long ago?"

"A lifetime. I was just a girl—as green as you are now. I played here, and learned here, and grew into a lady with all of my stubbornness and resolve. At that age, I'd have given anything to travel to a far-off land. To walk along the banks of the Seine. To see the pyramids at sunset. What had I to be afraid of? And when my parents died, I set out, still in mourning clothes, just as I'm wearing now. First, a year and a half in Europe. And then…" Her brow contracted, as if at a painful memory. "Do you know, as much as I wanted to be gone from this place, in my darkest hour I'd have sold my soul to see it again." She laughed suddenly—a startlingly bitter sound. "I rather believe I did sell it."

John didn't know what to say. He suspected she was remembering her husband. Grieving him.

"But I'm being morbid." She dashed the fingers of one hand against her cheek before turning back to him. There was a peculiar sheen to her eyes. "That's why I must have a companion to talk to. Someone thoughtful and sensible. Like you, John. Someone who won't be put off by all of the nonsense I talk, and who isn't afraid of the sharp side of my tongue."

He wondered if she realized she'd called him by his Christian name? He rather thought not. "I'm certainly not that. But I do wish I understood you better."

"So do I," she said. "More than you can possibly know."

Twelve

Thornfield Hall
Yorkshire, England
March 1844

"Who will light the fire this morning?" John asked several days later, standing in front of the children's makeshift desks in the darkened library. "Stephen? Peter?"

Stephen was on his feet in a flash, his chair scraping back upon the floor as he pushed it behind him. Peter trailed after his brother, both of them hurrying to the hearth for what was, undeniably, their favorite schoolroom task.

"Wait," John cautioned as Stephen retrieved the tinderbox. "Don't be careless. Remember, fire is dangerous. You must treat it with respect."

Having duly warned him, John stood back, giving Stephen independence to apply steel to flint. In no time at all a spark was struck.

"You may help him, Peter." John urged the younger boy forward, one hand resting gently on his back.

The boys knelt down in front of the hearth, and while Stephen lit the kindling, Peter blew on it to coax it into a flame.

John hadn't any idea why the activity was so enthralling to the pair of them. He suspected it was because they'd once been very cold. To them, a fire was a valuable thing, the ease with which they could now conjure one endlessly fascinating.

"Very good, boys," John said. "Now the lamps, if you please."

Stephen obediently lit two twists of paper, and distributing one to Peter, the two boys made short work of lighting the library's oil lamps. When they were finished, they threw the remains of their twists back into the fireplace before resuming their seats.

"Excellent. We shall need the light today." John brought out the watercolor paper and paints and set them before the boys.

Yesterday had been a particularly difficult day for them, working at their letters and sums. And then in the afternoon the rain had come in a furious gale, putting a stop to any outdoor activities.

John was determined that today would begin on a less dreary note. "We're going to paint a landscape this morning."

Peter glanced out through library windows at the bleak winter scene beyond.

"Precisely," John said, handing out their paintbrushes. "But we won't paint the lawn and the trees as they look now. We'll paint them as they looked in the summer."

Sitting down across from them, he demonstrated on his own piece of watercolor paper, deftly sketching in a sun and trees with leaves on their branches. Stephen and Peter watched intently, leaning forward in their chairs, as John began to fill in the sketch with light touches of watercolor paint.

"Do you see?" He took a bit of green paint onto his brush and gave a wash of color to the lawn. "It's not wintertime in our painting. There's no snow or ice. It's warm and sunny out. Just as when you first arrived here at Thornfield."

The boys briefly exchanged a look.

"Go on," John encouraged them. "You'll want blues, greens, and yellows. Bright colors for a bright summer day."

Standing up again, he busied himself about the library, organizing the books for their next lesson as the boys began painting. Intermittently, he stopped to assist them—helping Stephen to mix his colors, and guiding Peter in how to better hold his brush—but for the most part, he left them to their own devices. It was better that way, in his opinion. Not everything in drawing and painting should be minutely circumscribed. An artist must learn to trust his own interpretation.

When an hour had passed, he returned to look over their work.

"Was the sky really so blue, then?" John examined Peter's childish painting. "That gives me hope it might be so again. But what's this?" He took a closer look. There was a grayish cast over part of the landscape—a wisp of swirling vapor, unartfully rendered. "You've painted the Millcote mists," he said, smiling. "But the mists weren't here in the summer, surely. Fog and mist come with the cold weather. They derive from moisture in the air."

Peter blinked up at him.

"It's not a criticism." John squeezed the boy's shoulder. "Your work is very good. I especially like the way you've shaded the trees." With that, he moved to look at Stephen's painting.

Stephen still held his brush in his hand and was even now continuing to apply a wash of grayish white to his summer landscape.

"You've painted the mist as well." John frowned in spite of himself. He quickly schooled his features. He didn't wish the boys to think he was disappointed in them. "Is that the way you remember it? Your arrival here?"

Unsurprisingly, Stephen and Peter gave no answer. They merely looked at him in silent expectation, as if they were waiting for something. Praise, John thought. He gave it freely.

But he wondered, all the same.

Why was the mist present in their paintings? It must mean something. An indication, perhaps, of the boys' state of mind when they'd first come to Thornfield.

He mentioned this possibility to Mr. Fairfax that evening at dinner. The elderly butler only laughed.

"My word, sir, you do like to overcomplicate things."

John smiled. "Do I?"

"In this instance, yes. You see, the answer is quite simple. This past summer—July or thereabouts—when the boys arrived here, we did have the mists. Come to think of it, that may have been when they first began to appear."

John's fork froze halfway to his mouth. "In *July*?"

Mr. Fairfax nodded as he chewed a bite of mutton. "Faint-like, it was. The barest vapor in the beginning. But it did get stronger. We thought we were in for a rare summer storm, but it never did rain."

John slowly lowered his fork back to his plate. Mrs. Rochester had said the Millcote mists were something new. He hadn't realized just how new she'd meant. "Strange, that."

"It is, sir. But one gets used to it. Thornfield always was prone to fog and mist and the like. I've told Mrs. Rochester's guests to take care as they journey home. It's stronger after dark, and bound to cause a collision on the road one of these days if people don't take care."

Later, as John climbed into his box bed for the night, the mist was still very much on his mind. He knew little about weather patterns, and what he did know he had a devil of a time recalling.

Not that it made much difference.

Whatever knowledge he possessed was based on conditions in other parts of the country. Hertfordshire, London, and Surrey. Each place he'd lived had been different, just as Yorkshire must be.

Across the room the fire crackled low in the hearth. Lying on his side, a pillow bunched under his head, John stared at the dancing flames as he drifted into sleep. Since the night he'd become trapped in his box bed, he'd taken to sleeping with the panel open. He never again wanted to experience that level of panic.

Odd to think of it now—the fear he'd felt, then. Thornfield wasn't a frightening place. Not really. Only an old one. And yet…

That day on the grounds, Mrs. Rochester had looked at the house with such an expression on her face. It spoke of loathing—of hatred and regret. And something else. Something that was very like the look of someone staring down an impossible adversary. As if she was terrified down to her marrow, but resolved to not only face that terror but to prevail over it. To conquer and destroy.

A foolish thought.

He turned his head into his pillow. The fire slowly flickered and died. He hardly knew whether he slept, but he must have done, for some time later, he started wide awake at a peculiar murmuring coming from somewhere above him.

His pulse gave an anxious jump.

By this time it was pitch dark. He sat up in his bed, listening.

And there it was again—a vague rustling.

Rats, probably. Or the sounds of the wind.

More irritated with himself than afraid, he lay back down in his bed and tried to sleep. But his peace of mind was too disturbed. The clock down the hall chimed the hour. Two o'clock.

In that very instant a queer sort of noise sounded outside his bedroom. As if someone had brushed their fingers along his door as they passed down the hall. The exact sound he'd heard when he'd been trapped inside of his box bed.

He sat up again, heart racing. "Who is it? Who's there?"

There was no answer. Only silence. And then…

An inhuman laugh—muffled, low, and deep. Almost demonic.

It froze John to the heart.

He thought at first that the unnatural sound had come from outside of his door. But then it sounded again, this time as amorphous and disconnected as a phantom. It could have come from anywhere—the floors below or the floors above.

Good God, was it Mr. Poole? And was he possessed of some devil?

John's fear rapidly gave way to anger. Rising from his bed, he lit a candle and swiftly pulled on a pair of trousers and a linen shirt. If he was to confront the man, he'd rather not be in his nightclothes. Opening his bedroom door, he ducked his head out and looked up and down the hall.

His candle cast a dim halo in the darkness. There was no sign of Mr. Poole, but what John saw in the hazy light was far worse. The door at the end of the long hall was cracked open, and smoke billowed out from within.

It was Mrs. Rochester's room.

John thought no more of Mr. Poole and his demonic laugh. He flew down the hall with a single-minded intention. In an instant he was inside of Mrs. Rochester's chamber. She was asleep in her four-poster bed, the air all around her thick with smoke. One of the windows was open a fraction, and it seemed that the smoke was emanating from thereabouts. Had the curtains caught flame? It was difficult to see.

His sense of smell was equally obstructed. There was no acrid scent of burning wood or fabric. Nothing to sting at his eyes and nose. Indeed, the smoke seemed to have no fragrance at all. All John knew was that it had sucked all the oxygen from the room. It was impossible to breathe.

Gasping and sputtering, he went to Mrs. Rochester's side, only vaguely registering her state of undress. "Wake up! There's a fire!" He shook her by the shoulder, but she didn't move. For one horrified moment, he feared that she'd already succumbed to the smoke. That she'd suffocated there in her bed.

But no.

Her eyes opened in a state of bleary confusion. A cough racked her body. She brought her hand to cover her mouth. "What's going on?"

There was no time to explain. No time to ask her permission—or to beg her forgiveness. John gathered her up in his arms and carried her from the room. It was only a few strides down the hall, the danger of the fire spurring him on. But the urgency of the moment didn't numb him to the feel of her against him. Her unpinned hair falling about her shoulders, and her body free from the rigid constraints of a corset. She was warm and soft and inescapably feminine.

He'd have carried her a mile if he had to. Anything to secure her safety.

She came fully awake then. "John? What in the—?" She struggled against him. "Put me down!"

Stopping outside of his bedroom door, he set her on her feet. Only then did he register that she was clad in nothing but a sheer nightgown—a scrap of fine linen trimmed in lace.

His already pounding heart thumped even harder. "Your room is on fire," he said. "The smoke—can't you see it?"

She stared down the hall at the smoke billowing from her chamber. Her face paled in the candlelight. "How?"

"I don't know how it started," John said. "I heard Mr. Poole laughing outside of my door and—"

"*Mr. Poole?*"

John nodded grimly. But there was no time to sort out the particulars of who was to blame. For all he knew, the fire was still blazing. "Have you any water in your room? I suspect the bottom of the window curtains may have caught fire. I'm not certain, but if you'll wait, I'll try to put the fire out."

"I'll do nothing of the sort. Give me your candle. I'll investigate. You remain here." She flicked a glance at the closed door. "Is this your bedchamber?"

"It is."

"Go inside, light another candle, and shut the door. I shall be back directly." With that, she disappeared down the hall, her bare feet padding quickly along the carpet.

John hesitated only briefly before striding after her.

Mrs. Rochester may be his employer, but he was still a man. It went against his every impulse to remain behind while she faced the danger alone.

He arrived at her room bare seconds after she'd entered it. Covering his nose with his arm, he followed after her. Some of the smoke had cleared. He could just make her out on the opposite side of the bed. She was heading for the window.

He seized the silver water pitcher from her washstand. "Is it the curtains?"

She turned on him with a start. Her eyes blazed. "I told you to wait!"

"And let you walk into a raging fire? Not bloody likely."

"Infuriating man. This is the moment you choose to be a hero?" Coughing, she reached up to close the window. It slammed shut with an audible crunch of splintered wood. "Blast it. The latch is broken."

"Never mind the latch. What about the fire?"

She crossed the room to him through the rapidly receding smoke. "There is no fire."

"You managed to put it out?" He looked behind her. "The curtains—"

"I've taken care of it." Relieving him of the water pitcher, she pushed him toward the door. "Your assistance is no longer required."

He backed out of her room. "Mrs. Rochester—"

"Wait for me in your chamber. I'll be with you as soon as I make myself decent."

Heat rose in his face at the reminder of her scantily clad state. As if he could forget! Was it any wonder she wanted him out of her presence? "Yes, of course. If you're certain the danger has passed."

"I am," she said.

He reluctantly returned to his room. Finding the tinderbox in the dark, he struck a spark to a light a tallow candle.

Within minutes, there was a soft knock at his door. He opened it to find Mrs. Rochester on the threshold. She'd put on a flannel wrapper and slippers as a nod to propriety, but with her black hair curling loose down her back, she managed to look as tempting to him as she had in her nightgown.

"What happened?" he asked.

She didn't answer, saying only, "There's nothing more to worry over. But I need you to do something for me, John. I need you to wait here while I attend to something on the third floor."

He stilled. "You believe Mr. Poole was involved?"

"I mean to find out."

"Shall I wake Mr. Fairfax?"

"Why on earth would you want to do that? No, no. Let the man sleep. I'll sort this matter out myself. In the meanwhile, you must remain here. Bolt the door and don't open it for anyone until I return."

He opened his mouth to object, but she forestalled him.

"You don't have to understand the why of it, so long as you do as I say." With that, she abruptly took her leave.

John was no more capable of obeying her than he'd been before. And this time, it wasn't because he was afraid for her. It was because he was worried about someone else.

Two someones.

A pit of anxiety forming in his stomach, he slipped out of his chamber and made his way next door to the boys' room.

It might have been Mr. Poole whose laugh John had heard, but it was Stephen and Peter who enjoyed lighting fires. Stephen and Peter who gazed on the flames they'd kindled with twin expressions of rapture. It stood to reason that, if the fire in Mrs. Rochester's room had been started deliberately, it was one of them who must be to blame.

John's heart hated to admit to the possibility, even as his head recognized that the boys were obviously the most likely culprits. Indeed, John fully expected to find them awake, giddy from the aftereffects of their mischief.

Instead, on entering their room, his candle held aloft to illuminate his way, John found both Stephen and Peter tucked fast in their beds, looking as innocent as two sleeping angels.

He stared down at them, frowning.

Was Mr. Poole truly to blame for the fire?

Was anyone?

Perhaps it had been nothing more than a stray spark from the hearth or from an unattended candle?

The prospect did nothing to quell John's sense of uneasiness. He lingered in the boys' room only long enough to adjust their blankets and smooth the hair from their brows before returning to his own room. There, he sank down in a chair by his box bed and waited.

In short order, another soft tap sounded at his door.

"Let me in, John," Mrs. Rochester whispered.

He sprang up from his seat and unbolted the door.

She entered, her face even paler than when she'd left.

He shut the door after her, deeply conscious of the impropriety of their being alone together in his bedchamber at this time of night. On any other occasion he wouldn't have allowed it. At the moment, however, it seemed the least of their concerns. "Well?" he asked.

She stood in front of the cold hearth, arms folded at her waist. "It's just as I thought."

John was incredulous. "It was Mr. Poole?"

"He bears some responsibility, yes. But what happened tonight…it was in the way of an accident. I'm glad you're the only person besides myself acquainted with the details of the incident. You're no gossip, and know better than to breathe a word of it to anyone. As for the state of my room, you must leave me to explain that away to Mr. Fairfax."

"If you insist."

"I'll speak to him in the morning," she said. "In the meanwhile, we would do well to retire."

His brows lowered. "You're not thinking of returning to your bedroom?"

"What?" She frowned. "No, I don't suppose I should, should I? I daresay I must find somewhere else to lay my head tonight."

"Where?"

"The drawing room sofa, probably. There are other bedchambers, of course, but none that can be made ready without troubling Mr. Fairfax."

"Forgive me, but the drawing room sofa? It won't do, ma'am."

"Do you have a better suggestion?"

He did, though it was slightly indecorous. "Take my room."

She looked at him, the faintest hint of color rising in her cheeks. "*Your* room? And where will you sleep, pray?"

"In the nursery, with the boys. I can easily make a pallet on the floor."

She shook her head. "John—"

"It will be more than sufficient to my needs. Truly. And as for you…" He went to his bed and hastily straightened the pillows and coverlet. Heat crept up his neck. "I trust it won't be too unseemly for you to sleep here."

"Not unseemly, no."

"In that case…" He withdrew to the door. "I will bid you goodnight."

She seemed surprised. "Are you leaving me already?"

"I thought you said we should both retire?"

"Yes, but don't part from me yet, not in this formal fashion. Heaven's sake, John. You saved my life tonight. We can nevermore be strangers." She crossed the room to stand in front of him. "Come. Shake my hand." She extended it to him.

John took it without hesitation. He was keenly aware that they had never before touched without gloves.

"I owe you a tremendous debt," she said.

"You owe me nothing."

Her slim fingers curved around his hand, clasping it warmly, bare skin to bare skin. It was one of the most intimate experiences of John's recent memory. It made his mouth go dry. Made his heart somersault and his pulse thrum.

She gazed at him, her eyes bright. "I knew the day I met you that you would be of service to me. I saw it in your face." Her voice trembled. "But I didn't dare hope. Not until this moment."

John sensed she was becoming distraught. It was, no doubt, a delayed response to the harrowing events of the night. Perhaps she was only now fully appreciating the horror of a death by fire. "I was glad to be of assistance."

With that, he gently released her hand. Were she fully in her right mind, she wouldn't permit such intimacy, and he had no intention of taking advantage of her.

"Are you going, then?" she asked.

"It's late. And you must be cold." Indeed, it was a miracle she hadn't yet caught a chill. The window of her bedroom had been open, and there was a frost outside. "You'll want to get into bed."

His bed, he might have said.

And he may as well have.

The color in her cheeks heightened. It was almost a blush. "Yes. Quite." She inclined her head. "Good night, John."

"Good night, Mrs. Rochester."

He left quietly, making his way next door to the boys' nursery. They were still fast asleep, seemingly untroubled by the night's events. John gathered a blanket and pillow and lay down on the carpeted floor between their little beds.

Sleep was elusive. He tossed and turned until morning dawned, plagued by the thought that he'd missed something important about the fire. It was only as the sun rose, shining coldly through the nursery window, that he realized what it was that troubled him. It was that open window in Mrs. Rochester's room—the place from where the smoke had emanated.

And it was the smoke itself.

Had it not been for the way it robbed him of breath—making him gasp and cough—he might have thought it wasn't smoke at all.

He might have mistaken it, quite easily, for the Millcote mists.

Thirteen

On rising later that morning, John felt a keen longing to see Mrs. Rochester. The intimacy of the previous night seemed so much a dream to him. He needed to hear her voice, to see her face. Only then would he know if such emotion as she'd expressed—such a connection as they had shared—was strong enough to survive in the sunlight, and not merely the byproduct of a single dark and frightened moment.

He exited the nursery while the boys were still asleep. Sophie slept in a small bedroom adjacent to theirs and hadn't yet risen to wake them. John hoped the woman wouldn't feel too put upon that he'd stayed the night in what was, essentially, her domain.

Advancing into the darkened hall, he was surprised to find that the door to his own chamber stood open. He nevertheless rapped lightly on the doorframe before entering. When he received no answer, he entered and lit a lamp. It illuminated an empty room, the bed unoccupied, and the coverlet folded neatly at the foot of the mattress.

Mrs. Rochester must have risen even earlier than he had. Either that, or not slept at all.

But no.

On approaching the box bed, John caught the faintest scent of her exotic perfume. His stomach tightened. She had been here, in his bed. Though she must not have remained long.

He didn't know enough of her habits to guess where she'd gone. Riding, perhaps? Or down to an early breakfast? He rather hoped it was the latter. But having washed, dressed, and made his way downstairs, he found the dining room as empty as his own chamber. Only Cook was up and about, uttering her usual monosyllabic greeting as she served John his breakfast.

Lingering over his meal, he entertained a pathetic hope that Mrs. Rochester would appear and join him. She didn't, of course. Even Mr. Fairfax, also an early riser, was conspicuously absent. It left John with a distinct feeling of uneasiness.

When he'd finished eating, he returned upstairs to fetch the boys from the nursery. Servants were bustling in and out of Mrs. Rochester's chamber. A voice sounded from within.

"Put your back into it, Alfred! No need to be gentle."

John went to the door. A footman was kneeling in front of the fireplace, cleaning inside the chimney with a long brush. Soot fell down into his hair, blackening his face. Standing over him, issuing directions, was another footman.

They weren't the only servants present.

A large, muscular man stood at the window with a hammer in his hand.

It was Mr. Poole.

Clad in his usual plain garments, he was lining up a row of nails on the exposed window ledge, preparing to drive one of them home. He was wholly focused upon his work, his broad features giving no indication of the villain that lay beneath.

If villain he be.

Mrs. Rochester had said Mr. Poole was partially responsible for the fire. But in what way responsible? Had he unknowingly knocked over a candle? Failed to douse the flames in the hearth?

John supposed it was possible. And yet…

He could think of no good reason why Mr. Poole would have been in Mrs. Rochester's bedchamber last night.

Seeming to sense John's scrutiny, Mr. Poole looked up from his work. "Morning, Mr. Eyre," he said, inclining his head. The window behind him had been stripped of its curtains, exposing a paint-chipped white frame. Sunlight glinted through the cloudy glass.

"Good morning." John wondered how much, if anything, Mr. Poole would admit to of last night's events. "What's happened here?"

Mr. Poole hammered a nail through the window frame and into the casing. The glass rattled. "Only that old fireplace. It will smoke on occasion. Mrs. Rochester was abed when it started to blow. Alfred's giving it a good cleaning."

The kneeling footman grunted as he scrubbed inside the chimney.

"Is that all? A smoking chimney?" John cast a pointed glance at the hammer poised in Mr. Poole's hand.

"A broken latch," Mr. Poole said.

"Why not simply mend it?"

Mr. Poole continuing nailing the window shut. "The mistress says this'll do for the rest of the winter."

John was quiet for a moment before remarking, "A strange series of events last night."

"Aye. The mistress had quite a time of it, though none of us learned of the trouble until this morning."

"You didn't hear anything at the time?"

Mr. Poole again lifted his gaze to John's face. This time, John fancied he saw a certain alertness lurking at the back of the man's eyes. "You can't hear a smoking chimney."

"No, but if Mrs. Rochester was in distress, she might have called for help."

"The mistress isn't distressed by much." Carefully positioning the final nail, Mr. Poole hammered it home. The window frame shook with the force of his blow.

John stood there a while longer, amazed by the man's self-possession. He really seemed to have no consciousness of guilt. Perhaps he truly was innocent?

Having finished hammering, Mr. Poole reached up to check the bolts at the top of the window. As he did so, his right sleeve slipped back several inches onto his outstretched arm, revealing a brief glimpse of a heavy bandage at his wrist.

John gave him a sharp look. "Are you hurt?"

Lowering his arms, Mr. Poole hastily tugged his sleeve back into place. "An accident at the forge. Nothing to speak of."

An accident at the forge?

John's breath stopped. Had Mr. Poole burned himself during the fire? "Does Mrs. Rochester know?"

"Indeed, sir," Mr. Poole said. "It was she who wrapped it up in this bandage."

A rush of outrage took John unaware.

He no longer doubted Mr. Poole's involvement in last night's events. First, there had been the evil laugh in the hall outside John's room. Then there had been the way that Mrs. Rochester had hastened to the third floor in the aftermath of the fire. And now this.

Had Mrs. Rochester really bandaged the very wound that Mr. Poole had incurred in the fire? A fire that he was somehow responsible for? Doubtless she had her reasons, but at the moment John couldn't imagine what those reasons could be.

At length, he withdrew from Mrs. Rochester's room and made his way to the nursery to fetch Stephen and Peter.

The remainder of the morning progressed as on any other day, with nothing happening to interrupt the boys' studies. John nevertheless anticipated a sudden appearance by Mrs. Rochester at the library door, or by Mr. Fairfax, come to tell John that the mistress had summoned him to the drawing room.

A foolish expectation.

Nobody came to the library door. Indeed, the morning passed into the afternoon and evening much as it always did. There was no sight nor sound of Mrs. Rochester. Thornfield stood quiet as the grave, its inhabitants giving no indication of the tumultuous events of the night before.

At dinner John joined Mr. Fairfax in his small parlor where he was once again regaled with the story of the smoking fireplace and the broken window latch. John scarcely heard a word of it. He was too absorbed with puzzling over the character of Mr. Poole.

How to explain the events of last night and this morning? That Mrs. Rochester had in her employ a man who was capable of such mayhem? There seemed no rhyme or reason to the matter. Unless…

Good lord. Was it possible she cherished a fondness for the rough fellow? It would certainly explain why he'd been in her room last night. Why she tolerated his sinister freaks, and why, after the fire, she hadn't dismissed him out of hand. Yet Mr. Poole wasn't handsome by any stretch of the imagination. Nor did he seem to have any wit or intellect to recommend him. And Mrs. Rochester was a lady who appreciated lively conversation, as well as a comely countenance.

You're really quite handsome.

John's heart thumped hard as he recalled her words to him so many evenings ago. It had been an unexpected compliment. Especially as he knew himself to be rather plain. Not handsome at all, really. At the time, he'd thought it merely a provoking remark. A throwaway word to an inconsequential underling. But after last night...

He was no longer certain she hadn't meant it.

How well he remembered the way she'd addressed him as they'd stood in his candlelit bedroom, her in her dressing gown and he in his shirtsleeves. The way her eyes had burned into his with such peculiar intensity. How her voice had trembled as her hand clasped his—passionate, intimate.

Where was she today? Why had he not seen her?

When the last of their meal was cleared away, Mr. Fairfax poured out their tea. "You must drink something. You ate so little dinner. I trust you aren't becoming ill?"

"I'm quite well." John hadn't much of an appetite, it was true. But it wasn't illness that caused his discomposure. "I haven't heard Mrs. Rochester's voice in the house today. Nor have I seen her."

"You wouldn't have. She left at dawn, as soon as she'd breakfasted. I pray she'll have a safe journey."

John jerked to attention. "Journey? To where?"

"She has first gone to London to see her solicitor, Mr. Hughes. And then, on her return, I expect she'll stop at the Leas. The Eshtons have gathered a large party there, and have invited her to stay."

A *party*? After what they'd just been through together?

John forced himself to take a drink of his tea. It did nothing to calm the tumult of emotion in his breast. "When will she be back?"

"Oh, not for another week or more, I shouldn't think. She's a great favorite of the Eshton boys, especially the eldest. He'll endeavor to keep her there as long as possible."

John's throat closed on an unexpected swell of jealousy. It was as bitter as it was surprising. He'd seen the eldest Eshton son once from the battlements, and he was no boy. He was a tall, elegantly clad man. "Do you know him well?"

"George Eshton? I wouldn't say that I know him. But I've had many occasions to observe him. He used to call on Mrs. Rochester when her parents were still living. He was often her partner at the balls and assemblies hereabouts. The pair of them went riding together as well. They share a love of fine horseflesh."

"What is he like?"

"Handsome and wealthy, though not as wealthy as he would like to be. Indeed, as I understand it, the bulk of his fortune rests in his father's estate. He won't come into possession of it until the elder Mr. Eshton dies."

A grim thought entered John's head. "Mrs. Rochester's visit to her solicitor... It hasn't anything to do with him, has it?"

Mr. Fairfax's brow creased. "It hadn't occurred to me. But now you mention it...I suppose she could be speaking with Mr. Hughes about marriage settlements and the like. Then again, Mrs. Rochester isn't likely to consult with him on a subject of such a personal nature."

"Why not? Who else would she consult with but her solicitor?"

"In other circumstances, yes. But Mr. Hughes and Mrs. Rochester have long had a strained relationship. You see, he had partial control of her inheritance for the year following her parents' death. She wished to go away to mourn—to some exotic locale. But Mr. Hughes insisted she restrict her travels to Europe. To Paris and Rome. She spent more than a year there, doing as he advised her. It conjured a great deal of animosity between them."

"A year spent in Paris and Rome doesn't sound like much of a hardship."

"I don't say that she was miserable, only that it wasn't what she wanted. She wished for something more adventurous, away from the usual haunts of English travelers."

John hesitated to ask. It was none of his business, and he'd already indulged his curiosity enough for the evening. Nevertheless... "Is that where she met her husband?"

"Oh no. That was later. Somewhere in Egypt. She stayed there for a time before venturing on. She always was keen on far-off places, even as a girl. And who can blame her for wanting to travel? She was shut up here at Thornfield for far too long."

"She had a sheltered childhood?"

"I wouldn't go that far. Her father was a bit of an eccentric. Taught her to hunt and shoot, just as he would have taught a son. She was certainly as willful as a boy might have been. Some would say she ran wild here. But one couldn't blame her for her odd ways. She *was* kept at home for rather a long time, when other young ladies were having their seasons in London or attending the assemblies in York. Mrs. Rochester's parents were set on her marrying a local fellow."

John returned his teacup to its saucer with an unsteady clink of porcelain. "George Eshton?"

"Indeed." Mr. Fairfax helped himself to a biscuit. "But they didn't reckon for the strength of Mrs. Rochester's will. She had no intention of tying herself to Yorkshire. No sooner had her parents died than she was off—first to Europe and then to Egypt."

John wondered if she'd found the adventure she sought there. She must have found something. A measure of happiness, perhaps. Why else would she have married?

He finished his tea without tasting a single drop of it, and after bidding goodnight to Mr. Fairfax, retired to his bedroom.

A fire awaited him in the grate, and on the chest near the door, a tray holding the bottle of herbal tonic that Mrs. Rochester had given to him. He measured out a spoonful and swallowed it down, just as he did every night before bed. He didn't do it because he believed in the curative properties of the vile stuff. He did it for her. Because she'd asked him to.

Somehow, during the course of the past months, he'd come to respect her. To care for her. And he'd imagined that she had begun to feel the same.

More fool him.

Mrs. Rochester held no special regard for him. She'd left him without a word. Gone away to London, and then to a raucous house party attended by fashionable members of the gentry. And here he was. Left behind at Thornfield. An afterthought. A nonentity. As if last night had never happened at all.

Though his heart stung at the rejection, his head found it easy enough to understand. The truth was, despite their brief moment of intimacy, he *was* nothing but her paid subordinate. A humble tutor, with an equally humble salary of forty pounds per annum. He had no grand prospects. No expectation of wealth or property. He was, in short, no George Eshton.

In future he would do well to remember it.

Fourteen

*Letters from
Mrs. Bertha Rochester to
Miss Blanche Ingram.*

Krepostta Nosht-Vŭlk
Senniskali, Bulgaria
Monday, 13 March 1843

Darling Blanche, —

It's been too long since I've heard from you. Have you received any of my letters? Have you written back to me at all? Mr. Poole made the journey to the consulate again yesterday, and returned to inform me that none of your letters awaited me there. Indeed, there was no correspondence from anyone, which troubles me greatly, for I've lately written to my solicitor, Mr. Hughes, on a matter of grave import.

Should I continue writing, though my letters may never reach your hands? For all I know they've been cast to the four winds or are gathering dust on the shelf of some far-off way station. But I must write, and I shall write, for I have no one else in whom I can confide. Despite my marriage, and the constant company of my husband's sister, Mrs. Wren, I am very much alone here and missing you so very desperately.

You will, perhaps, wonder how things stand between Mr. Rochester and myself. I'm pleased to report that his alarming behavior of last month was naught but an aberration. He's long since apologized to me in the sincerest terms, and promised to never again let his temper get the better of him. We've been quite comfortable together ever since, though I confess there has been a certain distance between us. It's most evident in his lack of husbandly attention. He rarely visits my room anymore. Certainly not as often as he was wont to do in the early days of our marriage.

His own room lies adjacent to mine, and his headaches are such that he insists I not disturb him until after the sun has set. He's even gone so far as to lock the connecting door to prevent my accidentally waking him. I've had no luck in discovering anything that might alleviate his pain. Between you and me, I've come to suspect his malady owes more to a deep-seated melancholy than to an actual medical condition.

According to what I've read in the medical books available in my husband's library, the best treatment for melancholy is plenty of sunlight and fresh air. I tried to explain this to Mr. Rochester, that by locking himself away during the day, he's only exacerbating his problem. But he would have none of it. He's too long believed sunlight his enemy and refuses to entertain any other thoughts on the subject.

His unwillingness to heed sound advice isn't the only cause of strain between us. There's also the matter of my money and property. When he returned from his visit to his solicitor last month, he had legal papers he wished me to sign, all of them drafted in a foreign language. He says my signature on them will transfer ownership of Thornfield Hall into his hands. I told him that Thornfield was as good as his already by virtue of marrying me. And so it is, according to English law. But he continues to insist I formalize the transaction.

To own the truth, I may have become a trifle unreasonable on the matter. You know how I bridle at being forced into something. I refused to sign his wretched papers (how could I when I can't even read them?) and have written to Mr. Hughes, demanding he explain the legalities of marital property to my husband. In the meanwhile, Mrs. Wren has been working at me constantly—employing all manner of arguments—to convince me to do as Mr. Rochester bids me. If she knew me better, she'd realize that such methods do little more than solidify my resolve. I am no weak, wilting female to be bullied thus—not by my husband, and certainly not by his sister.

You will perhaps think me irrational. And if I am, it's no doubt owing to this strange night existence of mine. My nerves are frayed, and my temper pushed to the limit. What in Cairo and Athens was an exciting thing—being up all hours with Mr. Rochester and Mrs. Wren, and then sleeping the day away—has finally burnt me to a socket. I've begun to long for those dull, dreary days at Thornfield, awakened at dawn with a cup of tea, and then up and dressed for an early morning ride over the moors to clear away the cobwebs.

There is no riding in Senniskali. The region is plagued by wolves. One can hear them howling throughout the night. I've almost become used to their mournful songs. Yesterday, from a window high atop Nosht-Vŭlk, I even imagined that I saw a black wolf lurking. A giant creature, padding through the mist that swirls through the village. He stopped and raised his head, seeming to look at me from across the distance. And then he bared his teeth—razor-sharp canines glistening in the light of the waxing moon. The sight sent such a jolt of fear through me, I backed away from the window.

These are the fancies that plague a woman when she's far away from home, isolated in an unwelcoming land, and deprived of her sleep. Don't mistake me. I still care for Mr. Rochester, and I haven't yet come to regret my marriage. But I want to come home. To see you again, and to live at Thornfield, with all its familiarity and comfort. And I *will* return soon. That I promise you.

Until then, I pray that your days are brighter than mine, and your dreams sweeter.

Your loving friend,
Bertha

Krepostta Nosht-Vŭlk
Senniskali, Bulgaria
Wednesday, 29 March 1843

My Dear Blanche, —

I don't know if you will ever receive this letter. The last one I wrote is still stored away in a locked drawer of my desk, awaiting the moment Mr. Poole can again journey into Varna. As yet there has been no opportunity, and I fear there may not be one anytime soon. Relations with my husband have rapidly broken down. The cause of it: his continued insistence that I sign over my property to him, and my own stubborn refusal to do so.

Last night things came to an unfortunate head. As we were seated in the drawing room, I at the piano and Mrs. Wren at her embroidery, Mr. Rochester once again began to harangue me about signing those dratted papers. It prompted me to lose my temper in a fashion I hadn't permitted myself to do before. I told him that, if he was that set on owning an English estate outright, he should buy one of his own. Something newer and grander, with all the modern amenities. He certainly has the means to do so.

"It isn't so easy for a man such as I am to relocate himself to England," Mr. Rochester replied. "Besides which, I wouldn't like a new house. My family is an ancient one. Our bloodline stretches back, unbroken, for centuries. Your Thornfield Hall appeals to my sense of history. It is old and isolated. A place where one can have privacy. I would see my name on the deed before we take up residence. Otherwise, I cannot trust that I will be safe."

Here, I think there was some confusion in the translation. Mr. Rochester's English is generally very good, but he does at times say things that, I assume, mean something quite different in the original Bulgarian. This talk of "safety" and the difficulties of a man like him relocating to England made no sense to me at all.

Then again, perhaps the difficulty of understanding lies with me? Perhaps it's my own indignation at being pushed to sign something I can't read, and that my solicitor hasn't yet read, that makes me unable to sympathize? It certainly provoked me to address him rather sharply. I informed him that Thornfield was safe enough, and that no signature of mine would make it more so. "If you cannot understand that," I said, "you understand nothing."

At that, Mrs. Wren fairly leapt out of her seat, crying, "You will not speak to him with such disrespect!"

I was stunned by her rebuke, as you can imagine. Stunned, and really quite enraged. I'm almost ashamed to think of it now, but my temper roared to life. "How dare you?" I snapped back at her (or something to that effect). "Do you think to come between a man and his wife? I am mistress of this house, not you. I shall speak to my husband however I please."

Mrs. Wren's nostrils flared. She cast aside her sewing and turned to Mr. Rochester, appealing to him to intervene on her behalf. He silenced her with a wave of his hand, his gaze fixed on mine with a burning intensity. He asked me again if I would sign the papers.

In truth, I had been beginning to soften on the matter. To accept that I was, perhaps, being unreasonable. But in the heat of the argument, my annoyance got the better of me. I said that I would not sign them, and that that was my final word on the subject.

"Then I will know how to act," he replied.

That was only yesterday evening. Today he sleeps. I should be sleeping, too, but my anxiety woke me not long after sunrise. Some devil provoked me to try the door connecting our two rooms. As expected, it was locked. I shook it a little, my frustration building, as I reflected on all that I've had to put up with—all the sacrifices I've made—since first meeting Mrs. Wren and Mr. Rochester in Cairo.

In my youth, bouts of temper were easily dispelled by a bruising ride or a round of target practice with my rifle or my bow and arrows. Here, such activities are denied to me. The only outlet available is a brisk walk. And so I went to the main door of my chamber, intending to rouse Mr. Poole to escort me down to the village. However, when I tried the door, I found it bolted against me.

Rage overcame my senses. What manner of man was my husband that he would dare to lock me inside of my room like a recalcitrant child? I shook the bolt and beat on the door with my fists, calling for my maid, for Mr. Poole, for anyone who would listen. When that failed, I returned to the door that connected my room to Mr. Rochester's. I made such a commotion then, with my pounding and shouting, that it would surely have woken the dead. But my husband made no reply to me. Indeed, my calls were met with unbroken silence.

In a tempest of anger, I paced my room, wringing my hands. I don't mind telling you, Blanche, that as the reality of my situation sank in, I began to panic a little. For the first time, I viewed the incidents of the last several months with a dispassionate eye. My marriage. The journey to Senniskali. My husband's nighttime existence. And the constant presence of his sister, Mrs. Wren. It was no longer romantic. No longer a grand adventure. I felt a fool to have ever believed it was.

So great was my distress that—with no food or drink to sustain me, no hot cup of sugared tea to calm my nerves—I was quite tempted to resort to the only means I had at my disposal to bring myself under some semblance of control. Stored at the back of the bottommost shelf of my wardrobe, hidden behind a collection of old lavender sachets, were the two phials of laudanum remaining from Mr. Poole's injury. The ones given to me by the peasant woman in the village.

But if relief can only come at the expense of my alertness, then I must shun it. Better to remain on my guard than to drug myself into lassitude. If I sleep, I must be prepared to wake at the sound of a pin drop, ready to respond to the faintest whisper.

It's broad daylight outside, just approaching noon. A weariness has settled into my bones. The natural result of an upsetting event. I recall feeling similarly fatigued after Mama's death. I return to my bed now, wary of the sunset but resolved to hold firm against my husband and his sister. They will yet learn that my will is as strong as their own.

Your faithful friend,
Bertha

Krepostta Nosht-Vŭlk
Senniskali, Bulgaria
Friday, 31 March 1843

Blanche, —

I fear this may be the final letter I am able to write to you. The others are still secured in my desk drawer, this one shortly to join them. Mr. Poole will have to take them to Varna together, if he takes them at all. You may wonder why he wouldn't do so. The answer is simple: I have not seen Mr. Poole in days.

Once, I wrote to you that I was a veritable prisoner here, owing to the secluded position of the estate. Now, I find that I have become a prisoner in fact. But I mustn't get ahead of myself. I must start at the beginning else you won't understand. Perhaps you still won't. Perhaps you'll think I've at last gone mad. And you may be right. I shall leave you to judge based on the events I now transcribe:

After returning to my bed yesterday, I fell into a restless sleep. Hours later, as sunlight gave way to darkness, I woke to find Mr. Rochester looming over me. This was not a new occurrence. During the early days of our marriage, he often came to me in this manner, waking me with a kiss or a pleasurable embrace. But you must believe that this time was different. He had a look about him that had nothing to do with passion. Quite the reverse. I had the distinct sense that he meant to do me some violence.

I was up and out of my bed in an instant, drawing on my dressing gown. I asked what he meant by locking me in my room and demanded to know where my servants were.

His reply was nothing like I'd anticipated. He claimed that he hadn't locked me in my room at all. That he'd had no awareness of my captivity. Indeed, he blamed the whole of it on Mrs. Wren!

Appalled, and a little doubtful, I asked where Mrs. Wren was now, only to be informed that she'd finally left Nosht-Vŭlk. He said she was returning to her own home, a great distance away, and that I shouldn't expect to see her again. At this news I must confess I felt a sense of relief. Even at her most amiable, Mrs. Wren was still a third party in my new marriage. An oft-unwelcome appendage, who didn't scruple to exercise what she believed to be her superior claim on my husband's affections. Since marrying him, I'd frequently wished her gone.

Yet how could I rejoice at this turn of events?

"That doesn't explain where my servants are," I said. "Or where *you* were. Why you didn't wake when I called out for help."

He approached me, then, something almost hypnotic in his gaze and manner. I was struck again by how handsome he was. How very stimulating to all of my senses.

I reminded myself that this was no unfeeling monster. This was my husband. The man with whom I'd shared more intimacy than anyone else on earth. What devil drove me to be so unbending toward him? It shouldn't matter that his infernal documents were written in a foreign language. I was his wife. I should trust him enough to sign them.

But when it came to the point, I couldn't bring myself to trust him. Not implicitly. Fanciful or no, I couldn't dismiss the feeling that he wished me ill.

He told me that the servants had accompanied Mrs. Wren to Varna, and would return within the week. As for Mr. Poole, Mr. Rochester said that he'd sent him away with

Mrs. Wren as well in order to give the two of us a chance to "come to terms."

I knew then that he meant to force me into compliance. Why else would he have been standing over my bed in such a threatening manner? Why else would he have sent away Mr. Poole? I told him as much, giving voice to all of my suspicions.

"You know nothing of the threat I pose, my dear," he said. "But you will soon understand."

He continued toward me. My heart, at this point, was beating as swiftly as a hummingbird's. I had to stop myself from cringing, lest he discern the extent of my fear. For all his eccentricities, I didn't think my husband a wife beater, but in moments such as these, who can say what lengths a man will go to in order to get his way?

I told him that he had no right to send Mr. Poole away. That he was a faithful servant who only ever did what he was told.

"What *you* tell him," Mr. Rochester returned. "Am I not master in my own home?"

I said that he was, but reminded him that a wife was not without some authority.

"Your English law says differently," he replied. "You have told me so yourself. By virtue of marrying you, I have become lord of all you possess."

He had at this point backed me into a darkened corner. He stood over me, using every ounce of his masculine superiority—his height, his weight, and his build—to make me cower. To illustrate the fact of my physical weakness. My feeble femininity.

"We have pretended to be equals long enough," he said. "It has bred only discontent. Henceforward, you shall be an obedient wife."

In other circumstances, his words would have kindled my anger, but in this bizarre world in which I now found myself, his delusions of male dominance were the least of my concerns. I was far more troubled by his waxen pallor and the hungry look on his face. The sun had set, and I had yet to light a lamp, but I must tell you, Blanche, in the dim glow of twilight that shone through the high window of my bedchamber, Mr. Rochester's eyes looked as red as blood.

"The papers are on your desk. A mere formality. If you love me, Bertha, you will sign them. It is the only hope for you."

At that, he placed a hand upon the back of my bare neck. His flesh was cold to the touch. Colder still when his strong fingers closed and bodily turned me toward the papers. There was a moment when I feared he would crush my throat. Instead, he shoved me into the low chair in front of my desk and forced a quill into my resisting hand.

"Sign them," he commanded. "Do it now."

God forgive me, Blanche, but I did sign them—a stack of papers in a language I could neither read, nor understand. At the very least, I have signed away Thornfield, but I fear I have relinquished even more. All of my fortune, even that portion inherited from Mama that was left to me alone and should have been untouchable.

I trembled at what he might do next, but after my signature was affixed to the final document, Mr. Rochester's entire behavior changed. He once again adopted that old-world manner he'd used to woo me in Cairo and Athens. Pressing a kiss to my forehead, and collecting the documents, he took his leave of me as silkily as a courtier.

As he departed, I called out to him, telling him that I wanted to go home. He stopped in the doorway, but he did not turn around. He said that he would be visiting his solicitor in the morning, after which he would see to our passage.

He promised we would leave without delay. And then he was gone, closing my chamber door behind him.

I ran to it and tested the lock. Thank heaven he hadn't bolted the door. I was free to come and go as I chose. But at what cost?

This letter may never reach you, and if it does, perhaps you will think I have been headstrong and foolish. That I have provoked Mr. Rochester unnecessarily, and have deserved the physical manifestations of his anger. You always did believe a husband was a godly figure, the head of the family, and natural superior to his wife. But Mr. Rochester is not your vicar. He is a different kind of man. Sometimes, I wonder…

But I must end this now, before he returns. I pray I will find a servant in the house who will take it, along with the rest of my letters, to be posted. With Mr. Poole gone, so much is left to chance. Goodbye.

Your loving,
Bertha

Fifteen

Thornfield Hall
Yorkshire, England
March 1844

Nearly two weeks passed with no news of Mrs. Rochester. John was beginning to become accustomed to her absence.

Or so he told himself.

The truth was, as focused as he was on his duties, a small part of him was always alert for the sound of carriage wheels rattling in the drive, or for the arrival of the post, forever imagining that she might have sent a letter announcing her imminent return.

But Mrs. Rochester sent no letter. No message of any kind.

"I wouldn't be surprised if she went straight back to the Continent," Mr. Fairfax said one morning at breakfast, "and we didn't see her again for a year or more."

John lowered his fork to his plate, the sausage speared on its tines left uneaten. "Would she quit Thornfield in such an abrupt manner?"

"What's that?" Mr. Fairfax tilted his ear toward John.

John repeated his question.

"Oh, she might do, at that," Mr. Fairfax said. "I wouldn't put it past the mistress. You know how the gentry can be, craving excitement and the company of other fashionable people. She's never enjoyed the pace of life in this part of the country. She'd rather be abroad. And there's nothing to keep her at Thornfield, is there?"

Hearing this, John was conscious of an odd chill at his heart. For the briefest moment he permitted himself to feel it in full measure—that sickening sense of disappointment at learning he might never see her again. Not for a year or more.

And then he marshaled his wits.

There was no reason Mrs. Rochester's movements should be of any concern to him. No reason, save one. Or, more precisely, two.

"What about Stephen and Peter?" he asked. "Surely she must return for their sake."

Mr. Fairfax continued eating his breakfast, seemingly oblivious to John's concerns. "I wouldn't depend upon it. Not when she has you to trust to their care."

John's spirits sank. "Yes. Of course."

For the remainder of the week, he threw himself into his work. When he wasn't tutoring the boys, he was sketching and painting, or tiring himself out with long walks over the grounds. It was a melancholy period during which he did his best to keep up the appearance of an even temper, if only for the boys' sake.

The two of them were the brightest portion of his days. Brighter still as the second week of Mrs. Rochester's absence came to a close. On two successive nights, he'd heard them whispering to each other in the nursery, the sibilant sound of their voices drifting through John's wall in an unintelligible hiss. It unnerved him, just as it had the first time he'd heard it.

And then it inspired him.

On the following day, after they'd spent a successful hour at their sums, he summoned them to the piano that stood in the corner of the library. Music lessons weren't uncommon. He'd made several futile attempts at teaching them their scales. But this time, he didn't urge them to sit down in front of the piano and place their fingers on the keys. He sat down himself and began to play.

Stephen and Peter stood over him as John executed the beginning chords of a melody. It wasn't Mozart. And it certainly wasn't a religious hymn. But it was cheerful and bright. An old children's lullaby that had, about five years ago, been set to music.

"Today," John said. "We're going to sing."

At least, *he* was going sing.

He cast a glance at the door of the library, grateful—for the first time—that Mrs. Rochester wasn't in residence. He was no trained vocalist. No talented baritone to entertain guests at a party or engage in a pleasing duet with a lady.

But the boys wouldn't care about that.

Clearing his throat, John sang the first words of the lullaby in time with the music:

> *Twinkle, twinkle, little star,*
> *How I wonder what you are.*
> *Up above the world so high,*
> *Like a diamond in the sky.*

He played the melody with a flourish, adding a few extra notes and chords. His former piano master at the charitable school would have struck his hands with a ruler for such absurdity. It wasn't proper and correct. It was fun. Foolery.

"Sing, boys," he said. "Like this..." He vocalized the notes without words—rather like a child sounding out their vowels—before singing the next verse:

> *When the blazing sun is gone,*
> *When he nothing shines upon,*
> *Then you show your little light,*
> *Twinkle, twinkle, all the night.*

As he finished the second verse and continued on to the third and fourth, John felt Stephen draw closer on his left. At his right, Peter leaned in, his thin shoulder pressed against John's arm.

A guarded excitement built in John's breast. By God, why had he not thought of this before? Not piano lessons comprised of notes and scales, but music. *Song.* Something to inspire them. Music was, like art, universal. It transcended language. He prayed it might even transcend speech.

Pounding out the chords in anticipation of the final verse, he once again encouraged the boys to sing. "Come along, Stephen," he said, sounding out the notes. "And you, Peter. Like this..."

> *Tis your bright and tiny spark,*
> *Lights the traveler in the dark,*
> *Though I know not what you are,*
> *Twinkle, twinkle, little star.*

He'd no sooner finished the second line of the final verse than he heard it. A soft oohing sound, almost ghostly in manner. Not speech by any measure, but a vocalization. It came first from Stephen and then from Peter.

John's throat constricted with emotion. He swallowed hard. "Well done, boys. Very well done, indeed."

With that, he finished the song.

And then he started again from the beginning, fairly brimming with pride as Stephen and Peter oohed along with the lyrics like two howling wolf pups.

"Excellent," John said. "Brilliant."

He couldn't wait to share the good news with Mr. Fairfax.

When lessons broke at midday, John found the elderly butler in his parlor, partaking of a light luncheon of bread and cheese. He wasn't nearly as impressed by the boys' breakthrough as John had hoped he'd be.

"Humming, were they?" he asked as he sorted through the post. "But not speaking?"

"Not yet. But I feel confident that, in time…" John trailed off, his attention arrested by one of the envelopes in Mr. Fairfax's hand. "Has Mrs. Rochester written?"

The butler was squinting at the envelope's direction with particular interest. "This isn't from the mistress." He extended it to John. "It's addressed to you, from Mr. Taylor. The vicar in Hay."

John opened it and swiftly read the short missive within. It was little different from the previous notes Mr. Taylor had sent to him. "He's invited me to tea at the vicarage again. He asks if I'm free to come this afternoon."

"Does he?" Mr. Fairfax resumed his meal. "Well, you must go, of course."

"Impossible. The boys' lessons—"

"The boys will be glad of an afternoon to themselves. It's not raining. Sophie can take them for a ramble."

John rose and went to the window. Drawing back the curtain, he saw that the rain had indeed stopped, and the mists had receded back from the lawn. With any luck, they would have agreeable weather for the remainder of the day. "I haven't yet met Mr. Taylor. Is he a pleasant man?"

"Pleasant enough, but quite busy. He knows better than to waste his time in calling here. Though I fear that if you continue to refuse his invitations, he may well bestir himself to do so. Mrs. Rochester wouldn't care for the intrusion. Not if it occurred while she was in residence."

John glanced over his shoulder at Mr. Fairfax. "Well then," he said at length. "I suppose I'd better accept this time."

———

John unlatched the wrought-iron gate that led to the churchyard in Hay. It swung open on well-oiled hinges. He was early by more than a quarter of an hour, having walked the two miles from Thornfield at a rather brisk pace.

It wasn't because he'd been afraid. He'd had no expectation of meeting another wolf in the mist. Indeed, he'd long since accepted that his previous encounter had been nothing more than the unfortunate result of too much laudanum. Since he was no longer taking the drug, he was confident that such spectral visions were a thing of the past.

No. It wasn't fear that had spurred him on. It was merely a consciousness of time. In his note, the vicar had stressed punctuality.

John shut the gate behind him. He'd seen the churchyard before in passing—a neat and tidy area of rolling dirt and grass, scattered with well-kept graves that were marked with headstones of marble and granite. It was very different than the last graveyard he'd visited. That sad little plot of ground where the remains of Lady Helen had been consigned.

Beyond stood the church, as small and tidy as the graves themselves. It was a Gothic structure, made of stone with a tall, thin steeple. A spire rose atop it, stretching up to the sky. The same spire John had often spied from atop the battlements at Thornfield.

He strolled down the dirt path that curved through the graveyard, making his way toward the closed doors of the church. Mr. Taylor must be with someone. A parishioner, perhaps. John didn't like to interrupt. He lingered along the path, reading one faded headstone and then another.

A grave up ahead appeared newer than the others. Not only well-tended but liberally adorned with fresh flowers—a living accompaniment to the roses chiseled into the headstone. The symbol conveyed that the grave's occupant was a lady who had died in her full bloom. He stopped to examine the inscription. It read:

In Memory of
BLANCHE INGRAM
who departed this life 6th June 1843

The rest was obscured by the pile of flowers. He bent to move them aside so he could see the final lines. It was a scrap of poetry, not uncommon to find chiseled into a headstone:

Remember me as you pass by
As you are now, so once was I
As I am now, so you must be
Prepare for death, and follow me

"Ah," a voice sounded behind him. "I see you've discovered Miss Ingram."

John turned abruptly to find a gentleman standing behind him on the path. He was clad in a collar and cassock. A well-favored fellow, with short side whiskers and a shock of sandy hair flopping over his forehead. He was younger than John had expected. "You must be Mr. Taylor."

"And you're Mr. Eyre." He extended his hand, and John shook it firmly. "A pleasure to meet you at last. Have you been waiting long?"

"Only a few moments. I've been looking at some of the headstones."

Mr. Taylor came to stand next to him at the grave. "A tragedy, this. Miss Ingram was still young. Still beautiful."

"Was it an illness?"

"No. It was a riding accident that took her from us. A gruesome affair." Mr. Taylor cast him an enquiring glance. "You've not heard of it?"

"Should I have?"

"She was returning from a visit to Thornfield Hall."

John gave the vicar an alert look.

"It was last summer. Mrs. Rochester had just arrived home from the Continent and Miss Ingram had gone to call on her. The two of them were childhood friends, you know. As close as sisters. I'd have thought Mrs. Rochester might have said something."

"Not at all. I've never heard Miss Ingram's name spoken before. Not by anyone." John frowned. "She fell from her horse?"

"She was thrown, I believe, on the journey back to Millcote. Her horse arrived at the Ingrams' stables without her. She was found the next day, her neck broken from the fall. I pray she died instantly." Mr. Taylor's expression tightened.

"She was badly mauled about. The wild animals must have got to her in the night."

John winced. He wondered that Mrs. Rochester had never mentioned the loss of her friend. Then again, why would she? She wasn't obliged to confide in him.

Still, the manner of Miss Ingram's death was surely of note. Mr. Fairfax, at least, might have said something. The most John could remember him having communicated was that the Ingram family was lately in mourning, but he'd revealed nothing of the reason why, and John hadn't thought to ask. It hadn't seemed relevant.

Now, however...

John recalled Mrs. Rochester's words to him the day they'd walked together along the snow-covered lawn.

My dear Mr. Eyre, what makes you think that it's my husband for whom I wear mourning clothes?

Was it possible that she was wearing black for Miss Ingram?

"I'm sorry," he said. "I expect you knew her well."

Mr. Taylor's mouth twisted. "I was betrothed to her."

John took an involuntary step back from the grave. "I beg your pardon. I didn't realize."

"How could you if no one told you? You're new to the vicinity, aren't you?" Mr. Taylor turned back up the path to the church doors. He motioned for John to accompany him. "I'm glad you finally had time to spare for a visit. I regret I was unable to call on you myself."

"Not at all."

"We're a busy parish, here. And I haven't a curate to lighten my load. I confess it would be a relief if one were assigned to me. Especially, as now..." He gave a sad, self-conscious smile. "I haven't any official right to be in mourning for Miss Ingram. We weren't married. Even so, I feel as though I've lost my wife."

An image of Helen sprang into John's brain. Fair and beautiful and pleading with him not to leave her. He made an effort to dispel it. To remind himself that the guilt and the sorrow weren't his to bear. It was becoming easier to do so. Nevertheless…

"I understand," he said. "I've recently lost someone myself."

Mr. Taylor looked at him. "Not your wife, I trust?"

"No. She was a…a friend."

"My condolences. Loss is never easy."

"No," John agreed. "It isn't."

Mr. Taylor led him into the church. It was warmer inside, and brighter, too. The high windows angled the sun directly into the nave, illuminating the wooden pews on either side of the aisle, and the raised pulpit ahead.

A door at the back of the church opened onto a small garden, shared with an equally small house. "The vicarage," Mr. Taylor said, ushering John into the parlor. "You'll excuse the mess."

Books and papers were scattered on every available surface. Mr. Taylor swept up a stack from an overstuffed chair, clearing the way for John to sit down.

"My housekeeper's daughter is nearing her confinement. I gave her leave to take the month off. It seemed reasonable enough at the time, but as you can see, I've rather let things get out of hand." He caught a stray paper as it fluttered from his arms. "Do have a seat, Mr. Eyre. I'll be back in a moment with some refreshment. It's already prepared."

With that, the vicar disappeared into what was presumably the kitchen.

Sitting down, John looked about the cluttered parlor with frank curiosity. On a table nearby was another stack of books. They appeared to be of some antiquity, their covers worn and frayed with use. His gaze drifted over the spines, surprised by some of the titles he found there—and the language he found them in.

"Folklore," Mr. Taylor said, emerging from the kitchen with the tea tray in his hands. "I've been reading a good deal of it lately."

"In German?"

"I find it best to go to the source. It saves me from worrying whether certain points have been lost in a poor translation." He cleared another chair and took a seat. "Do you speak the language?"

"Not enough to mention."

Mr. Taylor poured out their tea, extending a cup to John. "But you must be familiar with their folklore?"

"A very little. Not as much as I'd like." John took the cup. It was chipped at one corner. "Most of what I know on the subject, I owe to the superstitions of my childhood nurse. We hadn't any books of fairy stories or folklore where I grew up, and there are none at Thornfield that I'm aware of, save an old copy of *Aesop's Fables*."

"Then you must take leave to borrow one of these." Mr. Taylor selected a volume and passed it to him. "This one is in English. You'll find it a riveting read."

"Thank you." John gave the book an appreciative glance before slipping it next to him in his seat. "I'll have a look at it this evening."

Mr. Taylor settled back into his chair. "As I was saying earlier, I regret that we haven't met sooner. You've been in residence at Thornfield since November?"

"October, actually."

"Ah yes. I'd heard Mrs. Rochester had employed a tutor for her wards. I was disappointed not to see you in church."

"As to that—"

"No, no. It's perfectly all right. I assumed you had some good reason for absenting yourself from services. It's why I've extended so many invitations for you to call on me at the vicarage." Mr. Taylor paused. "You will understand, of course, why I couldn't visit you at the Hall."

John recollected Mr. Fairfax's remarks about Mrs. Rochester not permitting the vicar to call when she was in residence. The old butler had never specified precisely why, only alluded to it being because the boys were ill and Mrs. Rochester was still in mourning. "No. Not entirely."

"I did call there once, in the days after Miss Ingram's death. Not my finest moment. I'm amazed you haven't heard of it."

"Indeed, I haven't."

"It's embarrassing, really. I went there, intending to condole with Mrs. Rochester, and found workers rushing about, refurbishing rooms and decorating the place. Things that might have waited until a respectful period of time had passed. Miss Ingram had died but days before. And there was no sign of mourning. No sign of respect. Mrs. Rochester wouldn't even receive me."

John shifted in his seat, not entirely comfortable with the turn the conversation had taken. "Grief manifests itself in different ways."

"Exactly right, sir. I told myself the very thing. Still, you'll understand why I've since kept a wide berth of Thornfield Hall." Mr. Taylor raised his teacup to his lips. "But all of that's neither here nor there in terms of your own spiritual well-being."

John inwardly sighed. He'd been expecting remonstrations about the state of his soul. It made them no less tedious to hear. He nevertheless listened politely as Mr. Taylor spoke of the value of attending services, of prayer and Bible study, and the dangers of evil influences.

"We've been seeking to explain the vagaries of evil for centuries," Mr. Taylor went on. "Consider these folktales"—he gestured to the book wedged into the seat cushion at John's side—"and the creatures that inhabit them. Dark figures conjured by human imagination to explain the inexplicable. Would that we would simply trust in God. There would be no need for superstition."

"You believe God to be the final word in matters that are otherwise incomprehensible?"

"I do," Mr. Taylor said. "I also believe that superstition runs deep in this part of the world. If I'm to understand my flock, I must understand those superstitions absolutely—even if I don't subscribe to them myself." He sipped his tea. "Take these strange weather patterns, for example. The fog and the mist, and the storm that never fully arrives. Some of the farmers contend it's the result of witchcraft."

John's mouth quirked. "Witches?"

"Quite." Mr. Taylor smiled. "And then there are our black dog legends. I expect you've heard something of those by now?"

"Mr. Fairfax did mention the Barghest to me."

"The butler at Thornfield Hall? Yes. I suppose he would know." Mr. Taylor's smile faded as he stirred his tea. "We've had several strange sightings of late."

"Of black dogs?"

"Of wolves."

There was a prickling at the back of John's neck. Foolish. He wasn't one of the vicar's superstitious parishioners. He was a man of reason. Of sense. All the same...

Wolves?

He recalled the black beast that had padded toward him out of the mist. "*You're not real,*" he'd told it. And it hadn't been.

Had it?

"Twice now someone claims to have seen one." Mr. Taylor extended a plate to him. "Biscuit?"

"No, thank you." John's throat had gone dry. He doubted he could eat one without choking on it.

"Yes, well, it's rather amusing, frankly." Mr. Taylor returned the plate to the tea tray. "I suspect there was alcohol involved."

John forced himself to take a drink of his tea, and then to swallow it, as calmly as his host. "Where was it seen?"

"Not here in Hay. Closer to your neck of the woods. I daresay that dratted mist is to blame. A man can become quite lost in it after dark. And if you add an excess of drink to the mix—"

"You completely discount the tales?"

Mr. Taylor lowered his cup back to its saucer. A shadow lurked at the back of his gaze. "Not completely."

"Then you believe—"

"Lord, no. There are no wolves in Hay, or anywhere in the vicinity. That much is certain. But I confess, I've sometimes feared that—" He stopped.

"What?"

"It's nonsense, really. No one has reported any cases of hydrophobia. But since Miss Ingram's death, I've often wondered if there might be an afflicted dog hereabouts. You see... when they found her body, it hadn't fallen victim to the usual depredations. It was a bit more serious than that."

John's hesitated to ask. "How serious?"

Mr. Taylor gave an ashen-faced grimace. "Her throat had been ripped out."

Sixteen

John arrived back at Thornfield well before sunset, a book of German folklore under his arm, and his thoughts consumed with images of black dogs, wolves, and gruesome deaths. Entering through a side door, he divested himself of his damp hat and overcoat. The rain had started again just as he'd passed through Thornfield's gates, a light but steady patter, hurrying him the remainder of the way to the house.

Straightening his coat, he crossed the hall to the stairs, only to stop short at the sight of Mr. Fairfax.

The elderly butler was descending the steps, one trembling hand clutching the banister. "Mr. Eyre. Back already?"

"Only just. Is everything well with the boys?"

"They had an agreeable afternoon with Sophie. She has them in the nursery at present, helping them to wash and change for dinner."

"I think I'll dine with them this evening," John said. "If you don't mind it? It might help to make up for my absence."

"As you wish." Mr. Fairfax came to a halt on the step above John. "Did you enjoy your tea with the vicar?"

"I did. He's very amiable."

"I expect he asked after the mistress?"

He had eventually. "He enquired about her health, and the health of Stephen and Peter." John paused before adding, "He regrets it isn't possible to call on them."

"I have every confidence that Mrs. Rochester will permit him to visit when the boys are well enough to receive him."

"She's unwilling to receive him herself?"

"Is that what he said?"

"He mentioned that he called here last summer. That he was turned away."

Mr. Fairfax's lips pursed. "Mr. Taylor is an amiable enough man, as you say, but like all vicars, he's prone to meddling. Mrs. Rochester had enough to contend with at the time. She was in no mood to indulge him." He resumed his descent, passing John with a nod. "If you'll excuse me, I must attend to my duties."

"Of course." Inclining his head, John continued up the stairs.

It was none of his business if Mrs. Rochester preferred not to see the vicar. None of his business if she never attended Sunday services, or never spoke of the death of her friend, Miss Ingram. She owed him no explanations, no confidences.

Nevertheless, he chafed at the mystery of it all. And he wished—stupidly, he wished—that she'd want to share her burdens with him. She had seemed to do so that night in his room.

But perhaps he'd imagined that brief moment of intimacy, just as he'd imagined so many other things of late.

Dining with the boys that evening in the nursery, it took an effort to redirect his thoughts to more productive subjects. By the time they finished their soup, he'd somehow managed to reignite some of the excitement he'd felt earlier when the boys had vocalized along with the piano. It had been, on the whole, a successful day, and John was determined to view it as such.

They were in the midst of eating their pudding when Stephen laid down his spoon with a clatter, and rising from his chair, went to the window. He drew back the curtain and peered out through the rain-streaked glass.

"What is it, Stephen?" John came to join him, with Peter close behind. "Did you hear something?"

John needn't have asked. Within seconds, he heard it himself. The clip-clop of horses' hooves in the distance, and the rattle of carriage wheels on gravel. It drew closer by the moment.

The nursery window looked out over the drive. It was lit by two lanterns, their glowing flame managing to push back the heavy mist that enshrouded it. Visibility was generally poor in the evenings, especially when it was raining, but John was able to make out the arrival of an elegant black-lacquered carriage. Pulled by a set of matched bays, it rolled up the drive, coming to a halt in front of the door. Another carriage arrived soon after, this one pulled by a set of four gray horses.

A footman leapt down from the box of the first vehicle, and setting down the steps, opened the door of the carriage. A gentleman emerged—tall and impeccably tailored. He turned to hand down a lady. An achingly familiar figure, garbed in a black traveling dress. As she stepped down onto the drive, she lifted her face to the house. Her features were briefly illuminated in the lamplight.

John's heart gave a heavy thump at the sight of her.

Mrs. Rochester was home at last.

But she hadn't returned alone.

The man—who now tucked her arm so masterfully into his in preparation for escorting her to the house—must be George Eshton.

John withdrew from the window before he was seen, and urged the boys to do the same. "Back to the table. Finish your pudding."

Joining them there, he made short work of his own portion.

It may as well have been sawdust.

He told himself that it didn't matter. Her arrival, whether on the arm of George Eshton or not, had no bearing on John's duties. Soon, he'd bid the boys goodnight and retire to his room to read his borrowed book. Perhaps later Mr. Fairfax would invite him for tea in the parlor?

Or perhaps…

But John dared not hope for it.

Who knew how long into the night Mrs. Rochester's guests would remain? In the past it hadn't been terribly long. And afterward, when they'd gone, she'd invited him to come to the drawing room with the boys. She'd encouraged him to talk to her.

But there was no guarantee he would see her tonight, nor even tomorrow.

Leaving the boys' room later that evening, he walked next door to his own. He was just preparing to enter when a floorboard creaked down the hall. It was Mr. Fairfax.

The elderly butler lowered his voice, addressing John quietly as he approached. "Such a to-do. The Eshtons have accompanied Mrs. Rochester back from the Leas."

John frowned. "Have they? Why?"

"On account of the rain, and the mist being high. They didn't like her to ride home alone, and insisted on escorting her. She says there was no way to dissuade them. And now here they are, all of them in the drawing room, as merry as if it were a party. I've had to rouse Cook to prepare something, for it looks as though they won't be leaving anytime soon."

"Can I be of help?"

"You wouldn't object?"

"Not at all." A tutor wasn't meant to be doing menial work, but John wasn't so full of his own self-importance that he couldn't roll up his sleeves on occasion and lend a helping hand.

Mr. Fairfax exhaled a heavy breath. "Thank you, Mr. Eyre. I knew I could count on your assistance. If you'll go down to the kitchens and see what you can do to smooth Cook's feathers, it will be much appreciated."

"Of course." John doubted he'd have much success. Up to this point, his interaction with Cook had been confined to perfunctory greetings at mealtime. The few servants employed at Thornfield weren't accustomed to treating him as a comrade. His position was considered far above theirs—though not far enough to merit any particular respect.

"And Mr. Eyre?" Mr. Fairfax added before he departed. "Use the servants' stairs. It will be quicker."

John responded with a stiff inclination of his head. The servants' stairs indeed. He supposed that put him on notice. A not-so-subtle reminder of his place in the household.

As if he needed reminding.

It shouldn't bother him. As a tutor, he'd long grown accustomed to being put in his place. And yet...

For the past months he'd had the run of Thornfield and had become used to exercising his authority. Even Mrs. Rochester had addressed him not as a servant but as a man who was worth knowing better. Someone of value.

Or so John had believed.

He used the back stairs to make his way down to the kitchens. There, he found the cook and her scullery maid busy preparing a tray. Alfred, the footman, stood waiting for it.

"See that Mr. Poole gets his pot of porter," Cook said. "And a double portion of that rare beef. He'll have a long night ahead of him what with all the commotion in the house."

"Bless him." The scullery maid added the items to the tray. "He gets good wages for it, I expect."

"The best," Cook replied. "And he has enough of it put by at the bank, he could retire if he wished."

"Why would he? He's a dab hand at his job, and strong enough for anything."

"He knows his business, I'll give him that much," Cook said. "'Tis not everyone could do what he does, not for any amount of money."

"Does the mistress not worry—"

The scullery maid might have said more, but at that moment, Cook's gaze lit on John. She silenced the maid with a nudge of her elbow.

John regarded the pair of them with wary interest. It seemed there was a further dimension to the mystery surrounding Mr. Poole. Not only did Mrs. Rochester keep him on, despite his tendency for malicious mischief, she also rewarded his dubious services with an exorbitant wage.

Were the man's skills at metalwork and furniture mending so valuable?

"Do you require something, sir?" Cook asked.

John came the rest of the way into the kitchen. "Mr. Fairfax thought I might be of use to you."

Cook's brows shot up. "You?"

Alfred took hold of the tray. "Is this ready?"

"Go on and take it up then," Cook said. "And don't dally." And then to John: "I don't know what Mr. Fairfax expects you can do, Mr. Eyre. You're no footman, and you know naught about trussing game or boiling a pudding." She squinted her eyes. "Do you?"

"I'm afraid I don't. But I can tote and carry if you need."

"Well…I suppose, if you want to make yourself useful, you can bring in more wood for the stove. It'll be burning all night at this rate."

John was glad to have something to do. A back door from the kitchen led out into the yard where the wood was kept. He raised the collar of his coat up over his neck as he ventured forth. The rain was coming in sheets now, a downpour unlike any he'd seen since his arrival in Yorkshire.

As he gathered an armful of firewood, a flash of lightning streaked across the sky, briefly illuminating the darkness. He scarcely needed the light. The small kitchen yard was easy enough to navigate. It housed only the woodshed, water pump, and privy. At the moment they were shrouded in mist.

But not mist.

It had become heavier at some point. Almost impenetrable. A proper fog.

Bending his head against the driving rain, John carried the firewood into the kitchen, and then turned to make another trip to the woodshed, and then another. The weather seemed to worsen with every passing minute. By the time he finished, he was wet through.

"That'll be enough," Cook said, shutting the door after him. "You sit down, Mr. Eyre. Take off your coat before you catch your death. I'll get you a cup of tea."

John stripped off his rain-sodden coat and hung it by the door before taking a seat at the old plank table. He ran a hand over his wet hair. It was hard to believe that only this afternoon the conditions had been mild enough to walk to Hay and back.

Where had the bad weather come from? There'd been mist, as always, and a light patter of rain upon his return, but nothing to compare with this maelstrom.

The scullery maid put a steaming mug of tea in front of him. "Listen to that wind howling, sir."

"I reckon the Eshtons won't like to drive back to Millcote in such a downpour," Cook remarked, stirring a pot on the stove.

"You reckon right." Mr. Fairfax entered the kitchen holding a tray on which stood an empty decanter of madeira and a plate of biscuit crumbs. He set it down on the counter. "Mr. Eyre? I'm afraid I must press you into service once more."

"Only tell me what you require," John said.

Mr. Fairfax half-leaned against the counter. He'd never looked wearier. "We haven't time to properly air the spare bedrooms, but there's fires to be lit and the beds will need fresh linens. It will take every set of hands in the house to make things ready."

John slowly stood, unable to conceal his dismay. "Mrs. Rochester has invited the Eshtons to stay?"

"She had little choice in the matter, given the conditions on the road." Mr. Fairfax straightened. His bones creaked at the joints. "Would that we'd had proper notice. We might have hired extra help for the occasion. But we must make do as best we can."

John wondered that any degree of poor weather could be enough to force Mrs. Rochester to submit to having overnight guests. After all, there were the boys to consider. She valued their privacy, didn't she? And what about Mr. Poole's erratic behavior? Surely it wasn't ideal to have people to stay with him creeping about?

"The poor weather might clear, given another hour or two," John said.

"Poor weather?" Mr. Fairfax stared at him as if he'd lost his wits. "Have you looked outside?" A clap of thunder shook the windows, bringing forth another torrent of rain. "It's the storm, Mr. Eyre. It's finally come."

Seventeen

The following day, the storm showed no sign of relenting. John was obliged to remain in the nursery with the boys. It was impossible to continue their lessons in the library. The house was too busy. Too merry, in spite of the foul weather. Around every corner, he heard voices raised in laughter and conversation.

Stephen and Peter heard them, too.

It was enough to bring back a shadow of the reticence they'd shown when John had first arrived at Thornfield. Worse than that, when a deep male voice echoed through the hall, John was certain he saw Stephen flinch.

"Guests can be disruptive," Mr. Fairfax said, passing John in the hall later that afternoon. "Trust that they'll be leaving as soon as the weather allows."

"Yes, quite," John replied with a touch of impatience. "But in the meanwhile, it might help if the boys were introduced to the Eshtons. It would show them that they have nothing to fear."

Mr. Fairfax appeared doubtful. "I don't think it wise myself, but I'll mention your suggestion to Mrs. Rochester."

John had no expectation that Mrs. Rochester would heed his advice. As the evening approached, he nevertheless made certain the boys were neatly clad, and that their hair was combed into meticulous order.

His efforts were not in vain.

At half past five, he received word from Mr. Fairfax that Stephen and Peter were to be brought to the drawing room after dinner, and that Mrs. Rochester had requested that John accompany them.

"She'll brook no refusal," Mr. Fairfax said.

John scarcely had time to shave and to change into a fresh coat and cravat before the appointed hour came. Collecting Stephen and Peter from their nurse, he descended to the drawing room.

It was presently empty, the party still lingering at dinner. But all was in readiness for them. The room was brilliant with light, a fire blazing in the hearth and candles flickering atop every available surface.

John drew the boys to a window seat, out of the way of the sofas and chairs that the guests would soon occupy. Sitting down, he was grateful for the brief moment of privacy so that they could get their bearings.

And not only them.

John felt a measure of apprehension as well. He hadn't encountered Mrs. Rochester since the night of the fire. And now he would see her again at last, not from an upstairs window but face-to-face. Close enough to hear her voice and to register the subtle changes in her expression.

Stephen and Peter seemed equally anxious for her arrival. They sat solemnly beside him, watchful and waiting, their little frames taut with tension.

John laid a hand on Stephen's shoulder. The boy looked up at him, a frightened question in his dark eyes. "You're quite safe with me," John assured him. "I won't let anyone harm you."

A soft sound emanated from the hall, drawing their attention. It preceded the arrival of the ladies: Mrs. Rochester, Mrs. Eshton, and another woman—quite young. They entered the drawing room together midconversation and at once sat down, making themselves comfortable in front of the fire.

Mrs. Rochester was wearing her usual black. A gown of silk and lace, with a fashionably low neckline. Her hair was drawn up in an elegant roll, secured with jet combs. At her throat, her silver locket glistened.

Her eyes briefly touched on John and the boys, half-hidden in their window seat, but no sign of particular warmth or recognition registered in her gaze. She resumed her conversation with the other ladies as if they had the room entirely to themselves.

John hadn't expected her to introduce him to her guests. To do so would have been borderline scandalous. He was only a tutor. A paid employee. He *knew* that. Nevertheless, he hadn't been prepared for her indifference.

Looking at her, he was painfully reminded of their last encounter. The way her voice had trembled as she clasped his bare hand in hers. So warm. So urgent. Her bronze-and-green-flecked eyes hadn't been indifferent to him then. They'd been brimming with unspoken emotion.

"Those are your wards, I suppose," Mrs. Eshton said, casting a cool look their way. "They're quite dark, aren't they?"

"Not at all English," the other lady added under her breath.

Mrs. Rochester leaned back against the sofa in that queenly way of hers. As if she were mistress of all she surveyed. A Bengal tiger might have lounged thus. A fearsome predator, thoroughly at home in her lair. "Stephen and Peter are from Bulgaria," she said. "I should be surprised if there was anything English about them."

John observed the three ladies as they talked. Mrs. Eshton was a large woman, aged somewhere between fifty and sixty, by his guess. Her hair was liberally peppered with gray, and she had a rather impressive double chin that was partially camouflaged by an enormous pearl necklace. Her smallest movement evoked haughtiness. A sense of superiority so innate that her upper lip was permanently curled.

The other lady—whom he soon learned was an Eshton cousin by the name of Miss Lynn—appeared just as haughty. Thin and sallow, she sat primly beside Mrs. Eshton, her aristocratically beaked nose lifted high in the air as she spoke.

Coffee was brought in almost immediately, courtesy of one of the footmen. Mrs. Rochester was pouring it out for her guests when the gentlemen entered the drawing room. A portly older man—Mr. Eshton, John presumed—and the two Eshton sons, George and Louis. The three of them looked thoroughly imposing in their evening black.

At the sight of them, Stephen drew closer to John.

"They're only men," John said, just loud enough for the boys to hear. "Do you see? They can't hurt you."

George Eshton took a seat next to Mrs. Rochester on the sofa, moving the folds of her skirt out of the way so he wouldn't crush them under his leg. It was a courteous impulse—and a presumptuous one. Who was he to make free with her person in such a way? As if he had the right to do so.

And perhaps he had.

He was a well-favored gentleman. Languidly elegant, with a pleasing countenance, thick golden hair, and a tall, athletic build. Looking at him now, John felt a sharp twinge of jealousy. He was no golden godlike man. He was an academic, plain of face and feature. Was it any wonder that Mrs. Rochester preferred the company of George Eshton to him?

The elder Mr. Eshton sank into a chair near to both the fire and his wife, and Louis Eshton sat down in front of the drawing room piano. It was a grander affair than the cabinet piano in the library. An expensive instrument made for entertaining. He tinkled the keys in a soft accompaniment to the clinking of coffee cups and lively conversation.

"Whatever induced you to take charge of two little waifs?" George Eshton asked Mrs. Rochester.

"Why shouldn't I have?" Mrs. Rochester asked. "I have room enough for them."

"Yes, but—"

"And they had need of me." She sipped her coffee. "There's no great mystery about it."

"Won't you introduce them to us?" Miss Lynn asked.

"On no account," Mrs. Rochester replied. "They're too shy of strangers at present. It's enough that they can observe you."

"*They* observe *us*?" Miss Lynn laughed. "I'd thought it the other way around. Isn't that right, aunt?"

"I did want to have a look at them," Mrs. Eshton admitted. "All of Millcote is anxious to see what sort of children you've brought back from the Continent. You can't blame our curiosity."

Mrs. Rochester smiled slightly. "Are my affairs so fascinating? I wouldn't have thought so. We lead a quiet life here."

"Too quiet," George Eshton said. "It isn't good for you, my dear."

My dear.

The casual endearment struck John like a blow. Were the pair of them so familiar with each other? So intimate?

"Nonsense," Mrs. Rochester said. "I'm content as I am. And if I grow restless, I shall take myself off again."

"And what of your wards?" he asked.

"What about them?"

Mrs. Eshton opened her fan and proceeded to wave it vigorously. "You should send them to school."

"I wouldn't dream of it," Mrs. Rochester said. "Not in their current state. It would be a cruelty."

"You will have to send them away when you remarry," the elder Mr. Eshton pronounced.

Mrs. Rochester took another sip of her coffee. "Will I?"

"If your husband wishes it." Mr. Eshton turned to George. "What say you on the subject, my boy?"

"I say nothing. I haven't any right to." George paused, smiling. "Though I have reason to hope that one day I shall."

"Oh, George!" Mrs. Eshton fluttered her fan in excitement. "You don't mean to suggest that you—"

"Enough," Mrs. Rochester said crossly. "Have we nothing better to discuss than my domestic entanglements? Even the most uncivilized societies have music to entertain them."

George grinned, flashing a set of strong white teeth. "She's right. We've teased her long enough." He called out to his brother: "Play something cheerful for us, Louis."

"And sing, won't you?" Miss Lynn asked Mrs. Rochester. "You have such a lovely voice."

"Pity Miss Ingram isn't here to accompany you," Mrs. Eshton said. "How well the pair of you sounded together."

George cast a measuring glance at Mrs. Rochester. "We won't speak of Miss Ingram. The recollection is yet too painful, I think."

Mrs. Rochester's face was void of expression as she finished her coffee.

John studied her in the moments when he was unobserved. She seemed animated enough in the company of her friends. As if she was enjoying herself. But there was something wrong. Something…off. He couldn't put his finger on it. It was merely an impression. A feeling derived from the unspoken energy generated by her and her guests.

It didn't help that the storm had worsened. Rain hammered against the drawing room windows and battered down on the roof in a relentless, and rather unnerving, assault. To hear it, one might fear they were about to fall victim to a return of Noah's flood.

"Dear Miss Ingram," Mrs. Eshton said on a sigh. "Such a tragedy."

"Will you sing in her stead?" George asked Mrs. Rochester. "I've always found your voice to be superior, even to hers."

"Oh, yes." Miss Lynn clapped her hands. "The pair of you must perform a duet."

"Will you?" George asked again, his deep voice gone silky and persuasive. "It would please me greatly."

"If you insist." Setting aside her coffee cup, Mrs. Rochester stood. "But I'll have no tepid love songs. If we sing it must be *con spirito*."

"As you command." George followed her to the piano, and taking his brother's place at the keys, commenced pounding out a boisterous tune.

Mrs. Rochester stood beside him, one hand resting on the piano. Her black silk skirts swelled out in a wide bell shape from her slim waist, the candlelight shimmering on her bare shoulders and throat.

The attention of the entire company was fixed upon her and George Eshton.

Now was the time for John to quietly slip away with the boys. They'd had enough. *He'd* had enough. And surely no one would notice if they withdrew. But just as he made to stand, Mrs. Rochester began to sing.

John found himself fixed to his place. Unable to move. Unable to breathe. She had a fine voice. Stirring and powerful. A rich contralto that seeped into his veins, and thereby, to his heart. With every beat he felt it resonating within him. Not the music or the song, but *her*.

It was a pleasure that swiftly turned to pain.

Taking Stephen and Peter by the hand, John exited the drawing room through a side door, the final notes of the duet sounding at his heels. A short passageway led into the hall and thence to the stairs.

Sophie was sitting on the bottom step, waiting. When she saw them, she jumped up.

"You see?" John said to the boys as he handed them off to her. "Nothing at all to be afraid of. Only people. They can't hurt you."

Stephen gave him a long look. If John didn't know better, he'd think the boy could read his thoughts. Children could be alarmingly intuitive.

"Go with Nurse," John said, urging them up the stairs. "I'll stop in to see you both before bedtime." He remained on the landing as Stephen and Peter ascended to the nursery, Sophie following close behind them.

A throbbing tension threatened at his temples and behind his eyes. The beginnings of a megrim. It had been nearly two months since his last one. He supposed the long reprieve was owing to the herbal tonic. Either that or a consequence of the happiness he felt in his new position. Thornfield was becoming a home to him; the boys his family. And Mrs. Rochester…

His throat tightened.

Behind him, the door to the drawing room opened and closed. Light footsteps sounded in the hall, accompanied by the rustle of silken skirts. A lady approached.

Steeling himself, John turned to face her.

It was Mrs. Rochester.

"Good evening, John," she said.

He caught the subtle fragrance of her perfume. Dizzyingly exotic. It did nothing to calm the erratic rhythm of his pulse. "Good evening, ma'am."

"I trust you've been well during my absence?"

"Quite well."

"And how have you been occupying yourself?"

"In doing my job. In teaching Stephen and Peter." How formal he sounded. How unfailingly respectful and remote. When all the while, he ached to tell her about the boys' singing. About his visit to Hay, and what he'd learned from the vicar. So many things had occurred since last he'd seen her. And he wanted, needed...

But it wasn't the time.

And he was in no fit state for conversation.

She took a step closer to him. "You've sent them to bed?"

"I have. They'd had enough."

"And you? What's your excuse?"

He was quiet a moment. "I wasn't aware I needed one. With the boys gone back to the nursery—"

"Return with me to the drawing room," she said. "You're leaving too early."

"I'm tired." It wasn't a lie.

Her eyes searched his. "What is it?" she asked softly. "Has something happened?"

He swallowed hard. "Nothing, ma'am."

"You don't like that I have guests staying, do you? Nor do I. But it's easier with you in the room. Knowing you're there... I find it soothing, somehow."

"I wasn't aware you noticed me at all."

Her mouth curved up at one corner in that wry way he'd come to recognize. "Don't be absurd. Of course, I noticed you."

"You were much engaged with your guests."

Her smile turned brittle before disappearing altogether. "My guests," she repeated. "Would that I could drive them all back to the Leas myself."

John was surprised by the edge of bitterness that sharpened her words. "In this weather? It's not fit for anyone. Least of all a lady."

"Don't let it fool you." She cast a dark look at the window above the stairs. "It's nothing but sound and fury. An illusion meant to frighten us."

"It felt real enough to me when I was fetching the firewood."

"You?" She looked vaguely appalled. "Don't tell me Mr. Fairfax ordered you—"

"I volunteered. I was glad to be of use." John wasn't ashamed to admit it.

"Well," Mrs. Rochester said bleakly, "I daresay that's what it's come to. Thornfield hasn't the staff to entertain. We must muddle through somehow." She drew back from him. "Retire if you must, but if my guests remain through tomorrow, I'll expect you in the drawing room again, and every night until we're free of them."

"Mrs. Rochester, it's hardly my place—"

"I see what you're about. You mean to play the dutiful subordinate. Play it, then. Do as you're told, without argument."

"I'm not playing at anything."

"Nonsense. We both of us are. What is this if not a farce? We shall perform our roles as written, and then, when my guests have gone—"

John held his breath for what she might say next. But her words never materialized. Her speech was arrested by the sudden arrival of Mr. Fairfax.

He appeared at the top of the stairs, half panting from the exertion. "Mrs. Rochester! Thank heaven I've found you. Another guest has arrived."

She turned to him, brows snapping together in irritation. "What are you mumbling about?"

"A hired coach from Millcote. It came not five minutes ago. Though how she persuaded the driver to bring her this far, I can't imagine. I daresay she must have paid extra for the privilege. She looks well-to-do enough for it."

Mrs. Rochester gave the elderly butler an arrested look. "She? What she?"

"I beg your pardon, ma'am." Mr. Fairfax withdrew a handkerchief from his pocket and blotted his forehead. "What with all the comings and goings, I'm a trifle overtaxed. But I've put her in the small parlor. She awaits you there. A lady by the name of Mrs. Wren."

Eighteen

*Mrs. Bertha
Rochester's Journal.*

6 April. Senniskali. — There is no point in writing any more letters. I have lost all faith in any of them being posted. Instead, I have resolved to write a true and thorough account here, in my journal, with hopes that one day, when I've at last returned home to Thornfield, I can share it with Blanche, or with my solicitor.

I have every expectation that I will see England again. My husband has, only last week, procured our passage. We leave for Varna, and thence to Athens, at the end of the month. Until then, we're obliged to remain in each other's company. Thus far, it has been an exercise in self-restraint.

On returning from his solicitor's last week, he apologized for his actions. He's sorry to have hurt me, and to have frightened me, and swears upon his honor that he won't do so again. What choice do I have but to accept his apologies and to forgive him? I'm in no position to do otherwise. Worse than that, I must pretend he's the same man I married and that my feelings for him are unaltered, for I sense with every ounce of my feminine intuition that—were I to confront him about his aggressive behavior—he might do me some greater violence.

As a result of this fear, Edward and I have commenced a silently agreed upon fiction. It enables us to interact as we did during the early days of our marriage. He is exceedingly civil to me. While I, in turn, do him the courtesy of pretending that he's never before laid his hands upon me in anger. That he's never threatened me or forced me to sign away my fortune.

It's this unspoken agreement that allows us to coexist in a house that is now absent its servants. Where have they gone? The way of Mr. Poole, I fear. Sent away so they can't bear witness to the mistreatment I may yet suffer at my husband's hands.

Only during the daylight do I receive any relief from his menacing presence. Tormented by his headaches, he inevitably retires at sunrise, emerging again only after dark. It is during those brief hours that I'm free to roam about the house. On the first day after his return, I went straightaway to the front door, only to find it bolted and chained against me.

I am a prisoner here, totally reliant on the goodwill of my husband. And of that goodwill, I can no longer be certain.

Does he love me? Did he ever love me? Or was it only my money and property he desired?

It's true I never loved him in return, but I own to mistaking his physical affections for something of a deeper nature. Not a communion of souls—I dared not hope for that—but a sympathy that transcended more mercenary concerns. I'm not the first woman to make such an error. Many before me have done so—a fact which makes the reality of my mistake no easier to accept.

I've been tempted to wallow in it. To excoriate myself for having fallen victim to the wiles of an unscrupulous predator. But I can think of no more unproductive way to spend my time. I'm an unwilling captive in a marriage—and in a house. The daylight hours can better be expended in formulating a way to extricate myself from this predicament.

And so I shall.

8 April. — The sun has risen and Edward has withdrawn to his room. I waited an hour before trying his door. It was locked, as it always is. On rattling the handle, I received no response, which assured me that he was asleep, and that Nosht-Vŭlk would be mine until sunset.

As yet, I've never fully explored the place. It's an intimidating structure, and Edward was adamant that I not stray to the darkest reaches of its upper and lower rooms. For my own safety, he said. But now…I wonder. Is there a means of escape through one of the doors? A way to call for assistance through one of the windows? There must be, surely.

Lighting a lantern, I ascended the drafty stone staircase to the floor above. There, at the end of a long, dark corridor, a door stood open. It led to a small room, which contained no furnishings, only a cold slab floor and a high stone-framed window barred with rusted iron.

The view from the window was breathtaking. It looked down from the very edge of the cliffs to the roiling Black Sea below. But I was in no mood to appreciate its beauty. I was interested only in escape. Leaving the room, I continued my exploration of the hall. It was lined with other doors, all of them locked. I rattled the handles, one after the other, with increasing urgency. All to no avail.

A wild sort of panic rose within me. I ran back down the stairs, trying every door that I passed. Locked. All of them locked. And where were the keys? My husband must have possession of them. But how to get them from him? I could see no way to do so. Not when he and I were on such precarious terms.

When at last I returned to my room, I imposed a forcible calmness on my body, commanding my pulse to slow and my breaths to come regular and even. I cannot descend into despair. I *will* not. An animal may gnaw off a foot to escape a steel trap, but I am not an animal. I am a woman.

11 April. — Edward knows I am his prisoner. And he knows that I know. Our interactions have taken on the air of a pantomime. When he rises at sundown, he asks me how I've slept, and presses a kiss to my cheek. I'm beginning to suspect that our situation amuses him in some perverse way. As if he's waiting to see me flinch—or to weep.

He spends his waking hours engaged in matters of business. Sometimes he leaves the house entirely, for where I do not know. When he returns, he generally brings back something to eat, and while I dine, he regales me with stories of his ancestors, and of the long-ago battles in the region. It is a land steeped in blood and conquest. A place that has rarely known peace for any length of time.

When Edward isn't engaged in a lengthy monologue, he's peppering me with questions about England. He wants to know everything about Thornfield Hall. How far is it from the nearest church? How close is it to the sea? He's particularly keen on the notion that the railway may soon come to Millcote. The idea of easy access to London appeals to him, though—as I pointed out—if he desires proximity to the city, it would be far more efficient for him to simply buy a house in town than to count on a railway line being laid all the way to Yorkshire.

It was during this particular conversation that he first informed me that his finances were not what they once were. Apparently, in the last several years, his investments in the West Indies have begun to suffer. I asked him to explain, but he would say nothing more than that British law made it impossible for his sugar plantation to make a profit any longer.

I suspect he must have earned his money there on the backs of slaves. Now that the vile practice has been abolished, it seems he's unable to acclimate himself to a new method of doing business. I had thought…

But there's no excuse for my ignorance. As soon as he said he had holdings in the West Indies, I should have interrogated him further. Instead, I assumed only the best, just as I did in every other regard. Was there ever a woman so ignorant? So certain she had evaluated a potential mate with a critical eye, only to discover that she's been as gullible as every other unwitting member of her sex?

The least I can say for myself is that, though I may occasionally make mistakes, I rarely make the same one twice.

14 April. — My nights with my husband have been passing much as ever, with only one marked change: I have lately seen him looking at me, studying me, when he believes I'm not aware. It's enough to raise the hairs on the back of my neck. He's up to something, and I fear that whatever it is, it bodes nothing but ill for me. My only advantage is one he hasn't yet surmised. He believes he is studying me, but it is *I* who have been watching him. Learning him. What use I can make of this meager knowledge, I don't know. Not yet.

Some hours ago, as the sun fully set, he departed on one of his mysterious errands. I stood in the hall as he unchained the front door.

"Why must you lock it behind you?" I asked.

"For your safety, my love," he said.

"Yes, but what if I should have some emergency? What if I'm injured? Or require help?"

He gave me a hard look. "You will receive no injury so long as you adhere to my rules. Stay close to your bedchamber, or to these rooms." He gestured to the hall and the adjacent library. "Do not venture any farther. My home is an ancient place, with stones and timber that have needed replacing these many years. I cannot promise you will be safe if you put a foot on the wrong step, or go through a forbidden door."

His speech chilled me. Was he aware of my daylight explorations? I didn't see how he could be. "Even more reason for you to leave the door unlocked," I said. "Or to trust me with the keys."

His lips curled in a mocking smile. "You may as well ask that I leave the door to my vault unlocked. I keep my treasures well protected. All of them." With that, he kissed me very hard on the mouth. So hard that the inner flesh of my lips was cut against my teeth, drawing a trickle of blood.

What my husband did next, I can hardly bring myself to put to paper. But I have promised a true account here, and so I must transcribe this aberrant behavior along with all the rest. It is this: as he kissed me, he lapped up the trickle of blood from my mouth with his tongue.

I stood there, stunned and repulsed, as he took his leave, shutting the door behind him. He drew the bolt from the outside, locking me in the house until his return.

What would he do, I wondered, if I were to fall upon the door, pounding with my fists and screaming? I feared the worst. This absurd pretense of normalcy was the only thing keeping me safe from him at the moment.

Lighting a lantern, I returned upstairs, but instead of going to my room, I climbed two flights to the topmost floor. It was darker there, and dustier, stinking of damp and rot. I checked the doors. Most of them were locked. But, much to my surprise, two of them were not.

The first opened stiffly as I turned the handle, swinging back with a shriek of rusty hinges so loud I nearly jumped out of my skin. Raising my lantern, I looked about the room. It was nothing very impressive. Some old furnishings, half covered with sheets. Rather like the furniture stored on the third floor of Thornfield.

Going to the barred window, I saw that it looked out over the courtyard, giving a rare glimpse of the path by which my husband made his comings and goings. He wasn't there at present, and there was no sign of any horses or carriages, nor of any servants that I could see. There was only a strange silver mist that had gathered in the darkness, rolling over the ground to the edges of the fortress. Somewhere in the distance, a wolf howled.

Resuming my investigations, I continued to the next unlocked door. It led to an even smaller chamber that contained nothing but a wardrobe and an old sea trunk. Dust lay upon the floor in a thick layer. I was conscious of leaving my footprints in it as I made my way to the window.

The view through the iron bars was nothing to speak of—only a glimpse of the sea below. All but one side of Nosht-Vŭlk was built at the very edge of the cliff, making escape from these windows impossible, even if I *could* manage to fit through the bars. Indeed, I was beginning to think that escape was impossible entirely.

After obscuring the evidence of my footsteps, I returned to my room, my mind in a tumult. At length, I came to the following conclusion: it is pointless to concern myself with thoughts of escape. Far better to remain in my husband's good graces until the day of our departure. Once I'm back in England, I will have a greater chance of extricating myself from his clutches.

Though I fear it is already too late for that. Whether locked inside of a remote fortress or not, a wife is a prisoner of her husband, confined by the legal bonds of matrimony. Such bondage knows no geographic boundary.

16 April. — My plan to appear a good and obedient wife has, so far, been successful. As a result, Edward has been kinder to me and has seemed less menacing. To keep him thus, I initiate conversation only on topics that are of particular interest to him, such as the history of his homeland or his collection of antiquities. He's always willing to expound on these subjects whenever he has a free moment. However, of late his free moments have become fewer and farther between.

He's busy from sunset to sunrise on some business venture of his own. It involves a great deal of letter writing, and a great many midnight errands outside of the house. He won't share the details of his enterprise with me, and I dare not press him too hard, lest I disrupt the tenuous peace we've come to in our marriage.

18 April. —Edward has been going into and out of his vault rather a lot in the past days, each time unlocking it and locking it again behind him. This morning, in the early hours before sunrise, I persuaded him to let me accompany him inside. Much to my surprise, he relented.

I've been inside the vault before. It's a cool room, dry and airless, filled with the most fascinating collection of antiques. However, as I looked about the walls, starkly brightened by lanternlight, I recalled that on my previous visit, the shelves housing my husband's treasures had been markedly fuller.

"Where is the rest of your collection?" I asked.

"Gone," he said.

"Yes, but where?"

"Gone," he said again. "Sold."

I noticed then that Edward's expression was unusually grim. He plainly wasn't happy to have parted with the pieces in question. "Why?" I asked.

"It was necessary," he said. "I required additional coin to purchase another item. A book."

"What sort of book?"

"Egyptian," he said. "Quite valuable to me. It may have come from the empty tomb in Thebes."

"And you bought it?"

"Not yet. But it will be mine." And then he added, very quietly: "I have been looking for it all of my life."

His words shouldn't have been ominous. I know the single-mindedness of some collectors. They'll happily bankrupt themselves to acquire a coveted piece. But I nevertheless felt a strange shiver of unease. "Is there something particular about this book that appeals to you?"

"You ask a great many questions," he said. "Take care. The answers may not be to your liking."

21 April. — Today, Edward was out again on another midnight errand. When he returned, he came to my bedroom, and summoning me to my little desk, placed before me a bottle of ink, a freshly sharpened quill, and several blank sheets of paper. "You must write two letters to your friend, Miss Ingram," he said.

My heart fairly leapt. "To Blanche? Do you mean to post them for me?"

"Indeed." He set his hand upon my shoulder, squeezing it so tightly that he caused me pain. "But you must write what I tell you to."

A chill settled into my veins. "What is it that you wish me to say to her?"

"Only this," he replied silkily. "In the first letter, you will tell her that you and I have left Varna. In the second you will say that we have boarded a ship for Marseilles."

I met his eyes, and he looked into mine, unflinching. There was a diabolical gleam in the depths of his gaze. I knew then that, were it up to him, I would never again see Varna, let alone England.

Strengthening his grip on my shoulder, he commanded me to date the first letter ten days hence, and the second for two weeks after that. When I'd done so, he collected the letters, along with the writing implements, and departed my chamber. I heard the bolt slide into place as he shut the door behind him.

I am again locked in my room. And unless I am very much mistaken, I have but ten days to contrive an escape. Or else…God help me.

22 April. — The pretense between Edward and I has been entirely abandoned. I know it now for what it was all along. A source of amusement to him. A means of toying with me, as a cat toys with a mouse, building the smaller creature's terror until that final moment when the cat at last makes a meal of him.

This morning, he returned at sunrise to unbolt my door. Where he'd been, I haven't the faintest idea. Yesterday, I might have refrained from asking in order to keep the peace. But today, I had no such concerns. I went directly up to him, and spoke in my most challenging tone. "What do you mean by locking me in my room? Have you no honor at all?"

His mouth curved into a lazy smile. "My English tigress. I see that a night in your cage has failed to subdue you."

Oh! If I were a man, I would have hit him. But I have no such power. Only words—the bulk of which appeared to have no impact on him at all. "It was never Mrs. Wren, was it? That first time I found myself a prisoner here? It was you all along. You locked me in my room then, just as you did last night." I looked him straight in the eye. "You coward."

His mood changed, swift as quicksilver. One moment he was smiling, and the next he had me by the throat. With one squeeze of his fingers, he cut off my air. "Have a care, dear lady," he said. "Lest I tire of you sooner than anticipated."

Blood roared in my ears. I daresay it deprived me of sense, as well as oxygen, for when he loosened his grip, I took only the barest breath before attacking him, once more, with the only weapon at my disposal. "Coward," I said. "Abuser of women."

His fingers tightened, crushing my throat as brutally as a vise. He lifted me straight up onto the toes of my slippers. "Say it again," he said softly. "I dare you to."

I was afraid. Of course, I was. But another emotion transcended fear. I saw my life flash before my eyes, as bright and brilliant as the pages of an illuminated manuscript. All those years yearning for adventure. All those years resisting marriage to worthy gentlemen. All for this—to end my days in the clutches of such a villain. And I wasn't frightened any longer. I was angry.

"Coward," I choked out. "Parasite."

At that, he roared his outrage like any animal and threw me across the length of the room with unbelievable strength. I hit the wall, banging my head sharply before crumpling to the floor. Dizziness assailed my senses, and a taste of bile rose in my throat. I feared I would faint, my lifeless body left entirely to his evil devices.

I willed myself to remain conscious, rising up to a sitting position against the wall.

For a moment, it looked as though he would come to me and finish the violence he'd begun. Instead, he drew back, his face a mask of controlled fury. "Count yourself lucky I still have need of you," he said.

And then he left me.

23 April. — The date of our departure is set for the first of May. That gives me seven days exactly. A feeling of desperation has made me conscious of every passing second. I've resolved to use my time as efficiently as I can.

I spent all of last night in my room, wary of venturing forth. Only this morning, when Edward finally retired to bed, was I able to go down to the kitchen to procure myself something to eat. The cheese and bread I found had gone moldy, and our small store of meat had begun to rot. My husband must be dining out in the evenings, for he has touched none of the food here. I shouldn't like to eat it either, but I must keep up my strength.

At present, there is no way out of Nosht-Vŭlk. No unlocked door, and no window from which I can climb. What I require most is a key. But how to gain access to it? Edward carries the keys on his person. I can't overpower him when he's awake, and while he sleeps, he lies safe behind the two locked doors of his bedchamber.

Returning to my room, I examined this lock on the connecting door. I knew it was strong. It had never so much as budged during all of my angry shaking and rattling. But was it a complicated mechanism? I knelt down on the stone floor in front of it and gave it a thorough looking over.

When I was a girl, Mama once confiscated a novel she caught me reading and locked it away in the drawer of her dressing table. Later, after much clumsy fiddling, I managed to spring the lock with a bent hairpin, and thereby retrieve my book. Would such a simple trick work on one of the locks at Nosht-Vŭlk?

Removing one of the hairpins from my coil of plaits, I bent it and poked it into the bottom part of the keyhole. As I rattled it about, a growing fear rose within me. What if Edward was to wake and catch me at my illicit task? But there seemed little chance of that. In all the months of our marriage, I'd never once seen my husband in the daylight. He was a sound sleeper—the soundest I'd ever encountered—and not likely to be disturbed by any amount of noise.

I continued my efforts, aided by the fact that, though strong enough, the lock was as old as everything else in the fortress. There didn't appear to be anything overly complicated about its interior mechanism. Surely nothing like the newer sets of locks and bolts that guarded Edward's vault.

After a time, in some frustration, I withdrew a second hairpin and inserted that into the lock as well. It took a great deal of trial and error. Rather too much. My patience had nearly run out when, at last, I heard the telltale click.

I can't describe the relief I felt. Wiping the perspiration from my brow, I stood and tested the doorknob. It turned in my hand. A little push, and the door creaked open. Holding my breath, I walked through it.

My husband's bedchamber was not unknown to me. Some nights, when first I arrived at Nosht-Vŭlk, the connecting door between our rooms had stood open. Then, I had curiously glanced inside, as any new bride might. Because of this, I recognized its grand furnishings: the twin wardrobes, marble-topped washstand, and stately four-poster bed with its heavy velvet curtains, drawn shut to block out the light.

My plan was simple. Moving as silently as a ghost, I would search his room for the keys. Where might he have put them? On the tall chest in the corner? In the pocket of his coat hung over the chair by his bed? I looked in the obvious places, but found no trace of them. I was about to commence searching the wardrobes when an unsettling thought occurred to me. What if the keys remained with him while he slept?

Steeling my courage, I approached the closed curtains of his bed. My heart beat so that I could scarcely hear myself think. I was deathly afraid he'd wake up and find me looming over him. However, when I finally worked up the nerve to draw back the bed curtain, I found—to my bewilderment— that Edward was not there at all.

How was this possible? He'd retired to his room at dawn, just as he always did. I'd heard the door in the hall open and shut. Had heard the lock turning. And yet…his bed was empty. Not only empty. It hadn't appeared to have been slept in at all. Not yesterday, nor the day before. Not in an age. The ancient coverlet and bolster were moth-eaten and covered with a layer of dust.

I backed away from the bed, truly afraid. If my husband hadn't been sleeping here all these months, where *had* he been sleeping?

More to the point, where on earth was he now?

Nineteen

Thornfield Hall
Yorkshire, England
March 1844

At Mr. Fairfax's pronouncement, Mrs. Rochester lost a good deal of her color. John had never seen her look so pale. So shaken. Not even on the night he'd rescued her from her smoke-filled bedroom.

"Tell Mrs. Wren I shall be with her directly," she said to Mr. Fairfax.

"Very good, madam."

She remained where she was until the butler departed, and then, gripping the banister with one white-knuckled hand, she sagged against the wall.

For an instant, John feared she would swoon. He reached instinctively to steady her, only to draw back at the last moment, mindful of his place. "Are you ill, ma'am?"

She looked up at him with wide, unseeing eyes.

A surge of protectiveness took him unaware. Damn and blast it anyway. What care had he for propriety when she was in such a state? "Here, lean against my shoulder. Let me help you." Putting his arm at her waist, he guided her to a silk-upholstered bench in the hall.

She sank down upon it, and taking his hand, drew him down beside her. He might have maintained a respectful distance from her, even then, but she didn't relinquish his hand. She clasped it tightly in hers, keeping him close. "Would that we were far away from here," she said. "Away from violence and danger. Removed from any recollections of the past."

"What is it?" he asked. "Tell me so I can help you."

"I fear I am beyond help."

"No one is beyond help."

"I am. And you'd realize it if you knew the half of what my life has been. What I've done. You'd run far and fast to escape me."

"Never," he vowed.

"You would."

"I'm not so fainthearted as that." He brought her hand to his lips and pressed a kiss to her knuckles. It was a reckless impulse. A rank presumption. But he couldn't bring himself to care at the moment. Not when she so desperately needed his reassurance. "There's nothing you could do that would drive me away."

She huffed an unsteady breath. It sounded vaguely like a sob. "I do believe you mean that."

"Of course I mean it. I told you that I would stand beside you. Don't you remember?"

"I remember everything," she said. "Everything."

"There you are, then. All that's left is for you to tell me what's wrong. What I can do to make this better."

She was quiet for a long moment as she visibly brought herself under control. "You can fetch me a glass of wine," she said at last.

"Done." When she released his hand, he rose and went at once to the dining room. It was empty, the table and sideboard still partially cluttered with the leavings from dinner. As he poured out a glass of wine from the decanter, Alfred entered to finish clearing. On seeing John with the wine, he frowned but made no remark. No doubt he thought John was taking it for himself.

Much that John cared for his opinion at the moment.

He returned to Mrs. Rochester. She was still seated in the hall, just as he'd left her. He offered her the glass of wine and she took it and drained it in one swallow. The ashen whiteness of her pallor slowly dissipated.

"I told you once that in matters of good and evil, I stand firmly on the side of good," she said. "Did you believe me?"

"I had no reason not to."

Her expression was grim. Remote. As if meditating on an unsolvable dilemma. "And what if someone were to tell you different? To say that it was, in fact, the opposite?"

He frowned. "I don't understand."

She leveled her gaze at him. "What would you do, John, if all of those fine people in the drawing room scorned me? If they accused me of some great evil?"

Under other circumstances, he might have been alarmed by the question. But not now. Now, she was plainly distraught and in need of comforting. "What evil?" he asked.

"Of being a cold, unfeeling creature, undeserving of the name of woman. Would you tender your resignation and abandon this house right along with them?"

"I care nothing for this house. But you…" His voice sank to a gruff undertone. "I wouldn't abandon you or the boys. No matter what the denizens of Yorkshire society had to say about it. What care I for their good opinion?"

She smiled slightly. "That loyal, are you?"

"To those who deserve it."

"Well then, I am on my mettle." Handing him the empty wineglass, she stood and straightened her skirts. "Enough dramatics. I'm fortified now. Another moment, and I shall venture into the dragon's lair."

John's brows lowered. "Is this Mrs. Wren a dangerous person?"

"Perhaps." Mrs. Rochester's mouth curved into another smile. This time it didn't quite meet her eyes. "But don't worry for me, sir. I can be quite dangerous myself when the occasion calls for it."

Later that night, John retired to his bed, unable to sleep. His thoughts were in disarray, his emotions confused. He worried over what might have happened with Mrs. Rochester and her mysterious guest. And he wondered if, when she'd concluded her meeting, she'd returned to the drawing room—and thereby to George Eshton.

The moon was full, a luminous silver disc shining through the slim cracks in his chintz window curtains. He stared at it, mulling over the way he'd kissed Mrs. Rochester's hand, and the way he'd vowed to stand by her, whatever the consequences. It had been all but a declaration. One he'd never made to any other lady before.

One he'd never made to Helen.

Why not? Had it only been because Helen was married? She'd been appealing in every other respect. Beautiful, sweet, and gentle. The epitome of feminine delicacy and grace. He'd admired her, certainly. Had been ready to stand her friend. But he hadn't been willing to brave public scorn to remain at her side. Hadn't been prepared to risk his heart—or endanger his soul.

How was Mrs. Rochester any different?

He may as well have attempted to enumerate the differences between sun and shadow. Between a tigress and a house cat.

Which was more puzzling still, come to think of it. Mrs. Rochester didn't need him to fight her battles. She was capable enough on her own. Why, then, did he feel a greater sense of protectiveness toward her than he'd ever felt toward Helen?

John couldn't fathom the why of it. All he knew was that he felt it. That it was real. It was no infatuation. No airy thread of romantic poetry. It was as earthy and fundamental as the blood coursing through his veins.

As the clock struck midnight, the guests at last made their way to their rooms. Voices sounded in the hall, doors clicked open and shut, and then all was once again in silence.

John slept briefly, awakening as the clock chimed three. It was the dratted moonlight shining in his eyes. He'd either have to rise and draw the window curtains more firmly or he'd have to shut the panel of his box bed. Given his previous experience, the latter option was distinctly unappealing.

He sat up, swinging his legs over the side of his bed, and then—

The night's silence was broken by a terrible, desperate scream.

It rang throughout the whole of Thornfield. A blood-chilling sound, enough to make John's pulse stop.

Who was it? And where was it coming from? It appeared to be emanating from somewhere on the third story. Was it Mr. Poole?

But no.

This was a woman's scream.

He leapt from his bed only to stand there, motionless, as the scream died. There was no repetition of it. How could there be? Such an outcry must have exhausted the lungs of the woman who uttered it.

Footsteps pounded along the floor above him, followed by several heavy thuds against the walls and the floor. And then—

John couldn't be certain, but he thought he heard the rattle of chains.

Foolish thought! There was no ghost lurking on the third floor, rattling its chains like a specter in a penny novel. There was only Mr. Poole.

And whatever poor woman had screamed.

"Mrs. Rochester!" a man cried out from above. "Mrs. Rochester, help!"

At that, John sprang into action. Lighting a candle, he tugged on yesterday's shirt and trousers, still draped on the clothespress. All the while, the noise outside continued. Doors opened and someone ran down the corridor, their light footfalls passing John's room.

"What's going on?" a gentleman demanded. "Where is Mrs. Rochester?"

"Was that her screaming?" an older lady asked.

"Heaven help us!" a younger lady cried.

John emerged from his room to stand at his door. The guests were milling around the hall in their nightcaps and dressing gowns. Sophie was among them. She hovered nearby, her eyes as large as saucers. "Go back to the nursery," John said. "Stay with the boys."

She nodded mutely before retreating back inside. John heard her lock the door.

"Check Mrs. Rochester's room, Mother," George Eshton was saying. "She might still be abed."

"You reckon she slept through that god-awful shrieking?" the elder Mr. Eshton retorted. "No one could!"

"She might have taken a sleeping draught," Miss Lynn said. "I often do."

Mrs. Eshton entered Mrs. Rochester's room only to come out seconds later, her face contorted in distress. "Her bed is empty!"

"Here I am!" Mrs. Rochester's voice rang down the hall. "I shall be with you directly." She strode past John without a glance, hurrying to join her guests. Like them, she wore a dressing gown over her nightclothes. Her black hair was disposed in a plait over her shoulder. Several strands had come loose to curl about her face.

"What in blazes has happened?" George Eshton asked. "Has someone been hurt?"

"No, indeed. A servant has merely had a nightmare." Mrs. Rochester took Mr. Eshton's arm, guiding him back to his door. "And here you've all disturbed yourselves for nothing. Come, back to bed with you. You too, Mrs. Eshton."

"But really, my dear," the elder lady began. "I—"

"I'll hear no more on the subject." Mrs. Rochester urged the older lady to her room. "I have the matter well in hand. Your interference will only embarrass the poor girl further."

John remained where he was until everyone else in the hall had been dispersed.

When the final door closed, Mrs. Rochester's gaze found his. There was nothing of calmness in her eyes. Only a glowing urgency. "Finish getting dressed."

He didn't linger to interrogate her. Withdrawing to his room, he put on his boots, slipped on a vest, and thrust his arms into the sleeves of his coat. He hadn't any idea what she might require of him, but he intended to be prepared for anything.

That scream had been no serving girl having a nightmare.

For one thing, they didn't have a serving girl at Thornfield, only the scullery maid. And she didn't sleep on the third floor. Add to that the tenor of the scream—the pure horror of it—as if it came from the throat of a woman damned to torment in the deepest pit of hell.

John shuddered to recall it.

When dressed, he returned to the door and cracked it open. Minutes passed. The house was quiet, save for the sound of rain pelting the roof and windows as the storm raged outside. It was well past three. The moon had begun to wane, casting his bedroom in darkness. He was grateful for the light of his candle.

A moment later, Mrs. Rochester's soft footsteps sounded on the carpet. She approached his door, fully dressed now in her black riding habit, gloves, and cloak. Her hair had been twisted into a hasty chignon at her nape. "Come with me," she said, holding aloft a small oil lamp. "Quietly, please."

John obeyed without question, accompanying her down the hall to the stairs that led up to the third floor. He was conscious of every creak of the floorboards, every groan of the steps under his booted feet. They stopped outside the same door through which he'd once seen Mr. Poole disappear. It was the man's lair, John presumed.

Mrs. Rochester produced a key from her pocket, and fitting it to the lock, opened the door.

John didn't know what he'd been expecting. An animal's den, perhaps. Something filthy and rank. This room was neither of those things. It was clean and spare, housing only a large curtained bed, a wooden chest, and a washstand.

On the opposite wall hung an enormous tapestry. A corner of it had been looped back, revealing a small hidden door. What lay behind it, John didn't need to guess. He heard, quite clearly, the faint rattle of chains and the muffled, preternatural laughter of Mr. Poole.

"Never mind that." Mrs. Rochester went to the bed and drew back the curtain. "Here, John. This is where I need you."

He came to stand beside her. As she lifted her lamp, he saw—to his astonishment—that a woman lay atop the bed. Her eyes were closed, her skin as white as a corpse. The bodice of her gown had been opened to the waist, revealing not only her corset and chemise but the blood-soaked bandage at her throat.

"Hold the lamp," Mrs. Rochester said.

John took it from her and raised it high, illuminating the poor woman's face. She was a stranger to him. A female of passing middle age. Her hair was sleek and dark, her eyes and mouth bracketed by faint lines. On the third finger of her lifeless left hand a sizeable ruby glinted, set in a band of gold.

Was this the mysterious Mrs. Wren?

Mrs. Rochester crossed the room to the washstand. Water splashed in the bowl, and there was a sound of tearing linen. When she returned, she blotted the woman's face with a thickly folded pad of wet cloth before using the same cloth to wipe away the fresh blood that trickled from the bandage.

The woman's eyes fluttered opened. "Am I out of danger?" Her words were strangely accented. John wondered if she was Bulgarian.

"Danger?" Mrs. Rochester gave a huff of impatience. "What do you know of danger? This is only a scratch. Don't be so fainthearted." She swabbed away more blood from the woman's throat. "Bear up awhile longer till the surgeon comes." Her eyes found his. "John?"

"Yes, ma'am?"

"I must fetch Mr. Carter from Hay."

"In this weather?" He couldn't imagine any of the servants being willing to go out on such an errand. Not at this time of night.

"I've little choice. But it won't take me long. No more than an hour or two. I intend to ride like the very devil."

Understanding sank in. "*You?*" He stared at her. "But… you can't. It isn't safe."

"Safer for me than anyone else. Don't argue. We haven't the time. I must go at once. In the meanwhile, I shall have to leave you here with this lady. You may continue cleaning the blood away as I have done. If she appears to be failing, bathe her face or offer her a glass of water."

The woman moaned softly. "Bertha…"

Mrs. Rochester stood over her, something vaguely threatening in her manner. "You're not to say a word to him. Do you understand me? Not a single syllable. If you dare defy me, I won't be responsible for what becomes of you."

A weak groan emerged from the woman's lips. Her eyes closed once more.

Mrs. Rochester put the pad of cloth into his hand. "Mind what I've told you. Remain here, within the four corners of this chamber, and venture no farther. Open no windows and no doors. And remember—not a word of conversation!"

With that, she exited the room, locking the door behind her.

Twenty

John's stomach sank at the sound of the key turning in the lock. He wasn't afraid. But he didn't much fancy Mr. Poole leaping out at him from inside whatever room was hidden behind the tapestry. Then again, John supposed that Mrs. Rochester must have locked that door as well.

He wiped another trickle of blood from the wound on Mrs. Wren's neck. Her eyes were closed, her mouth clamped so hard that her lips had gone blue. Was it loss of blood that made her hold herself so still? Was it pain?

Or was it fear?

He examined her more closely. Good lord, she hadn't fainted, had she? But no. Her hands were clenched at her sides, half-trembling with the effort. She breathed in shallow, shaking gasps, every exhalation prompting another pulse of blood from her wound.

What had Mr. Poole done to her? Had he attacked her with a knife? And why?

As if there could be a reason!

John cast a brief look at the small door in the wall. It was made of thick, light-colored wood, studded with large silver nails. A new door—newer, at least, than others he'd seen in the house. Its frame and hardware appeared new as well, as if the whole of it had been quite recently reinforced.

Was this where Mr. Poole was confined during one of his episodes? For what else could they be termed but episodes of madness? The man certainly wasn't out of his head the entirety of the time. Whenever John saw him in the kitchen or down at the stables, he appeared as unremarkable as any other servant.

And yet he'd attacked a woman who was easily half his size. Attacked and nearly killed her.

Mrs. Wren moaned as John swabbed her neck. The pad of cloth in his hand was hardly useful anymore. It had grown soaked with her blood. Rising, he went to the basin and rinsed it out.

When he returned, her eyes were open. Brown eyes, glazed with horror. They wandered around the room—to the small door and to the window—and then to John's face, searching, searching.

He wiped her brow again before cleansing the blood from her wound, all the while listening for sounds of stirring within the room behind the wall. He heard nothing now. Nothing save the steady downpour of rain, and the occasional rumble of thunder.

How would Mrs. Rochester manage in such conditions? Heavy fog and heavier rain would surely hinder her progress. She'd said she would ride like the very devil, but how swiftly could one travel on horseback when one was incapable of seeing more than a few feet in front of them at any given moment?

And what if her horse should slip in the lane as it had the day they'd met? What if she should be injured?

Or worse.

What if she were to fall and break her neck just as Blanche Ingram had? Her body left to lie until the following day, doomed to fall victim to ravening animals?

John was tormented by the imagery. As the minutes ticked by, it was all he could do to focus on Mrs. Wren. To swab her wound, and to rinse his cloth again, and then again, in water that was now clouded with her blood.

He passed an hour in this manner, all the while worrying for the safety of Mrs. Rochester—and for his own safety, near as he was to the menace lurking behind the door.

And he wondered how it was that Mrs. Wren had fallen victim to that menace. She was a stranger here, wasn't she? An unannounced visitor who had, only hours ago, been waiting in the small parlor to speak with the mistress of Thornfield Hall.

News of her arrival had struck Mrs. Rochester a blow. Indeed, on hearing of it from Mr. Fairfax, she'd seemed almost to be afraid. But in this room—the two ladies face to face—John had observed that it was Mrs. Wren who was stricken with fear. She looked on Mrs. Rochester with an expression of dread. But no. Not dread. It was more even than that. She looked on her with something approaching awe.

How was it that Mrs. Wren had found her way to the third floor? What was she doing here in the dead of night while everyone else in the house was abed?

Her eyes fell closed once more, and she seemed to drift into unconsciousness. John brought her a glass of water to revive her. She sipped it, whimpering.

He prayed that Mrs. Rochester would hurry. That she'd bring the surgeon, and that he would take over John's grim duties.

It was nearly another hour before he heard the sound of the key in the lock. Outside, the first cold glimmer of dawn threatened, its gray light streaking through the cracks in the heavy curtains as the door opened and Mrs. Rochester entered the room with Mr. Carter.

"Mind the time, Carter," she said. "The servants will be up shortly. I give you but half an hour to dress her wound and to get her downstairs and into the carriage."

Mr. Carter approached the bed. He was an older gentleman with a thick beard and side-whiskers. "Is she fit to travel, ma'am?"

"Of course. It's not a serious injury. Not but that you'd know it from the way she carries on." Mrs. Rochester opened the curtains, letting in as much of the early morning light as existed. "She's a nervous woman. Keeping her calm during the journey will be your main concern. You may well have to administer a sedative."

John withdrew from his place by the bed to make room for the surgeon. Neither Mrs. Rochester nor Mr. Carter had acknowledged him as yet. Neither by word, nor deed. There was an air of haste about them.

Mr. Carter bent to examine Mrs. Wren. His hands moved gently, but purposefully, to remove the blood-soaked bandage from her throat.

Mrs. Rochester joined him at the head of the bed. She regarded Mrs. Wren with an expression that was impossible to read. "How do you do this morning?"

Mrs. Wren gave a little cry as one of the bandages was pulled away. "He's done for me."

"Nonsense," Mrs. Rochester said. "You're not dead, are you? You've plenty of blood yet still pumping through your veins."

"She's lost a great deal of it," Mr. Carter remarked. "I wish I could have got here sooner."

"Will she live?" Mrs. Rochester asked.

John was startled by her matter-of-fact tone. He might almost have believed that she didn't care. That the life or death of this mysterious woman was of no consequence to her at all.

"It's too soon to say." Mr. Carter peeled back the final bandage. "What's this?" His face darkened like a thundercloud. "The flesh on her throat is torn, but this—! By God, these are teeth marks!"

"He bit me," Mrs. Wren murmured. "He struck like a viper."

"I warned you," Mrs. Rochester said grimly.

"I thought only to speak with him."

"You thought! I told you to wait until daylight—until I could be with you. Haven't you sense enough to be on your guard?" Mrs. Rochester looked to the surgeon. "Hurry, Carter. She must be off before sunrise."

"Give me another moment to finish cleaning the wound, madam. The bite runs deep."

"He sucked the blood," Mrs. Wren said. "He told me he would drain my heart."

Mrs. Rochester's face paled. "Be quiet, Felda. Don't repeat his gibberish." Again, she turned to the surgeon. "Have you nothing you can give her?"

Carter applied a fresh bandage, pulling it tight. "I'll administer morphia when she's in the carriage. It will give her some relief."

Mrs. Wren gave a pathetic cry. "His eyes!"

"Enough," Mrs. Rochester commanded. "You will not speak of it, do you hear me? You'll forget you ever came here. That any of this ever happened."

"I can't forget."

"You will. Once you're away from here—back wherever it is you came from—you may think of him as dead and buried."

"Impossible. You know that he—"

"*Dead and buried.*" Mrs. Rochester's voice was as cold and implacable as her countenance. "It isn't impossible. You may believe that."

"Bertha…" Mrs. Wren's eyes were bleary from pain, but it seemed to John that there was a glitter of accusation in her gaze. "What have you done to him?"

"She's becoming hysterical," Mrs. Rochester said. "Best give her the sedative now, Carter, before she does herself further injury."

"No!" Mrs. Wren cried. "No, you mustn't."

Mr. Carter went to his bag and withdrew a small leather case containing a needle and glass syringe. As he prepared the injection, Mrs. Wren tried to rise from the bed, only to slump back against the pillows, too weak to move.

Taking hold of her arm, Carter positioned the needle.

"No!" She struggled against his grasp, making a feeble attempt to evade the injection. All the while, her eyes were fixed on Mrs. Rochester. "What have you done, Bertha? What have you done to him? You…" Her words died away as the morphine did its work.

Mrs. Rochester stood, still as a statue, beside the bed, watching as Mrs. Wren slipped into unconsciousness. "I suppose," she said at length, "that loss of blood causes confusion."

Carter paused for a long moment before answering. "It can."

"Are you able to lift her?"

"It's difficult at my age. But perhaps your man might be of assistance?" He looked at John.

Mrs. Rochester looked at him, too. There was a hint of uncertainty in her face. As if she wasn't quite sure of him. "Will you carry her downstairs?"

John nodded. It was the work of a moment to scoop Mrs. Wren up in his arms. She was heavier than Mrs. Rochester had been, and far more encumbered with wire underpinnings. It made her form somewhat unwieldy, but not too difficult to bear.

"A post-chaise is waiting in the yard," Mrs. Rochester said. "We shall use the servants' stairs. I'll run ahead to see that the way is clear." She met his eyes. "No one can know of this. Not a single soul."

"I understand," he said. "I'll be as quiet as I can."

"I knew you would be." Mrs. Rochester exchanged another brief, whispered word with Carter before departing the room as swiftly and silently as a cat.

John followed after her, Mr. Carter at his side.

The stairs were dark, as were the floors below. It must be five o'clock or thereabouts. Though it was light outside, there were no servants in the kitchen as yet. John was able to carry Mrs. Wren out the back door without arousing any attention.

Rain fell steadily, wetting his hair and coat. He bent his head against it, half hunching over Mrs. Wren in a pathetic attempt to protect her limp body from the elements.

As promised, a post-chaise waited in the yard. Mrs. Rochester stood next to it, holding the door open. "You may put her inside."

John settled Mrs. Wren onto one of the padded seats. She slumped into a heap. Mr. Carter climbed in after her, shaking the raindrops from his tall beaver hat.

Mrs. Rochester shut the door of the post-chaise behind him. "Keep her with you for another day or two. I'll ride over on Friday to see how she does. With any luck she'll be fit to board a steamer."

"I'll look after her," Carter said.

The coachman—a faceless figure in an oilskin greatcoat with a hat tipped low over his brow—gave the horses the office to start. With a rattle of wheels and a crunch of steel-shod hooves on gravel, the vehicle drove off, leaving John standing beside Mrs. Rochester in the yard, the rain beating down upon them.

She didn't seem to heed it. Her thoughts were plainly elsewhere. "What a godless night!" she said at last.

"And a wet morning," he replied.

Her gaze cut to his. A flare of wry humor flashed in her eyes. "You must think me mad."

"Not mad. Only distracted." He paused. "Who was she?"

The humor in Mrs. Rochester's eyes vanished as quickly as it had appeared. "No one," she said. "Only a shadow. An apparition from the past."

"From *your* past?"

She gave a tense nod. "I'd never thought to see her again. Though I suppose I should have expected it." She didn't seem disposed to elaborate. Hoisting her skirts in her hands, she moved toward the path that led to the orchard. "Come, John. I know somewhere we can be dry."

Twenty-One

John followed Mrs. Rochester through the rain, down the muddy path that ran past the wood-fenced paddocks to the back of the Hall. The orchard lay ahead, and at its edge, half-hidden in the mist, a small arbor stood, twined with an overgrowth of ivy and clinging vines.

It was an old structure, composed of faded and splintered wood. The sagging steps creaked under Mrs. Rochester's half-boots as she climbed up to shelter beneath its roof.

"Here, John." She extended her hand.

He took it, holding it fast as he came to join her. It wasn't entirely dry inside the arbor. Raindrops blew in on the storm, splashing lightly on seats already cluttered with broken twigs and windblown leaves.

Brushing aside some of the debris, Mrs. Rochester sat down, drawing him down next to her. She didn't release his hand. "I know it isn't very warm here, but I must have a moment of freshness before I return to that mausoleum."

They sat, half turned to face each other, arms and knees almost touching. Her heavy skirts bunched against his legs, the hem pooling over his booted feet. It was intimate. Loverlike. Close enough to provoke a disconcerting simmer of heat low in his belly.

"Will you remain with me?" she asked.

"If that's what you wish."

"It is. Most assuredly." Her fingers twined through his. "We've passed a strange night together."

"The strangest." He swallowed hard. Her bare skin was silken soft, her slender fingers sliding through his to settle in a sensual clasp. It sent a tremor through his vitals. Rather like a minor earthquake. He cleared his throat. "What was Mrs. Wren doing on the third floor? Had you invited her to stay?"

"I had. She was meant to retire to bed in a room near to where the servants sleep. She should never have ventured beyond its threshold."

"She certainly suffered for her error. The poor woman looked as though she'd been mauled by a tiger. Or worse."

"You weren't afraid, were you? When I left you alone with her?"

"Not afraid, no. But I didn't much look forward to Mr. Poole coming out of that inner room behind the tapestry."

"You had no cause to worry on that score. The door was bolted."

"And what of the man inside the room?"

"What about him?"

"Will he live here still? Or have you made other arrangements for his care?"

A pensive frown touched her lips. "You're speaking of Mr. Poole."

"Who else?"

Her brows knit. She bent her head, her gaze lingering on their joined hands. "Yes, he'll remain here. But you needn't worry about him."

"How can I not? You must see that the man is dangerous."

"Things aren't always as they seem."

"No," he agreed. "Often they're worse."

She huffed a short laugh. "I thought you more optimistic."

"I am when it's called for, but in this case…" His thumb moved over the curve of her knuckle in an unconscious caress. "You're not safe with him here. No one is. If he can do such a thing to Mrs. Wren—"

"Spare your sympathy. Mrs. Wren will be fine."

"I trust she will be. But it isn't her I'm concerned with. It's you, and the boys. It's all the rest of us living here at Thornfield. If, at any given instant, Mr. Poole can lose his head, surely it must be better for him to be put somewhere?"

"I have the matter under control now. No one else will be hurt. I can promise you that."

"But you won't dismiss him."

"Mr. Poole is no threat to you. No more than I am." She drew his hand onto her lap. "But enough about him. Tell me, are you still taking your tonic?"

"I am."

"Good. Good." A breath of relief sounded in her voice. "I know you're wary of patent medicines, but I have faith in the mixture. Though I don't suppose it's helped your headaches as much as the laudanum."

"It has, actually."

She gave him a startled look. "Truly?"

"They come less frequently now. Some days not at all." He smiled, a little rueful. "I daresay it's because I'm happy here."

A flicker of emotion passed over her face, gone before he could grasp it. "*Are* you happy, John? Despite all of…this?"

"I believe I am. I'm proud of what I've achieved with the boys. And I realize it isn't ideal, not for a man in my position, but I must admit, I've come to care for them."

"Only them?"

His heart thumped heavily. He was silent for a long a while. And then: "You know what happened in my former position."

"Don't say you're comparing me to Lady Helen?"

"No. God, no. You're not at all the same. But *I* am. I'm still a teacher—a subordinate, if not in spirit, then in fact. And you're…"

"What?"

"Far above my sphere of life," he said. "So much as to be from a different world."

"I'm not."

"You are. Shared struggles have brought us closer—the difficulties with Mr. Poole and with the boys. But it's an illusion of intimacy. It isn't real."

"It feels quite real to me," she said. And then, before he could guess what she was about, she stretched up and kissed him, very softly, on the mouth.

John's breath stopped. His heart followed suit. He had a vague notion that he should draw back. That he should set her away from him just as he'd set Helen away during their single fateful encounter.

But Mrs. Rochester was no Helen Burns.

At the touch of her warm, half-parted lips, the simmering in his belly swiftly transfused to his blood—to his heart, and head, and loins. His breath stuttered to life, his pulse along with it. Without thought—without reason—he bent his head to hers, and returned her kiss in full measure.

It wasn't wrong. Not in that moment. It was perfect.

She was perfect.

Her eyes were closed, her lips soft and pliant beneath his. Though boldly initiated, there was a carefulness to her kiss. A trembling uncertainty. "We shouldn't." Her faint protest whispered against his mouth, their breath mingling.

"No. We shouldn't." Their fingers twined tighter. "John..."

"I know." His forehead came to rest gently against hers. "That was..."

"Yes." He loosened his grasp on her hand. But he didn't pull away from her. He hadn't the will for it.

It was she who pulled back, drawing away from him to meet his eyes. Her cheeks were flushed. "If you like, we can forget that, right along with all the rest of what's happened today."

"I think it unlikely that either of us will forget."

"No. Probably not." Releasing his hand, she stood, folding her arms at her waist. A gust of wind blew through the arbor. It stirred the loose strands of hair at her face. "Do you have a future in mind for yourself, Mr. Eyre?"

Mr. Eyre.

He slowly got to his feet, conscious of her changeable mood. He'd be a fool to presume anything from that kiss. Not only a fool. A cad. It was plain she was already regretting it. "What do you mean?"

"After you leave here. You must have an idea of what you'll do next."

He regarded her with increasing wariness. "*Am* I leaving?"

"Eventually. Stephen and Peter won't remain boys forever."

"True enough." He propped his shoulder against the damp wall.

"Well? Do you intend to seek employment elsewhere? Or have you some other plan?"

"I wouldn't call it a plan. But...I suppose, I'd always hoped that I might save enough money out of my earnings to set up a small school of my own somewhere."

She flashed him a look. "When?"

He shrugged. "Someday."

"Someday," she repeated. "That means never."

"What about you?" he countered. "What does your future hold?"

She walked to the edge of the arbor, her skirts brushing over the wet leaves on the ground. "You're familiar with Mr. George Eshton?"

A knot formed in John's stomach. "Quite familiar."

"He's handsome, wealthy, and amusing. A fine partner in a duet. Do you not think that he would make me a creditable husband?"

"You can answer that better than I," John said stiffly. "You've known him since you were a child."

"Who told you so? Mr. Fairfax?" She frowned. "It's true enough. There was a time, many years ago, I might have married George. It was the dearest wish of my parents—and of his." She shot him another look. "But perhaps you think it too late for me to find happiness."

"Not at all. I wish you every happiness in the world." He meant it, though it pained him to say it. "I pray that you'll find it. If not with Mr. Eshton, then with someone equally worthy."

"A worthy suitor. An estimable ideal, and one that George Eshton fits to a certainty. Would that my parents were here to see it. Had I been a more dutiful daughter, I'd have wed him while they were still alive." Her brow contracted. "Perhaps it *is* too late to try for happiness."

"I don't believe that. Not for you or anyone." Bitterness colored his words, but it didn't suppress them. "Love deferred is still love."

She made a scoffing sound. "What has love ever had to do with anything? Marriage, least of all."

John's gaze drifted over her riding dress. It was as black as every other garment he'd seen her wear. Mourning clothes, to the smallest detail. But not for her husband, she'd said. "Did Mr. Fairfax happen to mention to you that I finally visited the vicar in Hay?"

Her eyes narrowed. "No, indeed. When did this inauspicious event take place?"

"Two days ago." He hesitated before adding, "Mr. Taylor told me about the death of Miss Ingram."

She turned away from him to look out at the orchard, but not before he saw her flinch. "Did he."

"I saw her grave in the churchyard. I'd no idea you'd recently lost a friend."

"The vicar has given you an earful, I see. He's worse than any village tabby."

"He seems a pleasant enough fellow."

"Pleasant enough to you." Mrs. Rochester flashed him a humorless look from over her shoulder. "He's halfway to suspecting me of being a witch. Afterward...he all but accused me of being responsible."

"After Miss Ingram's death? I daresay he was distraught. She'd come to visit you, hadn't she? On the day you returned from the Continent? If she met her death upon leaving—"

"It wasn't the day I returned." Mrs. Rochester resumed looking out at the orchard. "That is, she *had* come on the day I arrived back at Thornfield. We had tea together. Talked for hours. But she came again the next day. Her return visit was...unexpected."

"It was then she had her accident? Riding home in the fog?"

"Her accident. Yes." Mrs. Rochester set both of her hands on the railing of the arbor.

"Is she the reason you're still in mourning?" he asked.

"I suppose she is, though our relationship hardly merits it."

"Mr. Taylor said you were as close as sisters."

"Not in the end." Her fingers tightened around the railing. "You think you know a person. All your life. But in the single moment you need them most..." She bowed her head. "May I ask you something?"

"Anything."

"If you heard a story from a friend—as outlandish as it seemed impossible—would you believe them?"

"I suspect that would depend on the degree of friendship. And on how outlandish the story."

"You'd sooner think your friend a liar?"

"No, but—"

"There can be no equivocation. You either believe them or you don't."

He fell quiet a moment before asking, "Is my friend in this hypothetical situation a woman?"

Her shoulders tensed. "Does it matter?" She gave him no opportunity to answer. "Of course it does. Women are emotional. Prone to mistaking intention. To misinterpreting the facts."

"I never said that."

"Yet you wouldn't believe your friend?"

He would have liked to reassure her. To tell her only what she wanted to hear. But it didn't feel like the time for calming platitudes. It felt like the time for honesty. "I don't know."

"What if this friend of yours had no evidence? Or worse— what if the outlandish story she told you was directly contradicted by someone else. By a man, in fact. A powerful man."

"I don't know," he said again. "How can I until that moment arrives? I'd like to think I would stand with my friend." He straightened from the wall, sorely tempted to go to her. "I'd stand with you if given the chance."

She turned to face him, one hand still resting on the railing. "You've already done so. Your help this morning—

it was invaluable to me. I won't forget it, you know. I don't ever forget a service. As for the rest of it... Well. I suppose it must all depend on me."

"I wish I could do something to ease your burden."

"Be careful what you wish for, sir." At that, her face spread into a smile. But it wasn't directed at him. It was aimed at someone beyond the orchard. "Ah, look. There's the Eshton brothers now, up for their morning ride. Rain and sleet have never stopped them from a good gallop." She flicked John a glance. "Best return to the house before they see you."

He stood there a second longer, feeling the full weight of his position in her life. Her paid employee. Someone to be dismissed the instant a worthier companion appeared.

But no. That wasn't it at all, was it?

George Eshton may have her smiles. Her singing and laughter. But John...he'd been privileged to see the real Bertha Rochester. A mercurial figure—dark and passionate—plagued by mystery. She was a lady in desperate need of an ally.

As he exited the arbor, he wondered if he was up to the task.

Twenty-Two

*Mrs. Bertha
Rochester's Journal.*

23 April, continued. — Having discovered Edward's bed empty, I was tempted to retreat back into the relative safety of my chamber. But there were still many hours left of daylight. Many hours while he slept—*if* he slept—during which I could make my investigations. I was determined that they wouldn't go to waste.

I conducted a painstaking search of every drawer before turning my attention to the first of my husband's two wardrobes. They were a matched set—centuries old, by the look of them. More like great oak cabinets with tall doors, wide enough for a person to step through. The front panels were plain, but carved above them were the same worn wolf figures I'd seen on the outside of Nosht-Vŭlk. I shivered to touch them.

The first wardrobe yielded nothing more than a collection of my husband's linens. Shirts, handkerchiefs, and cravats, neatly folded. My hands trembled as I slid my fingers through each stack, praying that a key might be tucked away inside. But there was no key. No sign of any hidden secrets.

Disappointed in my search, I moved to the second cabinet with little hope of success. Opening it, I was more disappointed still to find it empty. Worse than empty. It appeared to have been unused for a very long time. There was a distinct smell of rot about the interior. It nearly caused me to immediately shut the wardrobe door. It was that repellant. But I was resolved not to be so fainthearted. Holding my breath, I ducked my head and shoulders inside of the wardrobe and had a good look around.

I shudder to think what might have happened if I hadn't pressed on. Had I withdrawn immediately—had I given up—I'd never have spied the strange crack in the seams of wood. Never have recognized what I recognized in that moment: the wardrobe had a false back.

My heart beat so heavily I could scarcely hear myself think. A false door. Of course. This must be how he was departing his room each morning and returning to it each night. But where did the false door lead? I felt along the back of the wardrobe with my fingertips, pressing on the thin panel of wood in various places, until I heard a faint click. At that, the panel swung open, revealing a stone corridor and a steep stairway that led down into darkness. A waft of dank air emanated from its depths. It smelled of damp and decay. Of rotting flesh. As if an animal had crawled down below and died there.

I was both intrigued and repelled. Mostly, I was afraid. Too afraid to venture farther. I wasn't prepared for it. I had no candle to light my way. No weapon to defend myself. Closing the panel, I withdrew back to my bedroom to make a plan.

24 April. — It is perhaps a peculiarity of the marital state that, upon discovering my husband was sneaking out each night via a secret passage in his bedroom, my first thought was

John Eyre

that he must be guilty of violating his wedding vows. Did he keep a mistress in the village? Some local beauty whom he hoped to be reunited with once he'd drained me of all of my money and property?

Where else could he be spending his days? He was up all of the night, and he must sleep sometime. No doubt it was in a woman's bed somewhere. I wasn't jealous. Any ire I had was solely directed at myself for having been so foolish as to marry the scoundrel. My only hope was that the secret passage behind the wardrobe would serve for me as well as it did for him. If it led outside of Nosht-Vŭlk, I would soon be free.

Last night, at sunset, I listened at the connecting door, straining to hear the wardrobe open and close, signifying his return. I heard nothing—not a single breath or footstep—until he emerged into the hall. From there, he came to my room to bid me good evening. He informed me he was going out again on matters of business.

"What business could you possibly have in the middle of the night?" I asked.

"The business of living," he said. And with a mocking bow he swept out of my room.

I was nettled by his reply. What in heaven was he up to? I waited a moment before lighting a candle and slipping out of my chamber to the stairs that led to the floor above. There, I found my way to the room with the barred window that looked down over the courtyard. I stood at the edge, half-hidden behind velvet curtains that stank of mildew, and watched for Edward, waiting for him to exit Nosht-Vŭlk.

At last he emerged, coming to a stop in the courtyard. No carriage awaited him. No horse saddled and ready for riding. Where then did my husband go of an evening? Business, he said. The business of living. Perhaps that was another way of referencing his affair. A euphemism for sex, and drink, and other bodily indulgences. It seemed that his mistress *did* reside in the village. At least within walking distance.

It was a cold night, the mist drifting along the edges of the courtyard. As I watched him, he took a step toward it, and then another. And here I must catalog a strange phenomenon. I hardly know how to describe it. Indeed, I can't be sure I saw it correctly. My eyes were tired, and I was scared and hungry. Who can guess what illusions might plague a woman in this condition? Nevertheless, I feel constrained to record what I saw. It was this: Edward lifted his hands as he walked into the courtyard, and the mist seemed to swirl about him in a very specific pattern, circling around his legs and arms, enshrouding his body.

I don't mean to claim that my husband commanded the mist. It was something else. As if the mist were a part of him. An extension of his limbs. Of his very movement. It accompanied him across the courtyard, emanating from his person, a silvery vapor that thickened into a fog. I lost sight of him for a moment, and then, in the next instant he was gone, subsumed by the very fog he had seemed to create.

Gazing down at the empty courtyard, a sickening anxiety swelled in my breast. For the first time, I had cause to doubt my own sanity. If I could imagine this strange vision, what else might I have imagined?

I felt compelled to watch and wait for his return, if only to convince myself that I hadn't been dreaming. Settling myself into a corner of the window embrasure, I rested my head against one of the iron bars. Down below, the howl of ravenous wolves rose from the woods that surrounded Nosht-Vŭlk. It wasn't a landscape that was safe for walking. My husband may be able to navigate it somehow, but if *I* ever managed to escape, I would have to find a way to procure a horse and carriage.

On this thought, I must have drifted to sleep, for when I next woke it was to the sound of wailing. A pitiful noise. The cry of a child, quickly suppressed. By this time, it was well past midnight. Those early hours before dawn when the first glimmers of light begin to threaten. I sat up straight, leaning to peer out the window. I saw no one in the courtyard to whom I might attribute the sound, certainly not a child.

What I did see was the mist. It was there in abundance, blanketing the courtyard, and rising up along the walls of the fortress. It stretched its silvery fingers—up, up—toward my window. I drew back with a start, standing from the embrasure, and once again hiding my figure behind the mildewed curtains. But the mist remained, hovering there. I had the queerest sensation that it saw me.

24 April, later that morning. — The strange sights I beheld during the night convinced me that I'd too long deprived myself of adequate food and sleep. I slipped down to the kitchen again before sunrise and gathered what was left of the molded bread and cheese. There was a knife there as well—a dull instrument, good only for slicing cake. But it was better than nothing. I tucked it in with my food and returned to my room. There, I ate and then slept, attempting to conserve my strength for my journey into the secret corridor.

At sunrise, I was awakened by the sound of my husband's key scraping in the lock. His bedroom door opened and closed. A long silence followed, during which I imagined he was creeping into the wardrobe and making his exit through its back. I bided my time.

When another hour had passed, I dressed in my warmest traveling gown and my sturdiest pair of boots, and packed a few necessities into a leather satchel—the knife, my travel documents, and what was left of my food. If the opportunity to walk out of Nosht-Vŭlk presented itself, I intended to be ready.

As an added ward against evil, before leaving my room, I retrieved my silver locket from my jewel case and fixed it around my neck. At my husband's request, I hadn't worn it since my wedding night. But now I couldn't imagine proceeding without my parents' portraits to guard me and give me courage.

Lighting an oil lamp, I entered Edward's chamber through the connecting door. It was just as I'd left it, with no sign of where he'd been during the night—or where he was now. If I hadn't known better, I'd have thought he'd simply disappeared. Climbing into the wardrobe, I pressed open the false door and entered the stone corridor. The same rank scent assailed me. It seemed stronger this morning, enough that I was obliged to raise my scarf up over my nose and mouth lest I choke on the stench.

I descended the stairway, lamp lifted to guide my steps. All was in darkness. There was no natural light at all. And the smell! It only increased as I reached the bottom—two or three flights down by my estimate. I was met by another passage—a narrow, low-ceilinged corridor with a heavy wooden door at the end of it.

My throat tightened on a cry of frustration, for I feared I had reached the end of the road. But when I tried the door, I found it unlocked. It opened easily on well-oiled hinges—a good sign, to be sure. However, beyond it was only darkness, the fragrance of decay so pronounced that I gagged.

I haven't a fear of small places, thank God. If I had, I'd never have gone farther. The ceiling was low enough that I had to stoop as I walked. The stone slabs beneath my feet gave way to a dirt floor. The soil emitted a smell as foul as the smell of rot that had preceded it. Was it here that an animal had died? Somewhere in the darkness, curled up in a hidden corner?

This thought was at the forefront of my mind when I struck something hard with the toe of my boot. I leapt back, a jolt of terror nearly rending a scream from my lips. Shining the light at my feet, I was relieved to see that it was no animal carcass. It was nothing but an old suitcase, and next to it, a damp pile of faded clothing. Indeed, as I moved my lantern over the ground, I saw that there were many similar articles. Clothing and shoes. Even a lady's hat, the velvet ribbons long-devoured by some insect.

It must be storage. Old clothes and luggage. The sort of thing usually found in an attic. Why on earth would it be stored here? Left to the vermin and the damp? Raising my lamp, I ventured on, rapidly losing hope that I'd find an exit from my prison. But there must be some way out. Where else would my husband go when he came this way? He didn't remain down here in the darkness, surely. No human being would be foolish enough to do so. Not with all this stink and rot.

I advanced a little farther, my attention again arrested by the detritus in the dirt. There was nothing frightening about the remnants in and of themselves. Nevertheless, I found the sight of them to be exceedingly unnerving. Even more so, for as my gaze drifted over a piece of luggage, I was alarmed to find that I recognized it. It was a portmanteau of green morocco leather. The very kind my maid, Agnes, had been carrying when first we arrived here.

Crouching down, I opened it, expecting I knew not what. What I found was worse—far worse than I could have imagined. The clothing within had been hastily packed. Agnes's clothes. A pile of petticoats, crumpled dresses, and the new pair of gloves I'd given her last Christmas. And thrown atop the carelessly discarded heap: my Nock percussion pistol.

A numbness settled in my veins. Mrs. Wren had said that Agnes had hired a calèche and departed for Varna. That she'd had enough of exotic climes. But I understood now—as, perhaps, I should have understood then—that my maid had not left Nosht-Vŭlk at all.

25 April, morning. — Having found Agnes's belongings, I retreated back to my bedroom, too terrified to go farther. I cursed myself for being weak and afraid. Who knew what else the underground chamber might have held? If only I'd had the courage to continue on. But nothing is served by these recriminations. I must find a way to master my fear and carry on, lest I meet the same unfortunate fate as my maid.

At least I can congratulate myself on having the presence of mind to retrieve my still-loaded pistol. It houses only a single shot, which I've vowed not to waste. I've tucked it away in my wardrobe, along with what coin I have, my travel documents, letter of credit, and the two remaining vials of laudanum, leftover from Mr. Poole's injury. Which leads me to wonder: was the injury he suffered on the way to Varna truly an accident? Or was it a failed attempt at getting rid of him, just as my husband and Mrs. Wren got rid of my maid?

I would that Mr. Poole was here now. I could use his strength. But I must believe that, when their first attempt at disposing of him failed, a second attempt was made. He's likely as dead now as Agnes. Indeed, who is to say that their bodies aren't hidden under Nosht-Vŭlk along with the other detritus? It would explain the godawful smell of decay.

These thoughts and worse have plagued my mind since ascending the hidden stairway and returning to my room. When Edward emerged from his own chamber at sunset, he came to me, looking as suave and unruffled as ever. One wouldn't guess at the evil that lay beneath his elegant façade, but I sensed it now—emanating from him as surely as the mist had done.

I stood from my desk as he entered my room. Without a word, he approached, and sliding his arm around my waist in a lover's embrace, he bent his head into the crook of my neck and inhaled deeply.

"You've been wandering, my dear," he said.

My heart raced so I couldn't tell where one beat ended and the other began.

"Haven't I warned you that wandering is dangerous here?" As he spoke, his lips brushed my throat. They'd barely touched my skin before he recoiled back with a hiss. His fingers flew to his mouth, as if I'd done him an injury. "That necklace!" His eyes kindled with accusation. "I told you not to wear it."

I lifted a protective hand to my locket. "Don't be ridiculous."

"Remove it at once."

"I'll do nothing of the sort."

He took a step toward me, menacing me with his glare. "You will do as you're told. If you disobey me, I'll—"

"You'll what? Strike me? Throttle me? It will be no worse than what you've already done." To my shame, I felt tears burning in my eyes. I couldn't help but ask, "Why did you ever marry me?"

He continued to regard my locket with impotent fury. I was beginning to think he wouldn't answer when, at last, he said, rather sullenly, "You had something of what I required."

"Money?"

"That," he admitted, "and a certain vulnerability."

I took immediate exception to this. "I wasn't vulnerable."

"All women are. Only some are too stupid to realize it."

"But why me?" I pressed him. "There must have been others. Women of wealth and property. I can't have been the only one worth marrying."

He lowered his hand from his mouth with a wince. In the dim light, his lips appeared red as blood. Seared as if by a burning brand. "There were others. Of course there were. Women of a trivial nature, possessing neither souls nor hearts. And then I saw you in Cairo. A woman with an affect of strength. With a clear eye and a soul made of fire. A woman without protection."

I swallowed hard. "You were attracted to me."

He had the temerity to shrug. "It was, as much is in life, a matter of timing. Your English laws have harmed my investments. War has damaged my homeland. And the tomb in Thebes—empty. A perfect storm, isn't that what you call it in your language? And there you were, alone and so deeply, pathetically needy. Fancying yourself different from other women, but in every way the same. You made it quite easy, my love."

His words skewered my heart with ruthless precision. I thought of how assiduously he'd courted me, when all the while he'd been so cold. So calculating. And I, his willing victim. "And now?" I asked. "You'll abandon all this—your home, your people—for England?"

"This is not my home," he said. "The war with Russia has seen to that. And these are not my people. They're the creatures who arrived when my own people fled. A nomadic race, always eager to attach themselves to a powerful nobleman. They fear me enough to serve me, but they aren't of my blood. I have no connection to this place any longer. I shall be glad to start again in your country."

"With another woman?" I asked.

He seemed amused by the question. "What need have I of another woman? I am wed to you, Bertha." At that, he came closer—close enough to see me shrink back against the wall. His eyes flicked from my face to my locket and back again. "No, my dear. Your country has something superior to women. It holds the British Museum, and therein lies the book that I seek."

"I thought you said it was owned by another collector? That you were going to make an offer for it?"

"So I did," he said. "But the fool has refused it. It seems he'd rather the book end its days in a museum. I've had word of it from my man in Wallachia. And now my course is set."

"The British Museum will never sell it to you. They're not in the habit of giving up their treasures."

"I don't mean to buy it from them," he said. "I need only to read it. To learn its secrets."

It had been some time since my husband spoke to me in such a frank manner. No doubt he was only doing so because he'd already decided my fate. There was, after all, no danger in confiding in a dead woman. "What secrets do you believe it contains?" I asked.

"A cure for my illness," he said. "A recipe of old, the consumption of which will enable me to do what I have not done in an age."

"Which is?"

His mouth curled into a fiendish smile. "To walk in the sunlight, my dear."

25 April, later that day. — God help me, my hand is shaking so horribly I can hardly write down what I have seen. I'm back in my room again after having once more ventured through the wardrobe. But I must record every detail in order, as fantastic as it is.

After a night spent doing who knows what outside the walls of Nosht-Vŭlk, Edward returned at sunrise and retreated to his room. I waited an hour before I followed after him, with my satchel, lantern, and pistol. This time, I let neither the debris, nor the smell deter me. I descended into the darkness down the stone steps, through the wooden door, and into the underground chamber, navigating my way past the rotted clothing and stinking soil.

Beyond lay great piles of earth, heaped next to shallow holes in the ground. The sort that appeared as though made by a digging animal. But these weren't mole holes dug in an English garden. These were as wide and long as graves. My teeth chattered with fear as I passed them, shining my light into each one, and anticipating the absolute worst.

Anticipation did nothing to dull the horror of what I found. It was the body of a young woman. Or what had once been a young woman. Agnes, in fact. Tears stung at my eyes, bile rising in my throat, as I held the light over what was left of her. I paused to be sick.

But there was nothing I could do for Agnes. Not anymore. I continued on, suppressing the panic that built in my chest, as I found another body, and then another. They appeared to have been there for a long while, their remains consisting of little more than scraps of women's clothing clinging to desiccated bones. However, as I pressed forward, the ceiling slanting lower and lower, obliging me to bend at the waist, I saw a sight that I will remember until my dying day.

It was my husband—Edward Rochester—lying comfortably in a shallow grave. He hadn't the pallor of death. His face was in full color. Almost rosy with blood. His eyes were closed, his left arm resting across his waist, as if he were sleeping. Kneeling down next to him, I touched him lightly on the shoulder. He didn't move.

Was he dead? He must be so, for why else was he here? I pressed my fingers to his throat, seeking his pulse. And there *was* movement beneath my fingertips. A rushing feeling, like a mighty river. Such did I imagine his blood flowing through his veins. Not dead, then. But what of his heart? Why was it not beating?

I didn't linger to discover the answer. My brief moment of compassion was blotted out by the urgency of reality. Dead or no, he was unmoving, and I'd have been a fool to forego the opportunity to make a thorough search of his person. I slid my hands over his body, inside of his frock coat and his waistcoat. My efforts were rewarded, for there, in an interior pocket, I discovered a single key.

It wasn't what I'd been looking for. Not the house keys on their heavy ring. But it was something. My fingers curled around it.

In that same instant, Edward's eyelids slid open. He stared at me, unseeing in the lamplight. He was awake, and not awake—his eyes as lifeless as those among whom he made his bed. I didn't understand it. And I didn't remain long enough to investigate further. Snatching the key from his pocket, I leapt up in a tangle of skirts, and ran back the way I'd come as if the devil was at my heels.

Writing it all down now, I'd like to believe that I imagined it. Such horrors lie outside the realm of comprehension. But what I've seen cannot be denied. I've known for some time that Edward Rochester is no gentleman. Now, I must recognize that he is something worse. A murderer. A parasite who enriches himself on the wealth—on the very lives—of his victims.

Had he seen me? Was he even now rising to give chase? The thought provoked me to flee straight out of the secret panel in the wardrobe and up the stairs to the chamber with its window overlooking the courtyard. I suppose I had some hysterical notion to squeeze through the bars and fling myself out. Surely being crushed on the paving stones would be preferable to spending my final hours in that fetid graveyard beneath Nosht-Vŭlk.

But when I attempted to fit my body through the bars, I couldn't manage it. My shoulders were too broad. I was stuck there, head hanging out in the bright sunlight, choking back sobs of desperation. "Help me!" I cried. "Won't anyone help me!"

And God answered. For when the tears cleared enough that I could see, I beheld a familiar figure creeping into the courtyard, gazing up at me in abject astonishment.

It was Mr. Poole.

Twenty-Three

Thornfield Hall
Yorkshire, England
April 1844

John sat back against the broad trunk of the thorn tree, his sketchbook and pencil in his hand. His gaze intermittently lifted from the page to watch Stephen and Peter frolicking about the meadow. The pair of them were engaged in a haphazard game of battledore and shuttlecock.

It was a fine spring day. Warm and sweet-smelling. The mist had dissipated to the veriest vapor, clinging weakly at the edges of the Hall but coming no farther. John scarcely noticed it from his position.

He was in his shirtsleeves, his frock coat discarded at his side. It was hard to believe that only weeks ago a storm had raged at Thornfield. A strange storm, for it had ended within a day of Mr. Poole's attack on Mrs. Wren. A mere twenty-four hours later, the rain and thunder had ceased, and the light of the sun had broken through the clouds.

The Eshtons had left the following day, and Mrs. Rochester the day after that. She hadn't said goodbye to John. It wasn't her habit to inform him of her comings and goings. He'd had to hear it from Mr. Fairfax.

"She's gone to London again," he'd said. "To see her solicitor, I suspect."

John feared she was making preparations for her marriage. Not that it was any of his concern—kisses and confidences notwithstanding. But she'd been gone a fortnight, and he was conscious of every passing day.

His pencil moved over the page, shading in the landscape he'd sketched with rapid strokes. He was thus occupied when the echo of clattering hooves sounded in the drive.

It was Mrs. Rochester.

She cantered up on her great black horse, the drape of her heavy skirts floating behind her. A high-crowned hat was perched upon her raven tresses, a net veil shielding her eyes.

The coachman, Jenkins, came out to meet her. He held her horse as she dismounted. Having done so, she turned and looked out toward the thorn trees. After issuing a few words to Jenkins, she crossed the meadow.

John rose to greet her.

"John!" she called out. "Enjoying the fine weather, I see."

"I am, ma'am." He closed his sketchbook, and tucked his pencil away. "Did you have a good journey?"

"Good enough, but ultimately unsuccessful. How are the boys?"

"Very well." He paused. "That is, they *were* a bit distressed after the events of last month. I expect they heard the screaming. But I explained things to them, and they appear to be fine now."

Her mouth curved in a dry smile. "I hesitate to enquire what explanation you provided."

"Only that there was an accident, and that a guest had been injured."

"True enough." Her gaze drifted over his face before dropping lower.

He reached for his coat, but she forestalled him.

"You needn't stand on ceremony with me. Certainly not on an afternoon like this." With that, she removed her hat and wound the veil about the brim. "Suffocating thing."

"You might need it. The sun can be oppressive at this time of day."

"Nonsense. It's cool enough here. Come beneath the trees with me. Walk awhile."

He draped his coat over his arm. Despite his best intentions—all of his resolve to remain aloof and to remember his place—he found himself settling into her company as easily as breathing. "I understand you went to London."

"Much good it did me."

"Your solicitor was unhelpful?

"My solicitor?" She cast him a glance. "What has he to do with it?"

"Nothing, except that Mr. Fairfax told me you were visiting the man."

"I did visit Mr. Hughes. He's seeing to some tedious financial matters for me, settlements and so forth."

Settlements and so forth?

John's chest constricted. He'd been right, then. She *was* planning to marry. "I see."

"You don't. Mr. Hughes wasn't the reason I went to London." She squinted her eyes at the boys playing in the distance. "I went there to call on a particular gentleman. The same gentleman I call on every time I go into town. His name is Mr. Samuel Birch. He works at the British Museum."

Jealousy was temporarily replaced by curiosity. John gave her an interested look. "What do you want with him?"

"Many things. For one, he knows more about ancient Egypt that anyone else employed there. For another, he can read Egyptian hieroglyphs. He's working on several translations of ancient texts at the moment—though not quickly enough, as far as I'm concerned."

"Is that what you require? A translation?"

"Something like." Her arm brushed his as they walked. The briefest caress, however unintentional.

"I wasn't aware you had an interest in ancient Egypt."

"You must know I traveled there."

"Yes, but—"

"My father was an enthusiast. The kind who admires other men's adventures from afar. He subscribed to all the popular journals. As a girl, I often read them—the parts I could understand. The pictures caught my imagination. It seemed the grandest thing to travel there. To see the pyramids for myself. To observe a tomb being excavated."

"Did you? When you visited?"

"Oh yes. I did all of those things. It was glorious." A frown tugged at her mouth. "I met my husband in Egypt."

"I know."

"Mr. Fairfax again? He does rattle on about me, doesn't he?"

"He's very loyal."

"Well, that's something, I suppose. Loyalty." She sighed. It was a weary sound. As if the burdens of her life had finally got the better of her. "Tell me truthfully, John. How have you fared while I've been away?"

"I've kept busy with teaching the boys."

"And with drawing and painting?"

"That, too." He strolled a few steps in silence before adding, "I've rarely seen Mr. Poole about since that night.

Only once at the stable, busy at his forge. He addressed me as if nothing untoward had happened."

A scowl briefly marred her brow. "I told you not to worry about him. He has his duties, just as you have yours. Best to leave him alone."

"I certainly don't seek the man out."

"Good." Her arm grazed his again, warm and feminine. "Did you miss me at all?"

John looked straight ahead as they walked. He was painfully aware of her. Her womanly scent and shape, so endlessly alluring. The touch of her sleeve, and the soft rustle of her skirts, brushing against his legs. It was intimate. Unconsciously seductive. "I haven't any right to miss you."

"If you believe that, then your memory must have failed you."

"My memory is in perfectly good order," he replied. And then: "The boys missed you."

"Bah. The boys are as resilient as I am. They'll muddle through with or without me. It's you they've come to rely on. See how they look to you?"

"They're good lads. I hope I've been able to help them a little."

She laughed suddenly. "Is this John Eyre speaking? This humble creature?"

He bent his head, failing to suppress a short laugh of his own. "Yes, yes. I know. But I do *try* to be humble about my teaching."

"You're an excellent tutor, as we both know." The smile remained on her lips, but the one in her eyes faded. "I daresay you're an excellent man."

"Mrs. Rochester…"

"But that will keep, I trust." She turned abruptly back to the house. "I must go and change out of this dusty habit. Good afternoon."

He stood, still as a statue, as she walked away. It took a moment for him to remember to reply. "Good afternoon, ma'am."

"Bulgaria," John said. The library curtains were open, the midday sun illuminating the globe in its heavy wooden frame. "Can you find it for me?"

Stephen spun the globe one quarter turn, his finger tracing over the European continent. He pointed to his homeland. It wasn't the first time John had asked him to locate it on a map.

"Excellent," John said. "And you, Peter? Can you show me England?"

Peter used both hands to turn the globe in its frame, seeming to enjoy the spinning of it more than the actual lesson.

John stopped the motion with his hand as Britain came into view. "It's here. Do you see?"

The clock on the mantel chimed the hour, just as a shuffling noise at the door announced the arrival of Sophie. She was nothing if not punctual.

Stephen and Peter looked to her with anticipation. By this time of day, their stomachs were all but growling.

"Very well," John said. "Tidy your books, and then you may break for luncheon."

The two boys hurriedly organized their desks before racing off with Sophie to eat their small repast of toasted bread and cheese.

John watched them go, half smiling.

Mrs. Rochester's return from London had been followed by three weeks of relative peace. He'd initially expected her to set out again after a few days' time. Thornfield wasn't a place in which she seemed capable of finding peace.

But she hadn't gone.

She'd remained in residence. Even better, she'd taken to summoning him to tea each evening in the drawing room. There they engaged in long conversations punctuated by sharpness and humor. She took delight in sparring with him, and he'd come to enjoy it, too, almost as much as she did. It was becoming his greatest pleasure to laugh with her, and to make her smile.

The more he knew her, the more he found in her to esteem. She was a fascinating woman, regal and capricious. But it was her strength that defined her. He admired her for it. More than admired her. He respected her.

And that wasn't all.

He'd already known he was physically attracted to her. What he hadn't anticipated was feeling such tenderness. Such warm regard. Indeed, his affection for her grew by the day. But he dared not reveal the extent of his devotion. He was resolved to guard his heart—and his position in her household.

His insistence on clinging to a degree of formality between them seemed to needle her. So, she needled him in return, making veiled references to her impending marriage.

Yet there was no sign of George Eshton. He never came to call. And Mrs. Rochester hadn't journeyed to visit him at the Leas. The only evidence John could glean of their fast-approaching nuptials was in the constant correspondence with which Mrs. Rochester was engaged.

Letters arrived at Thornfield with regularity, and replies were sent out again, often the same day. Letters from London, Cairo, and—earlier this morning—even one from a town called Argeș in Wallachia. John had never heard of the place.

Still standing at the globe, he spun it back to Bulgaria. Wallachia was a vast region on its northern border, and one with which he wasn't very familiar. He skimmed the names of the cities and countries. Bucharest. Argeș. Transylvania.

Mrs. Rochester had once accused him of being a neophyte. A man who had never left the safety of the British Isles. It wasn't for lack of interest. He only regretted he hadn't made a greater effort to see more of the world. His lack of fortune and family weighed against him in that regard, but his profession was a mobile one. Many teachers removed to more exotic locales, usually in the guise of missionaries.

Collecting his sketchbook, John left the library. It was another fine day—odd at Thornfield. He was determined to take advantage of it. Climbing the stairs, he made his way to the third floor. Once there, he couldn't help staring at the closed door at the end of the darkened corridor.

The door to Mr. Poole's room.

A faint chill shivered down John's spine as he passed it. A memory of Mrs. Wren's ashen face and ravaged neck. Of her words, spoken in such desperate tones: *"He said he would drain my heart."*

When coupled with the book of German folklore that John had lately been reading, it was enough to sicken his stomach. He supposed he could blame Mr. Taylor for that. What did the vicar mean by lending out such disturbing fiction? Tales of bloodsucking creatures feeding on people while they slept. Of sharp-fanged sprites, sullen dwarves, and sinister changelings.

Did the people of Hay really believe such superstitious nonsense? John wondered.

He climbed the narrow flight of stairs that led to the attics. There, he found the trapdoor already open. Was Mr. Fairfax up on the battlements? Or someone else?

Pray God it wasn't Mr. Poole.

John hesitated at the ladder before steeling his nerves and quietly climbing up the rungs. Emerging onto the roof of the Hall, he saw someone seated in the distance, back propped against one of the chimney stacks. It wasn't Mr. Fairfax. Nor was it Mr. Poole.

It was Mrs. Rochester. She was weeping silently.

At the sight of him, she hastily wiped her cheeks with her hands. "What are you doing here?"

He lifted his sketchbook in silent explanation.

"Oh." There was a letter on her lap, the sheets of paper spread out over the folds of her black silk mourning dress. Gathering them up, she folded them back together and moved to rise. "Don't let me stop you."

His interest in drawing had disappeared the moment he saw her. He went to her and helped her to her feet. "What's wrong?"

She released his hand to brush off her skirts. "Everything."

"You've had bad news?"

"Nothing I didn't expect." She thrust the letter into the pocket of her gown. "You'd think I'd have been prepared for it, but I—" She broke off, eyes glistening.

His voice deepened with concern. "What is it?"

She walked to the battlements, turning her face to dash away another stray tear. "Only that I've reached an impasse. This problem I've been trying to solve. I thought I could conquer it. That I could win. Indeed, at times, I thought I *was* winning. But not losing isn't the same as winning. It's only a stalemate. And now I understand that I *can't* win. The best I can hope for is to maintain things as they are."

He stood beside her, his back against the battlements, facing her as she leaned over them. "Is that so terrible?"

"Yes. But…perhaps, if I went away. If I managed things so that I was no longer needed here save once or twice a year…"

A leaden weight settled in his midsection. "You want to leave again?"

"I do."

"For where?"

"Somewhere bright and happy. Paris or Rome or—" She broke off again. "Which would you recommend?"

A mild breeze whispered over them, bringing the sweet fragrance of newly cut hay and early spring flowers. It was strikingly at odds with the remnants of mist that still lingered about the grounds.

"You know I've never been anywhere," he said.

"But you've dreamed, haven't you? Where would you go if you were at your leisure?"

"Italy, I suppose. To tour the monuments and museums." He smiled at the impossibility of it. "It would be nice to see the ceiling of the Sistine Chapel."

"Nice," she repeated. "You think it would be *nice*."

"Glorious, then. Wasn't that your word for Egypt?"

She gave him a look—such a look. "Do you like me, John?"

His pulse briefly lost its rhythm. "Of course I do."

"Why?"

He studied her face, wishing he could read her as easily as he did the books in the library. That he could understand what it was that tormented her so. If he did, he might be able to help her. "Because you're strong. Intelligent and capable."

Her face crumpled. She looked out at the view again, visibly struggling to suppress another fall of tears.

"And because you're a good person," he said.

"I'm not."

"You are. I've seen it in how you care for the boys. In how you look after those you employ here at Thornfield." He brushed her silk-clad arm with the back of his fingers. The smallest stroke of comfort. "Please don't cry."

She turned away from him.

He withdrew his handkerchief and offered it to her. She took it without a word. "Miss Ingram's death wasn't your fault," he said.

"You don't know what you're talking about."

"I know about guilt. The way it can weigh upon you. Eat you up from the inside. I know what I felt when Lady Helen took her own life. Afterward...I didn't believe I could ever find peace again. But I have found it, here at Thornfield. And I want the same for you. I want you to be happy." He set aside his feelings. His love for her. And it *was* love, he recognized that now. But he wouldn't lay it upon her as another burden. "If Eshton makes you so, then I think you had better marry him."

"How magnanimous of you." She blotted her eyes. "He'll be relieved to know we have your blessing."

"You know what I meant."

"Yes." Her gaze cut to his, damp eyes brilliant in the sunlight. "I wonder what will become of you when I marry?"

He swallowed the lump forming in his throat. The truth was, he'd rather been wondering that himself. Indeed, during the past month, the thought of what he'd do when she wed George Eshton had kept him up at night far more than he'd once been kept awake by guilt over the death of Helen Burns.

"The boys are young yet," he said, a little hoarsely. "I'd hoped you would allow me to remain as their tutor until they're older."

It would be enough to be here with them at Thornfield. To see her, even if it *was* only once a year. He could make it enough if he had to.

At least, that was what he'd been telling himself. That her marriage didn't have to change anything. That a part of her, however small, could still be his.

"I mean to take the boys with me when I leave here," she said. "Didn't I tell you?"

He stilled. Whatever fragile hope he'd cherished in his breast fractured and cracked like so much glass. It was a feeling very close to physical pain. "No. You didn't."

"Well. Now you know." She crumpled his handkerchief. "What do you mean to do about it?"

He stared at her. "What *can* I do?"

She looked steadily back at him. "Am I not worth fighting for?"

"Is that what you what me to do? Fight for you?" He was incredulous. "To what end?"

"Do you only fight for things that are easy? Things that require no fight at all? I know you didn't exert yourself for Lady Helen, but—"

"That was different. *She* was different."

"How well I know it. Sainted Helen. Too good for this world."

He shook his head, troubled by her tone. "Don't."

"Helen, up there on her pedestal. But you're here with me now, John. Here in the dirt, among the living." She turned to him, tears still clinging to her lashes. "You told me once that you were my subordinate in fact, but not in spirit. Do you remember?"

How could he forget? It had been that morning in the arbor, words he'd spoken in the taut seconds before she'd kissed him.

"It's my spirit that now addresses your spirit," she said, "as honestly as if we'd crossed through the veil. Do you hear me, John? I don't want a lord and master. And I certainly don't want a long-suffering admirer. I need a man who will pass through this life at my side. A man who will be my equal— my second self, and best earthly companion."

His heart beat hard. He had the strangest sense that he was dreaming. That, at any moment, he'd wake up, alone in the darkness. "What about Eshton?"

"I'm not marrying George Eshton. I never was. I don't love him." Her mouth trembled. "The closest thing I've ever felt to love is what I feel for you."

A swell of emotion tightened John's throat. He knew what the declaration must have cost her. She wasn't a woman who often made herself vulnerable. He took her in his arms. She came willingly, setting her hands flat against his waistcoat. "Do you mean that?" he asked, his voice gone gruff.

"Yes," she said. And then again, more emphatically, "*Yes.* When I leave Thornfield, I must have you with me."

"In what capacity?"

"Whatever you choose. Tutor. Friend." She smoothed her palms over his chest. "Husband."

He bent his head to hers. "I don't want your money or property. I want only you, Bertha." He was conscious of using her given name for the first time. A heady feeling. "I do love you."

She pressed her cheek to his, her breath a soft, ragged whisper against his ear. "Then say you'll come with me. That we can leave this place together, along with the boys."

"Would that I could travel with you as your friend—or as their tutor—without damaging your good name." His hand moved gently on the corseted curve of her back. "But people will talk. You know what they're like. Your reputation would suffer for it."

"I don't care about my reputation."

"I care. I won't be the cause of your ruination."

She gave a strange laugh. "My darling. One day you shall marvel that you said such a thing." She pressed a lingering kiss to his cheek. "Husband it is, then."

He drew back sharply, his eyes searching hers. "Take care. I have nothing to offer you but myself."

"You're all I require," she said.

"Are you certain?"

"As certain as the grave."

He looked at her, deeply, every cell and sinew of his being yearning, yearning. Wanting her so very badly. A mighty surge of masculine emotion deafening him to the persistent flicker of warning that sounded deep within his brain. "Then marry me," he said. "Say you'll be my wife."

A look of almost savage determination crossed over her face. "I will," she said. "May God pardon me."

Twenty-Four

John straightened Stephen's and Peter's portfolios before stacking them on one of the library shelves. He'd already dismissed the boys for an early luncheon and was about to seek out his own midday meal when Bertha entered the library.

"Good morning." She was dressed in a black silk carriage dress, a black crepe-trimmed bonnet in her hand.

The sight of her never failed to make John's heart turn over. "Good morning." He crossed the room to meet her.

A week had passed since she'd accepted his proposal. During that time, he'd carried on much as he always had at Thornfield—teaching the boys and sharing dinners with Mr. Fairfax in the small parlor. The wedding was set for four weeks hence. In the meanwhile, John was taking no liberties.

But fair weather was upon them, and a fair mood along with it. In addition to summoning him for tea each evening, Bertha had begun visiting him in the schoolroom, often drawing him away for walks and picnics on the grounds. The boys always came along, providing a fig leaf of chaperonage.

As far as John was aware, no one at Thornfield yet knew that he and Bertha were to be married. And he had no intention of telling them. It was up to her to choose the time and manner of the announcement.

Apparently, today was that day.

"I've just informed Mr. Fairfax of our engagement," she said.

John failed to suppress a wince. He'd come to respect Mr. Fairfax. To look on him as something like a friend. The elderly butler's good opinion shouldn't matter—not in terms of whether or not John ultimately wed Bertha. Yet somehow it did. "How did he take the news?"

"He was surprised, naturally. But he soon came around." She smoothed John's waistcoat. "Don't look so worried. We'll need his help with the plans for the wedding. We'll never manage it so quickly on our own. Not if we mean to leave for Italy directly afterward."

"No. You're right. We can't keep it secret forever, can we?"

She gazed up at him, frowning. "You're afraid people will think you're marrying me for my fortune."

"Among other things."

"Let them. Who cares what anyone says? All that matters is our own happiness. Yours and mine, and that of the boys." Her hand lifted to cradle his cheek. "Are you having second thoughts?"

"Not about you." He bent his head to hers. "*Never* about you."

"Good. Because we haven't time for doubts. If you have a free moment, spend it as I am, on preparing to leave this place."

His gaze dropped briefly to her carriage dress. She was devoid of ornament, save for the ever-present silver locket at her throat. He knew now that it contained two small portraits of her parents. A dour couple who bore little resemblance to their daughter. It also functioned as a timepiece. There was a delicate clock set inside, which she often consulted. "Where are you off to today?"

"To Millcote to buy my wedding clothes. I've done with all of this black. It's time to shed my widow's weeds."

After glancing at the door to make sure no one observed them, John gathered her in an embrace. How well she fit in his arms. He could almost imagine that she'd been fashioned just for him. "How will I recognize you without them?"

"Foolish." She encircled his neck. "Wait until you see how smart I look in pastel-printed muslin. You'll fall in love with me all the more."

He kissed her fiercely. "Impossible."

After she'd gone, he made his way to the parlor where he often shared a midday meal with Mr. Fairfax. His footsteps slowed as he entered. The elderly butler was there, seated silently in his chair. A tray of tea and sandwiches stood untouched on the table beside him. He looked pale and grave, staring blankly ahead of him. Almost as if he was in shock.

A floorboard creaked under John's boot, announcing his presence.

Mr. Fairfax roused himself. "Mr. Eyre. Do come in. It seems that congratulations are in order. Though one can hardly believe it. Is it true, then? Do you really mean to marry the mistress?"

John took a seat in the velvet-upholstered armchair on the opposite side of the tea table. "I've asked her and she has accepted me."

"And you believe her?"

John frowned. "Shouldn't I?"

Mr. Fairfax regarded John with a troubled expression. "I couldn't say. That is, I expect you can believe it since she's told you so. But how will it answer? Mrs. Rochester is a proud and independent woman. Her marrying Mr. Eshton would have been surprise enough. But to marry you?" He surveyed the whole of John's person. "I can't understand it."

John supposed he should be offended. "Am I such a sad specimen?"

"No, indeed, sir. And Mrs. Rochester is fond of you, I daresay. I've noticed it myself. Many a time I've wanted to warn you to remain on your guard. Not everything at Thornfield is quite what it seems."

"I know that much," John said grimly, thinking of Mr. Poole.

How often since the man's attack on Mrs. Wren had John heard that blood-chilling chuckle of his? The rattling of chains and the scraping of wood coming from the third floor?

Bertha had said she was confident that Mr. Poole wouldn't hurt anyone again. John suspected that that confidence owed to some advanced level of confinement in the small room behind the tapestry. A place Mr. Poole was consigned during his moments of madness. Was he chained up now? Cuffed and collared like an animal, in addition to being locked in?

This was the same man John saw working diligently at his forge, or carrying a pint of porter and plate of cold pork pie up from the kitchen. A stolid, steady fellow, with no glimmer of insanity in his gaze.

It beggared belief.

"We shall be glad to leave for Italy next month," John said. "The climate will be better for the boys."

"Yes, the boys. You are to be commended, sir. They've improved a great deal under your care, and will improve even more if taken away from here. I've always thought as much." Mr. Fairfax's brows knit into a bushy white line. "Could you not travel with the mistress as their tutor? Must you marry her?"

"I *want* to marry her," John said. "I love her."

"What's that?" Mr. Fairfax cocked his ear toward John.

"I said that *I love her.*"

Mr. Fairfax's frown deepened. "Oh dear. That is unfortunate, for you see, I do fear there will be things that come to light that are far different from what you expect."

John was hurt by the insinuation. Hurt, and a little irritated. Did Mr. Fairfax truly think John had an expectation of wealth and property? That he'd forsake Bertha if her estate turned out to be worth less than it appeared? "I have no expectations," he said. "I want only to look after her."

"Well. I suppose your mind is made up. I pray that you won't be disappointed." Mr. Fairfax at last poured out their tea. He handed John a cup with an unsteady hand.

Some of the tea sloshed over into the saucer as John took it. He didn't drink. And when Mr. Fairfax offered him a sandwich, John declined it. He found that he'd quite lost his appetite.

Bertha remained in residence at Thornfield another fortnight—a blissful period of picnics, candlelit conversation, and stolen kisses—at the end of which she was called to London. Her solicitor required her to sign a few remaining documents relating to the administration of the estate in her absence.

John accompanied her out to the waiting carriage. "I still think he might have come to you."

"Mr. Hughes is pushing eighty. I daren't leave the final details of our departure to his feeble constitution. If left to his own devices, he'd make us wait another week, only to write and say he was too ill to embark on the journey." She held tight to John's arm as they descended the front steps. "No. I shall go to him in Fleet Street myself and see that all is in readiness for our departure. I'll be back the day before the wedding, no later. And then, the moment we're wed, we must fly. I won't tolerate a second's delay."

John gave her a look of concern. She was wearing a carriage dress of dark green silk trimmed in darker velvet—one of the many gowns she'd ordered on her visit to Millcote. The color set off her complexion to magnificent effect, and the wide flounced skirts and delicate velvet belt at her waist showcased her figure. He admired her in it, though it was still a trifle strange to see her out of her blacks. "You're anxious."

"With good cause. I've too often had the cup of happiness snatched from my lips not to be wary of divine intervention."

He gave her a reassuring smile. "If God intervenes, I trust it will be on the side of our union."

She didn't answer him. Instead, she turned into his arms, embracing him and pressing a hard kiss to his mouth—right there in front of Jenkins, Mr. Fairfax, and the boys. She broke away just as abruptly, permitting Jenkins to hand her into the cab of the carriage. He shut the door behind her, and leaping up on the box, set the horses in motion.

As the carriage rolled away, Bertha's solemn profile was briefly visible through the window. John watched her go, troubled.

Perhaps it was only bridal nerves. A common enough condition among soon-to-be-married ladies—or so he understood.

But Bertha was no virgin bride.

Nevertheless, in the past few days, as the calendar had advanced toward the date of their wedding, she'd seemed to become increasingly restless and distracted.

John's own state of mind was generally more optimistic. There were difficulties in marrying a wealthy widow, it was true. People would talk. They were bound to do so. And he didn't much relish being labeled a fortune-hunter. But the compensation of having Bertha Rochester as his wife would be worth it. Not her money or her property, but *her*.

He was in love with her. And though she hadn't yet declared her love for him—not in specific terms—he knew that what she felt for him was no passing fancy. He may not be dashing or daring. May not have wealth or breeding. But he was confident he could give her something of what she needed. Acceptance. Understanding. A shoulder to lean on when the next storm came.

It was impossible to solve her problems for her. He wouldn't presume to try. But he could stand by her side. He could be there for her as an equal. A second self, as she'd said.

As for all the rest of it, John was resolved to be patient. There would be time enough for her to confide in him after they were married.

He retired to his room that night wearier than usual. In Jenkins's absence, John had been tasked with supervising Stephen and Peter at their afternoon riding lessons.

Fortunately the boys required little instruction. Indeed it was clear that they'd ridden before. Once in the saddle, their confidence rose. John supposed it derived from the ease with which they could kick their mounts into a gallop and swiftly escape any perceived danger.

But there was no danger here. Not for them. They never went about unescorted, and they never ventured onto the third floor. It was surely only the memory of danger that plagued them.

Standing in front of the washstand in his bedroom, John bathed his face and dried it with a clean towel. A single flickering candle illuminated his reflection in the mirror that hung over the basin.

Sometimes he hardly recognized himself anymore. He looked older. Graver. Good lord, there were even a few faint lines at the corners of his eyes. He leaned over the basin, drawing closer to the mirror in order to see them.

And suddenly another face appeared in the glass, shrouding John's own face like a caul.

He jerked back in alarm. His heart jerked, too, leaping hard against his ribs.

What the devil?

Spinning around, he searched the darkness, all the while knowing what he would find.

There was no one else there, of course. It had been a trick of the candlelight. But such a trick! The face had been fearful. Ghastly. Possessed of a countenance that could never have belonged to a human being.

Was it some sort of premonition?

Or was it merely a side effect of his tired eyes and equally tired brain? It must have been, for when he looked into the mirror again, the face was gone.

It didn't stop his pulse from racing. And later, when he finally climbed into his box bed, it did nothing to ease him to sleep. Instead he lay awake for hours, attuned to the slightest movement, the faintest noise.

When Bertha returned at the end of the week, John met her carriage at the gates. It was approaching twilight, the very hour when the mist was at its utmost. Seeing him, Jenkins stopped the horses. Bertha alighted, waving the coachman on without her.

"You needn't have done that," John said as the two of them met in the road. "I know you must be tired."

"Not at all. I'm glad for the opportunity to get some fresh air. It's been a long, stuffy journey." She stretched up to kiss him, raising one hand to curl around his neck. Her lips shaped softly to his, their breath mingling sweetly.

John held her fast. "I've missed you."

"And I you." After another deep kiss, she drew back to look at him. "What is it? What's wrong?"

"Nothing, but—"

"Something's happened. I can see it in your eyes."

"It's nothing," he said again. "Only my imagination getting away from me."

"Ah. Is that all?" She linked her arm through his as they turned to walk up the road back to Thornfield. "It's the eve of our wedding, John. You had better confess all to me."

He heaved a sigh. "It's ludicrous. I'd blame the laudanum if I could. I often had strange visions while taking it. But since I've stopped, the visions have ceased. That is, they *had* done, until the night you left."

"What happened? What did you see?"

"I was standing at the washstand, looking into the glass. And…a man's face appeared."

"A *man's* face?"

He nodded. "It wasn't a reflection. It simply materialized like vapor, floating there over my own face, nearly transparent—but not so transparent that I couldn't see the horror of his countenance."

"Describe it."

"It was all over in a blink, mind you, but he seemed a fashionable gentleman. Handsome, even, with elegant features and waving ebony hair combed back from his forehead. But there the semblance of humanity ended. The image he cast was malevolent. The face of some poor creature damned to the pit."

Her gaze jerked to his. "Why do you say that?" she asked sharply. "Why do you call him a poor creature?"

"He was white as death, with blood flowing from his eyes and ears to stain his face. And such eyes he had. Red as hellfire." John grimaced. "Do you know, he rather reminded me of one of the foul specters in that book Mr. Taylor lent to me. One in particular: the German vampyre."

Bertha's footsteps faltered.

John caught her swiftly round the waist to steady her. "I beg your pardon. I shouldn't have gone into such gruesome detail." He looked down at her. "Have I frightened you?"

"No. Of course not. I'm only a little tired, that's all." She stepped back from him. Her face was pale in the waning light of day. "What happened next?"

"Nothing. The vision disappeared. Gone as quickly as it had come. Though I confess it left quite an impression. I didn't fall asleep until dawn."

"Understandably so." She brushed a stray lock of hair from her face. Her gloved hand was trembling.

"Bertha—"

"Don't fuss. I'm perfectly all right."

"Have you dined?"

She shook her head.

"Take my arm, then, if you please. I'll get you home and fed." He waited for her to slip her hand back into the crook of his arm. When she'd done so, he continued back toward the house, albeit at a slower pace. "You see why I didn't want to tell you."

"Yes. It's all quite fanciful." Her bell-shaped skirts swayed against his leg. "Are you sure you haven't taken any laudanum?"

"Not a drop. Nothing but that herbal tonic of yours since February."

"Strange. It should have put an end to bad dreams."

"In addition to headaches?" He smiled slightly. "You have a lot of confidence in the mixture."

"A guarded confidence. It's a new recipe. I only discovered it earlier this year. An obliging chemist made it up for me in London."

"You've never mentioned what it contains."

She hesitated for an instant. "Various things. Wild rose. Garlic. Tincture of silver nitrate. An imprecise concoction. So much of this is trial and error."

He looked at her with a start. "Silver nitrate?"

"Trace amounts. Not enough to harm anyone. Perhaps therein lies the difficulty." She rubbed her temple, as if to stave off an impending headache. "Oh, why do we have to linger? Why can we not leave this place immediately?"

"For Italy?"

"Yes. For Rome or London. Anywhere but here. I don't want to wait another night. But we must, mustn't we? We can't leave until we're married." She stared ahead, her gaze fixed on the house looming in the distance, swathed in its veil of mist. "Will you do something for me?"

"Anything."

"Will you spend tonight in the nursery with the boys? Sophie won't mind it." She paused before adding, "You'll never sleep properly in your own room. Not after such a nightmare as you've described. And I want you to be well rested for our wedding."

He frowned. "If that's what you want."

"It is," she said. "And John? Be sure to bolt the door."

Twenty-Five

*Mrs. Bertha
Rochester's Journal.*

26 April, morning. — After a fraught night, I am again alone in my chamber. Mr. Poole has gone, with promises to return to the courtyard today at noon. In the meanwhile, I've entreated him to hide himself as best he can. I believe he comprehends the danger. Indeed, when he saw me leaning out the barred window, he confessed that he'd thought me already dead.

Apparently, he was set upon when he was returning from accompanying Mrs. Wren to Varna. He routed his assailants and walked the rest of the way back to Senniskali. I don't flatter myself that he's loyal. He's not even passing clever. But Mr. Poole is strong as an ox, and he knows who it is who pays his wages. I've promised to triple his salary if he assists me in escaping this place.

"Avoid the mist," I called down to him as he departed yesterday. "Hide yourself at night as best you can. And on no account let my husband see you."

The small key I'd found in Edward's waistcoat pocket was still in the pocket of my skirt. I hadn't the time to investigate what lock it might fit into. The sun was rapidly slipping beyond the horizon. Soon my husband would wake, and I dared not risk him catching me with my pilfered prize.

He rose at sunset, and much to my relief, seemed to have no idea that I'd spied him in his unnatural sleep. Neither did he seem to realize that his key was missing. He disappeared for the evening, returning at dawn with more foreign papers for me to sign. I did so without objection, even as my heart threatened to sink into despair. But what was the point in arguing with him? I was still his captive.

Only when the sun rose and he once again retired to his lair did I venture from my room to test the key I'd stolen. It was a daunting task. Most of the doors in Nosht-Vŭlk were locked. It would mean trying every one of them.

I first went to the front and side exterior doors—the doors that, if opened, would grant my freedom. There was little hope of success. The front door was barred with a heavy bolt, and the door from the kitchen was equally secured. Neither the key, nor persistent poking with my hairpins, produced any effect.

Discouraged but not defeated, I tried various doors off of the main hall before extending my search to the opposite side of the fortress. It was there I found the key's natural home: my husband's vault. When inserted, the key opened the lock with a decisive click.

Suddenly I understood why my husband had kept this key separately on his person. He valued the items in his vault more than anything else he possessed. I hadn't much time before he realized his key was missing. After that, it wouldn't take long for him to determine the likely culprit of the theft.

Swinging the door of the vault open, I cautiously entered, my footsteps silent on the rich Turkish carpet that covered the floor as I lit the two lanterns which gave light to the small room. I'd never before been inside on my own. Never had the leisure to thoroughly inspect the treasures within—what was left of them. It appeared he'd sold off even more since my last visit. All that remained were bits of pottery carved with odd words and symbols; figures of gods and goddesses; and a few delicately bound books and scrolls protected behind glass.

I slid the interior bolt in place, if only as a precaution, and using the key, I opened one of the glass cases to take out a scroll. It was Egyptian, that much I recognized. But I hadn't any notion what the writing said. As for the images, they seemed to depict a kind of funeral rite.

Examining the other scrolls and books, I saw that they were much in the same vein. Texts from ancient civilizations—each with depictions of burial and rebirth. It's a common enough belief in mythology, the idea of rising from the dead. But given Edward's recent revelation about a book which would enable him to walk in the sunlight, I felt a distinct sense of unease.

Was this the belief that currently possessed my husband? That he was some manner of deity who would soon rise again? I couldn't help but make the comparison. The way he slept in the dirt, among his many victims—like a pharaoh entombed with slaves for the afterlife. It was a sort of delusion, I supposed. A mania, such as one read about in the sensation papers. With no doctors to take him in hand, his delusion had been permitted to advance to a gruesome conclusion. To murder and mayhem.

But what of the way he'd interacted with the mist that I'd seen from the window? What of his eyes that night in my room, as red as the devil himself?

I was puzzling over these very things when a faint—and quite persistent—scratching sound commenced. It set my nerves a jangle. I couldn't tell where it was coming from and didn't remain to find out. Returning to my room, I dined on the last of my store of spoiled bread and cheese, and while I waited for the clock to strike twelve, I began to formulate my escape.

26 April, later that day. — I've sent Mr. Poole on an errand, equipped with enough coin (tossed down from the barred window) to see it through. I pray he'll have success. It's a foolhardy thing to have asked him to do. A reasonable woman might have simply commanded him to go to the authorities. However, Mr. Poole has informed me that Senniskali is all but empty. And even if there were a local policeman or magistrate hereabouts, what could they possibly do to help me?

Edward Rochester is stronger and more powerful than I am, both in law and in fact. This is his homeland, not mine. His people, no matter that he chooses to disavow them. While I have no allies save Mr. Poole. If I'm to escape this place, it must come down to my own ingenuity.

27 April, midday. — I write this entry with an unsteady hand and a heart that has twice, this long night, come close to beating its last. In making my plans to escape my husband, I failed to appreciate the true nature of the man I was dealing with. Man, I say. But he is no man. He is something else entirely. I pray to God that I—

But I must calm myself and start at the beginning or risk my account sounding like the deranged ravings of a lunatic. No one will ever believe what I have seen—what I have done—if I cannot relate it clearly. Would that there was a drop of laudanum remaining to steady my nerves!

My ordeal began yesterday at sunset. I knew my husband would eventually discover that I'd taken the key to his vault, but I hadn't reckoned for how severe his reaction would be.

Indeed, it was out of all proportion—or so I believed at the time.

At sunset, when he rose from his slumber, he came to my room. I stood to meet him, a branch of candles flickering on the desk at my back. I was as wary of his presence as ever, but no longer strictly afraid. Hope of escape had made me bold. That was my first mistake. Had I been more on my guard, I'd have noticed right away that something was different about him. He looked sated. As if he'd just partaken of a nourishing meal—something I hadn't enjoyed for many days. It was a mistake to provoke him.

"You have something that belongs to me," he said.

"Such as?" The key to his vault was still in the pocket of my skirt, along with my Nock percussion pistol. I longed to reach for it, if only to give myself additional courage.

"You have my key," he said, approaching me slowly. "Give it to me now."

"What key? Not the one to the front door, else I'd be gone by now." I sidestepped away from him. "By-the-by, where are the house keys? I've had no luck in finding them."

"I warned you—"

"They must be secreted away somewhere. I know they're not on your person."

"Bertha—"

"You'll need them to unlock the front door and bolt it again when we leave this place. It's but three more days until the date of our departure. Have you forgotten?"

He circled around me like a wolf stalking its prey. All the while I edged closer to the door. "You came to me when I slept," he said. "Do you deny it?"

"Why should I?"

"Because, my dear, it means your very life."

A chill went down my spine. I took another step away from him. "From the moment I married you, was my life ever anything but forfeit?"

His eyes gleamed with an unnatural light. "No, indeed. But I might have kept you awhile longer as my pet." He came closer. "You saw me at rest. What else did you see?"

Try as I might to present him with an innocent countenance, the expression on my face must have told him all.

"Did you see my brides?" he asked. "The ones who came before you?"

Women of a trivial nature, he'd called them. Women possessing neither souls nor hearts. I'd thought he'd meant his prior lovers. Ladies he'd met who hadn't been worthy of marriage. Good lord, had those desiccated bones with their scraps of feminine clothing truly been his former wives?

I stared at him in slow-dawning horror. By this point, I was disposed to think him a veritable Bluebeard. "I saw bones." My voice shook, betraying me for the coward I was. "I saw Agnes."

The name didn't appear to register with him.

"Agnes," I repeated with growing anger. "Did you not even mark her name? She was my maid. An honest and hardworking servant girl who you killed in cold blood."

"I assure you, there was nothing cold in the way I disposed of your maid. She felt the full warmth of my embrace before she exited this life. And quite happy she was to experience it."

My jaw went slack. Such shock I felt. Such disgust. And with it, an incandescent rage that he should do such a thing—that he should get away with it. When next I spoke, my voice no longer shook with fear. It trembled with fury. "You contemptible beast. What sort of man are you?"

He paid no heed to my words, only stalked toward me with a single-minded intent. "Enough of these games. Where is my key?"

Something in his face told me that he was no longer capable of distraction. In a moment, he would make a physical search of my person, finding both the key and my pistol. That, I couldn't abide. Clutching my skirts, I feinted toward my bed, only to dart around him and out the door of my room.

He reached for my throat as I ran past, and he might have subdued me if not for the presence of my silver timepiece locket. After touching the chain with his palm, he drew back with a muffled oath, allowing me vital seconds to get away.

I plunged down the stairs with my heart in my throat. His heavy footfalls sounded behind me. This, I knew, was the end of the road. I couldn't outrun him. He would soon eat up the seconds I had gained. And then he would take the key. He would disarm me, and he would kill me.

There seemed only one way to ensure my survival. Reaching into my pocket, I pulled out my pistol at the same instant I reached the landing. I spun around, my back against the wall. He was there on the stairs, midway down and still in motion. Raising the pistol in my hand, I aimed for his heart and pulled the trigger.

The bullet fired straight and true. Edward's face contorted—more with surprise, I think, than with pain. And then, he crumpled and fell down the stairs. He landed beside me, his neck bent at an odd angle. He didn't move again, nor did he appear to draw breath.

A surge of unimaginable relief tore through me. All those years of target practice at Thornfield. Those many seasons hunting with Papa, learning to wield my rifle. If only I'd known I was preparing for such a day! And now, here I was.

And here Edward was—in a heap at my feet. He was dead. I had killed him.

One hand at my midriff, I descended the rest of the way to the hall, trying to catch my breath. I was standing there—slowly going into shock, I expect—when my attention was arrested by a bone-chilling sound.

It was him. My husband. He rose to his feet before my eyes. Unharmed. Undead.

"*You*," he said. His gaze fixed on me with murderous intent.

And I ran for my life. There was no time to reason any of it out. Like any hunted animal, I could focus only on escape.

In a fortress filled with locked doors, there was but one place that offered a chance of safety. My husband's vault was nearby. I fumbled for the key as I approached it at a dead run, my palm so damp with perspiration I feared I would drop it. Somehow, I managed to insert it in the lock. Opening the vault, I slipped inside and slammed the door behind me. I was just sliding the interior bolt when my husband's fists connected with the door.

He hit it so hard that it rattled in its frame. "Bertha!" he roared. "You can't hide!"

I cowered in the darkness at the opposite end of the vault. For a man who had just taken a bullet, Edward seemed to have enormous strength. He'd break down the door, I knew it.

Trying desperately to calm my racing pulse, I inhaled great gulps of air. My knees were weak. I leaned on the wall for support, very much in danger of collapsing.

But it wouldn't do. There was no time for cowering weakness. As my husband shouted my name and pounded on the door, I rallied my wits and what was left of my courage.

The tinderbox and two oil lamps were easy enough to locate by feel in the darkness. I lit them both. The light immediately helped to dispel some of my panic. When next my husband shook the door, I called out, "I wouldn't do that if I were you."

"Open it, Bertha," he said. "Or I'll tear it from the hinges."

Indeed, I believed he could. It was beginning to sink in that my husband was an unnatural thing. Worse than a fortune-hunting parasite. Worse, even, than a wife-murdering Bluebeard. He was truly some variety of monster. "I wouldn't do that," I said again. "Not if you value your collection."

That was enough to give him pause. "By all that's sacred, if you touch a single artifact—"

At that, I hoisted a small statue of Osiris from one of the shelves and pitched it against the wall. It shattered with a sound loud enough to make me flinch. I can only imagine how it must have sounded to him.

"Damn you!" he cried in something very like anguish. This was followed by a stream of invective—oaths and slurs against women that I'm loath to put to paper. Suffice to say, he was in a towering rage. He gripped the door and pulled it so hard the hinges creaked in protest.

In response, I gave an old Etruscan urn the same treatment as the statue of Osiris. At the sound of its demise, Edward ceased his attack.

"Can you hear me?" I asked. "Every time you attempt to break down that door, I'm going to smash another and another."

"I'll tear you to pieces," he said. This was followed by more harsh words in a language I couldn't understand, and then: "You'll scream to your god for mercy."

"Perhaps. But can you do it before I set the entire room ablaze? I have two oil lamps in here, and these scrolls will make marvelous kindling."

That quieted him for another long moment. "Think of your family," he said at last.

"I have no family. Isn't that why you chose me? Because I had no one to protect me? No one to care if I died in mysterious circumstances?"

"Think of your homeland. If you damage another item, I'll come down on England like a plague. Your countrymen won't—"

"What care I for England? It's my own well-being I'm concerned with." I heard him pacing outside the door. My eyes darted over the shelves. There weren't enough artifacts left to continue smashing them all through the night. And as boldly as I spoke, I really didn't relish the thought of setting myself on fire along with his books and papyri. What I needed—*all* I needed—was to hold him at bay until dawn.

He muttered something in Bulgarian, or possibly Romani. I could no longer guess. "I would have given you an easy death," he said. "A lover's kiss. But you've lost the privilege of it."

My stomach tightened with a fear I dared not show. "What's this?" I mused in a loud voice. "A ceremonial wine goblet?" Picking up another artifact—a cup carved with strange symbols—I held it at the ready. "From a funeral rite, I think. Pity it must meet its end."

"No!" he cried. "Don't harm it!"

"Then stop threatening me. Stop beating at the door. I will *not* be terrorized." My words were greeted with dead silence. I was silent, too, for a time—very much concerned with what he might be planning next. And then I asked, "Why were you not injured when I shot you?"

"Your aim was poor."

"My aim was excellent. I know I struck your heart. Why were you not killed outright?"

"I cannot be killed," he said.

I choked on a sound of disbelief. "Nonsense."

"Believe what you will. As long as you open the door."

"Not at present." He didn't need to know that I intended to stay in the vault all night. "Not until your anger has cooled."

"I'm not angry. Not anymore." At that, his tone gentled, becoming almost seductive. "Remember how it was between us in Egypt? In Athens? The two of us in harmony, with none of this arguing. Remember the pleasure I gave you? It can be so again. Only open the door."

I wondered if this was how Eve had felt when tempted by the serpent. Such was my husband's voice—it wrapped around me, a low, persuasive baritone intent on weakening my resolve. Reiterating over and over again his single request.

Open the door.

"Enough," I said. "You can't trick me into acquiescing. I've shot you, and you've threatened me with a painful death. As far as I'm concerned, our marriage is over."

It didn't dissuade him. He kept on, pacing and muttering at the door for hours.

The best I could do was to block him out of my thoughts and to focus, instead, on what I was going to do next. In a cold sweat, I sank down into a sitting position on the Turkish carpet. Opening my locket to check the time, I saw that it was still early. I had many hours to go until sunrise. Many hours in which to formulate a plan.

Edward had said he couldn't be killed. A fantastical claim! Yet I couldn't fully discount it. How, then, was I to defeat this man? This creature?

I took a mental account of what I had learned thus far of his weaknesses:

      I. Sunlight
     II. Silver
    III. Laudanum

Whether these weaknesses were real or imagined, I didn't know. My husband claimed them as such. Since the first day I met him in Cairo, he'd assiduously avoided the sun. As for silver, he can't bear to touch it. On our wedding night, he said it was toxic to him. That it caused a painful rash whenever it came into contact with his skin. Then, I'd suspected it of being a mere fancy. But now I wasn't so sure.

Days ago, when his lips had brushed the silver chain of my locket, he'd drawn back as if scalded. His mouth had looked redder afterward. Almost scorched. And then again today, when he'd attempted to grab my throat. Had it been the silver that thwarted his efforts?

And what of his intolerance for laudanum? A strange allergy, to be sure. The very smell of it repulsed him. He couldn't abide to be near it. I'd tasted but two drops of the stuff and it had been enough to repel him.

Of course, there was a good possibility that these weren't weaknesses at all. That they were nothing more than Edward's crazed imaginings. He was plainly a madman. A deviant who made his bed among the corpses of his victims.

But I couldn't dismiss an incontrovertible fact: I had shot him and he hadn't died. Not only that, he appeared to have suffered no injury at all. He was outside that door. Vigorous. Relentless.

I realized then that escaping him wouldn't be enough. We were married, and I had signed away to him even that part of my fortune which was to be mine irrespective of marriage. Wherever I went, he was bound to follow, demanding his legal rights over my money, property, and person. The only hope I had was to kill him. And since that had failed so spectacularly, there was but one course remaining. I must conquer him somehow.

The prospect was daunting. I was mulling it over—imagining all sorts of outlandish scenarios—when I heard a faint scratching sound. The same scratching sound I'd heard when last I'd visited the vault alone.

The fine hairs rose on the back of my neck. But this time I couldn't run away. I was stuck there with it.

Muffled as the sound was, it only became more insistent as the next hour ticked by. Where was it coming from? I performed a cursory search of the room. In the meanwhile, Edward appeared to have gone. To where I didn't like to think.

I looked behind the shelving as best I could, scanning for hidden spaces in the lamplight. There was nothing. Not a single crack in the plaster. "Is someone there?" I called out softly.

Scratch, scratch.

My pulse skittered wildly. I stood, stock still, in the center of the vault, straining to listen over the sound of my blood pounding in my ears. But the vault had fallen quiet again. I sank back down on the carpet, legs too unsteady to bear my weight. And then I heard it once more.

Scratch, scratch.

I realized then, with a jolt of fresh horror, that it was coming from below. As if someone—or something—was underneath the very ground I sat upon. Crawling away from the edge of the carpet, I began to roll it back. It came up easily, revealing a sight as ominous as any I'd seen since my time at Nosht-Vŭlk.

There was a door in the floor. A simple square with a bolt set into it. I drew the pads of my fingertips over the latch.

And something beneath responded.

Scratch, scraaaatch.

My heart stopped. Was it one of Edward's victims? Another servant he was in the process of disposing of? Or was it something else? Something worse?

Withdrawing the vault key from my pocket, I tested it in the lock, both relieved and disappointed to discover that it fit. My constitution couldn't handle much more. I'd been frightened enough for a lifetime. But if some poor soul was entombed below—a living victim that I could render aid to—then I knew my duty.

Unfastening the latch, I lifted open the door.

Twenty-Six

Thornfield Hall
Yorkshire, England
May 1844

The first of May fell on a Wednesday. A bright and blooming morning, rife with the fragrance of spring. It was the ideal weather for a wedding.

His waistcoat buttoned and his cravat arranged in an elegant knot, John shrugged on his new frock coat and made his way downstairs. His trunks were already packed and corded. By this time tomorrow, they'd be on their way to Rome, right alongside the trunks belonging to Bertha and the boys. She would be Mrs. Eyre, then. His wife.

John still found the reality of it difficult to believe. When he'd left Lowton, he'd had no expectation of forming a family, let alone falling in love. And yet, in less than a year, Bertha and the boys had become his whole world. What doubts he had were eclipsed by the great love he felt for them.

Entering the hall, he found the doors standing open. Outside, Jenkins waited with the carriage. Someone had hung a wreath of bloodred roses on the door and twined rosebuds into the horses' manes.

Strange that. John's wedding to Bertha wasn't a grand occasion. Indeed, she'd several times referred to it as a "mere formality." A tedious but necessary ceremony that would enable them to set off for Europe without delay. There would be no guests at the church, save the two people who were obliged to witness the affair.

"Mr. Eyre. Good morning." Mr. Fairfax came in from outside where he'd been exchanging words with Jenkins. "Have you breakfasted?"

"Not yet." John consulted his pocket watch. He supposed there was still time. Enough, at least, for a cup of tea and some porridge. "Have you seen Mrs. Rochester?"

"Here I am." Her voice sounded from the landing. She came down the stairs to join them, the full skirts of her cream silk dress held in her hands. It wasn't a wedding gown. Not of the sort worn by young ladies embarking on their first marriages. But the delicate embroidery on the bodice, and trim of finely wrought Brussels lace on the collar and cuffs, gave it the richness and radiance of a queen's raiment.

John's gaze drifted over her. His soon-to-be bride. She was breathtakingly beautiful.

Bertha greeted his perusal with a slight smile. "Come." She extended her hand to him and he took it. "I shall give you five minutes to eat something, and then we must dash."

He followed along after her to the dining room, careful not to tread on her skirts. "Have *you* eaten?"

"I had a tray in my room at dawn." Releasing his hand, she took a seat at the table.

He made himself a modest plate at the sideboard before sitting down in the chair beside her. "So early?"

"I'm accustomed to rising with the sun." Her mouth quirked. "Why? Did you think it was nerves? That I've been up all night, pacing my bedchamber with anticipation?"

He laughed. "Having second thoughts, more like."

"Never." She gave him an arch look. "And you? Have you—"

"Been pacing? My God, yes." He poured himself a cup of coffee. "But I haven't had any second thoughts."

"Not a one?"

He shook his head. "No regrets. No changes of mind."

"Regrets." She paused. "Now those I *have* had."

His hand stilled, his coffee cup frozen halfway to his mouth. "Not about me, I hope?"

"Specifically about you." Her faint smile turned rueful. "I regret that I never met you before."

"Before when?"

"Before I married Mr. Rochester. Before I became the woman I am now."

He slowly lowered his cup back to the table. "I adore the woman you are now."

Her expression softened. "Ah. But you didn't know me then. I often wonder what you would have made of me. And what I would have made of you."

"Were you so very different?"

"I was innocent. Disposed to see the best in people—and blind to the worst of them." A shadow crossed over her face, briefly dimming the light in her green-and-bronze-flecked eyes. "But I don't mean to distract you with my melancholy reflections." She motioned to his plate. "Eat, please. The carriage is waiting."

John made short work of his breakfast. Ten minutes later, they were settled into the cab of the carriage, rattling down the road toward Hay.

Mr. Taylor had agreed to marry them at his church. A generous gesture considering that he and Bertha didn't like each other very much. As far as John was aware, the two of them hadn't seen each other since Miss Ingram's death.

Was that the cause of Bertha's dark mood?

She gazed out the window, tense and still, frowning at the gathering mist that clung to the trees and shrubs that lined the road.

"Is something troubling you?" John asked.

She turned her head to look at him. "Such as?"

"I hope you aren't apprehensive about seeing Mr. Taylor. I know the two of you have had your differences. And after the death of Miss Ingram—"

"Mr. Taylor is the least of my concerns," she said. "I'm merely impatient. Everything feels as if it's taking hours longer."

His brow creased with concern. "Is that all? Truly?"

"Don't ask me that now."

"If not now, when?"

"When we've been married a year and a day. Ask me again then, and I shall tell you about my troubles. Every cursed one of them. Until that time, you mustn't press me, John." She turned back to the window. "Oh, but I do wish Jenkins would drive faster!"

He studied her profile, trying to suppress the creeping uncertainty that threatened his sense of well-being. It was his wedding day. He should be happy. They both should be. There was no time for doubts. Indeed, it was rather too late for them. "We're nearly there."

As the carriage came to a halt in front of the church's wrought-iron gate, John's attention was drawn to the rolling graveyard, with its headstones of marble and granite—a reminder that death was ever present.

The specter of it had been with him for as long as he could remember. A grim companion on his journey from childhood all the way to the night of his arrival in Millcote. Even then, Helen's ghost had stood at the crossroads, her hand held up in warning.

It seemed a distant memory now. A nightmare from which John had slowly awakened during his time at the Hall.

And he *was* awake now. Fully conscious of what it was that mattered in life. *Love* mattered. Love for the lady sitting across from him, and for the two lads waiting back at the house. Stephen and Peter. The first martyrs, Bertha had called them. Sophie was to have them ready to depart the instant John and his new bride returned. And then they would leave Thornfield Hall, and their new life together could begin.

Jenkins opened the door of the carriage and lowered the steps. John climbed out first to assist Bertha down. She gripped tight to his hand.

He sank his voice. "Are you sure—"

"Yes, yes. Let us go in," she said. "Mr. Taylor will be waiting."

They passed through the iron gate and down the path through the graveyard. At the end of the path was the church, its front doors standing open. Garbed in his white surplice, Mr. Taylor was positioned in front of them. His posture wasn't one of welcome. Quite the reverse. He appeared to be barring them entry.

A black-suited gentleman was at his side—a sober-looking fellow of passing middle age. The two men wore twin expressions of gravity.

Bertha's grip tightened on John's hand with a convulsive strength.

"Mrs. Rochester. Mr. Eyre," Mr. Taylor said. "Forgive me. This gentleman has only just informed me that there is an impediment to your marriage."

"An insuperable impediment." The stranger was as somber as an undertaker. "This woman has a husband now living."

John's breath stopped, right along with his heart. He absorbed the words like a blow.

But it couldn't be, could it? It must be a mistake. Some confusion over Mr. Rochester having died abroad.

Turning to Bertha for reassurance, he found her countenance as hard as chiseled marble.

"Who are you?" she demanded of the stranger.

"My name is Briggs, madam. I'm a solicitor from London, hired to investigate the matter. I have certain documents in my possession proving the truth of what I say."

Bertha's eyes kindled. "Hired by whom?"

"What documents?" Mr. Taylor asked at the same time. "I'd like to see them."

Mr. Briggs withdrew a folded paper from his coat pocket and read it out to them:

> *"I affirm that on the 11th of November 1843, Bertha Antoinetta Mason, of Thornfield Hall, in the county of Yorkshire, England, was married to my brother, Edward Rochester of Senniskali, Bulgaria, at the Villa Striges in Athens, Greece in a civil ceremony. I was witness to the union and have a copy of the marriage record in my possession. Signed, Mrs. F. Wren.'"*

Bertha scoffed. "That proves I've been married before—a fact of which I've made no secret. But it doesn't prove that my first husband is still living."

"He was but two months ago," Mr. Briggs replied. "I have a witness who can swear to having seen him." He turned to the open door. "Mrs. Wren? Come and join us, if you please."

A lady in a voluminous gown and feathered bonnet emerged from the dark interior of the church. John recognized her at once. It was indeed Mrs. Wren.

What little color Bertha had left drained from her face. "Good God, you dare to show your face here? And inside a church no less!"

Mrs. Wren crept into the doorway, coming no closer. Her words issued in an unsteady undertone. "On my brother's behalf—"

"Speak up, worm!" Bertha commanded. "If you would accuse me, I'd have you do it with some conviction!"

"Please, ma'am, I beg you," Mr. Taylor said severely. "Remember where you are."

"Did you hear him?" Bertha asked Mrs. Wren. "Are you aware this is a house of *God*?"

Mrs. Wren trembled but she did not back down. "I know my duty."

"Go on, madam," Mr. Briggs encouraged her. "Tell the vicar what you have seen."

"Mr. Edward Rochester is now living at Thornfield Hall. I saw him there in April. I am his sister."

"You're a liar," Bertha said.

"He's there," Mrs. Wren insisted. "He resides in a small room on the third floor, under constant guard. She has made him her prisoner."

John's blood ran cold. He looked to Bertha. She didn't deny it.

A smoldering flame glinted in her gaze. She glared at Mrs. Wren in taut silence as if, at any moment, she would do the woman physical violence. And then: "Close the church, Mr. Taylor. There will be no wedding today."

John's heart plummeted like a stone. And yet he'd known that something was bound to go wrong. A feeling of foreboding had troubled him ever since he'd fallen in love with her.

He'd anticipated her growing bored with him. Of leaving Thornfield, or of marrying George Eshton. Never once had he thought that she was already married to a living husband. Never once had he contemplated the possibility of bigamy.

"You've no doubt heard whispers about the strange goings-on at Thornfield," Bertha said to Mr. Taylor. "About my man, Mr. Poole, and the lunatic he's charged to look after. A distant relation of my late husband, or so I would have my servants believe." Her hand held tight to John's, for all that she wouldn't look at him. "What this London solicitor and his invertebrate client say is true. Edward Rochester still lives. If you can call it living. He's plagued by insanity. Consumed by delusions. And possessed with a silver tongue that would convince even the most rational person that *he* is the victim, and *I* the oppressor."

"It's not true," Mrs. Wren said. "He is not insane."

"He's a man who believes himself something akin to a deity. An immortal. A vile parasite who would slaughter his own sister to restore his strength. Do you doubt it?" Bertha pulled John along with her as she strode down the aisle. "Come, Mr. Taylor, Mr. Briggs. Come and see this creature that I have made my prisoner."

It was a stony drive from the church, all of them bundled inside the carriage—Mr. Taylor, Mr. Briggs, Mrs. Wren, and Bertha. John held himself under tight control, unable to utter a single private word to the lady who should now be his wife. There was no opportunity to do more than clasp and unclasp her hand, his palm dampened with apprehension.

The carriage rolled to a lurching stop in front of the entrance to Thornfield Hall. One by one, they disembarked. Mr. Fairfax stood at the open door. Sophie was next to him, Stephen and Peter arrayed at her side, waiting to welcome back the newlyweds.

"Away with you all," Bertha said as they entered.

John forced her to slow her pace. He met Stephen's eyes, and then Peter's, giving the boys what he hoped was a bracing look. "It's all right. Go along with Nurse back to your rooms. I'll come and see you before the day is out."

Stephen looked past John to the figure of Mrs. Wren. At the sight of her, he visibly blanched, shrinking back from the door. Peter followed suit.

John's gaze cut sharply to Mrs. Wren. She wouldn't meet his eyes.

"Do as he says," Bertha ordered Sophie. "Take the boys to the nursery and lock the door." She tugged on John's hand. "This way, everyone else. You too, Mr. Fairfax. We all of us have no secrets any longer."

As a group, they trudged up the stairs to the third floor and down the darkened corridor to the tapestried room John had visited on that fateful night in April. Rapping once at the door, Bertha entered.

Mr. Poole was inside, seated in a high-backed chair by the fire. He got to his feet, eyes narrowing at the strangers who accompanied his mistress.

"How is he today, Mr. Poole?" Bertha asked.

"Restless, ma'am. Seemed to know something was afoot. Been muttering to himself all morning and pacing the room to the length of his chains."

"You keep him chained?" Mr. Taylor asked.

"He's violent," Bertha said. "And strong. He'd as soon kill you as look at you. Chaining him is a mercy, and far gentler than the treatment he'd be served in an asylum." She stiffened her spine. "Unlock the door, Mr. Poole."

John looked at her, and for the first time since they'd stood together in front of the vicar, she met his gaze. He saw determination in the depths of her eyes. Bone-deep resolve. And something else. Something that made goose-flesh rise on his arms.

It was fear.

The sort of fear one only felt in the face of extraordinary danger.

"Stand back," Mr. Poole warned as he drew back the tapestry and unbolted the hidden door. "You wouldn't know it by looking at him, but he can move fast as lightning when the spirit takes him."

The small crowd of interested onlookers withdrew a safe distance. Even Mrs. Wren—Mr. Rochester's own sister—stepped back, taking refuge behind her solicitor.

Only Bertha remained where she was, holding John fixed to her side. "Scared, are you?" she asked Mrs. Wren. "You should be. It was here your brother attacked and bit you."

"He bit you?" Mr. Taylor sounded appalled.

"He wasn't himself," Mrs. Wren said. "He didn't know me."

Mr. Poole drew open the door, revealing a small windowless room. There were no lamps. No candles to brighten the darkness. The only light provided came from the outer chamber, illuminating the front half of the cell, but leaving the back in darkness.

In that darkness a figure lurked, his movement announced by the same rattle of chains John had often heard while lying in his box bed at night. A sound that had resonated from the floors above. He heard it now, unmuffled—a metallic scrape and clink that quickened his pulse.

"Edward!" Mrs. Wren called out. "It is I!"

The shadow moved, seeming to rise up on its hind legs. A deep baritone voice emanated from the cell. "Come closer."

Mr. Briggs laid a staying hand on Mrs. Wren's arm.

"You come to us," Bertha said. "Step into the light. Show these fine people what you are."

"Bertha," the voice said.

"Are you Mr. Edward Rochester?" Mr. Taylor asked. "Can you affirm your name?"

A long pause. And then: "I am Edward Rochester."

"And do you have a wife?"

"A wife?" Familiar laughter rippled from the darkness. Cold and mirthless. The very laughter John had attributed to Mr. Poole. "Many."

"Many wives?" Mr. Briggs's brows lowered. "Enough nonsense, sir. Can you tell us if you're presently married? And, if so, to whom?"

"She is there with you now. I can smell her." The voice drew closer. "*Bertha.*"

Bertha's hand tightened on John's. "Your sister wishes to take you away, Edward. This very moment, along with her solicitor. It's midmorning. Can you tell the time of day anymore? Never mind it. You will soon feel the sun on your skin."

Mr. Rochester shrank back with a hiss, accompanied by a loud clang of chains and a stream of muttered words in a language John couldn't understand.

"What is he saying?" Mr. Taylor asked.

"I believe," Bertha replied evenly, "that he's calling me a bitch or a whore. He often does."

"He doesn't know what he's saying," Mrs. Wren said. "She's starved him."

Mr. Briggs gave Bertha a sharp look. "Is that true, madam?"

"I've starved him of blood," Bertha said. "Of anything else he's welcome to eat his fill. Tell them, Mr. Poole."

Mr. Poole nodded. "Aye, sir. He's got the bloodlust something fierce. I bring him up rare meat, and all manner of things, but he won't partake of much. Would rather bite and drink from me if he could manage it—and he has done once or twice, the cunning fellow. Just as he bit this lady, here."

Mr. Taylor shuddered, and Mr. Briggs turned the color of parchment. "Human blood?" the latter echoed.

Mrs. Wren shook her head. "It wasn't like that. He didn't know what he was doing. Leave him with me a day or two and you shall see how soon he recovers—"

"Would you like to go with your sister?" Bertha called loudly into the cell. "She can take you now, straight out into the sunlight."

Another hiss.

"No, no," Mrs. Wren protested. "It isn't how it seems. We must come back after dark. He'll be stronger then and can tell you his side of things. If you'll permit him to explain—"

"After dark?" Bertha gave a scornful laugh. "Oh yes, by all means. Come again when all is in darkness and he can strike with efficiency."

"I think not, madam," Mr. Briggs said. "Daylight will suffice. We're safer in his presence when we can see."

"I've seen enough." Mr. Taylor paused before calling into the darkness, "Unless you would say something more on your own behalf, sir?"

"Come closer," the voice beckoned. "I thirst."

Mr. Taylor's lip curled with thinly veiled revulsion.

"As you see, he is mad," Bertha said. "He has been so for some time. If you doubt it, ask Mr. Carter, the village surgeon in Hay. He's heard many of my husband's insane ravings and accusations—though he wasn't aware at the time that his patient *was* my husband. No one was. Least of all this good gentleman."

"Is that true, Mr. Eyre?" Mr. Taylor asked. "You had no knowledge that Mrs. Rochester had a husband now living?"

John's mouth was dry. He shook his head. "No. I didn't."

At last Bertha released his hand. "Mr. Eyre is innocent in all of this. I deliberately kept it from him, and my servants were instructed not to let him into their confidence on the matter."

John flexed his fingers. He felt like a boat, untethered from its moorings. She was letting him go. Releasing him from his commitment to her. He wasn't certain he wanted to be released. Not until he understood the full picture.

But events moved quickly.

"Bigamy is a grave sin, madam," Mr. Taylor said. "That you would contemplate such a course—"

"Can you blame me?" Bertha's gaze came to rest on John's face. "Look at this gentleman. Handsome, honest, and kind. A good man who loved me well and could have made me happy. And now look at my husband—if you can see him in the darkness. Look at the unnatural creature I am tied to for the remainder of my life."

"You are his legal wife," Mr. Briggs said.

"Wedding vows are not to be taken lightly," Mr. Taylor agreed. "They cannot be cast aside when adversity strikes."

"No?" Bertha cast Mr. Taylor an unreadable look. "Not even if one's husband is a brute? A monster?"

"Marriage can be difficult, I'm aware," Mr. Taylor said. "But as his wife, you are obligated by God to stand by him."

"If that be the case, then let me exercise a wife's control over this lunatic. Leave him with me, not with a sister who has no knowledge of how to manage him. And not in an asylum where he would be neglected and abused. Leave him here, and permit me to continue to care for him in the manner I see fit."

"You don't understand." Mrs. Wren was becoming frantic. "It isn't what it seems. She's twisted the truth to suit her purpose. Her fortune belongs to my brother, and he must be set free—"

"Let us depart, madam." Mr. Briggs took her arm. "We can discuss the possibility of any further legal action on the return journey. Nothing more can be done today."

Mrs. Wren shrugged free of him. "I would stay a moment longer."

"As you wish." Mr. Briggs turned to go. "Mr. Taylor?"

"We will speak again on this subject, Mrs. Rochester," Mr. Taylor said as he departed with the solicitor.

"Bolt the door, Mr. Poole," Bertha commanded. Mr. Poole hastened to obey her. "Mr. Fairfax? You may show the gentlemen out."

"Yes, ma'am." The elderly butler followed after the two men. "This way, sirs."

The moment they were gone, Mrs. Wren turned on Bertha with trembling anger. "*You!*"

Bertha faced her. "Have you something you wish to say to me?"

"You treacherous witch. All your talk of laws. Of treating Edward gently. But you and I both know the truth of it. What you've done is disgraceful. It's outside the laws of man."

"But I'm not a man, Felda. I am a woman, and your brother—if that's who he is—was very foolish to meddle with me. Did you truly expect I'd go quietly? That I'd simply disappear and leave the pair of you to my money and property? Well"—Bertha's expression was implacable— "you know better now."

Mrs. Wren backed up. "I believe you are insane."

"Believe what you will," Bertha said. "But know this: if you ever set foot in this house again, I will show you no mercy. I will deal with you exactly as I dealt with him." She loomed over Mrs. Wren, as righteous and beautiful as an avenging angel. "Now run back to London with your solicitor before I really lose my temper."

At that, Mrs. Wren spun on her heel and fled the room.

Twenty-Seven

John withdrew from the tapestried room in a fog. Bertha made no effort to detain him. He simply drifted away as she exchanged words with Mr. Poole. Something relating to Mr. Rochester's care.

Mr. Rochester.

The full horror of it hadn't sunk in yet. Indeed, as John retreated to his bedchamber, locking the door behind him, he felt a sense of preternatural calm settle over him. He sank down into a chair and rested his head in his hands. His forehead was warm to the touch. Perhaps he had a fever? Or some other encroaching malady?

It was impossible to tell what was wrong with him. A broken heart? A fractured soul? He was overheated and yet odd chills racked his frame. It was the shock of it, surely. The painful sharpness of the loss of her. Of happiness, so nearly his, only to be snatched from his grasp at the final moment.

In time, he rose and stripped off his new frock coat, waistcoat, and cravat. He changed into the plain clothing he'd worn when he'd first arrived at Thornfield. The humble garb of a village schoolmaster. Like it or not, he must accept that his time in the sun was over. There would be no more thoughts of love and romance. No more possibility of marriage. Of family.

He'd have to visit the boys' nursery soon, if only to temporarily reassure them. And after that...

Good God, what was he to do?

One thing was certain: he must leave Thornfield Hall. His love for the boys—his love for *her*—notwithstanding, he could no longer remain. Not after having come so close to marrying her. Not after learning that her husband still lived.

She'd lied to him from the beginning. Had led him to believe—

But no. He wouldn't think poorly of her. Not when she'd found herself wed to such a man. A violent lunatic with a thirst for human blood.

John shuddered to think of it. Of Mr. Rochester hiding in the shadows of that small room behind the tapestry. Of the sound of his voice, beckoning and threatening by turns.

Knowledge of his presence in the house cast the events of the previous months in a new light. The sounds John had heard—the laughter, the rattle of chains, and scratch of fingers.

And worse.

Had Mr. Rochester been responsible for setting Bertha's room alight? He must have been, for John knew now that Mr. Poole was no villain.

What else had Mr. Rochester been responsible for? How often had he escaped from his prison to wreak havoc among the household? It was a miracle that no one had been killed.

John sat back down in front of the cold hearth, letting his aching head rest against the back of his chair. He needed to think, but he was too weary in spirit to do more than accept that he must leave this place. After a long while spent staring into the empty fireplace, he closed his eyes.

And he must have drifted off, for when next he opened them, the clock on the mantel was striking two o'clock.

No one had come for him. Not Mr. Fairfax with a cup of tea or a tray for John's luncheon. Not Bertha. She hadn't followed after him. Hadn't stopped at the door to enquire if he was all right.

In the space of so many hours, he'd become a secondary concern to her. Or, very probably, no concern at all. He'd been right to feel that she'd let him go. The moment she'd released his hand—a hand she'd clutched like a lifeline all the way from the church to the room on the third floor—their romance had ended. Their friendship, too, by the look of it.

Rising, he went to the door and unbolted it. He'd make himself a cup of tea and some toast, and then he'd go to the boys and offer some form of explanation. It wasn't ideal. But what choice did he have?

He opened the door and passed through it, only to stop short. His heart leapt in his chest.

Bertha was there.

She was seated in a chair in the hall, a small leather-bound book on her lap. At the sight of him, she stood. "At last. I feared you would stay inside until nightfall."

He swallowed hard. "What are you doing here?"

"Isn't it obvious? I'm waiting for you." She surveyed him with a frown. "Why did you not remain in the room with me upstairs? Shout at me or demand some kind of explanation?"

"I've had my explanation. You told Mr. Taylor and Mr. Briggs about your marriage to Mr. Rochester. About his madness. And I understand."

"Then why—" She broke off, her gaze dropping to his clothing. "I see. You've already made up your mind." Her mouth trembled. "You're leaving me."

He wanted desperately to reach out to her. To offer her some form of reassurance. But there was nothing he could do to make this any easier for her, or for himself. "You must see that I can't stay here. Not after what we've been to each other."

"You speak in the past tense."

"Yes."

"But you don't know the whole of it…" She came closer to him. "What I told those gentlemen about my husband… it wasn't the truth."

John's brows snapped together. "I beg your pardon?"

"Not entirely the truth. Just a version of it. One they were most likely to believe. The real truth is here." She held the small book out to him. "Take it."

He reluctantly obliged her. "What is it?"

"It's the journal I kept during my imprisonment."

John stilled. "Your *what*?"

"In the months after my marriage, my husband made me his prisoner. He rid me of all of my servants. Soon, all of his were gone as well. It was only the two of us alone inside his fortress on the cliffs overlooking the Black Sea—he in his madness, and I in my captivity." She pressed his fingers closed over the book. "It's all there, John—to a point. The unvarnished truth. Will you read it?"

"Bertha…" He shook his head. "It won't change anything."

"Please. If you ever loved me—"

"I still love you."

Her face spasmed with emotion. She visibly brought herself under control. "Then read it," she said. "And when you've done, come and find me."

The branch of candles in John's bedroom guttered as he read the final lines of Bertha's journal for a second, and then a third time.

There was a door in the floor. A simple square with a bolt set into it.

The description conjured an image in his mind. A long-ago charcoal sketch that had made little sense to him. A sketch that had upset Bertha so much that she'd thrown it into the fire.

Unfastening the latch, I lifted open the door.

There, the journal entry ended with a blotch of smeared black ink. As if Bertha had been interrupted before she could finish. The truth to a point, she'd said. It wasn't enough truth for John's taste. He was beginning to suspect what had happened next, but he needed to know for certain.

Taking hold of the branch of candles, he exited his bedchamber and made his way to the drawing room. It was ablaze with light—a multitude of candles and lanterns holding back the encroaching darkness of evening.

Bertha was seated on the settee. She'd changed back into her widow's black. Her countenance was solemn, her eyes faraway as she gazed into the embers of a dying fire.

It reminded him of the first evening she'd called him to join her there. The way she'd looked—so queenly and remote. So utterly invulnerable.

"Was it the boys?" he asked.

Her gaze lifted to his. "You've finished reading?"

"I have." He placed the branch of candles on a table by the door before coming to sit down across from her. "Was it?"

"Yes." Her bosom rose and fell on a deep breath. "When I opened the door in the floor, I found them there, half-drained of blood. Village orphans, I assume. Romani children, not from Senniskali, but from somewhere else. They were weak and frightened. Scared to muteness. I still don't know how long they'd been down there."

"You'd heard a child's cry some days before."

She gave a terse nod. "I suspect it was one of them, but it may have been a different child. One I was unable to save."

"Earlier, in the hall, the boys seemed to recognize Mrs. Wren."

"I daresay they did. She was gone from the fortress during the time I found them, but I assume they knew who she was, just as the rest of those in the region did. She was recognizable, if not by her face then by the ruby ring on her finger." Bertha's thumb stroked the base of her own third finger, absent any wedding band. "She isn't his sister, you know. He's far too old to have a sibling still living. I'd be amazed if the two of them were related at all."

"Then who—"

"She's his creature. His procurer. He requires a loyal servant to do his bidding by day. Someone to assure his safety while he sleeps, especially when he's traveling as he was when I met him in Egypt."

"I don't understand."

"Don't you?"

"How can I? You ended the journal so abruptly."

"Yes, well…there wasn't a great deal of time to write after that. I had much to do in order to save us all, and not many hours of daylight in which to do it."

"Will you tell me the rest?"

"I don't know." A weary sadness glimmered in her eyes. "Is there a chance you'll believe me?"

John's heart clenched. She'd asked him something similar once. A hypothetical question posed in the arbor, in the stormy, early morning hours after a wounded Mrs. Wren had been sent off with Mr. Carter. "Did you tell Blanche Ingram?"

"I did."

"And she didn't believe you?"

"No. She did not." Bertha's mouth curved in a bitter smile. "More's the pity."

"I'm not Miss Ingram," he said.

"No. But your reaction will be the same. You'll think me insane. Either that or a fantasist. Some soft-headed fool obsessed with otherworldly claptrap."

He gave a humorless laugh. "Good lord, Bertha. Do you have any notion of the things I've seen since I've come to Thornfield? That I've *imagined* I've seen?"

Her eyes met his. "Such as?"

"The wolf you describe in your journal. I encountered him once myself on the road to Hay. It was the day you fell from your horse."

She frowned. "The wild dog you mentioned?"

"I wasn't likely to admit to having seen a wolf, was I?"

"But you did see one?"

"As plain as day. A great black creature, with glistening fangs. He was coming through the mist. And that's not all I've seen."

Her gaze sharpened. "Go on."

John told her about the night he'd arrived at Thornfield, seeing Helen standing at the crossroads with her hand raised in warning. He told her about the sounds he'd heard—the fingers scraping on the panels of his box bed, and the rattle of chains from the floors above. He even told her about those bleak sleepless nights in the weeks after his arrival when his guilt had conjured Helen's image, kneeling at the foot of his bed in silent accusation.

"And you know about the face I saw in my shaving mirror," he said. "I didn't imagine it."

"No. I don't suppose you did." Her brow furrowed. "I've seen strange things myself. Though nothing too terrifying since I've come home to Yorkshire. He's too afraid of me to toy with me overmuch. After what I did to him in Bulgaria—"

"What did you do?" John asked. "What happened after you found the boys?"

She stood abruptly and walked to a nearby table. A tray reposed upon it, containing a decanter of wine and several cut-crystal glasses. She poured herself a measure and took a long drink. "It smelled of death, that chamber where he kept them. Just like the lair where he slept. I believe there may have been bodies there, too. Other victims. Other children."

John's stomach tightened. "In there with Stephen and Peter?"

"Yes." She lowered her glass. "They didn't want to come to me. I had to coax them out one by one, with whispered words and empty promises. How they clung to me, then! It broke my heart. But I hadn't the luxury of tears. I had to be strong for them, and for myself." She took another drink. "At sunrise, I emerged from the vault, knowing that I took my very life in my hands, and theirs along with it. If Edward had been awake—if he'd dared to brave the sunlight to capture me—I knew I wouldn't stand a chance. He was too strong."

"But he wasn't there," John said.

She shook her head. "I took the boys to my room. They were so weak after climbing the stairs, I had to let them lie down upon my bed. While they rested, I went to the chamber with the window overlooking the courtyard and waited for Mr. Poole."

"In your journal, you said you'd given him coin the previous day and sent him on an errand."

"I had. I sent him to buy a horse at the twice-monthly market outside the village—two horses if he could find them—and to procure as much rope as he could. And he did, God bless him. He came back midmorning in a cart pulled by two enormous Bulgarian drafts. He used them, along with the rope, to tear the front door of Nosht-Vŭlk straight off its hinges." She stared into her empty wineglass, her expression meditative. "That's when the real difficulty began."

"Tell me," he urged her. "Please."

"I went back through the wardrobe and down the secret stair. But first I retrieved the two phials of laudanum from my room. I gave a few drops each to the boys and Mr. Poole, then took a few drops myself."

John recalled the patent medicine the boys had been taking. How angry Bertha had been when she learned John had put a stop to it. And what of her reaction to his own laudanum use? She'd been relieved to hear of it. As if the knowledge of it had assured her of him somehow. "Did you believe it would repel him?"

"It had seemed to work before. What did I know but that it might work again? After dosing everyone, I collected some rope and a lantern—and Mr. Poole, of course. He was obliged to accompany me, poor devil. He despises small spaces. And there was a chance it would all be for nothing. That we'd find my husband's lair empty. But he was there, much to my astonishment. Asleep, just as he'd been when last I dared enter. He hadn't taken any precautions at all. Hadn't been afraid in the least." She refilled her glass. "It was his fatal mistake, underestimating me."

The embers in the grate crackled and snapped, sending sparks up the chimney. It startled John. Made him aware that he'd been all but holding his breath as he listened to Bertha's tale.

She crossed the room, her crepe skirts rustling over her petticoats. "While he slept in that strange sleep of his, unable to fully wake, unable to do me harm, I poured a whole phial of laudanum down his throat. And then—with Mr. Poole's help—I bound him with rope and dragged him out into the sunlight."

John stared at her, momentarily speechless.

"You think me hard," she said. "I have had to be."

"Not hard, but—"

"Any compassion I might have had for him dried up the moment I saw what he'd done to Agnes. And then, when I found the boys...the anger within me grew. It burned so bright, all other emotion was reduced to cinders. I prayed the sun would put an end to him."

"But it didn't."

"Nothing can." She raised her glass to her lips, but didn't drink. "He opened his eyes and writhed about, as if the torments of hell had been unleashed upon him. For the barest moment, I wondered if it was only the madness. The depth of his self-delusion. But his exposed skin began to turn red, as if the sun had burned him. It *did* burn him. He was weakened tremendously by the exposure. But he did not die."

"Was there no one about? No villagers loyal to him who could have stopped you?"

"Not a one. Those who might have intervened were at market day. Besides, I had Mr. Poole with me—an intimidating fellow at the best of times. We loaded Edward into the cart and covered him with a tarpaulin. While Mr. Poole stood guard, I fetched my belongings—my money, letters of credit, and travel documents—and collected the boys. I made them sit up front with me, wrapped up in one of my cloaks. A more ramshackle lot you couldn't imagine. But we hadn't time to do better. By early afternoon, we were on the road to Varna."

"And when it grew dark again? What then?"

"Ah. That was a trick. I knew he abhorred the touch of silver. In the next village we passed, I paid the smithy a small fortune to have a pair of silver manacles cast. It took most of the silver available in the vicinity, including every piece of silver jewelry I had in my possession. All but this." She touched her locket. "I'd no idea if it would work. I knew my husband was strong, and that what powers he had derived from darkness, but—"

"Powers?" John couldn't keep the doubt from seeping into his voice. "You can't truly believe he's an unnatural creature?"

"Can't I? You said yourself that you saw the wolf on the road to Hay. How do you think such visions manifest?"

"I don't know. But—"

"And what about the mist? You've seen it here, the way it clings to everything hereabouts, irrespective of the season. It nearly suffocated me the night it came into my room."

He stared at her. "I thought that was smoke. From the fire."

She huffed. "There was no fire. It was the mist, come in through an open window. That was him, John. And so was the thunder and lightning that came the night the Eshtons were obliged to shelter at Thornfield."

"You're telling me that he has the ability to influence the weather? To conjure the storm?"

"No." Her face was grave, her tone ringing with certainty. "I'm telling you that he *is* the storm."

Twenty-Eight

John's brow contracted. His initial reaction was one of utter disbelief. And then...

And then, he reminded himself of all he'd seen since coming to Thornfield. All he'd experienced. And he thought of *her*—looked at her. Bertha Rochester was no fantasist.

Her face fell. "You don't believe me."

"I do." He paused. "That is, I want to. I'm only trying to understand."

"I don't fully understand it myself," she said. "All I know is that he's powerful, and that he possesses arts unknown to human men. Before I captured him, I suspect he was capable of transforming himself into the mist or a wolf or any creature of the night. The legends say he can. But since I've bound him in silver and deprived him of nourishment, he's lost that ability. All that's left is a remnant. A shadow of what he once was. It seeps out of him. And when he's able to taste a drop of blood—as on the night he bit Mr. Poole's arm—he gains the ability to direct that shadow. To render it lethal."

John recalled the night the mist had come into Bertha's bedchamber. The way it had seemed to absorb all of the oxygen from the air. It was why he'd thought it was smoke.

And what of the following morning? John had assumed the bandage on Mr. Poole's arm had hidden a burn from starting the fire. But it hadn't been a burn at all. It had been a bite wound, rendered by Mr. Rochester.

The realization left John cold. He struggled to accept it—to believe it—even as every particle of sense, every logical precept ingrained in him from his youth, rose up in protest at the impossibility of it all.

"What of the weather?" he asked. "The storm?"

"The rain and the mist…they're a manifestation of some sort. A projection of his very essence. So, too, the black wolf, and the feeling that he's there with you in your room. Even the image you saw in your shaving mirror. The stronger he is, the stronger, and more real, the projection. And he *is* strong, John. It's why, even at his weakest, the mist stretches all the way to Millcote."

John endeavored not to sound as skeptical as he felt. "And yet you were able to subdue him? To manage him the whole of the journey home?"

"We traveled by day, exposing him to the sun as much as possible. It was cruel, I know, but it kept him weak and pliable. At night we took turns sleeping, while one of us watched over him—bound in his silver manacles." She set down her glass, leaving the remainder of her wine untouched. "From Greece, we conveyed him to England by ship. What a fearful voyage I had, with such a monster in the vessel! Mr. Poole knew only that my husband was a madman. A dangerous lunatic. He knew nothing of Edward's true nature. But I—*I* knew what he might be capable of if he got free of us. I was ever on my guard."

"Mr. Poole has no notion of what Mr. Rochester is? What you *believe* he is?"

"None whatsoever. Nor has Mr. Carter, or any of my servants. Before you, the only one to whom I ever told the truth was Blanche Ingram."

A sinister chill traced down the back of John's neck. "Did Mr. Rochester kill her?"

Tears glistened in Bertha's eyes. She blinked them away. "Yes."

"But…how? You're not saying he got free of you?"

She shook her head. "Blanche came the day I arrived home. I told her all. She was doubtful but wouldn't outright call me a liar. She said she must think on it, and that we would talk again. But I knew when she rode away that she wouldn't come to any conclusions in my favor. She hadn't seen the things I'd seen. Couldn't bring herself to believe me."

"I'm sorry."

"Don't be. It was my own fault for confiding in her. I put everyone at risk, her most of all. She came back the next day, unannounced. I was engaged with the boys, and Mr. Poole had stepped away from the third-floor room for a moment. I'd told Blanche where my husband was kept. She crept upstairs to speak with him. I presume she wanted to hear his side of the story.

"It was the space of minutes. Less, probably. He must have beckoned her inside. Convinced her to try to release him. It was enough time for him to snap her neck and tear out her throat. He was starving, you see. Insensible with want. We were able to get to her before he drained her dry, but not soon enough to save her."

John's stomach roiled. "Good lord."

"Yes, it wasn't very pleasant. That night Mr. Poole took her body from the house and left it on the road to Millcote.

Later, I released her horse to run home on its own. Everyone believes she broke her neck in a riding accident. But Mr. Poole and I know—and now you know—that my husband was to blame."

He looked at her in dismay. "How could you bear it? She was your dearest friend."

"How could I bear anything? One does what one must. Besides, I hadn't time to grieve. There was much to be done to make Edward secure. Mr. Poole fashioned stronger silver chains and manacles at his forge. And I had workmen out straightaway to replace the door to my husband's cell with one of ash wood reinforced with silver."

"Why ash?"

"Folklore and legends." She toyed with her locket. "I've been learning these many months, writing letters and traveling everywhere I could, trying to find answers. It hasn't been easy. There were peasants along the way from Varna, and later, gentlemen at universities and museums who have tried to help me in the abstract. Have told me stories of men cursed to walk in darkness. Men who must drink the blood of humans in order to maintain their vigor."

"Vampyres."

"Yes, very like. I must assume my husband is one of them. But not the kind from folklore and legend. Not entirely. He's not immune to troubles. Indeed, most of his problems are very human. At the time I met him, he was suffering pecuniary difficulties—a result of spending too much on his collection of antiquities. And he had no way to recoup his losses. The abolition of slavery impacted the income generated from his sugar plantations in the West Indies. And the wars with Russia made his homeland unstable. He needed to get out. A wealthy English wife was just what he required."

"In your journal, you mention a book at the British Museum. Something he claims to have been searching for all of his life."

"*The Book of Going Forth By Day.*"

John blinked. "Is that what it's called?"

"It's an Egyptian funerary text. *The Book of the Dead*, some call it." She grimaced. "Yes, I found it. Mr. Birch, the gentleman from the antiquities department at the museum, has been translating it for me. It contains spells and so forth. Incantations that will allow the dead to walk among the living. To endure the sunlight. My husband seems to think one of them might heal him of his affliction."

"What do you think?"

"I haven't the faintest idea. I'm not searching for ways to render him more human. I've been searching for answers to the opposite question."

John went still. "You're trying to find a way to kill him."

"You needn't look so appalled. No such method exists. No spells or incantations. No magic potions. Edward Rochester will outlive us all. God only knows how old he already is. One hundred years? Two hundred? Such a creature cannot be killed."

"You can't know that."

"But I do. The sun hasn't managed to put an end to him, nor has the silver. My last hope was in an old book kept at a monastery in Argeș. But even that proved disappointing."

John rested his elbows on his knees, his fingers pushing through his hair. She'd been reading a letter from Argeș the day he'd found her weeping on the battlements. The day she'd first broached the subject of marriage. How happy he'd been then. How hopeful for their future together.

And now, here he was. All these months of building a life here, only to be faced with the same dilemma that had driven him from Lowton. An entanglement with a married lady.

But no. This wasn't the same at all.

Bertha Rochester didn't need him in the way that Helen Burns had needed him. She didn't want a savior. She needed an ally. Someone to stand by her side. To support her. To *believe* her.

Yes, she'd lied to him. She'd hidden the truth. By God, she'd have committed bigamy! But under what provocation? Her husband was no husband at all. He might not even be human. The existence of such a creature defied belief. And yet...

John had witnessed the strange happenings around Thornfield. The manifestations. Mist and wolves and ghoulish images in the looking glass.

She'd been facing it all alone, with no one to confide in. No one to trust. And he wanted to be that person for her. Not because he was particularly brave or heroic, but because he loved her. Admired her—even more so after reading her journal.

He couldn't leave her as he'd left Helen. And he couldn't abandon her to that creature lurking within the tapestried room. He wouldn't.

"You haven't tried everything," he said.

"Not everything." She sighed heavily. "Doubtless I could spend a lifetime on testing out various ancient concoctions."

"No." He sat up. "I meant...you haven't tried *everything*. The usual methods."

"I shot him through the heart, John. If he can survive that—"

"And you're certain you hit him? The pistol didn't misfire or—"

"My aim was true. The bullet struck him. It knocked him down. I saw it with my own eyes."

"But you haven't tried anything else?"

"What else is there aside from driving a stake through his heart, or cutting off his head and filling his mouth with garlic?" Her mouth tightened with distaste. "Good God, can you imagine? I want to defeat him, but I could never explain such conduct to anyone. Even Mr. Poole isn't likely to turn a blind eye to butchery."

"Is that what you were advised must be done?"

"It's part of the old legends in that region of the world. Heaven knows if it works. Nothing else has. I've exposed him to the sunlight. Bound him with silver. Deprived him of blood. And still he lives. Granted, he can no longer tell night from day, but he's more than capable of doing mischief. I'd convinced myself that he could be left here in Mr. Poole's care, while you and I—" She broke off. Her mouth tugged downward. "But now, it's you who are leaving."

John was silent. He was struck by an idea as unsettling as any he'd heard thus far. Under normal circumstances it wouldn't bear thinking of.

But these circumstances were far from normal.

"I'm not going anywhere," he said. "Not yet."

She regarded him warily. "I don't understand."

"I have an idea of something that might work," he said. "A way you might be alleviated of your burden, without any gruesome aftermath."

Deep in her gaze, a spark of hopefulness flickered. "Go on."

Rising to his feet, he offered her his hand. "Perhaps it's better if I show you."

The small, rigid leather case stood open on a chest in John's bedchamber, revealing the more than two dozen glass phials of laudanum within. Bertha withdrew one of them, examining it with a frown. "Where did you get all of these?"

"A village doctor in Lowton. He prescribed it for my headaches. I thought I'd explained."

"I knew you were taking laudanum when you arrived, but this…" She returned the phial to the case. It settled into its compartment with a delicate clink. "This is a great deal of opium, John."

"Enough to kill a man, I suspect."

Her eyes met his.

He stared back at her, his heart beating heavily.

"Would it work?" she asked finally.

"You tell me." His bedchamber was shadowed, lit only by a single taper candle and the dim evening light filtering in through his window curtains. It cast half of Bertha's face in darkness.

"I don't know," she said.

"But you've given him laudanum before. It helped you overpower him."

"That was naught but a single small phial.. And it didn't exactly put him to sleep."

"What effect *did* it have?"

She wandered across the room, her brows knitting in thought. "It seemed to affect his senses. He was less reasoned, and a bit uncoordinated. A bit…less human."

John leaned back against the chest. "But weaker?"

"Yes, but I don't know how much of that was because of the laudanum and how much was because of the sunlight. When I captured him, I used every tool I had, all at once. It's difficult to tell which was the most powerful. Indeed, it's all so much chance."

"You said the laudanum repulsed him," John reminded her. "He must fear it for a reason."

"I daresay it's because it pollutes the blood of his victims."

John suppressed a grimace. "If he drank it, would it render him insensible?"

"I suppose it might. But put him to sleep forever? I don't know if it's possible." She stopped her pacing to stand beside his box bed. "How would we even manage it?"

He considered a moment. "Have you a needle and syringe?"

"Heavens no. Only Mr. Carter possesses such things. And he isn't likely to lend them to us. Even if he did—can you imagine what he'd think if my lunatic husband was suddenly to die of an overdose injection of laudanum? He's a good man, Carter, but I wouldn't wager on his condoning murder."

John recoiled at the word. "It wouldn't be murder. Not if Rochester is what you say he is."

"It doesn't matter what I say. All that matters is what people believe. And no one is going to believe he's an unnatural creature, least of all the local magistrate. Philosophical arguments about the nature of humanity are beyond his purview." The glimmer of hopefulness in her eyes flickered out. "No. I don't believe we can use laudanum, any more than we can employ a stake through the heart."

"What, then?"

"Nothing. There's nothing that *can* be done. Our only hope is to leave this place with the children." She remained where she was, back propped against the wall of the box bed. "Will you reconsider? I know we can't marry now, but there's no reason you couldn't accompany—"

"There *is* reason. It would be the end of you."

"My reputation, you mean." Bitterness sounded in her voice. "What care I for that anymore?"

John ran a hand through his hair. Outside the sun was setting. How long ago it seemed he was in this very room, rising at dawn to dress for his wedding. "I want to do what's best for you, and for the boys. But…I need to think on it."

Her shoulders slumped. "Yes, of course." She stood up. "Will you stay here tonight, at least?"

"I believe I must. It grows late already."

It seemed there was nothing more to say. Head bent, she moved briskly to the door.

He caught her hand as she walked past. She stopped, frozen where she stood as he brought it to his lips and pressed a lingering kiss to her wrist.

Her throat worked on a swallow. "I'm sorry, John."

"I am, too," he said.

Sliding her hand from his, she exited his room in a flurry of black crepe skirts, shutting the door behind her.

John was left alone in the shifting shadows. He took a ragged breath. And then, standing from the chest, he went to the basin and splashed cold water on his face. It did little to revive his spirits, but it was sufficient to awaken him to his duty. He'd promised the boys he'd stop in to check on them. And he always kept his promises.

Minutes later he entered the nursery to find Stephen hunched in the window seat. Peter was crouched on the floor below, huddled near the foot of the chair where Sophie sat, sewing by lanternlight. She looked up at John.

"Mr. Eyre!" She lowered her needlework, speaking in heavily accented French. "There, you see? Did I not tell you he would come?"

Stephen rocked back and forth in the window. He was emitting a soft sound—a continuous low moan. It was so faint that John hadn't heard it upon entering. But he heard it now. It sent a jolt of alarm through his system.

Crossing the room in three strides, John came to sit beside him in the window. "What's wrong?" He laid a hand upon Stephen's shoulder. "Are you hurt?"

"That man," Sophie said.

John's gaze jerked to hers. "What man?"

"The man up there." She pointed to the ceiling. "The bad man. Stephen hears him speak."

Bloody hell.

Was it true? Had Stephen heard Mr. Rochester's voice? Had he recognized it?

John leaned over Stephen's small frame, his posture protective. "Is that so? Did you hear him?" He rubbed his back in gentle circles. "No matter. He won't harm you. I promise you that. He'll never harm you again."

Below, Peter rose from his place on the floor to lean against John's leg. He clutched John's trousers in one small fist.

John ruffled his hair. "You're all right, Peter. You're both safe and well."

"That woman," Sophie remarked. "The brunette lady who comes today. They know her, too."

"She's gone now," John said. "Everything is back as it should be."

Sophie snorted as she resumed her sewing.

John ignored her. Holding the boys close, he offered soothing words and caresses. All the while, the anger built within him. That such a monster should reside on the third floor! In the very house with those he'd previously made his victims. It was a cruelty to Stephen and Peter.

A cruelty to Bertha, too.

John wanted to go to her. He wanted to tell her that he'd made up his mind. That he'd leave with her straightaway, along with the boys. What other choice was there?

But his emotions were such that he couldn't trust any decisions made in the moment. Better to confront the matter in the morning, with a clear head.

"It is past time for dinner." Laying aside her needlework, Sophie stood from her chair. "Will you dine here, sir?"

"I believe I will." John urged the boys up. "Go with Nurse and wash for dinner. We'll all feel better after we've eaten."

A short while later, dinner was delivered to the nursery by Alfred and Mr. Fairfax himself. The elderly butler cast John a sidelong glance as he deposited a tray on the small nursery table.

"That will be all, Alfred," he said. When the footman had withdrawn, Mr. Fairfax turned to John, addressing him in a low voice. "My dear Mr. Eyre. I swear to you, I had no knowledge of the true identity of our unfortunate tenant. I thought him a distant relation of Mrs. Rochester's late husband. It never occurred to me that he was Mr. Rochester himself. We kept it from you, it's true, but only for the boys' sake. What tutor would take employment in a house with a lunatic in residence? I hope you can forgive—"

"You're forgiven," John said. "Pray, speak of it no more."

Mr. Fairfax appeared relieved. "Very good, sir. Will you be sleeping in the nursery again tonight?"

John's gaze flicked to the boys. The pair of them were pale and drawn, all of the progress he'd made with them vanished in the space of a single day. He was sure they'd rally tomorrow, but for now... "I will. The boys are a little distressed this evening."

"Indeed." Mr. Fairfax inclined his head. "I shall be in my parlor if you require anything else."

When Sophie and Mr. Fairfax had withdrawn, John attempted to engage the boys' attention. Retrieving the tinderbox, he prompted them to light a fire in the hearth. They did so, albeit with a trifle less enthusiasm than usual. Afterward, the three of them sat down to dinner. None had much of an appetite.

John was glad when the time came for bed. Sleep would be a welcome reprieve from the horrors of the day. Not just for the boys, but for all of them. After making his pallet on the floor, he reached to turn off the oil lamp.

From his bed, Stephen made a sound of protest.

"Very well, we'll turn it down, but not off." John lowered the wick until the flame was reduced to a tiny glow. "How's that?"

Stephen and Peter were silent.

John supposed that was answer enough. Lying down on his pallet between their two narrow beds, he rested his head on his arm. He was still in his trousers and shirt. It was a concession to Sophie being abed in the connecting room. He daren't offend her sensibilities.

An odd consideration given the reality of the situation.

His thoughts were consumed by that reality. By everything that Bertha had told him. So much so that it seemed he would never find any rest. Sleep was, indeed, elusive, but it came eventually—though not a deep sleep. He drifted in and out of it for several hours, tossing and turning on his pillow.

Sometime after midnight, he was vaguely conscious of the creak of bedsprings, and the light tread of footsteps on the carpeted floor. There was a clink and a scratch somewhere near the fireplace. And then the sound of the nursery door opening and closing again.

John sat up, at once wide awake. The light of the oil lamp still glowed faintly from the bedside table. He turned up the wick and the glow brightened to illuminate the room.

His eyes went first to Peter's bed. His small form was outlined there beneath the blankets. John then looked to Stephen's bed. It was empty.

Stephen was gone.

John leaped up and quickly tugged on his boots. He caught hold of the lamp by the handle and raised it high, giving a cursory look around the room as he strode to the door.

There was no sign of Stephen hiding anywhere. No sign of anything. And yet John had the distinct sense that there was something else he should have noticed. Something important.

As he exited the room, his gaze moved swiftly over the nursery one last time, only to land on the mantelpiece with a gut-wrenching jolt. Realization struck him like a thunderbolt.

Good God.

Stephen had taken the tinderbox.

Twenty-Nine

It took no more than a few minutes to rouse Sophie and Peter and urge them to get dressed, but they were crucial minutes. Advancing into the hall, John caught the acrid scent of smoke.

Bertha's bedroom door opened. She came out to join him, still tying the belt of her chintz dressing gown. "What's going on?"

"A fire. And a real one this time." He quickly relayed the particulars. "Dress and wake the others. Get everyone out of the house."

"Can't it be put out?"

"I don't know. I'll try. But I want you safe." He bent his head and kissed her, hard and brief, before striding away down the hall.

"Where are you going?"

"To the third floor. To find Stephen." John took the stairs two at a time. Smoke billowed through the corridor, accompanied by the crackling of flame. It was coming from one of the storage rooms next to the room where Mr. Rochester was held. The old furnishings within had provided ready kindling. Stephen appeared to have set their holland covers alight.

John shielded his nose with his arm. "Stephen?" he called. "Stephen, where are you?"

The door to the tapestried room opened. Mr. Poole stepped outside, looking about in confusion. "Sir? What the devil—"

"It's a fire, Mr. Poole!" John shouted. "Get out of there!"

Mr. Poole appeared to hear him—to register the smoke and the flames—but he didn't flee. Instead, leaving the door open behind him, he ducked back into the room.

The blasted fool.

John hadn't a moment to spare for the man's idiocy. Making his way through the smoke, he continued calling for Stephen. And he prayed—prayed like he hadn't done since before Helen had died. Since before he'd lost his faith. He prayed that Stephen would be all right. That he was safe somewhere, clear of the flames.

God, please protect him.

But prayers didn't exist in isolation. They must be accompanied by intent. By action. He sprinted up the stairs to the attic. He even climbed the ladder that led to the trap door. "Stephen!"

But there was no sign of him. Not in the attic, nor on the roof. Only the ever-increasing smoke that burned John's lungs and stung at his eyes, blurring his vision.

Coughing, he managed to find his way back to the third floor. He had a faint hope remaining that Stephen was hiding in one of the storage rooms. He might have been frightened after setting the holland covers alight. Perhaps even feeling guilty.

John raised his lantern. "Stephen!"

In that moment, a blood-curdling scream broke through the darkness.

John stumbled to a halt. It wasn't a boy's scream, thank God. It was a man's scream. And it was coming from the tapestried room.

Good lord, it was Mr. Poole.

John's pulse throbbed in his ears. His vision narrowed to a point. For an instant, all he could see was that open door. There was no time to close and lock it. No time to do anything but run.

And not even that.

A figure emerged from the room. Tall and lean. An elegant gentleman with black hair swept back from his brow. He was rubbing one of his burn-reddened wrists. And then he stopped, his gaze fixing on John like a wolf fixing his attention on a rabbit. His eyes glimmered red amid the smoke. "Mr. Eyre," he said. "I've been waiting to make your acquaintance."

John backed away, his heart pounding like a drum. "Mr. Rochester."

"You know who I am? How gratifying." Mr. Rochester's mouth curved up in a mockery of a smile. His lips were stained with blood. "*I* know who *you* are. I've heard you these many months. I've smelled you." His eyes blazed. "Where is my wife?"

John's gaze darted to the storage room where the flames were now licking out of the door to run along the wall. The silk paper hangings in the corridor were curling away from the wood. "Stephen!" he called hoarsely.

"Stephen. Peter." Mr. Rochester advanced upon him. "The first martyrs, isn't that what she calls them? Peasant boys she saved from a fate worse than death." He gave a low chuckle. "You mustn't believe everything my wife tells you, Mr. Eyre. Women are prone to exaggeration."

Out of the corner of his eye, John saw a glimmer of movement in the chamber directly across from the burning storage room. A small figure in a long white linen nightshirt.

Stephen.

Relief tore through him. As he backed past the door, he held out his hand. "Now, Stephen!"

A small hand shot out of the smoke. John gripped it hard, and turning around, he broke into a run toward the stairs, with Stephen close at his side.

"Don't look back," he said in a litany. "Don't look back."

They'd nearly reached the landing when a loud thump sounded behind him, and Stephen's hand was ripped from his own.

John spun around to find Stephen on his knees, a bunched piece of carpet tangled under his feet. His small face was white with terror. Whiter still as Mr. Rochester closed the distance between them.

"*John!*" Stephen cried out.

There was no time to contemplate the fact that he'd spoken for the first time. No time for emotional displays. John's response was fueled by pure adrenaline. By a soul-deep determination to save Stephen from harm.

This inhuman monster had hurt them enough. *All* of them. But no more.

Bertha and the boys were John's family now. His to love and to protect.

And John *would* protect them, even at the cost of his own life.

He darted back to Stephen, grabbed him by the hand and pulled him to safety in the same instant Mr. Rochester lunged to strike.

In his opposite hand, John raised the lantern. He flung it at Mr. Rochester with all his might. The glass shattered, the paraffin oil splashing over Mr. Rochester's ragged clothes. He looked at John with an expression of horrified amazement and then promptly burst into flames.

A sense of savage triumph coursed through John's veins.

But he didn't linger to admire his handiwork. Half carrying Stephen along with him, he descended the stairs to the hall and raced out onto the lawn. Bertha was already there with Mr. Fairfax, Sophie, and Peter. The other servants were nearby, milling about in various stages of undress.

"John!" Bertha flew into his arms. "Thank God you're safe. I was about to go in after you."

He held her fast as he scanned the lawn, feeling her heartbeat against his breast, as swift and wild as his own. "Is everyone here? I don't see Jenkins or the footmen."

"Alfred has gone to summon the engines from Millcote. Jenkins and the others are seeing to the horses. The only ones unaccounted for were you and Stephen. And Mr. Poole. He wasn't inside, was he?"

A breath shuddered out of John. "Mr. Poole is dead."

She drew back to stare at him. "*What?*"

"I think he was trying to unchain Mr. Rochester in order to get him out of the house. He must have thought he was saving him from the fire. You said he didn't know what Mr. Rochester was. That he believed him to be nothing more than a lunatic."

Bertha's eyes lit with dawning horror. "By God, John, you don't mean to say that Edward got free?"

"He killed Mr. Poole. He must have taken his keys and unlocked himself. I saw him on the third floor. He spoke to me. Tried to take Stephen."

"Where is he now?"

"Still inside the house. I threw an oil lamp at him and he caught fire. I thought he'd given chase—"

"Heavens above!" Mr. Fairfax pointed to the battlements. "Who's that on the roof?"

As one, they all stared upward. It was a black, starless night, but Thornfield stood out against the darkness in a growing conflagration. Its upper stories were consumed by flames. They licked out from the third-floor windows, and higher still, reaching toward the roof.

Along the battlements a figure moved against the night sky, his body consumed by fire.

It was Mr. Rochester.

Stephen gave an inarticulate cry, and Peter's face crumpled. John pulled them closer, circling them with one arm while the other remained securely around Bertha's waist. The boys clung to him, leaning against him as she did, drawing strength from his nearness.

"His face," Bertha said under her breath. "He's burning."

And he was. John could see it even amidst the chaos of the fire. Mr. Rochester's skin was blackening to ash. As they all watched, he yelled something out in a strangled voice and sprang from the roof, as if in a desperate attempt to escape the pursuing flames. He landed on the paving stones with a loud crack of bones and thud of flesh.

The servants screamed, and the boys buried their faces in John's shirt. John would have liked to hide his face as well, but he forced himself to look. To bear witness.

He wasn't alone.

Bertha, too, refused to avert her gaze. She regarded the bloody heap on the ground. The creature who had once been her husband. Her bosom rose and fell on shallow, trembling breaths. "I must go to him. I have to be certain."

"No," John said. "It isn't safe."

"Come with me, then." She slid her arms from his waist, and hoisting her skirts, picked her way across the lawn.

"Stay with Nurse," John said to the boys. "Mr. Fairfax? Watch over them. They've had a fright."

"As you say, Mr. Eyre."

John went after Bertha. She was standing over her husband's body, staring down at it with an expression that was hard to read. He came to a halt beside her, following her gaze. His stomach recoiled in protest.

Mr. Rochester's skin had flaked away, but the blood inside of him—his final meal—seeped out of him and into the paving stones in a steady stream.

"Mr. Poole wouldn't have let him perish," she said. "It would have meant an end to his position here. And he liked his wages too much to give them up."

"It was his choice to go inside. He must have known the danger."

"I'd given him tonic to drink. It should have worked as a repellent. Indeed, I thought it would." Her brow creased. "But it doesn't work, does it? Not reliably. It didn't work the night the mist came into my room. The night Edward bit Mr. Poole. I should have realized then—"

"It isn't your fault," John said. "And perhaps he didn't take the tonic as often as he was meant to."

"Perhaps, not. But it *is* my fault, for all that. I hadn't the courage to put an end to my husband, and now poor Stephen must bear the burden of having done it." She gave John a bleak look. "There will be an inquiry. I won't be able to prevent it. After what happened with Mrs. Wren at the church, people will suspect the worst. And if the district coroner should want to see the body…"

"I wouldn't worry on that score," John said.

A cool night breeze drifted over the landscape, carrying away some of the flakes atop the growing pile of ash. At this rate, there would be nothing of Mr. Rochester's body left for the coroner to examine. Nothing to hint at his having been anything other than a dangerous lunatic, charred to cinders in a fire.

"Do you suppose Stephen knew how to destroy him?" Bertha asked. "That the boys have always known?"

John smoothed a curl of silvery-white hair back from her face. "I wouldn't mark it down to any particular knowledge. Stephen has always had an interest in kindling fires."

"Well, he's certainly kindled one now." She glanced up at the Hall. "He's destroyed Thornfield. It won't survive the morning, not even if the engines do manage to arrive before dawn."

"He was terrified," John said. "Don't be angry with him."

"I'm not angry. I'm relieved." Her mouth twisted. "My nightmare is finally over."

Curling his arm around her waist, John drew her away from Mr. Rochester's rapidly disintegrating body. The boys were looking at them intently, waiting for them to return.

"What now?" she asked.

"You can rebuild," he said.

"Thornfield?"

"Your whole life."

"A daunting prospect. I'm not entirely sure I can face it alone."

John bent his head to hers. "You won't be alone."

She turned to look up at him, forcing him to stop walking and meet her gaze. "Do you mean that, John? You're not just talking about the boys or—"

Leaning down, he captured her mouth with his. He kissed her fiercely, with all of the emotion roiling in his soul. She softened against him, arms sliding to circle his neck. For an instant, her lips yielded to his, and then she stretched up, returning his kiss with as much passion as he gave it.

She wasn't a passive participant in anything. She was his equal. His second self.

"I trust that answers your question," he said against her cheek.

She gave a soft, breathless laugh. "Yes. It does."

Arm in arm, they crossed the lawn to rejoin the others. The fire brightened the night sky, illuminating the landscape around the Hall.

Something was different. A feature John had come to accept as being part of Thornfield and its vicinity was gone. Gone as though it had never been. "Look," he said. "Do you see that?"

Her gaze drifted over the grass and trees. "The mist. It's disappeared." A sheen of tears sparkled in her eyes, reflecting the flickering flames. "He truly is dead."

"He is," John said. "Whatever he was—whatever power he had—it's all over now."

She looked at the heap of ash on the pavement. "Consumed by fire."

He held her firmly against his side as they rejoined the boys. Stephen and Peter ran to him, clinging at his shirt. John felt a profound depth of responsibility for the three of them. It eclipsed all other concerns.

"We don't have to stay here," he said.

"I must," she replied.

"Leave it with Mr. Fairfax. Trust him to manage. He always does in your absence."

"But Edward was my husband," she said, a quaver in her voice. "I have a duty—"

"Not anymore." John's arm tightened around her. "Let me take you away from this place."

She turned her face into the curve of his neck. Her uneven breath was warm on the bare skin exposed by the open collar of his shirt. "To where?"

"Somewhere safe." He brushed a kiss to her temple. "Let me take care of you."

She made a choked noise against his shoulder. It might have been a sob.

"It's all right." His words were a husky murmur at her ear, meant for her and her alone. "You don't always have to be strong, my love. You can lean on me awhile."

She swallowed and nodded her head.

John exchanged a few brief words with Mr. Fairfax. The butler was more than capable of meeting the engines and seeing to the servants' welfare. They would be in no danger. The fire was confined to the stone walls of the Hall.

Bertha cast it a final look as John drew her away. He urged the boys along with them toward the stables. The riding horses had already been evacuated. Two half-dressed footmen struggled to control them at the edge of the drive.

The carriages had been evacuated, too; rolled out into the stable yard, both the larger coach, and the old one-horse gig that had brought John to Thornfield so many months before.

Jenkins was hitching the coach to a team of bays.

John addressed him quietly. "I need to get Mrs. Rochester and the boys to an inn for the night. Somewhere in Hay."

"We're taking the horses to the Three Bells," Jenkins said.

John was familiar with the place. It was a clean, respectable establishment, with plenty of room to house the displaced residents of Thornfield. "That will suffice," he said. "Once you've delivered us there, you can return for the others."

"Right-o, sir." Jenkins opened the carriage door and set down the steps.

John assisted Bertha up into the cab and lifted the boys in with her. He climbed in after them. Jenkins shut the carriage door.

Inside the darkened interior, neither Bertha nor the boys wished to be apart from John, not even by so much as an inch. They all huddled together on the same upholstered seat, Stephen and Peter at John's left, and Bertha at his right, her head resting on his shoulder, and her arm circling his midsection.

Jenkins hopped onto the box and gathered the ribbons. The coach gave a shudder as the horses sprang into motion. And then they were rolling away down the drive, the flames that consumed Thornfield Hall dancing in the carriage window at their back, and ahead of them, an endless expanse of perfect night—free of mist, free of evil.

John gathered his family close. Soon, he had no doubt that the shock would set in for all of them. But for now, they were together, and they were alive. It was a blessing. A miracle. And he was resolved to view it as such.

Epilogue

*Mrs. Bertha
Eyre's Journal.*

7 May 1845. Val d'Arno, Italy. — It's been a month to the day since we settled into our new home in Florence's river valley. The Villa della Agnello is nothing very grand—merely an old farmhouse, formerly owned by a wool merchant. For us, however, after a year spent wandering the length and breadth of Italy, the quiet comfort of the rambling property is something very near to heaven.

There are no villagers nearby to disturb our peace. No busybodies to ply us with questions. Our closest neighbors are the monks at the local monastery. Good and pious men. I can sense their eyes on me when we pass on the road. I wonder if evil leaves a mark? A stain, readily observable to those of true and honest faith? If so, that stain is daily fading.

The boys have already begun to heal. They spend their days out of doors, basking as much in the sun as they do in John's company. Their skin, no longer pale as death, has been burnished to a deep bronze. One might easily mistake them for native Florentines. They can even speak creditable

Italian, finding more confidence in the rounded vowels and melodic rising-and-falling syllables than in the languages of their past—a past we are all of us trying to forget.

In that, John is our lodestar. He draws us out of ourselves, out of the villa and into the sunlight, no matter how low our spirits. If his own spirits suffer, he doesn't show it. It's only on rare occasions that I've observed him looking solemn and pensive, his pencil stilled over his sketchpad, as if a stray memory has caught him unaware.

When that happens, it's up to me to take him by the hand and bring him back to the present. To the love and laughter of our little family, safe here in the Italian sunshine, far away from the horror and uncertainty of the past. It's a choice we make daily, for ourselves and for each other—to choose light rather than darkness.

We all of us bear deep scars from what we've suffered. From the loss, betrayal, and physical pain. From the guilt in believing we might have behaved differently—might have tried harder, done more. But such thoughts serve no purpose anymore except to rob us of our precious peace. And we deserve peace after what we've been through.

"We need never go back," John said to me this morning when I was in his arms. "We can stay here forever."

The idea greatly appealed to me. If only it could be so! But I refused to be selfish. "You'd give up your country?" I asked. "Your home?"

"You're my home now," he told me.

I had no reply. Too moved for words, I could only kiss and embrace him. My friend, my husband. This decent and honorable man who has helped me to rebuild the shattered pieces of my life. I love him so very dearly.

Perhaps that's the true secret of our happiness? This deep love we hold for each other, and for the boys. We have been through fire together and come out the other side, not unharmed but stronger for the experience. And we *are* stronger. I know that much for certain. If evil should ever come again into our lives, we will face it together.

And we will defeat it.

Author's Note

At this point, some of you might be wondering why on earth I would ever combine Charlotte Brontë's *Jane Eyre* and Bram Stoker's *Dracula* in a retelling. I had many reasons for doing so (which I'll elaborate below), but the simplest is this: in the text of *Jane Eyre*, there are several references to monsters, bloodsucking, and even vampires. They include the following:

1. After Bertha attacks and bites her brother, Richard Mason, Mason tells Mr. Rochester: "She sucked the blood: she said she'd drain my heart."

2. Jane tells Mr. Rochester that the gruesome-looking figure who crept into her room one night reminded her "Of the foul German spectre—the Vampyre."

3. During another conversation, Mr. Rochester relates the difficulties involved with getting Bertha home to Thornfield, stating: "To England, then, I conveyed her; a fearful voyage I had with such a monster in the vessel."

From those lines (which I included in *John Eyre*) and others, it was easy for me to imagine that the person locked away on the third floor was, in fact, a monster.

Similarly, my decision to make Mr. Rochester the villain, was based on actual scenes from *Jane Eyre*, as well as on my evolving view of the character himself. When I was younger, I used to think *Jane Eyre* was a deeply romantic novel, and Mr. Rochester an equally romantic hero. However, on subsequent readings (and with my own advancing years), I began to notice all the ways that Mr. Rochester exploits Jane's innocence and takes advantage of his position of power. He also speaks disparagingly of every other woman he's been with, employing the age-old tactic of implying that Jane is "different" from them, and therefore, worthier of better treatment.

Where does *Dracula* fit into all of this? There were already vampire connections between *Jane Eyre* and *Dracula* to play with, but I also really liked the idea of Bertha facing a situation somewhat similar to that faced by Jonathan Harker. Except, unlike Harker's mentally and physically debilitating experience as prisoner to the Count, Bertha's imprisonment ultimately serves to reveal the full, magnificent extent of what she's capable of as a woman.

And that's the final element of inspiration for *John Eyre*: strong women. Though John is, in many ways, the main character, it's Bertha who holds power as the story's true heroine. I began writing *John Eyre* during the height of the #MeToo movement. Several predatory men were being dragged, vampire-like, from the shadows and made to face the sunlight. The women who accused them were rarely in positions of power. They'd previously been doubted, demeaned, or dismissed. Others had kept silent for years for fear of the same. It made me think a lot about allyship and the importance of women having friends and partners who listen to and believe them. In many ways, that's the role John serves for Bertha—not her savior, but her ally.

John Eyre is my first effort at a retelling/reimagining/fanfic of a classic novel. When writing it, I wanted to keep the basic framework of *Jane Eyre* to provide a feeling of familiarity that would (hopefully) make the supernatural gothic bits seem scarier as they blended into classic elements of the story. To that end, you can be sure that if I used a description or piece of dialogue from *Jane Eyre* I did so with specific intention.

I understand that some of you might prefer that authors not tamper with the classics. But here's something I've learned as a reader: none of the stories in the huge canon of retellings and fanfic take away from the originals. Quite the opposite. In most instances, the retellings are borne of a deep and abiding love for the source material. That's certainly true in my case.

I love *Jane Eyre* and I adore *Dracula*. Spending time immersed in their worlds was enormous fun. And during this sad, grim, awful pandemic year of grief, fear, and loss, I needed something fun to take me out of myself. If you found the end result a bit bonkers, you can blame it on that, and know that regular programming will resume with my next Victorian romance novel, *The Siren of Sussex*, coming in 2022 from Berkley/Penguin Random House.

As always, if you'd like more information on nineteenth century fashion, etiquette, or any of the other subjects featured in my novels, please visit the blog portion of my author website at MimiMatthews.com.

Acknowledgments

This novel was written entirely for my mom. She's a huge fan of *Jane Eyre* and *Dracula*, and of every print, movie, and mini-series retelling or adaptation thereof. Last year, we began joking about a gender-flipped *Jane Eyre* retelling called *John Eyre*. Talking and laughing about all the possibilities for the story got us through many difficult times. For that reason, and many others, I owe my mom a debt of gratitude.

I'm also grateful to my dad for his patience. During all the discussions my mom and I had about *John Eyre*, he never said a word (though I'm pretty sure he thought we'd both lost our minds).

Thanks are also due to my brilliant editor, Deb Nemeth; to my cover designer, James Egan; and to Colleen Sheehan for formatting.

Last, but not least, extra special thanks go out to my wonderful beta readers: Sarah, Rachel, Clarissa, Courtney, and Renée—authors and readers extraordinaire. Thank you for your feedback, your kindness, and for the valuable gift of your time. I promise that the next book I ask you to beta read won't have vampires in it.

About the Author

USA *Today* bestselling author Mimi Matthews writes both historical nonfiction and award-winning proper Victorian romances, including *Fair as a Star*, a *Library Journal* Best Romance of 2020; *Gentleman Jim*, a *Kirkus* Best Indie Romance of 2020; and *The Work of Art,* winner of the 2020 HOLT Medallion. Mimi's novels have received starred reviews in *Library Journal, Publishers Weekly*, and *Kirkus*, and her articles have been featured on the *Victorian Web*, the *Journal of Victorian Culture*, and in syndication at *BUST Magazine*. In her other life, Mimi is an attorney. She resides in California with her family, which includes a retired Andalusian dressage horse, a Sheltie, and two Siamese cats.

To learn more, please visit
www.MimiMatthews.com

OTHER TITLES BY
MIMI MATTHEWS

NONFICTION

The Pug Who Bit Napoleon
Animal Tales of the 18th and 19th Centuries

A Victorian Lady's Guide to Fashion and Beauty

FICTION

The Lost Letter
A Victorian Romance

The Viscount and the Vicar's Daughter
A Victorian Romance

A Holiday By Gaslight
A Victorian Christmas Novella

The Work of Art
A Regency Romance

The Matrimonial Advertisement
Parish Orphans of Devon, Book 1

A Modest Independence
Parish Orphans of Devon, Book 2

A Convenient Fiction
Parish Orphans of Devon, Book 3

The Winter Companion
Parish Orphans of Devon, Book 4

Fair as a Star
Victorian Romantics, Book 1

Gentleman Jim
A Tale of Romance and Revenge

The Siren of Sussex
Belles of London, Book 1

Lightning Source UK Ltd.
Milton Keynes UK
UKHW010633210721
387524UK00001B/179